## Praise for *A Death in Shonagachhi*

'Rijula Das has evaded the prevalent tropes of writing. The book manages to achieve everything that good literature does while at the same time being entertaining'

**2021 JCB Prize Jury**

'*A Death in Shonagachhi*, through its finely developed characters and settings, takes us deep into the hidden and harsh universes of the layered city of Calcutta. Using her fly-on-the-wall method, Rijula Das accomplishes a level of interiority that can compare itself to Upton Sinclair's seminal novel, *The Jungle*'

**Sarnath Banerjee**, author of *Corridor* and *All Quiet in Vikaspuri*

'Addictive and hilarious. Rijula Das is a writer to watch'

**Avni Doshi**, author of *Burnt Sugar*

'Rijula Das surprises you with everything in this book – the writing, the scenes, the characters, the story. A debut you cannot stop reading'

**Arunava Sinha**, translator of *Chowringhee* and *Tiger Woman*

'From its electric opening to its sobering end, and even thereafter, Rijula Das's *A Death in Shonagachhi* will colonize your mind. Here, set within the form of a murder mystery, is a deeply sensitive portrait of life (and death) in a red-light district. Rijula is unafraid of accessing interiorities and of where they take her. Decades ago in France, Jean-Patrick

Manchette called the crime novel the great moral literature of our times. This novel seems to take that maxim to heart'

**Tanuj Solanki**, author of *Diwali in Muzaffarnagar* and *The Machine is Learning*

'A hard-hitting portrayal of life and death in [a] red-light district'

***BusinessLine***

'A gem of a novel … a superb debut … it deserves every prize, accolade and palm frond that comes its way'

***India Today***

'A pointillist story about a sex worker's life, *A Death in Shonagachhi* is a skilled debut'

***Hindu***

'Riveting … Das weaves threads of pathos, humour, squalor and kindness into her narrative. She flits in and out of the minds of characters, hoping to leave you with different vantage points'

***Firstpost***

'This debut novel eschews a smart script in favour of the real, messy world … Das enters this world boldly'

***Scroll.in***

'Finely calibrated … Bold and unflinching in its portrayal of the hapless lives of sex workers and their vulnerabilities, their "unheaved sighs" and unexpressed sorrows, their sense of defeat and fatalism – made worse by a system that maltreats them, handles them with contempt and derision – the novel urges us to face up to some unpalatable truths'

***News9***

'This novel transforms and gradually unravels an honest and unsettling narrative of Shonagachhi's inner life. It pulsates with some unforgettable characters and heart-warming friendships … A truly genre-bending [novel]'

***Feminism in India***

# A Death *in* Shonagachhi

Rijula Das received her PhD in Creative Writing in 2017 from Nanyang Technological University, Singapore, where she taught writing for two years. She is a recipient of the 2019 Michael King Writers Centre Residency in Auckland and the 2016 Dastaan Award for her short story 'Notes from a Passing'. Her short story 'The Grave of The Heart Eater' was longlisted for the Commonwealth Short Story Prize in 2019. Her debut novel *A Death in Shonagachhi* won the 2021 TATA Literature Live! First Book Award for Fiction and was longlisted for the 2021 JCB Prize for Literature. She is from West Bengal and lives in Wellington, New Zealand.

# A Death *in* Shonagachhi

*a novel*

Rijula Das

PICADOR INDIA

First published 2021 by Picador India
First published in paperback 2022 by Picador India
an imprint of Pan Macmillan Publishing India Private Limited
707 Kailash Building
26 K. G. Marg, New Delhi 110001
www.panmacmillan.co.in

Pan Macmillan, The Smithson, 6 Briset St, Farringdon, London EC1M 5NR
Associated companies throughout the world
www.panmacmillan.com

ISBN 978-93-90742-87-5



3 5 7 9 8 6 4 2



Typeset in Fairfield LT Std by R. Ajith Kumar, New Delhi

Printed and bound in India by Replika Press Pvt. Ltd.

*For Baba and Dadubhai – first friends in a new world*

# 1

LALEE HAD LEARNED THE WORD 'PHANTASY'. FOR REASONS he couldn't articulate, this made Tilu very jealous. Tilu Shau – obscure writer of erotic fiction – had been visiting Lalee for almost six months now, on every second Wednesday, given his book sales and assorted hustling yielded enough cash for him to afford Lalee's door fees. He was a slight man, and nothing much to look at. It didn't matter to him now, but he still remembered all those little ways his heart had sunk when he was a schoolboy and a pretty girl wouldn't deign to give him a second glance. Especially now, as Lalee stood leaning on her door frame, smoking a cigarette, face averted from him.

Not too long ago, he had read a book on the mysteries of the human psyche. Everything, it said, had its origin in childhood. And though Tilu couldn't fault his mother for more than an occasional smack across the head and a haphazard sort of neglect, he understood that now it was de rigueur to blame mothers for one's adult failings. He, therefore, speculated that his troubles began with his mother not being able to remember exactly when, during her two-day labour pains, the tiny, wrinkled body of Trilokeshwar Shau had touched the earth. Or, that he didn't quite touch the earth, but plopped unceremoniously into the hands of the buxom nurse with the prominent rabbit teeth who scrunched up her nose and, pressing her front teeth down on her lower lip, said '*Eh ma*' in a nasal falsetto, before holding him up for his mother's benefit, who, he was led to believe, had croaked a little. Such was the music of his passage onto this earth, and had set the background score for the rest of his life. His father was proud of him nonetheless – first male heir and so on. Parental pride had eventually given way to bitter disappointment, but at the time of his birth, overcome with emotion, his father foisted upon him the name 'Trilokeshwar' – god of three realms. The family name, however, could not be remedied. Still, there were all kinds of benefits in being low caste these days. At least he'd get a government job through some well-meaning quota, Tilu's father had thought.

Not only did Tilu fail spectacularly at getting that government job, but he also started writing erotic novellas at a dangerously tender age. As it happened, Tilu Shau wanted to put his theoretical knowledge to practical use. Since he was no prince, had no idea how to talk to women and possessed all the charm of a leftover roti, the usual routes of courtship normally earned him one brandished slipper and a volley of threats from both the object of his attentions and all the local thugs, dadas and old coots of her neighbourhood. After some stellar fiascos, Tilu did what every failed Romeo did in Calcutta. One early evening, clad in a mostly white pyjama-panjabi, Tilu stood in front of the Dinatarini Maa Kali temple and mumbled 'Ma, Ma' a few times before hitting his forehead thrice in quick succession on the grime-plated sacred floor.

He walked purposely to the half-broken, non-AC Baroda Bank ATM and withdrew a conservative amount of cash, hiding it surreptitiously in the right front pocket of his Rupa briefs. He looked around himself, but grown men with hands inside their pants was such a commonplace scene in metropolitan Calcutta that no one had paid him any attention. His first time in Shonagachhi was an adventure and a battle that had led him to Lalee's door. Tilu hadn't looked back. That was a long time ago. And now, Lalee had gone ahead and learned the word 'phantasy'. It was the way her mouth arranged itself when she said it, how she ducked her chin as she moved her neck to a decidedly sexual angle, the curl of the upper lip, a momentary half sneer baring an incisor. It beguiled Tilu. Lalee made him pay for what she called the 'Phantasy Speshaal' before letting him through the door.

'Since when?' he asked. After all, he had been coming to Lalee for quite a few months now. Every second Wednesday like clockwork, and whenever he had a small windfall. But today when he arrived, at 7 p.m. on the dot, Lalee turned up her nose (the gall of the woman!), and dragged on her cigarette. And said he needed to pay extra for what he was about to do. This was an outrage. He'd been on the special rate for returning customers, and now this. Almost double. The bitch!

'Why?' he asked, and she said, 'Phantasy sex will cost you more.' Tilu hadn't realized until then that his particular sexual predilections came under 'fantasy' ratings. He decided not to quibble over Lalee's pronunciation. If she wanted to replace her F's with Ph's, that was her business entirely. But Lalee went on to give him the breakdown of her new rates: Fantasy

Mild, Fantasy Special and Fantasy Double-decker. He was almost sure she was making this up, but arguing with Lalee was not the way he wanted his evening to go. In the ensuing silence when Tilu was afraid to ask what this last package entailed, Lalee took the opportunity to inform him that what he had been doing all along would very much attract the Fantasy Special rate and that he owed about a few thousands in back pay. Tilu Shau's heart sank to his stomach. He had always known that his pocket and his penis shared a magical connection. When he got paid, days few and far between, he was always quite tangibly delighted to meet her.

This, coupled with the look of unmitigated awe that glazed Tilu's eyes every time he sneaked a look at Lalee's bursting décolletage (not that Shau was aware of it, but women are good at noticing things like this, collecting them and storing them away for future use), encouraged Lalee to feel a sense of unprecedented control and power over him. Consequently, she had no respect for him. Tilu assumed that his loyalty would flatter Lalee. But his romantic devotion had backfired. Although Lalee herself was enough to give Tilu a lifetime's worth of erections, it was the thoughtfulness behind his preparations that should have earned him some special treatment if there was any justice in the world. Sadly, there wasn't. And Lalee treated Tilu with the contempt of the strong towards the weak. She didn't have to please him. She only had to drop the end of her saree and there he would be, saluting away to her glory. Her indifference burned a hole in Tilu's heart. But it had never stung as much as it did that evening, when, bold as brass, sucking on that cigarette, she demanded double the rate. Fucking fantasy! This was the problem with

English words – you stuck one on and it started costing fucking more. He tried to put it out of his mind, but in the middle of a particularly stinging larrup, his heart started hurting. All these months of nothing but the utmost loyalty, yet not even a 5 percent discount. And then came the jealousy, not in a tidal wave as he had feared, but trickling in like the dripping of the leaking tap he heard every morning and every night in the dump he called home. 'Who taught you this word?' She said it was none of his business.

This was not a good answer at the time. Tilu was slipping off character. 'Which sonofamotherfuckingbitch taught you that word?' She hedged. She told him he must pay for what he got, that nothing was free in the world. Nobody did it better than her. Tilu knew this was true. She was hiding one fact with another. How come this had never occurred to her before? She was happy enough to do what he wanted for the regular fee. Until now. She gripped his balls in a vice. Tilu whimpered. There were tears in his eyes as Lalee's face remained frozen in contempt. He no longer knew if he was crying from pleasure or pain. Why did he have to love a nasty bitch? He could have eaten better with the money. Lord knows there wasn't much of it. Under his leaky roof, on rainy days he was forced to move the bed around in a room that couldn't hold two lizards at the same time. He felt sad for himself. Someone, after all, had to. Unsure and out of breath, he shouted at her, '*Khaanki maagi, chutiya magi* – whore.' She slapped him before grabbing him by the neck. In the heart of his rage and bubbling self-pity, Tilu Shau was intensely aware of her beauty; it pierced through the fog of his pain.

She was riding him like the autumnal goddess rides her lion, him – Trilokeshwar Shau – the poorest excuse for anything. She was resplendent. Her black-and-brown skin glistened, dark coils of oiled hair reached down her back and spilled onto his navel, her breasts hung loose as she moved. She went for his throat and bit as if to draw blood, pressing tighter and tighter. He couldn't breathe. She smiled as though it was an act of mercy. She might have loosened a tooth with that slap. The traitor in him whispered that double the rate was, after all, worth it. In pain and pleasure Tilu Shau whimpered and sighed, but someone a wall's width away started screaming absolute bloody murder.

Lalee bolted from her perch faster than a fourteen-year-old's ejaculation. Confused and almost climaxing, Tilu had to remember to breathe. He followed Lalee as she walked out the door, hastily wrapping a loose robe around her body. Tilu stood at the doorway naked and dazed, Lalee's back blocking his view. Then he saw the blood trickling in a line slowly towards Lalee's feet. She turned around and pushed him aside. 'Get the fuck out of here, now,' she hissed at his face, open-mouthed like a dead fish on the monger's slab. 'NOW!' A few people had begun to gather. He grabbed his clothes and ran out of Lalee's hovel, embarrassed and terrified. Stark naked, clothes gathered at his chest, Trilokeshwar Shau hurtled down Lalee's street before disappearing into the even darker alleys of Shonagachhi.

What had happened exactly? He was too scared of Lalee to ask. He felt ashamed at his own lack of courage, of manhood, his inability to face a difficult situation. He realized that even though it was cold and he was naked, and running down the streets of a whore pit, after being packed off by a woman he undeniably and hopelessly loved, he still had a raging erection. He also realized in the burnt-out bottom of his tattered heart that if Lalee was somehow in trouble, he'd fail her. He stopped and fell to his knees. Alone and crouching, Tilu Shau came, and then he cried a little for himself in the streets of Shonagachhi on that sultry, stifling June night.

# 2

LIKE A LOT OF MEN WITH OMNIPOTENCE OVER A LIMITED universe, Samsher Singh enjoyed making a show of it. A few months after he was made Officer-in-Charge at Burtolla Police Station – temporary home to Shonagachhi's pimps, touts, madams and petty hooligans that crawled the underworld – he had his own special lavatory installed. This was strictly out of bounds to everyone. For them was the generational graffiti, unflushed cigarette ends and the stench of the communal toilet. Every morning, he sidled through the tin door that never opened fully, and into the narrow confines of the makeshift toilet.

Almost as soon as he had squatted down, Naskar knocked on the shiny tin door. He was the newest recruit and was therefore always tasked with unpleasant errands.

'Syaar?' he called tentatively, in the kind of velvety voice that would have better suited a singer of romantic ballads. Samsher grunted. Naskar's voice had an ingratiating quality that made every word sound like a proposition. And it was the last voice Samsher liked to hear at these inconvenient moments.

'What?' he asked in English, something he did only when he wanted to make no secret of his anger.

'Ah, syaar, please don't mind me disturbing you, syaar … I mean, syaar, I have a koschen and—'

'Do you think this is the best time for koschens?' Get Balok-da.'

'Actually, syaar, Balok-da asked to get you, syaar, for the murder case but I don't know …'

Samsher turned off the tap.

'What? *Murder ho gaya?*'

'Yes, maane, syaar, it is a prostitute.'

Moments later, Naskar heard the water run. There was a fumbling with the latch which had a tendency to act up in crucial situations. Naskar heard muffled expletives and half-hearted kicks. Eventually, Officer Singh emerged sucking on a bleeding index finger.

Naskar tried to fill the silence. He got off to a promising start with 'uhmm', then proceeded to a placating 'syaar', drawing out the first syllable and modulating towards the end. Under Samsher's impatient glare, the survival centres of his brain kicked his legs into motion and made him blurt out, 'I'll get Constable Ghosh syaar,' before making a run for it.

Constable Balok Ghosh took one last drag from his bidi and squashed the dog-end under his boots.

'Maity is on his way, syaar,' he said.

'But what happened, exactly?' Samsher asked.

'*Khoon*, syaar. Murder.'

'Victim?'

'*Rendi magi*, syaar. Prostitute. One of the Blue Lotus

whores, you know, the place across the road from the NGO office. A-category, high-class. One of Shefali Madam's girls.'

Samsher knew Shefali Madam, not well, but their paths had crossed in the complex warp and weft of bribes and arrangements that held together the world of Shonagachhi. The woman ran her own kingdom in a five-storey building called The Blue Lotus. No one knew the actual number of women she harboured in there. In a place like Shonagachhi, where each building had anywhere from twenty to fifty rooms and countless girls within, it was hard to keep track of what went on where. She had kept the machine well-oiled enough that the law didn't bother her. Samsher always felt uneasy in front of this large and female autocrat.

'A-category means she would have a pimp? Which pimp?'

Balok Ghosh spread his arms, shrugged.

'Could be anyone, maybe Chintu.'

Samsher raised an eyebrow, trying to bring to mind a face that might match the name.

'I've called Maity; it might be him. All the girls have mobile phones these days – they go over the heads of pimps and handlers, make their own deals. Lot of bad blood, I hear. Maity might know something,' Balok said.

Samsher nodded thoughtfully. Mobile phones had changed the landscape of prostitution. The girls themselves had a window unto the world without the pimp, without the madam, and the natural order of things had been compromised. 'Escort Services' had sprung up like mushrooms and they poached on the girls; the hierarchy of bribes, cuts, rates and negotiations that Shonagachhi thrived on, was changing. The girls would switch pimps, or find clients on their own, cut deals with police officers on their own. Balok waited for a few moments, then said, 'Maity will be here sir. These days he's flying a bit too high, but he'll know something.'

Rambo Maity sat ill-at-ease on the hard-backed governmental chair, staring vacantly at the regulation portrait of Gandhi smiling at him from the wall behind Samsher Singh's desk. Maity drew a pack of Marlboros from his shirt pocket and offered one to Samsher. His gold-rimmed aviators stayed on his face.

'Arrey saab, nothing to worry about, everyone knows it was Salman Khan,' Maity said, his mouth stretching into an oily smile.

Samsher's arm stopped halfway to the pack of cigarettes.

'The film star? What has he got to do with this?'

'Arrey na, syaar. That's the babu. Used to be her customer at one point of time, worked as a tout in Sudder Street, sold ganja and girls to the foreign tourists. You've seen him around.'

'Nah, I can't remember.'

'Oh, you would if you saw him.'

Samsher leaned back on his chair and gave Rambo a long, scrutinizing look. Rambo Maity was a pimp on the rise. Until recently, he used to be a bottom feeder, but Samsher had always found him to be an amiable informer, a lightweight insecure enough to readily volunteer information. Of late, he seemed to be doing well. His general beggarly manner had dissipated, as had his customary penury. Nowadays his catalogue came laminated. He boasted of the largest collection of Virgin College Girls, or so Balok had relayed one day in passing. Last month, he even had business cards printed and had proudly presented Samsher with one.

Now Rambo took his aviators off. Samsher watched with satisfaction as the green discolouration from the cheap metal stained the bridge of his nose. *Typical*, thought Samsher. *Can't buy class after all.*

'Look, syaar, they'll sort it out on their own. No point getting involved. This kind of shit happens once a month – you know how it is.'

Samsher felt relieved, though he was careful not to show any emotion. He would certainly prefer to not get involved. The Byzantine network of crime and violence and cuts and bribes was just too much to deal with, and for what reward? OCs like him were a dime a dozen, and no one cared about Burtolla Police Station.

'You're still doing well, I see,' said Samsher, eyeing the nearly full pack of Marlboro Lights.

'Oh this is a present for you only, syaar.' Rambo pushed the box towards him. 'I thought to myself: "Our OC syaar likes a good smoke. Let me bring him something." After all, I'm seeing you after such a long time.'

'Did you know the girl?' Samsher asked, as he noticed the obvious hesitation on Rambo's face.

'You know how it is,' Rambo offered. 'Seen her around. One of Shefali Madam's. Nice girl, A-category, as they say, making good money, till the notebandi happened.'

'Fucking demonitization,' Samsher muttered. The government had invalided 500-rupee notes, and it had hurt them where it mattered. But he couldn't say what he thought, or even voice his doubts in front of his own subordinates. Who knew which cocksucker belonged to which party and, more importantly, whom they spied for. At least you didn't have to worry about that with criminals.

'Don't worry, syaar, I'll keep an eye out. As soon as there's any development, I shall report back. But there won't be any. Open-and-shut case. Guy got jealous and killed her, I have no doubt. What red-blooded man is going to accept his girlfriend doing … doing that stuff for money.'

'All the babus in Shongachhi do. In fact, they take a cut.'

'Of course, of course. But I won't keep you in the dark, syaar, you can depend upon it.'

After Rambo had gathered his aviators and walked away from his office, Samsher sat quietly in his chair. He wasn't the fastest thinker, he would be the first to admit, and he had never needed to think very fast. But what was it to him? There were no phone calls, no orders from the head office, no one cared, and neither should he. He got up and kicked the stray mongrel that often slunk around the station. The moth-eaten thing whimpered and retreated behind the chairs to lick his many wounds.

Constable Balok Ghosh knocked softly on the door and poked his head in. He'd been listening, something Samsher both expected him to do and was frustrated about. Coughing theatrically, Balok said, 'Acid, syaar. Motherfucker emptied the whole bottle on her and then pushed the bottle down her neck.'

Singh sat down, played with a globe-shaped glass bauble on his desk.

'It's all been quiet so far. Our boys went right after it happened. Nothing to see. I'll go get some tea for you.'

'Balok-da,' Samsher said, not looking at anyone or anything in particular, 'how far will this go?'

Balok Ghosh looked straight ahead. 'You don't need to bother about it, syaar. These things tend to sort themselves out.'

Samsher nodded. He picked up the pack of cigarettes Rambo had left behind and inhaled deeply. *Sala, these English cigarettes smell expensive even without being lit.* He closed his eyes and smiled, thinking about his wife, her distended stomach, the nervous glow, the sheer terror of death and glory, an all-in gamble of progeny and oblivion.

# 3

MOHAMAYA. THAT WAS HER NAME. SHE WAS BARELY TWENTY.

Lalee had to shut her door because she could not take it anymore. Mohamaya had lived next door to her for almost a year. The girl before Mohamaya had run away, and Lalee never knew what became of her. Then one day, Mohamaya moved in. In the beginning, she didn't say much. Lalee had gathered – a little from her and a little from the others – that Chintu had found her wandering around Sealdah station, and the demands of hunger and shelter were strong enough for her to follow him to The Blue Lotus. She looked young. Lalee had, of course, known girls far younger – some of them seven – but Mohamaya had an inviolable air of calmness about her that Lalee found discouraging. It felt wrong to be crass around her. Mohamaya reminded Lalee of a young bride she had seen once in her village, a very long time ago. Mohamaya was an old-fashioned beauty, doe-eyed, long-haired and fair-skinned. As if she was made to be wrapped in red-and-gold silk, bejewelled, calmly ruling over a prosperous household. In her presence, Lalee wanted to hide her dark hands, her angular face, the bitter smirk that seemed to always hang around her lips, and the cuss words that they formed more naturally than anything else.

Mohamaya was good to her. Called her Laal didi, a little smidgen of genuine affection in the soft lilt of her voice. Lalee sighed, and shook her head. *What a waste of such beauty*, she thought – all of it spilled on the floor, swollen face and a broken glass bottle stuck in her throat spewing blood like a spigot. There was a time Mohamaya had gone away. She had never confided in Lalee but everyone knew she had been transferred to the quarters upstairs. They were special quarters – Lalee hadn't seen them herself; they were only for those amenable to the Madam's wishes. But she had heard about them. Of course she had run into Mohamaya from time to time in the labyrinthine alleyways of The Blue Lotus. But Mohamaya had only smiled politely and walked away. Lalee, in those moments, had felt a jab of jealousy – she wasn't beautiful enough for the luxury quarters, not pliant enough, not woman enough. All of that seemed so futile now. Now, when the women came in waves, asking about the girl that died last night, so unquietly, so callously drawing attention to herself lying in a pool of blood. 'Mohamaya, Mohamaya, Mohamaya,' she kept repeating, telling anyone who wanted to know her name. 'We called her Maya.'

Lalee hadn't slept very much after walking into Mohamaya's room. Before the crowd of women could take in what was in front of them, Shefali Madam had the room barricaded. A thick wall of men, some Lalee had known and many she didn't, edged her, Malini, Amina and the others out of the room. Before the windows were shut and the door bolted, Lalee only managed a glimpse of Shefali Madam's broad, capable back obscuring her view of the dead girl on the floor.

A group of women, Lalee among them, milled around outside waiting to know what happened. Amina burst into tears while Malini sat seething in a corner, knocking again and again on the locked doors.

No one answered. Eventually, a man Lalee had never met – a well-dressed middle-aged man wearing glasses – came down the stairs from The Blue Lotus' upper quarters and asked the women very politely to go to their rooms and ask the customers to leave.

'Please go and compose yourselves,' he said. 'This is a difficult moment, but we all must keep calm, yes?' He had the kind of capable voice that could get the group of nervous and bewildered women to do as instructed. Though Malini glared at him, Lalee tugged at Malini's arm until she finally left with her.

'There's nothing to be done now,' Lalee whispered in Malini's ears.

'Of course,' Malini seethed. 'They won't leave anything that would help us do something. I run the Sex Workers' Collective; I should have been there. Shefali Madam can't have it all her own way. Sweep a murdered girl under the carpet like some dirt. You just wait and see what I do.'

Lalee found it hard to believe that Malini or anyone else could do much for Maya. The girl was dead, there was no helping her. In time, more would die – perhaps not so openly, perhaps they would just slip through the cracks into some viscous oblivion where no one would remember their names or what they looked like, but they would, all the same, be lost. Lalee wanted to have Malini's absolute faith, her recalcitrant rage and bullish optimism, but she had learned her lesson well – there was no hope, no escape.

She paced up and down the narrow corridor connecting all their rooms. Memorizing the spaces where the paint had peeled, the glimmer of spidery webs, lines of dust – as if all this anguish was some kind of antidote to death, a talisman against memories of slit throats.

Sitting on her haunches on the red cement floor, Nimmi was feeding her two children. She called out, 'Oi, ledki. What are you doing?'

Lalee glanced at them, the two children were staring at her, hypnotized by her ambulations.

'You've quietened my babies,' Nimmi said. 'I've never had it so easy before.'

Lalee leaned against Nimmi's door frame. All their rooms were stuck side by side, a narrow rectangle of space enough to fit a bed and a clothing rack. Nimmi's bed was slightly larger and elevated, resting as it did on two thick bricks. Her children slept under it when she was with customers. Lalee stared at them. Maya's room was two doors down from Nimmi's and yet here she was, feeding her children like it was any other day.

'Don't let it get to you,' Nimmi said.

Lalee felt her temper flare up. She hadn't always played nice with the other girls, not been a pleasant person, but she hated to think that Nimmi and the rest of the girls could doubt her grief so easily, as if nothing could shake her from her acrid self-centredness.

'Rest up – you'll have to go and stand out there after

sundown, just like every other day,' Nimmi said, rolling a ball of rice mixed with dal and pushing it into her boy's reluctant mouth.

Lalee looked away from them, retraced her steps to her room. It was sultry. A damp heat seemed to climb out of the uneven cement floor. The Blue Lotus was an old building. The rent kept rising every year, but everyone in Shonagachhi was too busy to do any repairs. Shefali Madam had once said to her: 'The houses here are like women. They're to be rented out, so money can be made; they don't have time to be mended.' The dark alleys inside The Blue Lotus got narrower and darker over the years Lalee had spent within it. The insides were cool, even in the worst of summer. Some of the girls wet gamchhas during the long afternoons, spread them out on the floor and slept on them. In the evening, business resumed as usual. Heat and sweat caused the make-up to slide, but customers came, and the girls stood outside, no matter the weather.

She heard a familiar cackle outside her door. A small head clad in a red baseball cap bobbed up and down, arms animatedly gesturing to the world.

'Ai babua,' Lalee called out.

The tiny head jerked towards her and the boy gave her a wink and a smile. Babua, at nine, had the smile of a man who had the world figured out, and knew where the cracks lay, where the lever could enter, push and crack it open.

'Come here,' Lalee said.

'Ai Lalee didi, give me some cash, no? You're looking so well these days.'

Lalee made a mock gesture of slapping off his red cap. Babua moved, raising up his hands in self-defence.

'Where did you get that cap?' Lalee asked.

'Foreigner tourist, Lalee didi. They were shooting with big video cameras – they say us kids will be able to go to a new school, get mid-day meals and all that.' Babua laughed.

She went back to her room, feeling the shape of the migraine descending behind her eyes like a raincloud. She spent the rest of the day either laid up in bed or pacing the narrow confines of her room. She wanted to do something, but she didn't know what. She wanted to scream, and she wanted to cry, she could urge Malini and maybe the Collective to do something, or maybe she could run down the road to the nearest police station and tell them everything – about the girl, barely twenty, who had died last night and that nothing at all remained of her this morning, not even the frayed poster of her favourite Bollywood star on the walls. But Lalee didn't do any of these things, she remained confined to her room, with a hammering pain waiting to explode behind the darkness of her eyes.

# 4

KUMARHATTA, KANKINARA, PAIKPARA, ICHHAPUR, RISHRA, Kamarhati, Kolikata – Tilu Shau whispered the names as they streamed past his barque, slow as glaciers. It was March of 1495 and he was sailing down the Hooghly, its dark waters rippling around him under the latticed shadows of tall coconut trees. Men, women and yes, there they were, the children, gathered around the bank staring at his vessel, standing like a coiled, frayed human thread. Black bodies, baked in the sun, naked children with rotund bellies and sickly limbs gathered in the arms of half-naked mothers, watched his barque move slowly down the river, their teeth big and protruding, cheekbones rising like plateaus from their starving faces. He looked down at his own hands, plump, hairy-knuckled, decked with gold rings that cut into the flesh. He puffed on his hookah and twirled his luxurious moustache with one hand. His hookah-bardar, crouching at his feet, looked up at him in fear. He kicked the man lightly, just enough to make him crawl away some distance.

This was all wrong. They had got the timing all wrong. He looked at his shoes: fine Persian slippers touching his bloated feet, the fat pearls sewn on them with gold thread dazzling his eyes in the sun. He moved his huge, fat body one way, then another. This was an anomaly in the narrative. It is 300 AD, perhaps earlier – how could he have found Persian slippers?

Tilu Shau turned fitfully on his old rickety bed in his dilapidated ancestral home at Sovabazar, less than two kilometres south from where Lalee lived. It could have been the mosquito, circling him and whining. It could have been the unpredictably talkative geckos that tik-tik-tikked their tongues or the cockroaches that sometimes flew around his room like joyful, fearless birds, but the discography of Tilu's world chanted *Manasamangal* in the nasal singsong of his long-dead widowed aunt. Tilu Shau flailed around his bed like a man at sea. Where was Champak Nagar? Where even was the Karatoya? He was the wrong Chand Saudagar, going the wrong way, afraid that the swamp-loving snake goddess would devour him alive.

Kana Haridutta, Narayan Deb, Purushottam, Bipradas Pipilai and, the last of them all, that Bijay Gupta – they were all writing this dream. One bard added a detail here, another added a flourish there and they pushed his large barque all the way south towards Sri Lanka to trade silks, gems and spices. But before his journey, he would worship at the feet of the other dark goddess. Not the swamp thing of slithering snakes, but the other, the naked black Kali of Kalighat some three hundred years before the East India Company would christen it Colegot. 'Colegot, Colegot,' breathed Tilu Shau, tossing on his bed, turning in his ornate ship. The villagers stared at the passing leviathan. Kumarhatta, Kankinara, Paikpara, Ichhapur, Rishra, Kamarhati, Kolikata – settlements now swallowed by the metropolis. He dreamt of the tiger-infested abode of Kali as the passing settlements and its peasants stared at his passage.

It wouldn't end well. Tilu Shau knew *Manasamangal*. In the grips of his hubris, the wealthy Chand Saudagar would refuse to worship the wild, vengeful swamp goddess Manasa. In retribution, Manasa would send her snakes to destroy all that Chand Saudagar held dear and take his son's life on his wedding night. Tilu cried in his sleep for the son he didn't have. But, from the banks of River Hooghly, Tilu Shau's dream changed course, and suddenly he was in a room, alone with a naked woman – her hair flowed like a dark halo behind her, snakes crawled all over her body. He couldn't tell if it was the goddess Manasa or Kali, but the terrifying spectre grew larger and larger until Tilu Shau lay dwarfed at her feet. He looked up to see Lalee's giant face on a dark, snake-wreathed body. She opened her mouth to swallow him and a giant red tongue obscured his world.

Tilu woke up sweating and whimpering softly, shaking his head to dislodge the dream. If he closed his eyes, he could still see Lalee's giant face, her vermilion tongue descending upon him. In his head, the rhythm of the poem played over and over in the same meandering nasal tones of his long-dead aunt, but he could not remember the words. He wanted to forget Lalee; Shonagachhi was too dangerous for him, and, if he were to be honest, so was Lalee. He didn't have it in him.

He walked bleary-eyed to the tap outside his room. In the distant past, this was a narrow corridor connecting all the rooms on this floor. A lengthy court case between the many claimants to the house had waged on for at least three generations and was set to carry on for quite a few more, with the result that odd corners were now serving as kitchenettes and washrooms. With each generation, the number of claimants had only grown. Originally, three brothers had fought for the sole ownership of the house; as they had children and their children had children and so on and so forth, all that had happened was that many lawyers in the city made a respectable income from the litigious clan that fought as a matter of tradition for increasingly smaller areas of inheritance.

Tilu Shau's father was one of these many claimants. After his mother's death, Tilu's father was the sole occupant of the room next door. Father and son had not spoken to each other in many years. Tilu was a great disappointment of a son, an emotion his father was prepared to air loudly and frequently to anyone who would listen. After he had bribed a considerable number of people to admit Tilu to a mechanical engineering course, Tilu had diligently failed his way out of college, focusing instead on ganja and subversive poetry. His father then tried to teach him the ropes of the family business of automobile spare parts. But Tilu's muse was hiding behind the door, waiting to distract him from such worldly pleasures. He quarrelled with his father and spouted the little bit of Chairman Mao he had learned by osmosis during his short-lived college days. Tilu's father had promptly shown him the door. Neither man knew how to go about a reconciliation, so it had faltered and rotted away into a cavernous silence.

He wrote poems when he was in college. The men he sat with at roadside tea stalls outside the university, men who debated poetry and politics while he nodded quietly with a frown on his face, periodically arranged poetry readings. Once, to fill the afternoon slot before the famous poets arrived, Tilu was invited to read his poems in front of a restless audience at the Little Magazine Festival under the strained awnings of the outdoor stage in Nandan. He would never forget the madness of those moments, just before he heard the announcer call out his name. The admission list outside the college had helpfully declared each student's caste next to their name and Tilu always knew, no matter how congenial the air in the tea stall or how many times the Mukherjis and the Chatterjis slapped him on the back mid-discourse, they were generously forgiving his lack of erudition, overlooking his non-existent savoir faire. Poetry was supposed to be his salvation. Each piece of paper that bore his name in printed ink was a talisman that would bring him veridity. But he had mumbled the lines, revealing the hollow penury of each word, and he told himself over and over again that he had written nothing, nothing of importance or value. He had stopped after that. But he remained loyal to his bedraggled band of poets, dressed like them in faded khadi kurtas and open slippers, even grew a rough beard. It was through them that he had met Amulyaratan Chakladar, proprietor of Ma Tara Publishing Works. Chakladar never published his collection of poetry, but he had given Tilu Shau a job.

Chakladar had handed Tilu five history text books, one in English and four in Bangla, and told him to write chapter synopses in his own words. The pay was negligible and the deadline was a week. 'The language must be high-level,' he told Tilu. 'If a student doesn't have the dictionary open next to him, what is the fucking point of a guidebook?' Tilu started by copying the words, and then, like a classical singer, went off in riffs, flying in the face of facts and peppering the text with moral precepts that would guide young footsteps through the thorny pathways of life. Surprising himself, Tilu stood in front of Chakladar's shop before those seven days had passed, clutching the handwritten guidebook manuscript. In his other pocket was the first draft of *The Naughty Sister-in-Law*. Sweating profusely, he slipped that other manuscript between the chapters on the Nanda dynasty and the one on the legacy of Chandragupta Maurya. Chakladar frowned, and after an hour, sent Bhoga with ₹500 and a whispered commission for the next instalment of the Sister-in-law series. That history guidebook sold well and its back cover bore the picture of a bespectacled bald man, a Professor T. N. Roy, gold medallist. Although there was no mention of what the medal had been awarded for.

He was no poet. But creative energy, like a gassy stomach, will make itself known. Idly, and only to entertain himself, he tried his hand one day at writing the slim, erotic novellas that he read so often. Once written, he had an unstoppable desire to show the manuscript to someone else. That first reader was Bhoga, Chakladar's printing assistant. He was a boy, but a boy who had expanded his considerable vocabulary with the help of the erotic fiction that was the most profitable aspect of Chakladar's business, second only to the brisk trade he did in printing wedding cards and wedding menus. Tilu marvelled at the copies of his book he saw in odd corners, aboard the daily commuter trains and at country liquor joints.

Thus far, he had written four for Ma Tara Publishing Works

in his ever-popular Sister-in-law series. He had produced *The Naughty Sister-in-Law*, *Sister-in-Law in the Moonlight*, *After the Bath* and *Monsoon Has Come, Sister-in-Law*. In an idle moment he had even begun a translation of *Sister-in-Law in the Moonlight*, which he thought was the most romantic and playful of his quadrology. He dreamt of pitching it to English-language publishers, but the more he worked on it, the more he despaired at his own inability to translate the magic he had so finely wrought in stylized, Sanskritic Bangla.

He spent hours flipping through the pirated copies of the latest bestsellers and prize winners on Park Street pavements and old copies he could find in crammed College Street bookshops. He had two obsessions, Lalee and literary fame. He would write something big, something so epic and vast in its scope and literary audacity that would leave the world dumbstruck. He waited for it to happen. He read aggressively, going through the dusty old tomes at the National Library about a bygone era. He became quite obsessed with the accounts of dead sahibs, their anecdotes of a wild, newborn Calcutta and its historical records. Of course everyone knew that Calcutta was a British invention, and for years he had been content to know it as Calcutta, eschewing the Bengali 'Kolkata'. But then he began reading about all the names it had been called before it was Calcutta, and where their boundaries lay. In time, it seemed to him that it did not matter what names we gave to places, politics be damned. Once this place had been Dihi Kolikata, a small village of no importance at all, and then it had been 'the settlement', as the first colonial settlers had called it before it was christened 'Calcutta'. He shivered with excitement when he found out that Chowringhee, the most godawfully congested and populated thoroughfare of modern Calcutta, was a tiger-infested jungle even in the early 1800s. He read somewhere that native servants of those grand British houses on Chowringhee would strip their European uniforms and run through that jungle every evening, braving bandits and tigers, back to their homes. The Chowringhee he knew bore no resemblance to that primal place. Old, imposing buildings, bus depots, hundreds of small and large businesses and thousands of people crossing its street had quite taken away any chance of encountering the kings of the jungle.

The shabby decline of this mythical Chowringhee into a middle-class hodgepodge of pavement stalls, beggars and countless daily passengers hurt Tilu's sense of grandeur. Sometimes he would hear Holwell in his brain, noting dryly in 1752 that there was no need to fret over Chauringi Road which only led to the pagan temple of Cály at Colegot and to Dee Calcutta. But he advised that the native market held on the road might be of some cultural interest. *So many names*, thought Tilu Shau, *for one spit of land*. Calcutta, Golgotha, Colegot, Dihi Kolikata, Khal-khatta, or whatever her true name was, was spilling her tales to him. He need only listen attentively. Perhaps he was her chosen scribe. Let those Mukherjis and Chatterjis of his youth keep their Derrida; all he ever needed was this city.

Once or twice, in vulnerable moments, Tilu had tried telling Lalee some of these tales from the past, but she wasn't a good listener and demanded money for any time she spent with him. It broke his heart. One day, when his great book was launched into the world, Lalee would stand by him at award ceremonies and poetry festivals while famous doddering old poets would leer at her and envy Tilu Shau. One day, he reminded himself, there would be recognition and vengeance.

Every time he closed his eyes, the memory of a giant, red-tongued Lalee haunted him. Tilu sighed and, lighting the kerosene stove, pulled the misshapen aluminium pan from a rack and held it under the tap. There was a cotton rag tied around its mouth so the water wouldn't spray in all directions, so it now trickled slowly through the cloth. Tilu waited for the water to boil, watching the swirls of iron staining the corners of the sink, wishing he had a cigarette to go with his cup of tea, but he didn't even have two coins to rub together at the moment. He would have to go to College Street today, to get an advance payment. The thought made his heart palpitate wildly; any time he had to deal with Chakladar, his publisher, Tilu wished he was a different man, one with nerves of steel. On the other hand, what he really wanted to do was to visit Lalee. But even then, he would need those steely nerves. Lalee alone was enough to make him tremble, but after the horrible death of that girl, Shonagachhi was no longer a safe place.

To distract himself from the macabre events of the previous night, Tilu Shau walked, steaming mug in hand, towards his desk and opened the curtains. Weather-beaten, bleached and bent out of shape, an old billboard for a mattress stared balefully at him. 'Dutta's Fantasy Mattress, The Sleep of Your Dreams', the herald proclaimed. The copy, though in English, was written in Bangla script in keeping with the neighbourhood's reading abilities. Every day, a baking sun and torrential rains in the monsoon swept through the billboard. A pretty girl, clad in a translucent saree, sat gingerly on a giant white mattress, inviting the spectator with a sly smile. *In some world*, thought Tilu Shau, *there are invitations like this*. One day, when he is rich and famous, Lalee might sit on a humongous white mattress, inviting him to bed.

He sighed, and turned over a new page in his notebook, picked up an old fountain pen and began writing. Job Charnock had come to him in a waking dream. In that dream Charnock appeared as a six-foot-three hero of newborn Calcutta, as unlike him as imaginable. *But*, Tilu thought in idle moments, *wasn't there a Job hiding inside every red-blooded man?*

Not what Tilu was, but what he should have been. A leviathan of a man, adventuring his way through a world that demanded to be ravished, to be discovered and awakened. A man of strength and resolve, a man who tamed the wild earth and the passions of wild women with throwaway ease. Tilu could have been that man.

While he struggled with sentence construction, his hero Job fought a dozen Thugs in the wilds of Chowringhee some hundred and fifty years ago. Job was braving indescribable odds in his pursuit of a forty-carat diamond that had been stolen by dacoits from a local king's palace. He was at the moment deep in the territory of Thugs armed with nothing but his hunting crop. The deadly Thugs were gypsy robbers who would throw a noose around their prey and strangle him to death. Tilu knew from his obsessive research at the National Library that while some historical records show Thugs to be an organized group of itinerant tribes travelling through South Asia between the thirteenth and nineteenth centuries, other records suggest that they were disenfranchised farmers under British rule, who, left with no land and no other means of sustenance, took to robbing and murdering with nothing more than a loose kerchief as a weapon. These emaciated men would sit crouching under the jungle foliage, waiting for the lone traveller, sometimes for nothing more than a few paise. In a way, Tilu's heart went out to them, but for the purpose of his bone-chilling adventure series, he preferred the first version.

This morning, his writing wasn't going as well as he had hoped. The events of the night before and the cursed image of Lalee were flooding his mind. Every five minutes or so, Job's great perils notwithstanding, Tilu Shau's mind drifted off to the small room in Shonagachhi. The dastardly leader of the Thugs threw a deadly garrotte at Job – Tilu Shau thought of Lalee's lips dangling a long white cigarette – Job grabbed it long before it could reach his neck – Lalee turned around and looked deep into Tilu's eyes – Job pulled at the noose so hard that the leader fell flat on the ground and – Lalee lay like an exquisite silken rug under Tilu and closed her eyes in pleasure – Job landed heavily on top of the Thug and broke the man's jaw in one blow – someone screamed, Lalee ran – Job wiped the blood from his knuckles – Lalee's back obscured his view and a thin red stream moved like a snake towards Lalee's feet. Even in his room in Sovabazar, Tilu Shau could smell the acid and the blood – a curious smell, at once pungent and sweet. He put his head on the table.

He had so little self-control. Tilu must go see her at Shonagachhi. What if she was in trouble? What had happened last night? What if the same thing ended up happening to Lalee? That woman didn't know what was good for her. This is when Tilu should be at her side, to protect her from harm. It all sounded plausible in his head but the minute Lalee appeared before his eyes, he lost the plot. He couldn't deceive himself anymore. He could have gone to other girls in Shonagachhi but by some strange alchemy the only door he had ever knocked on was Lalee's. And would the woman reward such loyalty? No. What a fool he was to love a woman like Lalee. He toyed with the idea of visiting her, but what if Shonagachhi today, after that girl's murder, was unsafe? What if he was ambushed by some gangs, beaten and robbed? The more he thought about it, the more nameless dangers he conjured and the less appealing Shonagachhi seemed. He opened his wallet and looked inside. There was one hundred-rupee-note, a ten and a twenty. Some coins fell out of his trousers. He peeked at the shaded area of the balcony where one electric heater and an aluminum rack served as a kitchen. Supplies were running low. Tilu sighed. He shook off the previous night's clothes vigorously, as if aggression could dislodge the smell of perspiration and the nameless, ghostly odour of blood and death. He wished he had enough clothes so he never needed to wear these again. He slipped his wallet into his front pocket and walked out to the street where he would take a bus to College Street.

# 5

WHEN SHE GOT ON THE BUS, MALINI WASN'T THINKING. There was only a relentless force pushing her forward. She walked for a long time, not even looking at the buses that passed her by, conductors shouting destinations into the sweltering air. When she saw a familiar number, Malini waved down the minibus like a madwoman, running after it as if her life depended on it. 'Rokke … Ladies,' the conductor shouted as the minibus lurched to a stop. Malini climbed up the wooden stairs amid curious looks. When she found a seat in the ladies' section, Malini tried to concentrate on what she was going to say. She'd been to the police station quite a few times, as a collateral of a raid, or as a consequence of a poor client's inability to bribe strolling constables at Victoria Memorial. Those days were long gone; ever since she became involved with the Collective and with Deepa madam, she had less and less time for the business.

All she could think of was the heat. That and Mohamaya's face. She panicked at her inability to focus on what she needed to say to the police. There was no point, it was fruitless, no one would care – but she had to try. If she didn't, if they didn't, what was the point of all those years she had slaved for the Collective, pushing past mountainous obstacles and painting an invisible target on her back. She noticed she was opening and closing her fists. On clenching them, she felt the slippery sweat of her palms. The woman next to her gathered her jhola and scarf to herself, away from Malini. She turned her head to the window.

Outside the Burtolla police station, Malini stopped before entering. She wasn't herself, her body felt alien, a lifeless, heavy thing that she had to drag through the doors. A few constables, who were outside smoking and sipping cups of tea, looked at her askance. Some of them seemed familiar. But Malini couldn't concentrate enough to make out their faces. She walked in.

When Malini left the police station, she felt herself walking in a daze. Her head felt lighter, and she looked around herself at the variously staring, frowning and sniggering male faces around her in khaki uniforms, smiling awkwardly. She found she couldn't move. The force that had propelled her since the morning, the vision of that cauterized flesh that had haunted her through the night, the irrepressible restlessness that had dragged her by the hair, had suddenly and without warning abandoned her completely. She looked down at her feet. Her slippers needed mending. The nail on her big toes was chipped diagonally, still bearing tiny maps of residual nail polish from months ago. The hem of her saree was dirty, tracking something that looked like rotten food, unrecognizable to her.

She walked. One foot, then another. She walked slowly, as if she was remembering how to do it. Outside the station gates, where some of the policemen gathered and congregated at all hours of day and night, Malini blew on the bricks, extruding from the broken boundary wall and sat down. She looked at her wristwatch – it was just before noon. She watched the sun climb down towards the horizon and, eventually, nightfall.

# 6

LALEE SURVEYED THE YOUNG MAN IN FRONT OF HER. THE hunched shoulders, the arms that looked too thin, emaciated almost, and the nape of his neck, bent forward, giving up under the immense pressure of the world. He hadn't shaved for a few days, and the stubble hid his sunken cheeks, filling in the shadows raised by his cheekbones. She wanted to tell him to stay, to rest for a month. She could feed him, watch over him. He had been little when Lalee left. He was the youngest, and the only son. Whatever their father had thought of the gaggle of girls that came before him, he had been proud of this male heir. He was the only one their father had never hit, never even let the wind blow too hard on him. Lalee had loved him from the moment he was born. He had large eyes, forever staring at the world in wonder. Looking at him now, something gigantic and insoluble settled in the pit of Lalee's stomach. She washed the daal a second time and then a third, running her fingers slowly through the red grains, muddying the grey water.

'There are the girls,' he was saying in a voice barely above a whisper, a man defeated even before he had begun. 'If I don't pay for the books this time, they won't be able to go to the school anymore. At least there the mid-day meals …' his voice trailed off.

Lalee sighed, and then replied with some anger, 'Why would you even think about making them not go to school? Have I ever said that you need to make them stop?' She wanted to add that if all else failed the girls could come to her. There was a school here for the children, and whatever anyone said about it, she knew the truth. She knew children of sex workers had gone on to live other lives, better lives; one of them was even a doctor, and another a journalist. But that would not happen. Even now her brother, twelve years younger and as close to a son as she would ever have, would not stay the night. His wife, Lalee imagined, would rather slit the girls' throats and throw them in the river than send them here. Lalee didn't begrudge her that. What she felt instead was a stab of pride. She had never met the woman her brother had married, but when he came to tell her, she made sure he left with a pair of gold earrings for his bride. She wondered if he had given them to his wife, or if he had said where they came from, or if the woman even knew about Lalee, but she hadn't asked.

'And there is the roof,' he continued. 'Last monsoon a part of it came down during the storms. I meant to put it up but that year the moneylender's men—'

'How much?' Lalee asked, cutting him off.

He hesitated, looked at Lalee, who had turned her back on him, coaxing the small gas burner to life.

'Fifty thousand,' he said in a voice that broke Lalee in places no one would ever see. She blew on the burner, huffing and puffing with a rage that hid her face, waging a war on invisible blockages, on burnt bits and recalcitrant grime.

Afterwards, when Lalee sat next to him and watched him eat, she said, 'Give me a month. Let me see what I can do. Can you wait a month?'

He nodded his head, pushing great mounds of rice into his mouth.

Lalee forced more rice on his plate, and the rest of the vegetables. He looked up when he heard the scrape of the spoon against the steel bowl, that hollow screeching utensils made when they were empty. They both knew that sound. Their ears were trained to hear it, a sound they had heard over and over again since early childhood.

'Ma is alright. A little better this month. The arthritis doesn't go away, but she is okay.'

Lalee nooded. She never asked about their mother, but he would slip it in just the same before taking his leave. His stubble was grey in places. Lalee marvelled at that untimely sign of age. Somebody had taken her sickly, stick figure of a brother, with his wide eyes and snotty nose, and compressed him in a chamber, ageing him until he looked like a weary, defeated man – a man who would always, simply and quietly, lose.

Lalee didn't know how he had found her. One day some of the girls brought him in, saying he had been looking for her outside. His head was shaved and he wore a white loincloth, sullied during his journey to Calcutta. Lalee stared at him. Reaching under herself like she was an ocean and bringing up a memory that could have been a dream, a non-thing, a figment that she had made up. Then she had cried, and the shock had worn off. Malini was there that day, and she had held Lalee in a suffocating hug that felt like the only thing in the world that kept her in place, that kept her from drowning in a grief she didn't fathom. Later he had told her about their father's death. In her head that man had died a long time ago. The evening they had taken her away, when he had sold her, she saw him in a ditch by the river, drunk. Lalee could have sworn he was dead, the flies hovered around him like they did around dead kittens in the far end of the fields. Maybe she had made that up, or maybe he really had died, and his body had simply gone on, piloted by something her mother's incessant worship and prayers had conjured up. To Lalee, he was the memory of a man in the custody of flies and dead, rotting things. But her brother had come back, found her and visited – not often, but enough times – to remind her that she had a story that began somewhere else. That she hadn't just existed here, in this nowhere place where all the girls had flowed like blood collecting in a butcher's drain pipe.

She watched him drink from the steel tumbler she had placed next to his plate, upended into the air, high above so the water flowed into his waiting mouth. She felt a stab of anger at the sight – he could eat here but his lips remained untouched by her utensils. Until she realized that this was exactly how their father used to drink. Now his son drank in much the same way, holding the glass unnecessarily higher than it needed to be, and then washed his hands on the plate with the lees.

Before Lalee had finished doing the dishes and leaning them against the wall to drip-dry, he had his bag in his hand. A frayed, dark maroon jute shopping bag bearing the scrubbed-out scroll of some shop; a plastic bag poked out of it. Lalee walked him out of the door, until he began to look hesitant, glancing at the women around him who'd had an early start to the evening and were already talking to customers. Lalee slowed, watching him speed up, walking with his head bowed, determined to not see any more than the track of dirt that led to the main door.

The man was dozing off. Lalee shoved him back to his senses. Telling him his time was up, she climbed off the bed. He opened his eyes and looked at Lalee. He didn't make any attempts to stifle his yawn, staring at Lalee through bleary eyes. Lalee sighed, averting her face from him. His clothes were those of a workman; he looked like a man in need of sleep. Maybe he had worked all day, digging earth for new homes, or repairing cars, and once he left from here, he would probably go where men like him go to sleep like the dead. Lalee tied the knot in her salwar and dropped the kameez on top of it. She held the door open for him to leave.

Conversations trailed into her room from the street outside. Some voices sounded familiar, or maybe it was the conversations that were familiar. The high-pitched laughter, the voluble haggling. This last customer hadn't paid a lot, but he had put on a condom without any resistance. She took out the money and straightened the damp notes. Two of them were the new 200-rupee notes. Lalee spread them tight between two fingers. They were new and still had the crackle in them, though the man's sweat had made them damp. She took the money and put it in her handbag. She checked her phone, scrolling past the text messages and, for a moment, wished there was a message from Tilu. It would save her from going outside, standing in the doorway and having to talk to someone new. She put her hand on her forehead, shutting her eyes against the chaos of the street outside. Someone had turned up the volume of the music player. Lalee suspected it was the young man who ran the small store outside The Blue Lotus. Lalee counted the hours it had been since Mohamaya was lying dead next door. She felt breathless. A wave of nausea whirled in the pit of her stomach, clouding her vision. She pushed herself from the bed and ran out of her room, standing outside the door that belonged to Mohamaya. The door was pulled shut, the iron bolt was fastened, but not locked. Lalee touched the bolt, wondering if she should open it, and if she opened it, what she would find inside. Would Maya have remained in a place like this? Would she have hovered in the foetid air of this room, stuck in some unearthly limbo, in a place that could be hell or home.

She felt a hand on her shoulder and almost jumped out of her skin.

'It's only me,' Amina said. 'Get away from there,' she added.

The two of them walked slowly towards the door. Nimmi was standing under the yellow bulb over her door talking to a man, a cobweb just above them forming latticed shadows on her face. She leaned against the door in a red saree draped between her breasts like a river between countries, letting her eyes slide off Lalee and Amina. Their voices were low, and Lalee looked away.

'Do you have any Crocin?' Amina asked quietly.

Lalee looked at her. Amina's eyes were drooping, and a listlessness burdened her body. *Thin*, Lalee thought. *Too thin.*

Maybe she sent all of the money home, to those two children she had left behind, to that brute who had once married her and left her here because there was no more money to be squeezed from her parents.

'Do you have a fever?' Lalee asked and placed a palm on her forehead, nearly knocking Amina off her feet. She put her hand under Amina's ears and on her cheeks.

Amina shrugged.

'Did you have any customers tonight?'

Amina nooded. 'That phoolwallah came again,' she said. 'The flowers were wet, dripping all over me. Almost two hours though.'

Lalee knew the man. A small, respectable-looking man. A man who looked like a high-school teacher or a small business owner. One evening, many years ago, he had come to Lalee with a large plastic bag held in one hand. He had adjusted his spectacles and stared at his feet a lot. The only time he had looked directly at Lalee without taking his eyes off her was when she had worn all the flower jewellery he had brought. Stark naked, bedecked with garlands of tuberoses and marigolds and bracelets of hibiscus blooms. Flowers dripping beads of water that seeped into her skin and dropped on the bed. He didn't want Lalee to touch him.

Lalee remembered she had made a joke, a sarcastic, barbed remark about how Hindu brides were supposed to wear flowers on their wedding night. The man had not come to her again. These days, once every few months, she saw him at Amina's door. Amina was younger, softer. Lalee had not fit whatever fantasy the man carried in his own private, askew universe.

'You shouldn't have sat with those wet flowers on you. Was

the fan on? Of course you'll come down with a fever like that. It'll suck the fever right out of your bones.'

Amina looked at her for a moment and then closed her eyes. They were sitting on the steps outside The Blue Lotus watching the girls on the street and random pedestrians.

'Did your brother come today?' Amina asked and Lalee felt herself tense up.

She didn't want advice from people. She didn't want them to know much about that part of her life, or what used to be her life. It was a dead thing. She didn't say anything.

'How much?' Amina asked again.

Lalee stared straight ahead. The intense beats of the music from the shop next to them finding purchase within her blood, against the thump thump thump of her chest, deafening her.

'I'll go get that Crocin from my room,' Lalee said and stood up. Walking away, she looked back at Amina sitting on the doorstep. The yellow bulb silhouetted her, the light spreading through the wisps of her hair, sticking out from her braid. *This is also a kind of family*, she thought. *No, this* is *the family*. These are the ones who stand and remember and maybe even cry when you're lying on that floor. She left Amina bent forward, her skinny spine protruding from her curved back, and went to her room.

# 7

LARGE CARDBOARD BOXES FULL OF CONDOMS WERE stacked outside the Cooperative Bank. Lalee waited outside the open door, the interior hidden from her view by a flimsy pink curtain, the print on the fabric had long dissolved under the sun. She leaned back on the iron railing of the first-floor verandah which served as the waiting room for the bank's customers. Someone inside was shouting. Lalee could make out the words, but she didn't listen, allowing her mind to drift. It was the same story – she didn't need to know the details.

A woman Lalee didn't recognize strode out of the room, her whole body shaking with anger. She flicked a hand swiftly across her face, wiping her eyes. Lalee went inside.

In front of the small, simple signboard, Bharati-di was sitting at her desk, a mini table fan aimed directly at her.

'Where is Malini-di?' Lalee asked.

Bharati looked up and gestured Lalee to a chair and went back to the file in front of her.

'She's at the police station.'

'Why?' Lalee asked compulsively.

Bharti sighed, looking up at Lalee to ask if she had come for an idle chat.

'She's sitting in front of the thana until they take her report. She went yesterday and they didn't do anything about it. Some girls are joining her today. You can go.'

Bharati pushed her slim spectacles upwards. The last part of her sentence had the slightest hint of a barb that didn't escape Lalee. The Collective's women, and their Cooperative Bank liked the girls to be involved, and Lalee's apathy wasn't welcome.

'What do you need?' Bharati asked, not looking at Lalee. 'Let me tell you right now that the best we can do is 4,000 rupees, and we can do it next week.'

Lalee felt lost.

'But that is what you said three months ago. You said the notebandi had made things very hard but in three months' time you can give me the full amount.'

'What's the full amount?'

'I need 50,000.'

Bharati looked up. She took her glasses off and placed them very carefully on the paperwork in front of her.

'It hasn't got better for us. Surely you remember what it was like. You're B-Category, right?' Bharati sighed. 'It hit you girls in the worst way. A-Category too – not in the beginning but eventually. But you girls who charge less than 500 …' Bharati shook her head.

Lalee remembered. The streets had been silent and eerily empty last November, not one customer in sight, except of course, she recalled, Tilu. God alone knows where he found the money, but he came, reliable as clockwork. Even before a customer would look at her or any one of the other girls, they asked, 'You're taking 500 notes? You're taking 1,000 notes?' She lost count of the number of times she had to say no. Everyone was looking to shed the banned notes, and what better way than an hour's pleasure. Shonagachhi had stopped. The A-Category girls charged a lot more. Maya, she couldn't help remembering, charged at least ₹5,000 for an hour. They survived, but eventually it got to them too.

'Haven't you recovered now? You said that in three months you would manage and everything would be back to normal.' Lalee asked almost desperately, unable to keep the note of pleading from her voice.

Bharati pointed at the edges of the cardboard boxes outside the door.

'We used to sell a hundred of those cartons a month. Now it's difficult to even sell twenty. Our deposits are down from 4,00,000 rupees a day to barely 70,000. It's not just you girls, you know. When it hits you, it hits us too. They banned the notes, they didn't ban our needs.

Lalee looked down at her hands. A tendril of ire raised its head somewhere in the sea of despair. She was going through options – there had to be other places she could go, other people who could help her.

'Whatever you do, don't go to the moneylenders. The interest rates they charge, you'll be in permanent debt and they'll own you, body and soul.' Bharati paused for a second before giving Lalee a once-over.

'What do you need the money for?'

Lalee got up from the chair and slowly started walking to the door.

Bharati called out after her.

'Go see Malini at the thana if you can. It's time we all stood up for something.'

# 8

ONTO ONE OF THE PAVEMENTS AT THE FIVE-LANE crossroads before which the bus screeched to an abrupt halt, Tilu got off and looked around. Across the road stood Sukhi's world-famous paan shop. On one of the other pavements, Babul the pimp waited around 5 p.m. The second turn to the right from his waiting spot led to the front door of The Blue Lotus. Tilu walked as nonchalantly as possible, wondering if Babul had spotted him yet. He didn't want to draw attention, or invite any trouble. Sukhi never gave trouble, having once told him, 'Writer saab, when a man is happy, he'll pay twenty-five rupees for one sweet paan. But I am a dharmik man, if I charge people that much, I make sure to put the best stuff in.' Tilu Shau, on occasions when his pockets were flush, like that time he got paid for the *Sanatani Cookbook with 1001 recipes for Hindu Wives*, had tried Sukhi's deluxe paan. Sukhi had laid out a slew of pots, irregularly shaped and colourful as if they held misshapen djinns inside them. What they held – Tilu watched with fascination as Sukhi's hands moved fast and light like a roadside magician – were variously coloured gels and goop that he smeared on the paan, always with his fingers. A drop of this and a smudge of that. Maybe if it all went well, if Lalee was nice to him today, he would reward himself with a paan *and* a cigarette before going home. The children played without bothering to look at him, stopping only to beg and cajole when a car stood at the cross-section. A tall, lanky sort of man was staring at him, mindfully scratching his crotch with a concentrated frown on his face. Shonagachhi, the day after a murder, could mean all sorts of trouble. Tilu quickly crossed the road over to the other side, turning his back on prying eyes. Sukhi looked up at him and asked if he wanted a cigarette. Tilu put his hand inside his pocket and felt two 5-rupee coins in there.

'One Pataka bidi,' he mumbled. A smoke would buy him some time.

He found a narrow ledge on the pavement, blew the dust away and sat down. He lit his bidi slowly with a match. His surreptitious hand reached towards his pelvis, trying to feel the contour of the two notes in his back pocket. He felt relieved that they were still there, that the pickpockets had spared him today. Would that be enough? Lalee's new rates would kill him. And Lalee, damn her, would probably laugh at his face. He sighed – there seemed to be no way out. He got up and walked about a bit. The air was sweltering. It was mid-June already and there was no sign of rain. When he was a boy, rains would flood the narrow alleyways outside their house for weeks. They flooded basements and first floors so people would have to seek shelter elsewhere. And now the burning sun blazed overhead, melting his skin off. He craned his neck upwards, shielding his eyes with his hand. A lone crow was cawing to the wind right above him. Across the road, Tilu noticed the tall man whispering to a woman standing next to him, pointing at Tilu. He started walking briskly.

His treacherous feet trod the very path they knew so well, and soon Tilu was standing outside The Blue Lotus. The women were out – variously leaning, squatting and sitting on the pavements that jutted out of the doors of the ground floor. He waited for a second, scanning the faces for Lalee's, or at least a familiar one. Out of the corner of his eye, he saw a big group of women outside The Blue Lotus shouting and raising a fuss. He peeked at them from his hiding spot. A crowd had gathered, happy to catch some street drama. A squat woman, one end of her saree wrapped around her considerable midsection, was shouting at invisible people on the upper levels of the building, urging them to hurry up. A group of girls came out of one house and started walking towards the Collective's office. Behind them, Sunil, The Blue Lotus' cook, came rushing with a roll of papers cradled in his hand. He saw Tilu and smiled broadly at him. Tilu cleared his throat.

'Eh, yeh, Lalee …?'

'Inside. Didi is in her room, just saw her come back.'

Tilu pointed at the roll in his hands.

'Oh this? These are all, what do they call them, posters. These madams are going to the pulish station.'

Tilu's heart gave a quick, involuntary shudder. 'Police' was not a word he liked to hear, especially after what he had seen on that terrible night.

'Pulish?' he wheezed.

'Oh don't worry, writer babu, they're going to join our Malini didi there. She's at the station, teaching those pulish babus a lesson. The Collective's madams will be all there. Nothing to fear.'

Sunil caught up with the group of women, walking shoulder to shoulder past the small shops and the steady stream of street girls, towards the small building with the Collective's signboard on top of it. Tilu looked at his watch – it was still a good few hours until evening, when Shonagachhi would truly come alive. Perhaps these girls would come back from where they were headed before the evening truly took off. Looking nervously to his left and right, he bowed his head and started walking towards The Blue Lotus.

A couple of girls he had never seen before accosted him at the entrance, grabbing him by the hand and jabbering at him. He stared at them, bewildered. Most of the girls here knew him by face and didn't bother him. He mumbled something about having a woman inside waiting for him, and then, in the middle of their taunts and jeers, he walked into the courtyard.

Tilu looked around, disoriented, like a man who had just woken up. The girls around him gave him strange stares. He wondered if he should leave. Everything was okay, Lalee was clearly not in danger, maybe he could just go now, not see her face, not confront the roiling bottomlessness that besieged him every time he saw the woman. Why torture himself? He could just walk out now and no harm would be done. He breathed out, unclenching his sweaty fists, and then he looked up to find Lalee watching him from the far end of the courtyard. She smiled at him, a genuine, relieved kind of smile as if she had expected to see him there. And a crater opened in the pit of his stomach, draining all the air in his lungs.

Lalee beckoned to him before walking up the flight of stairs. When Tilu reached the top of the stairs, she glanced at him and went into her room. Tilu followed her inside like a man hypnotized as Lalee shut the door behind them.

# 9

SAMSHER HEARD THE WAILS AND CURSES FROM INSIDE JUST AS he was about to knock on the door. He sighed and bowed his head against it. He could hear his mother haranguing the gods and anyone within earshot. All he wanted was peace and quiet when he came home. To take a long, cold shower, empty half a bottle of talc under his armpits and flip through the twenty-four-hour news channels where everyone screamed at each other. He held that image behind his eyes for a second and knocked on the door.

'You mark my words, beta,' his mother roared, nostrils flaring. 'It will be a girl. Sharmaji has never been wrong, never been wrong in twenty years, and he has spoken. And that's final.'

Samsher's mother believed in truth by repetition. If she said something enough number of times, it would, inevitably, apotheosize into idiomatic truth. In the corner, leaning against the dark kitchen wall was his wife. They had married recently, about six months ago, after a lot of viewings and judging and negotiations about dowry which his mother had spearheaded. At last, she had found a daughter-in-law she could tolerate, or so Samsher had hoped. In the end he was ready to marry a goat if he could only get the interminable negotiations over with. His mother had taste, he had to admit. His bride was lithe, fair-skinned and long-haired. She hardly ever spoke, even behind closed doors, and had perfected the art of keeping her eyes lowered and the sari covering her head. He liked her. She was young and treated him with an awe-filled apprehension, as if he was a lion only marginally sedated with opium.

After all the sorting, however, his mother still found fault with his wife on a daily basis and harangued everyone in the household. It gradually dawned on Samsher that she wanted a daughter-in-law she could torment, not like. And that was fine, as long as his mother kept him out of her feuds. But this she refused to do.

'What is it, Amma? Why must you yell all the time?'

'Oh, I'm yelling? Am I? It's all my fault, then? I'm only looking out for your future and he comes home and the first thing he does is point the finger—'

'Amma,' Samsher cut her short, 'will you just tell me what happened?'

'She's going to have a girl!' Samsher's mother pointed a finger at his cowering wife like a one-woman mob at a witch trial. 'Sharmaji said there is no doubt about it.'

Sharmaji was a gifted charlatan. Samsher daydreamed about handcuffing the old toad and dragging him to the cells one day. But the thought of having to move out of his own home or spending the rest of his life listening to his mother's curses deterred him. Her faith in Sharmaji exceeded her faith in God. He was the family astrologer. Every Tuesday she showered, put on a clean, pressed sari and went to visit him to discuss her household owes and seek guidance for the future. Sharmaji had once told his mother that Samsher would never get into the police force and do well to seek employment as an electrician. When Samsher proved that prophecy wrong, Sharmaji predicted that he would die in a car chase or be murdered by a whore. This augury had brought on peals of motherly curses and, for a time, daily keening. No amount of fact or proof of the man's travesty could shake his mother's faith in him, and Samsher had developed an abiding hatred for the man.

'He cannot predict the gender of the child, Amma,' Samsher tried to soothe her. 'Only doctors can do that, and they're not allowed to.'

She rounded on him like an avenging angel. 'I've seen her eating lemons, oh yes, I have!' she said triumphantly. 'And tamarinds! I've seen her with my own two eyes. Don't you tell me that doesn't mean anything. I know the signs. She's glowing!' His mother pointed an accusatory finger at his wife.

Samsher fled quickly into his bedroom, glancing briefly at his wife who was receding slowly into the dark of the kitchen.

Later in the night as she lay uncomfortably next to him, shrinking herself as much as possible, Samsher felt moved to say something.

'Don't worry,' he began, 'Amma is just … Amma. Her bark is worse than her bite.'

He heard soft sobs, disappearing stealthily into the pillows before they could be heard. He turned on his side and gingerly placed a hand on her head, stroking the black strands that had escaped from her long plait. A moment later he heard her speaking, softly and apologetically, 'But what if she is right?'

Samsher draped her waist with his other arm and brought her closer to himself, brushed his lips against her neck and said, 'I'd love a daughter. I'd love that very much.'

# 10

NASKAR LOOKED AT HIS WRISTWATCH. IT HAD BEEN TWO hours since he had checked it last. Officer Singh wasn't in yet and Constable Balok-da was furious. The women were still there, and it seemed to him that every day the crowd increased a little more. He counted the heads – one, two, three ... thirteen – and he lost count again. They kept moving, holding the posters in front of them. From time to time they took out tiffin boxes, their shiny steel reflecting in the midday sun. They talked among themselves, laughed, and sometimes Naskar thought he felt a festive gaiety in the air. Who'd think they were here to protest a murder, if one didn't look at their placards? He shook his head. They had taken the spot where Balok-da usually smoked his foul bidis when Officer saab wasn't around. As long as the women were here, Balok-da would stew. Some of the women left in the evening, which didn't surprise Naskar given their profession. If his mother knew, she may not allow him to come to work. He said a short prayer, folded his hands and touched his forehead twice in quick succession. The faster all of this got sorted out, the better it would be for everyone. If only Officer saab would do something to get rid of these women.

# 11

THE ROOM WAS DARK AND COOL. LALEE'S EYES, STILL blazing from the glare of the June sun, took a few minutes to adjust to the gloom. The hum of the air conditioner was so low that it was completely inaudible. This was a room designed for sleep, for relaxation. Lalee imagined rich housewives lazing in serene rooms like this one, escaping the blinding sun of other worlds, other lives. It was a beautiful room. When the summons came, Lalee was wary, unsure why Shefali Madam wanted to see her. She considered refusing, sending Nimmi off with a curt rejection back to Madam, but it would be a childish, futile tantrum. She locked her room and followed Nimmi to Madam's quarters on the top floor.

Shefali Madam sat on a large velvet armchair in a corner of the room, directly under the AC, pointing a battery-powered mini-fan at her chin. A young chhukri dipped a rag in a bucket of ice water, squeezed it with all the might her scrawny hands could muster and sponged Shefali Madam's back with depressing enthusiasm.

'The wicked,' Shefali Madam announced to no one in particular, 'have no peace.'

She looked at Lalee.

'Ki re, chhukri, what did I just say?'

'The wicked have no peace,' Lalee repeated.

'Understood, girl? Now look at me.' Madam waved the tiny fan at herself. 'Cannot abide the heat, not when my body is telling me to become an old woman, haha. But we keep at it, eh, Lalee? In this life it's better to be dead than old. No customers, no babus, no lovers, no one to fight with – what is life for? You should know, you're almost there. Another fifteen–twenty years and it will be time for you too. I wish for your sake that when the time comes you have a room like this to cool your lady parts in. Those traitorous things are just waiting to turn against you, like a ticking time bomb. Tick-tock, tick-tock.'

'You wanted to see me?'

Madam took her feet off the stool in front of her.

'I have a job for you.'

Lalee knew Shefali Madam, perhaps a lot better than either of them realized. It must have been what, nearly twenty years that they had known each other. They had been enemies, antagonists, compatriots, protectors. She held her tongue – silence bothered Madam more than anything.

In a minute, Lalee was quietly satisfied to see Madam fidget.

'Good,' she said. 'You don't have questions. I don't like questions.'

She removed her feet from the velvet ottoman. Lalee noticed that her toenails had been freshly painted a bright blood red.

'Tonight, I want you to pack up your stuff and move up here.

I'll get one of the boys to sort out a room for you. Get your things and in a couple of hours, go find Chintu. He'll tell you what to do.'

Lalee didn't move or reply. Shefali Madam made a face.

'I heard you went to Cooperative Bank for a loan.'

'What is it to you?' Lalee said without thinking.

'What is it to me? It's good business. You remember what it was like not six months ago with that whole note ban? The last time I saw these streets so empty was in 1992, after they demolished the mosque. We would stand outside as early as ten in the morning. Nothing, nobody anywhere. And when one of us had a customer – oh, the jealousies, the fights we had. Anyway, we're managing to keep our heads above water, and if you are smart about it, you'll take my offer.'

'And what happens to my room, my regular customers? And what will you take?'

'What – that writer man?' Shefali Madam laughed. 'Listen, chhukri, I'm throwing you a lifeline. I won't ask you why you're begging for a loan month after month, that's entirely your business. We'll continue our adhiya system. No need for room rent; you'll be working from here, and you'll go out too. My cut will be the same – 50 percent.'

Lalee imagined what it would be like to go out. Maya used to do that, but Lalee never quite knew when or how. Maya had a pimp of course and she got pretty good jobs and good clients. Once or twice, Lalee had thought of asking her what it was like outside, but she couldn't work up the courage. She smiled – there was one thing she could say that would raise Madam's hackles.

'This is the same deal you made with Maya, the thing that

ended up killing Maya, this thing that ends up killing everyone. One way or another.'

Shefali Madam's lips pursed in a smile. A single drop of red betel juice began a slow trickle from the corner of her mouth. She rubbed it off with her thumb, glancing at it for a moment. Then she said:

'In your first month, you made a friend. I don't remember her name. I had high hopes for her. A perfect village girl. They don't make girls like her in the city anymore and half the village girls who end up here have already had a good roll on the hay before they got here. Ah well, those were different days. That girl, that friend of yours. I tried to keep her intact, seal unbroken. She tried to run away before the month was out.'

Madam shook her head, laughing softly.

'And when we got her back, she tried to run away again, and again and again. Oh she was a one, always plotting her escape. As if she had anywhere to go.'

Shefali Madam paused, spit out the pan in an ornate bowl and took a cigarette from a mangled cardboard box. Lalee watched Shefali Madam's slow, deliberate movements, holding her breath without realizing it. She pointed the long, white stick towards Lalee.

'You remember what you did?'

'Nothing,' Lalee replied, in a slow, steady voice. 'I did nothing.'

'Exactly.'

Madam brought the cigarette to her lips, lit it with a plastic lighter and exhaled a perfect ring of smoke.

'I know she asked you to run away with her, but you didn't. Not once. Neither did you tell anyone that she was going to escape. We knew it, of course. All these girls, half of them will try to escape. The other half – well the other half are like you. Intelligent. Remember your little friend who tried to run away again and again. People like you survive, people like her don't.'

Packing in her room, Lalee did remember what happened to her friend who tried to escape. Jigri, that was her name. Lalee could hardly understand what she said, her thick, rural dialect from some obscure village in Jharkhand made no sense to Lalee. She was nine and Lalee was ten. They were terrified and alone, and spent the first three days side by side chained to a rickety wooden leg of an ancient charpoy. When they both stopped sobbing, sometimes they could hear the soft buzz of drilling termites invading the old wood, and the scurrying of cockroaches under their feet where Jigri had urinated herself.

Jigri spoke in urgent, short deluges. As if those were the last words she would be allowed to utter as a person, as if the words would be taken away from her if she did not use them. She gestured with her head when Madam tied both her hands and feet after the first escape. She asked Lalee again and again to run away with her. To run to the nearest bazaar, grab the first policeman they saw and to go home. Lalee didn't know if it was that one-year difference between them or if she had been a broken thing even before she got here, but she never believed Jigri. She never believed there was anywhere to run, and Jigri's failures were both Lalee's vindication and shame. She'd been right, but she was also a broken thing that deserved this place because she didn't think there was anywhere in the world that wasn't another kind of hell.

Lalee remembered very well what happened to Jigri, though she was sure Madam didn't remember Jigri's name. What happened to Jigri was one of many things that Lalee didn't think of anymore.

# 12

SAMSHER SAT SHAKING HIS LEG IMPATIENTLY AT THE doctor's office, staring at a large medical chart of a burgeoning baby in a woman's womb. He marvelled at the curve of the sinews falling and rising around the crouching child. He glanced at his wife, sitting modestly next to him. A few strands of her frizzy hair had escaped her braid and were sprouting around her face haphazardly. Samsher watched her wipe a droplet of sweat from her forehead, looking down at her lap the moment their eyes met. He smiled to himself. The pregnancy had brought a nice glow to her face, flushing her pale cheeks and plumping the rest of her. He remembered the skinny, scared girl he had married six months ago, trembling next to him as the priest bound their hands together with a sacred thread.

He cursed the doctor in his head for not installing an AC. The man was a gynaecological surgeon with a private practice and affiliations with two major private hospitals. He probably made ₹30,000 a day on average, and still rented this shitty two-room chamber with stained walls above an umbrella-repair shop. Samsher sighed. He really should have taken his education more seriously. He wouldn't have had to hang out with pimps and petty criminals if he had, even if he only amounted to a dentist, as all the failed sons of rich, ambitious fathers do. He'd have been respectable, had a smarter, convent-educated wife and taken her to the multiplex on weekends to watch overpriced movies while eating flavoured popcorn.

He touched his wife's hand. She shivered and stiffened. All in all, he was a lucky man. This was a good woman. Soon her lap would be full with a bouncy baby and she would be complete. The sour-faced receptionist called out his wife's name. She stood up nervously, walking slowly towards the doctor's chamber. Samsher remained where he was. This wasn't a man's job. His mother had refused to come, and his wife's family was nowhere to be found. As per tradition, they should have come and taken her away long ago. In time, Samsher would have gone to her parents, enjoyed their hospitality and brought his wife and child back. His mother felt rightly robbed of this incredible convenience. And still Samsher could not let himself do nothing. Someone, after all, had to take this girl to her doctor's appointments, take her to the hospital when the time came and nurse both mother and child.

As she emerged from the chamber, clutching a wad of papers, Samsher could see the bent head of the doctor behind her. A wheezy old man, sitting with his feet on the cheap chair, gathered to his chest, began coughing violently. Samsher looked at him with distaste. He could go in and have a talk with the doctor, make sure everything was going alright. He could also maybe ask if the doctor knew the gender of the child. On the one hand, he could easily get away with it as a policeman, while on the other, if the doctor was one of those annoying types, he could raise a fuss over the fact that Samsher was asking for something illegal. He tried to crane his head to peek inside the doctor's chamber through the slowly swinging door, trying to make up his mind. But the wheezy man was shuffling his way into the room, dragging a young woman behind him. Samsher gave up, walking ahead of his wife, waddling under the weight of her enormous stomach.

As soon as he had closed the door after his wife inside the taxi, his phone began to ring. A cautious-sounding Constable Balok Ghosh urged him to come back to the station immediately. Samsher looked at his wife, who smiled back at him.

'What did the doctor say?'

'Everything is good, I should have a normal delivery,' she replied shyly.

Samsher hesitated for a minute. 'Are you scared?' he asked.

She shook her head slowly, looking down at her belly which she was cradling with her hands, the tips of her fingers pressing one another. Samsher felt overcome by a wave of tenderness suffusing his insides. He was going to be a father; this woman and their child would become his world. He would live his life with them for them and they would know him better than anyone in the world and he would protect them from it.

He put his hand on hers, clutching it all the way back to his house, where he left her at the door and told the taxi driver to drive to Burtolla police station.

Samsher hid his face in his hands as Balok Ghosh briefed him. He was hoping it would blow over, just like these cases usually did. Shonagachhi had its own way of dispensing justice, and the police seldom needed to get involved, except when people like this woman created a fuss over it. Samsher kneaded his temples with his knuckles.

'So who is she?' he asked his constable.

Constable Balok Ghosh looked at a card in his hand, and said with contained distaste:

'Deepa Marhatta, syaar. Runs an NGO in south Calcutta, mainly with the Collective in Shonagachhi.' He lowered his voice as he said the last bit. 'We told her you're busy, but it's no use, she won't listen.'

Samsher Singh groaned behind his hand.

Balok Ghosh looked at Samsher's bent head. The man was so big, but had the brains of a farm animal, with all the blunt doltishness of a bull. In his considerable experience, Samsher wouldn't go very far. That he was a duty officer was already a miracle. Balok cleared his throat.

'My advice is to hear her out, and do whatever it takes to get her out. These girls are like poison. Like ... like syphilis, syaar. Hard to shake off. Plus, there's the horde of whores right outside the thana. We have to manage the situation.'

---

'Arrey madam, come, come, please take a seat, tell me how we can serve you. Ei Naskar, bring two special cutting chai. Will you take some refreshments, madam? They make very good Moglai porota here ...'

Deepa smiled sweetly at Samsher, disarming him. He had a composite image in his mind of what he thought of as 'lady social workers'. Samsher hated them, and would not admit that he was mildly, inchoately afraid of them. Shouty, belligerent, unmarried women of a certain age, who in some way – Samsher felt sure – were ruining the sacred family and social structure. Who knows why? Maybe because they couldn't get married themselves. A bunch of ugly harpies. But this one – Samsher didn't have a box he could fit her into. He couldn't tell her age. She could be in her late thirties or mid-forties. She looked striking, had a nice smile and was, very clearly, a few rungs of social status above him. Her clothes were plain, but Samsher knew that kind of plainness. It sold at a premium in small, palm-terraced boutiques that displayed their wares on reclaimed antique furniture in old art-deco houses, shunning anything as crass as a shop.

Deepa held up a hand.

'Please, Officer, thanks for the offer. But I'm rather in a hurry and would like to lodge a report please. I understand that these women outside are protesting the fact that you won't file a report for a cognizable offence?

Samsher smiled like a man martyred.

'Madam, you're educated people, cream of society. But we understand things also. Just some phone call telling us unverified information cannot count as grounds for a solid FIR, na?

He would have carried on but Deepa cut him short.

'These women outside were not making phone calls, sir. They have been sitting here for four days now; so you can do the bare minimum, like register a first information report.'

Samsher opened his mouth, but Deepa thrust a hand in front of his face. He instinctively moved back, his shoulders sagging a little against the hard-backed chair.

'Anyway, I'm not here to argue legal technicalities with you. I have some excellent colleagues in the National Human Rights Commission who'd be much better at that debate than me. I also have some friends in the judiciary who encourage us – you know how it is these days – to report such incidences of the police not filing FIRs.'

'But madam, this is the first time we are hearing about any such occurrence,' said Samsher.

'Of course. Of course, you're hearing it for the first time. I wish to lodge a police report about the matter.'

'Certainly, if that's what you would like to do. But you know how these things work.'

He opened his hands in an expansive gesture hoping that Deepa would fill in the blanks of his omissions.

She stared at him, blank-faced. Samsher did not know how to respond to Deepa's silence. Her kind of women annoyed Samsher. Just by sitting quietly she challenged Samsher's authority. He was a man, he was bigger than her, he was a police officer. She needed him. And yet, she sat there, cocooned in her privilege, her English, and made him feel inferior. He took out the new iPhone from his pocket, turned it around a few times in his hand and put it on the table. He chanced a look at Deepa from the corner of his eyes, checking to see if the sight of such an expensive thing would change her expression. He thought better of it and quickly swivelled in his chair.

'Madam, it's very difficult to track down these things. She might have just run away with her babu or some young man who promised to marry her.'

He waggled his finger playfully.

'You can't trust them. As soon as a man comes around and says, "Hey I'll make you my wife", they rush after him and give him all their money, and they are never seen again.'

He paused, growing more confident in the apparent silence of the woman sitting opposite him.

'What can we do, madam? Can't run after every whore in the country trying to stop her from making a fool of herself.' He smiled.

Deepa stared at him, her face relaxed and neutral, and that, most of all, unnerved Samsher. He looked down at his boots, until he heard her speak again.

'I understand. You can do this, officer, you can take down a complaint lodged by me, Deepa Marhatta, resident of Flat no. 4B/1 Ballygunge Circular Road, Calcutta 700019, that Miss Mohamaya Mondol, twenty-three, known to me personally, was murdered by a person or persons unknown on last Friday, the 3rd of June, at The Blue Lotus in Shonagachhi. A bottle of carbolic acid that she kept in her own bathroom was smashed on her face and then pushed into her throat. She died as a result of those intentionally inflicted wounds.' Deepa paused. 'And now will you please take down what I have just said, and give me a copy of that complaint?'

Samsher Singh swivelled in his chair, looked around his office like a cornered animal, threw his hands up in the air and said, 'Well, madam, we are your servants. We're here to protect you only.'

He raised himself slightly and looked around for a minute, before shouting, 'Ei, Balok-da, Balok-da? Take madam to Naskar and take an FIR, okay?'

Deepa smiled one more time at Samsher. A smile she would

have given a casual acquaintance at a dinner party, flattering and completely insincere. She put a hand forward, which seemed to mystify Samsher.

'Lovely to meet you, officer. Have a great day.'

Samsher Singh leaned backwards and forwards, testing the chair's creaking hinges, his mood entirely spoiled by the distasteful encounter. Yes, it was true that they knew. But what did they expect him to do? Rush in on his own and save society from ruin and injustice? When the fingers are pointed, they will turn towards the girls of the red-light district. It's not for nothing that they put them in one corner, in these floating towns where they can remain among their own folk and not be a part of normal life. *And I'm supposed to be their fucking keeper?* thought Singh. He pinched the bridge of his nose, massaging his temples with his knuckles. He thought of calling his wife, sending the police jeep to bring her, taking her to Mitra Cafe for some afternoon tea and fish kobiraji, and then maybe they could go for a drive in the police jeep along the Ganges, maybe he would buy her an ice cream and they would sit, side by side, holding hands. But she did not have a mobile phone – his mother would not allow it – and she wasn't allowed to answer the phone at home either. His mother was ever watchful, as if she was all that stood between propriety and the utter dissolution of her domestic order. Samsher sighed – an evening with his wife was not worth tiptoeing around his mother's silent, simmering wrath. Balok Ghosh poked his head through the door and asked him if he would like a cup of tea. Samsher nodded, staring at the jumble of electric wires and crows outside his window.

# 13

LALEE STARTED BY FOLDING EVERY PIECE OF CLOTHING, fitting them in neat rows at the bottom of the two large plastic bags since nothing else could be found. She wondered if she should have gone and asked for a suitcase, or at least a large kitbag from one of the girls down the corridor. But she didn't; she didn't want to answer questions, or invite inquisitiveness, especially when she didn't know what to expect. She sat down on the bed, throwing to the floor the folded blouse she had been holding in her hand. She was making a deal with Shefali Madam, a deal that was neither spelled out nor outlined. She looked around the room – her things were strewn everywhere – and felt a heavy desolation coming on. It was unnerving, to give up her own space. It was expensive and infested with cockroaches, and it had taken a long time for her to be able to afford her own four walls. Sometimes she felt that the room was slowly sucking her soul out. It required monthly libations, and she spent her days earning to keep a place she wanted to escape. And yet it was hers. It was the only thing in the world that was truly hers. The audacity, the sheer possibility, of being able to close the door on the world. Maybe it was how Malini felt about all of them, about the Collective and how so many of the women felt about their lives here. It was not a good life, not always, but sometimes it was, and despite everything else, it was theirs. In moments like this, Lalee could almost understand Malini. Her relentlessness and her obstinate, daily labour.

Outside the newly painted door, standing in front of the rooms in Shefali Madam's private quarters that Lalee thought of as 'Upstairs', she hesitated for a moment, and then, with an emotion that crossed the border between vindictiveness and impotent frustration, threw the door open hard enough for it to crash against the wall. She dumped the two big plastic bags on a pristine bed. Chintu had pointed her through the plush lounge area to a small room. She noticed that it could be locked from the inside. The door was heavy and painted a dark red. There was a large double bed which claimed most of the space. Its beautiful milk-white sheets were a far cry from the bare, unsteady bed with its cheap printed cotton sheets that Lalee had lived and worked on most of her life. The floor sparkled and the room smelled faintly like flowers. A new AC had been placed directly above the bed.

At first, tearing through her fog of formless helplessness, Lalee felt a surge of relief, as if she had been walking miles in the oppressive heat in the heart of summer and someone had pulled up next to her in an air-conditioned car, allowing her to sink into respite. But she knew Shefali Madam, and she knew this place. She'd seen girls clutch desperately at sudden pieces of luck, a promise of marriage, a declaration of love, a long-standing rich babu who paid the rent and you never had to stand on the street again. Such largesse of fate was short-lived and Lalee knew that failed hopes hit harder than changing circumstances. Or maybe she had simply lost the ability to believe in anything good. Something, after all, had to give. Hope was a bad survival strategy in Shonagachhi. Lalee thought about unpacking her bags. She had far more clothes than she thought she did; they seemed to crawl out of the walls like rats once she'd begun to gather her things together. She walked around the room with a handful. They looked cheap and flimsy, as if whispering to her that she didn't belong in this well-appointed room. There were no cupboards, almirahs or even a steel trunk to keep them in.

She poked her head outside, hoping to find someone she could ask where she could put her clothes. Chintu, who was standing outside, told her that a car was waiting. 'Where?' she asked. Chintu walked ahead and Lalee followed him to a black sedan and entered, closing the door behind her. She watched, through the dark windows and the freezing air of the car's AC, as the city around her slowly flowed past, viscous and blood-like.

Lalee looked around the restaurant, slowly and without apparent self-consciousness at the dark-red walls, the carved Chinese dragons, the emerald booths and the plastic bamboo trees that dotted the restaurant. Rambo sat opposite her, and next to him was a white woman Lalee had never seen before. Their heads were bent over a phone screen. After a perfunctory nod, Rambo was pretending not to notice Lalee. Lalee watched his face as he laughed easily and ingratiatingly at the mem next to him. She had long, golden hair. Lalee noticed the dark brown undertone that seemed to augment its paleness. She thought about the times she had coloured her hair, using dye from a box that Maya usually bought. The smell lingered in her hair for days, a cloying fragrance of fruits mixed with a strong chemical stench. Lalee watched the light slither on the mem's hair, falling past her shoulders and onto her breasts. She was saying disjointed things like 'no, not this one Rambo darling' and 'yes, I like that' as Rambo's thumb flicked the surface of the phone. Lalee felt at once ignored and on display. She stood up, clutching her handbag to her like a weapon. She disregarded the mem staring up at her with a curt smile on her lips and spoke to Rambo.

'Why am I here?'

Rambo put his phone on the table and Lalee caught a quick glance of a woman's photo. Rambo watched Lalee's face with smirking amusement.

He beckoned to the waiter and without waiting for Lalee's input, ordered two vodkas with cranberry juice. When the drinks arrived, he pushed one glass towards Lalee.

'What is this?' Lalee asked.

'Just a vodka with juice – haven't you had one before?'

'I'm not talking about this, I mean ... all of this,' Lalee said, gesturing. 'What is happening?'

Rambo smiled.

'Madam told me you needed money,' Rambo said, leaning over the red table, reaching for the small platter of salted peanuts. He raised an eyebrow, 'This is your trial night. Let's see if you can do it.'

Lalee sat down. She had stepped out of Shonagachhi,

not often, but it had happened sometimes. A regular would request a home visit, or a good client would want company for a friend. But they had been quiet affairs. Stealthy entrances into someone else's home, slipping in and out of respectable neighbourhoods. Lalee had not been to a dance bar like this one. Rambo was looking at the mem beside him. She turned to Lalee and extended her right arm.

'This is Shaka,' Rambo said, smiling at Lalee. 'She's Russian. Do you know what's her rate for a whole night? Seventy thousand.' He laughed with – Lalee was surprised to note – genuine glee. As if this was his personal achievement.

The mem frowned. In the very next second, she pushed Rambo playfully and leaned on his shoulder, with one languid, bony arm around him. The momentary annoyance that crossed her face didn't escape Lalee's attention, and she found a tiny, shimmering sliver of joy in her annoyance at Rambo.

'Oh, you think everyone is Russian, Rambo darling. Because you couldn't name another country with a gun to your head.' She said in a strange accent that Lalee didn't entirely understand. She turned to Lalee, 'Just call me Sonia. Anyway, my dancing name here is Jasmine.' She swept her hair back over her shoulders, bent sideways and dragged her handbag up to the table. Then, as if she had forgotten something, she asked, 'Are you hungry? They make a very nice chilli babycorn.'

Lalee shook her head. 'I haven't brought any money.'

'Don't worry about it.'

Rambo turned around and beckoned to the middle-aged man in a white coat, red-and-white turban and cummerbund with such casual disdain that Lalee scanned the man's face for a trace of irritation. But his face was expressionless as he walked slowly towards their table.

Sonia placed the order. 'One chilli babycorn, dry, and one stir-fried pork.' She turned to Rambo and winked.

When the waiter had retired to the recesses of the restaurant, Sonia took out an oblong box from her purse and placed it in front of Lalee. Lalee opened it and took out a sleek rectangular piece of chrome and glass.

'Turn it on,' Rambo said.

The phone sprang to life. Lalee looked as a clean, new screen lit up, dotted with a few apps. She turned it around and noticed a few dents and scratches on its body.

Sonia got up from her chair and walked to where Lalee was sitting, standing behind her and leaning over the phone. Once she had explained the basics of how the phone worked, Lalee took out her own battered cell phone. A long crack ran diagonally across its face. She said, annoyed, 'I've seen a mobile phone before.'

Sonia backed away with raised palms, mimicking terror.

'Oh excuse me then, but I doubt you've used any of these apps before. Anyway, let me explain: this phone is where the clients will call you. We'll make the connections, and the service will give out this number for clients. But, more importantly, this is where you will receive the money. How do you think your friend Maya was doing so well when the rest of you girls were busy turning down clients with 500-rupee and 1,000-rupee notes, huh? She'd been doing this for years. Smart girl – she caught on fast.'

At the mention of Maya, Lalee's heart sank. She listened in mystified silence as Sonia opened each app on the phone and explained how mobile wallets worked.

'Once a job is confirmed, the client or the service will

transfer money to your phone wallet, you understand? You can see the money here. Then the contact numbers and locations are shared on WhatsApp, got it?'

Lalee nodded her head, entirely at a loss as to see how this money could be real, how she could have something she didn't physically possess. She kept looking from Rambo to Sonia, both of whom kept insisting that it was in fact real money which she could transfer into her bank account, buy food with it, even pay Shefali Madam her cut, and while Lalee sat listening to them, she wondered how many times these two had given this same speech to how many women like her. She thought about the old man who brought vegetables in a wooden cart every Wednesday morning, and wondered if he too would take this unreal money.

Sonia continued, and Lalee still struggled to understand the lilt in her accent, and all of the English words she used. 'Maya and some other girls even have card-swiping machines with them. No one likes to carry that kind of cash on them these days – how else do you think they were making so much? Digital is better than physical, always remember that. Anyway, it'll be a lot clearer after tonight.'

Rambo placed a small bag in front of Lalee.

'There's a dress in there, and some other stuff.'

Lalee frowned, 'What other stuff?'

Rambo waved his hands vaguely, 'Face wash, lipstick … girl things.'

Sonia chimed in, both her and Rambo's bodies leaning over the table to face Lalee, their faces eager and, Lalee imagined, tinged with some anxiety.

The waiter showed Lalee through a door and silently turned

on the lights. Without a word, he shut the door behind him and left.

She looked around the dingy bathroom. A white tube light lit the pale green walls, and two cockroaches scuttled away from the shadows. A toilet stood in the far corner. Against an old, water-stained washbasin, a giant mirror reflected back a spotted image of Lalee.

There was a black dress in the bag. It felt warm, as if it had been taken off someone's body. Lalee brought it to her nose. It smelled like stale perfume, a spicy, floral whiff mixed with the smell of dead nicotine. The small bag contained a random selection of make-up, face wash and a small vial of perfume. It also had packets of condoms. Lalee placed the new smartphone on the washbasin, and then, hesitating, she put it back in the bag and zipped it shut.

When she walked back into the restaurant, Sonia and Rambo were discussing something intently. Their heads were so close together that they could be mistaken for a couple on a date. Some of the restaurant's customers were openly staring at Sonia but the waiters paid them no attention at all.

They were busy moving the chairs around. What that revealed, Lalee noticed with mild surprise, was a dais in the shape of a semi-circle. Some men, not in waiter's uniform, were busy putting plastic sprays of yellow flowers around the stage. Rambo and Sonia stood up as Lalee came towards them. Then, gesturing for the two women to follow him, Rambo walked to the door.

# 14

TILU STOOD OUTSIDE LALEE'S DOOR, BLINKING FAST AND wiping the sweat off his forehead. The light-blue tin door, with its paint chipped in places and the moss-lined wall next to it, was still there, left slightly ajar. A boy, no more than five or six, peeked out of the door, staring at him wide-eyed. Tilu could see a woman folding clothes inside, while wrangling another child with her left hand. She saw him looking at her and came to the door.

'What do you want? The shop's not open yet.' She smirked at him, pulling the boy back inside.

'Lalee?' Tilu mumbled, wiping his forehead with a handkerchief.

The woman twisted her lips in distaste.

'Lalee's not here anymore – gone.' She walked away, dragging both children, who were staring at Tilu again, back into the room.

He knew he should leave, but couldn't find the strength to do so, not knowing what he should do next. The new woman who was moving around the familiar room – the room that until a few days earlier had belonged to Lalee and was the stage on which his grand romance had played out – was looking at him askance.

A woman's voice called out, and he didn't realize she was calling to him, feeling unsure in the commotion of the communal courtyard. Amina came up from behind and tapped Tilu on the shoulder, and to her secret amusement Tilu actually flinched at her touch.

'You are Lalee's babu, no?' said Amina.

Tilu wished it were so, that Lalee was exclusively his and shared her bed only with him. It wasn't so, but it felt good to imagine otherwise. He couldn't afford Lalee and Lalee wouldn't have him, but the idea that someone may have thought him worthy brought a smile to his face.

'Yes, yes, I am,' Tilu agreed readily.

'She hasn't told you?' Amina frowned. 'She's not here anymore.'

Tilu's heart sank. Surely this was linked to that murder, surely Lalee was in danger, why would she disappear otherwise?

'Where have they taken her?' Tilu hissed, shaking slightly from nerves, fear and unaccustomed courage.

Amina gave him a long stare. She lowered her voice and moved closer to Tilu. Anyone watching them would think Tilu was a customer Amina was trying to seduce. She whispered in his ear, clutching at his shoulder.

'Taken her? What do you mean by that? She's just working some outside jobs.'

Amina gave Tilu a once-over, taking in his faded kurta that had clearly shrunk from washing, his unshaven salt-and-pepper stubble, the cheap glasses.

'She'll be charging a lot more,' Amina said, pointing to the upper floors.

'They deal with ... high-end clients.'

Tilu blinked at her. He felt at a loss, but vague apprehensions began to surface in his foggy brain.

'Where is Lalee? I need to see her.'

Amina looked around, sweeping the room with a glance, pretending to laugh at what Tilu said.

'Call her if you want. But can you afford her? She'll be going away, for a while. Has she told you about that?'

Amina turned around to leave but Tilu grabbed her hand, desperate for answers. Amina could see the panic spreading on his face.

'I don't think you should come back here.'

Tilu walked away from The Blue Lotus as fast as he could, keeping his face half hidden with his handkerchief. He walked aimlessly for a while. He couldn't understand himself anymore; a number of feelings – some he didn't even know existed – tumbled around his head with slow, depressing repetition. He had never felt so powerless, so needy in his life. If he saw Lalee again, he wouldn't know what to say to her. Yet there was so much to say, and so little that he could articulate or even understand. He couldn't explain why he felt afraid; Tilu Shau knew Shonagachhi, and Tilu knew Lalee in Shonagachhi. Tilu knew the Lalee of Shonagachhi. Outside, would she be the same Lalee? Then it all fell into place for him: the longer cigarettes, the higher rates, the new hardness in her eyes – she had slowly been moving away from him, becoming someone he didn't know.

# 15

TILU LOOKED UP AT THE GREYING SKY ABOVE. TALL BUILDINGS, each studded with a rectangular screen of light, glimmering brighter than stars could ever hope to shine in a strangulating city. Tilu looked until his neck hurt, until unhappy commuters shoved him, bumped into him and wondered aloud why mad men were allowed to proliferate the streets during rush hour.

Park Street had once been Burial Ground Road where the first-ever chief justice of the Supreme Court of Calcutta, Sir Elijah Impey's deer park ran amok. Not many knew this, but Tilu did. Waiting for the sweltering metro train in the cavernous emptiness of Central station, Tilu felt the same thrill he did when he was a teenager, running away from the familiar drabness of his north Calcutta home to the expanse of the shaheb para. The sky felt bluer, the smog felt fragrant, the women and the lights, the streets and the smell of food, a secret, alluring world opening its doors to him. Now, balding and knock-kneed, he could still feel the shape of his adolescent desire wrapped around these foreign parts, so far and alien from his brick-bared home – that immense, beckoning seduction of a life unlived.

In the suffocating intestine of the metro, Tilu felt two women crash into him. They were both giggling, talking loudly, unconcerned and careless with their bodies. He turned his head discreetly, stole a glance, letting his eyes measure their fullness. The loudest, perhaps barely eighteen, was in a red top, the contours of her breasts brushing against the crowd, her thighs exposed in denim shorts. It was scandalous, and secretly thrilling. Tilu could not look at the girls directly; it felt wrong, like a forbidden, nasty thing, but he liked to know there was such abandon in the world, such invitations, even if they were not laid out for him.

The Park Street metro station spat him up as it did thousands other commuters, tired wage slaves, small cogs in giant wheels, pleasure seekers, tourists. Tilu stepped sideways, separated from the tide of bodies and asked for one single Marlborough Light from the guy selling cigarettes and fake Calvin Klein perfumes from a kiosk on the pavement. *This is what Lalee's lips must taste like*, he thought, *this burn, this tinny taste of counterfeit foreignness, this exceptionally white-bodied cigarette*. But it was easier to think about Sir Elijah Impey, his deer park and the funeral processions that in their day had passed this land. A long time ago, this road of abandon was a thoroughfare leading to the Park Street Cemetery that lay beyond it. Only two lordly houses dominated this place, and it is to Sir Impey's deer park that the street owed its name. Tilu felt he was a man born out of his time, in a plebian age of pen pushers and small-time clerks. The glory days of Calcutta, with its wild bands of Thugs, Kali-worshipping dacoits, pale-faced British cartographers and vicious malarial mosquitoes was the age he really belonged to. He could have made something of himself then.

He looked up at the old homes in the upper storeys of the street-level shops. Their facades, though crumbling and moss-bathed in recent years, bore the imperial English grandeur of the past. Tilu approved of faded glory. The very new and green sign that proclaimed Park Street as 'Mother Teresa Sarani' got in the way of Tilu's antiquarian reveries. He snorted loudly, turned towards the man who sold him the lone Marlborough and was now trying to hawk fake Gucci perfumes to a couple of girls, and said, 'See this nonsense? We have to call it Mother Teresa Sarani now. Huh, the sisterfucking mayor now tells us what to do. This place was great once, but with peasants like that mayor, what can you expect?'

The vendor of cigarettes and perfumes stared into the distance and replied philosophically, 'What's in a name? Whatever you call it, the street is the same street.'

That bastard mayor, after attending a ceremony where he was asked to unveil the statue of Mother Teresa in Naples, had promptly renamed Park Street after the sainted lady upon his return. If the papal sanctification had been carried out properly, the street should have been called Beata Teresa Sarani, but the mayor, having judged that Beata might be too much for even a race as pretentious as the Bengalis, had wisely stuck to the more homely 'Mother'. 'This mother-loving place will one day go to a mother-loving dump,' Tilu mumbled loudly as women began to edge away from him on the pavement. He came to a stop in front of Trinca's, advertising its Bloody Mary and Pina Colada at ₹200 a pop. Tilu stared at the board for a while, craning his neck to peek at the gaudily dressed crooner inside. He shook his head; such paltry shows of today could not hold a candle to the gentlemen's clubs such as The

Golden Slipper in their heyday of the fifties and the sixties. Rheumy-eyed octogenarians still remember those years, their faces grew warm at the memory of its forgotten nights. Tilu wished he could have seen the dancing girls of The Golden Slipper, smoked Cuban cigars in stuffy upper-class rooms. He knew that when these distinguished, cravat-wearing gentlemen were smoking cigars in the velvet-draped private rooms of Park Street and swapping tales of their youthful exploits in Oxford or Cambridgeshire, Tilu's forefathers were fighting ancient unassailable battles with mosquitoes, recalcitrant tubewells and nightly power cuts. He loved Park Street with the hankering of the dispossessed.

June was hot and heavy, smothering Calcutta under a blanket of unheaved sighs. Tilu Shau wondered if the rainclouds would ever descend upon the city. This was his favourite time of the day – the gloom of the sky, the grey-blue of the oncoming evening and the headlights on the well-trodden streets completed his urban fairyland. He took out his carefully folded white handkerchief from the breast pocket of his cream half-sleeve shirt and wiped his forehead. He walked slowly, deliberately away from the metro station exit, still spewing unbelievable numbers of people onto the streets, into narrow unknowable alleyways to a familiar destination.

The Nepali boy was lighting the kerosene lamp at the front door when Tilu Shau reached the Bangla liquor shack. It was dark and more people were flocking towards it in solitary ambles, like members of a secret melancholy church. The bald, skeletal man who sold the best mutton brain curry in small dried-leaf bowls with extra green chillies and rock salt, was smoking a bidi, sitting on his haunches. The man who sold hot rotis and vegetable curries was only just beginning to knead the huge mound of dough in front of him, dripping sweat into his day's work. Tilu Shau loved all of this. One day, he knew, one day, he'd put all of this in words and it would all be redeemed, made magnificent and immortal in a way his soul knew it already was.

It may have been an hour or five, Tilu couldn't tell anymore. Time became more viscous, trickling like blood through sand in this loud and swampy place. A large man – as fat as he was tall – sat companionably next to Tilu. He had a plate of hot chickpeas in front of him and a pint of clear liquid in a glass bottle that he shared generously with his newfound friend. He had read all the books in Tilu's Sister-in-law series and enjoyed them immensely. Tilu was delighted despite himself. He wished he was known for something better, he wished he'd someday stand in the glittering orb of an expensive yellow light in Park Street's Oxford Bookstore where beautiful women in translucent saris would wait in a line for an autograph from him. But on balance, he felt, a drunk fat man was better than nothing. His father would never know the secret magic of meeting in a dank corner someone who'd read your words.

'This boudi then, who's this naughty sister-in-law you write so much about? I think she needs to be punished.' He laughed without making a sound, his large belly quivering.

'She's no one, someone imaginary.'

'Oh come on! I'm sharing my hard-earned pint with you here, dada. You have to reveal the identity of this talented lady.'

'She is …' Tilu faltered. Dark skin and long hair and the smell of sweat and the fumes from the fire burning in his throat, all seemed to coalesce into one figure. 'She is a woman I know. She's ... an untamed thing.'

'Give me the address, brother. I need to meet her at least once before I die.'

'Don't, my friend. She's an addiction. You have a wife, children – don't start a habit you cannot sustain. There are easier ways to kill yourself.'

'Hahaha! And who wants those? I've been married sixteen years, dada, I've done it in and out, I have done the kids, the maternity wards, the Choitro season sales, the in-laws, Jamaishoshti. It isn't worth it. It's one long way to wait for death to come and take you. Nah, I say. Fuck that shit. Fuck a woman who'll make you feel alive.'

*Yes*, Tilu thought; the image of Lalee, hips jutted to a calculated angle, dark back exposed through a revealing blouse underneath her sliding saree, long, dark hair falling to a side like some sort of taboo night magic, drawing on a long, white stick of cigarette. Tilu closed his eyes to hold that image behind his eyes, to burn it into the dark space.

'She's gone. She's gone from where she used to be.'

# 16

LALEE ADJUSTED HER DRESS WHEN NO ONE WAS LOOKING. Sonia was standing by the window, leaning against the wall, arms crossed around herself. She was whistling something that sounded vaguely familiar. It reminded Lalee of a lullaby, a tune from another time and another life. Hearing it here in this cold, barren room felt wrong. She felt a heat rise from her neck. Rambo was fiddling with the large camera in his hand. He probably didn't know how to use it; Lalee allowed herself a smirk. Sonia seemed removed from it all. Rambo muttered under his breath.

Lalee didn't know what to expect when she was led – Rambo at the front and Sonia behind her – up the dim stairs to a room above. She saw the number stuck on the door. She whispered, '212, 212, 212,' to herself until she noticed Sonia looking at her strangely. It felt important to remember. She wondered why she had been brought there. For a moment, she considered turning around and running for it. She would get out of the door, maybe even further, get on any bus and then … and then, where? There were times, especially in those early days, when she had dreamed of a place that came after 'then', someday – Lalee clenched her hands imperceptibly – there will be a place beyond here, that absent horizon that had to exist somewhere, but it wasn't here now.

Rambo looked at her and clicked his tongue.

Lalee frowned. Rambo said, 'Oh, not you. This cocksucking thing doesn't work. Too many settings.'

He pointed the thing at Lalee, the white-hot flash startling her. She tried to lean on her hands, placed slightly wide behind her hips and closed her eyes for a moment. The room smelled like disinfectant. The cold white light pervaded everything. Rambo had said something about a catalogue, a higher grade of clients. He had pointed to Sonia and said, 'Do you know how much this bitch makes? For a night, 70,000; for just a dance, 10,000; extra for happy endings.' Lalee had stared at both of them. Sonia had simply smiled and walked away. Lalee didn't believe him. She hadn't seen that kind of money in one place, at one time. The white cotton sheet felt cold under her skin. Even half of that – 25,000 a night – meant in two nights she would have 50,000. What would that buy? A new roof? Brick walls? A tubewell? Education? She dared not plan, but it was nice to be able to dream. Tilu's face surfaced in her head, like a flower floating over a polluted river. The constant smallness of being, the haggard face, the hunched shoulders and the inevitability of defeat that ruled his soul, and was imprinted on his body. She opened her eyes.

'Not too bad. With some focused yellow lighting, I think I could make something of it,' Rambo said to Sonia. Her blond head knocked against Rambo's dark, oiled one, peering over the camera's tiny screen.

'Alright, I have to go now, darling,' Sonia said to Rambo. His face broke into a smile Lalee wasn't prepared for. Sonia turned to go, her hair brushing against Rambo's forearms as Lalee looked at his face – the naked absolution, the eyes withdrawing quickly as Sonia turned around. Lalee blinked. Idiot Rambo, he was in it, knee-deep and without a map.

Afterwards, standing in a dark corner as Sonia whirled under the multi-coloured, roving lights, Lalee felt a sharp twang of piercing metal somewhere deep inside her. The tall, blonde woman sparkled like a rare stone, being showered in banknotes like goddesses were showered with shredded marigold petals. She wore a small, blue bustier and a pink, embroidered ghagra, her flawless white body and perfect belly button encased in gold chains. The men around the restaurant stared at her, clapped with her and blew a confetti of banknotes at her feet. The drunkest among them tottered forward and tried to dance with her, awkwardly moving to the strange exotic music like ill-formed primates. Sonia – composed and alluring – smiled at them tolerantly, unknowably, skewering them with her direct, seductive gaze that Lalee recognized without mistake for the knife's edge it was.

She was watching Rambo too. Half of his face lit by the fragments of the second-hand spotlight that landed on him, and the rest lit by something internal, something that felt dangerous and unmappable. It was either foolish love, or the kind of greed that got people killed. It could have been the goddess dancing in front of Lalee or the numerous, scattered notes that seemed to rend the air around them. Lalee hated them both in that moment. Hated Sonia, hated Rambo and all these punters throwing away cash like it was nothing but dust. There was more money lying on that floor than Lalee had ever seen at one time, more than families she knew would make in a year. And she wondered how they ever managed to keep a tab on what they earned and what was simply lost in the dark, musty undersides of the couches, for rats and cleaners to find.

Once in a while men came up to Rambo and started talking to him. Lalee watched their heads bend together, each trying to scream into the other's ear. Rambo was grinning wildly, taking out his phone and showing something to these men. Lalee moved closer and realized he was scrolling through pictures of girls, but the men's backs blocked her view and she couldn't make out the faces. She wondered if her photos were being peddled too. She had felt hesitant, afraid and extremely suspicious when Sonia and Rambo had brought her to that room and asked her to pose for the camera. Sonia had sat down on the bed, urged Rambo to leave them for a while and explained very calmly to Lalee that the kind of customers Rambo was going to get her, the kind of customers that Madam wanted her to get, did not punt out large payments without seeing what they were likely to get. She said little, leaving Lalee to embroider her imagination, leaving the details to be mangled by her own greed, desire, desperation and envy. Lalee wasn't oblivious, she was simply incapable of resisting that powerful cocktail. When she had stopped resisting, Sonia calmly adjusted Lalee's dress, redid her makeup and invited Rambo back into the room.

Sonia was a dancer. Looking around the room and watching the men get drunker and the few stone-faced waiters standing unobtrusively in the corners, Lalee thought she had solved the Sonia puzzle. This is what she did, probably even serviced rich men, and Rambo featured in some way as a broker of sorts.

Between the two of them, they had it figured out. This was the reason for Rambo's recent flashiness, and if a fool like Rambo had won big, she could only imagine what Madam had made of this. Perhaps there were more like Sonia, mems and near-mems who earned more than B-category girls like her, maybe even more than A-category girls like Maya.

Lalee's heart stopped at the thought. Maya – there she was again. The melted face, the gushing neck and that smell. Lalee felt her head spin for a second, and her stomach twist. The room was already speckled with dark lights, the smell of sweat and booze, and now awash with the ghastly smell of burning flesh. Lalee knew how people burned. A man on fire tried to run, fell down, crawled a few paces, got up again and tried to run. Once there was a peaceful village balanced precariously on the edge of Hindus and Muslims. It took one ember, and the peaceful village charred itself. Lalee knew, but she didn't remember. It felt like a dream that had happened to someone else. She had nothing to do with it anymore. She had reawakened in a small room partitioned by plywood where a younger Shefali Madam owned a Godrej almirah full of shiny synthetic sarees and ghagra cholis, and she had seen a steady stream of girls like Jigri replicating themselves endlessly like an ancient curse, coming and going out of her life. Like Maya had come, and how Maya had left.

# 17

NASKAR HOVERED AROUND THE DOOR BEHIND THE SMALL, shrivelled body of Balok-da and Samsher's hulking back. They were blocking his view but he wouldn't dare say anything. His two superiors were also standing a little to the inside, carefully hiding their faces in the interior gloom of the thana. The crowd of women outside the station had swelled considerably. Once or twice, when neither Balok-da or Officer saab was around, Naskar had taken a flask of chai to the women outside. More commonly, he had handed out bottles of cool water. It was June after all and he didn't want to see them collapse in front of the thana. It was a lot harder to evade Balok-da's ever-roving eyes and his network of spies than it was to escape Officer saab's notice. Officer saab didn't concern himself with mundane events; he wasn't petty either. Balok-da, on the other hand, was a much larger threat in Naskar's world.

From what he could see, the TV journalist was quite pretty. She was talking to all the women. Some other people whom Naskar hadn't seen before but Balok-da had unequivocally tarnished with the 'NGO folks' label, had come today. The pretty journalist was adjusting her dupatta while standing in front of the camera. She held her microphone and began to speak. Naskar could hear her clearly, but her interview was frequently interrupted by Officer saab's interjections.

*We're bringing you this report from the streets of Shonagachhi.*

It's Burtolla police station, idiot.

*These women have been on a strike …*

What strike? Idiot. This is not the cocksucking Writers' Building.

*… for several days. They demand that their friend – a young mother and sex worker called Mohamaya Mondal who was murdered on June 3rd – receives a fair and thorough investigation from the police.*

Bnara natok! 'Fair and thorough investigation.' Cocksucking media journalist.

*We have with us a senior worker from the Nari Shakti Vahini, who have joined these women from the Collective, in their fight against injustice.*

*'Madam, why are you here? What are your demands?'*

*'Our demands are very simple. We want the public and the police to wake up to the reality of this situation. These women like Maya are a target of daily assault and violence. How many girls and how many women need to die before we wake up?'*

*'So, Madam, today, what do you think is the road ahead?'*

*'Raid-Rescue-Rehabilitate. There is no other way. The police need to conduct fair, transparent raids with honesty and not shield the guilty parties. We need to find these girls, rescue and protect them and then we should put all our resources into rehabilitating them so that they can find their place in society. Human trafficking is an organized crime, and we need to be organized to fight it.'*

*'In your opinion, madam, how bad is the situation right now?'*

*'You can see plainly how bad it is. Mohamaya was a bright young girl who had been brought here against her will. She had two children, and she wanted to provide them with good education and a good future. She was trying to leave this life behind but people who sell women and girls do not care about that.'*

Haan, the victim narrated her janampatri to you, sala idiot.

*'Every man in a khaki uniform in the area of Shonagachhi has earned off their backs. Either directly, or by fining the johns or getting a cut from the girls, the madams and their pimps. They know everything that goes on there. For example, they know very well that a fresh consignment of girls has arrived recently. A full load, from Nepal, Bangladesh, Bihar and even a few from Myanmar. We have been waiting at various posts outside Shonagachhi. There are girls as young as seven in there … Seven! Speaking from a lifetime's experience, I'll give her a year. They don't always survive beyond that. And yet we prefer to save the perpetrator rather than the victim.'*

Samsher turned around and nearly knocked into the craning figure of Naskar. He gave Naskar a look that could have burned him down. Fucking raid-rescue-rehabilitate! Did they think he was busy plucking his cock hair here all day?

This news would go on TV. And then the assholes would gather five half-dead aantel bumboils to debate this issue endlessly.

There was little activity in the station. Two drunks sat dozing on the lone wooden bench, their hands tied together with rope, and a constable was talking desolately with them. Most of the personnel were focused on the circus going on outside. Samsher drummed his fingers distractedly on his desk, frowning at the greenish glass globe that ubiquitously held errant paperwork in all government offices. This thing was going to go the distance, now that the media had got a hold of it.

He looked up and saw Balok Ghosh hovering in the doorway. He gestured for him to walk over. Balok came and stood next to Samsher's chair, staring stoically ahead.

'Did someone go to The Blue Lotus when that … thing happened, Balok-da?' Samsher asked.

'Yes, syaar, I went with Junior Constable Biswas, syaar. She was dead, of course. The thing happened around midnight, I think; we went around two in the morning. They didn't want to hand over the body but since there were no relatives and it was a murder case, I told them the body had to go to the police morgue, syaar. I made a call and some people from the Knatapukur police morgue came and took it away.'

'Evidence? Did you seal the crime scene?'

Balok Ghosh frowned slightly and then gave a shrug.

'No, syaar, we were just there. Things had been somewhat cleaned away by the time we arrived. You know how it is, they take care of their own business. Everyone swore that some customer did it but no one had seen him or any other person enter. She was soliciting as usual in front of the building, and there's always a lot of people around. Son of a bitch broke an entire bottle of carbolic acid on her face and then pushed the bottle into her throat. Broken glass all over the floor.'

'What happened to that? Did you confiscate the glass?'

'No, syaar. They even moved the body, cleaned up the blood. Didn't want to leave it for two hours, I suppose.'

Samsher Singh gave a long sigh. Balok waited for something more from his boss. After a few minutes, he decided to dole out some more information. He believed, very firmly, in drip-feeding intelligence to his superiors.

'Biswas is on duty in the booth outside Shonagachhi, on the big crossing in Sovabazar, syaar. He said two media vans came in today about an hour ago. They're going to get their money's worth out of this.'

Samsher groaned.

'And we have no evidence of any kind? The bottle could have had fingerprints, my man! If this blows out of proportion, which I think it will, what am I going to say when Lalbazar calls?'

Balok Ghosh shrugged again, as if to say that he had seen a lot of fingerprints in his time and didn't think much of them.

'Well, it'd be a case of a needle in a haystack, syaar. How many people will you be running after? The fingerprint is hardly going to be matched and there would probably be a dozen different sets of prints anyway.'

Samsher nodded. Fingerprints and clues and body lines only worked in American television serials, or when someone really high-profile got murdered and the Central Bureau of Investigation led probes. Then the Special Branch and the Crime Branch all became super-efficient to bring the criminal to justice. It wasn't going to happen for some whore in Shonagachhi, who saw god knows how many men in a day, and he was certainly not going to take up the task.

'Who informed us about the crime?'

'No one, syaar. Biswas was on duty, he saw some johns running away, commotion and shouting, so he went to see what the matter was, then two girls told him what had happened. I don't think the NGOs came until the morning. Though I'm sure they knew on the night itself. Some of those girls there are in constant touch with them, call them on mobile phones.'

Samsher nodded.

'Is the body still there?'

'At the Knatapukur morgue. They did the post-mortem even though the reason of death seems to be pretty clear. No one has claimed the body, of course. Such girls ... they don't have many people willing to take them to the crematorium when the time comes.'

Singh drained the last of his tea and got up from his swivel chair, put on his regulation khaki cap and picked up his baton.

'All right, Balok-da, you're coming with me. Let's go and have a chat with the people at the morgue. Have they sent us a report yet? Ask the driver to get the jeep out.'

Samsher Singh and Constable Balok Ghosh, not suitably motivated, marched out of the Burtolla police station to see a dead girl.

# 18

IT WASN'T THAT SHONAGACHHI WAS NEVER IN THE NEWS. Every once in a while, there was a murder, or some newspaper would decide to write a feature on the life of Shonagachhi girls or their children and the much-needed work the dedicated NGOs were doing in the area. And the news channels would bring around their vans when some hot and immediate crime had taken place in South Asia's largest red-light district. Lalee watched the girls on the lower floor lining the balcony, bending over the concrete railings to look at a news channel journalist recording an interview. Lalee sighed quietly to herself. It must be Malini. There was something about outsiders coming into Shonagachhi, commenting on the things that happened here, that unsettled Lalee. She was aware that the local NGOs and even the Collective encouraged the right kind of media coverage – but Lalee knew in her bones that talking heads on a TV screen debating the state of Shonagachhi's women knew very little of life in these fabled streets. At best, they understood the strife, the visible and invisible traumas that scarred the people who lived here, but they were blind to the laughter, the friendships, the minutiae of daily life that flowed here as it did in countless respectable neighbourhoods.

It was late when she came back with Sonia the night before. Lalee didn't entirely understand what Sonia did and how her business worked. Sonia moved in a mysterious world of money, of dancing bars and rich clients. But Lalee was beginning to get the idea that there was more to it than they revealed to her. There was also something strange about Rambo's involvement that Lalee couldn't quite put her finger on. Girls like Sonia didn't need pimps like Rambo. Neither did they need people like Shefali Madam. Lalee had known Shefali Madam a long time and she had a feeling that there was a reason Shefali Madam wanted Sonia to spend time with her, but she couldn't tell exactly what it was. If she asked, she may or may not get an answer, and whatever that answer was, Lalee might not be able to believe it.

After her performance last night, Sonia dropped Lalee off at The Blue Lotus and drove off in the car. Lalee didn't ask where she was going. During the car ride, Sonia had once more and patiently showed Lalee how to accept money using mobile wallets, how to make payments and transfer the money to her bank account. The engorged numbers in Sonia's own accounts, or what she had shown to Lalee, seemed unreal. Part of her couldn't shake off the notion that it was all an elaborate hoax.

She had foolishly walked to her old room. The sight of a new woman in her room had shaken something inside her. She stood outside that old door, staring vacantly at the familiar walls, the posters someone else had pasted on them, the spot in the alcove where a pot of mustard oil had once spilled. Then she had dragged herself upstairs and slept in an unfamiliar room which didn't belong to her.

She decided she would go out to the small shop across the road, buy a few things she needed, maybe a cup of tea. On her way there, she could go meet the new resident of her room.

She knocked roughly on the door. A voice answered:

'It's open – you just have to push it hard. The damn door keeps jamming.'

Lalee pushed open the door and saw a young woman sitting on a double bed facing the window with a handheld plastic mirror, doing her make-up.

'What's your name?'

'Chanda.'

Lalee asked a little tentatively, unsure how to frame the question, 'Are you new here? One of Shefali Madam's girls?'

Chanda looked at her and nodded distractedly.

'Just took up this room – it was yours, no? Madam told me I could have it on adhiya.'

Chanda laughed and Lalee noticed that the girl's cheeks dipped in two little spots on either side of her mouth. A dimpled smile that made her look even younger.

'Shefali Madam must be minting money. I do all the work, and she gets half without even dropping the end of her saree. At least I don't have to pay rent. Do you know that Category-A girls can get paid up to 70,000 rupees now?'

'I'm Lalee.'

'I know who you are.'

Chanda concentrated on tracing the line of her lower lash with a black pencil that didn't seem to move very smoothly. She pointed to the news van standing outside.

'Have you heard? They've been here since morning, asking people all sorts of things. That's Tara News – they're here because of the candlelight march that the Collective is organizing. Are you going? Or is that something upstairs girls like you are not supposed to do?

'I don't know.'

'All of Shonagachhi is going to be in the march. Malini came here with five others and spoke to Shefali Madam – all of us are going.'

Lalee was thinking about this when Chanda spoke again, flashing a finger to the room next door.

'You know it happened in this room?'

She pointed a finger at the floor and for a second Lalee almost expected to see a dead woman lying there. Chanda continued, oblivious to what Lalee already knew.

'Oh, it's horrible. I didn't see her. I didn't want to see her but I heard what happened to her face. Oh my God. I heard Mohamaya had two kids. I never knew. Apparently they stay with her parents. They didn't know what Maya did. They thought she worked in the city. Her husband died, so they had no money, and her parents are very old. You know the NGO woman, the tall one who comes with Malini?'

Lalee nodded.

'She showed us a picture of her kids. One boy, one girl – the girl is very pretty, has big eyes. I felt very sad, you know. So young, and none of it is their fault.'

She stopped to take a long breath and then continued.

'Did you know Maya auditioned for a role on a television serial? That NGO, she was a peer-educator for them. Maya used to go to the girls and tell them about AIDS and give free condoms and all that. Shefali Madam didn't like it very much, but she didn't say anything. Must have been because of Malini. That NGO woman apparently helped Maya audition for that TV role. Wouldn't it be great if one of us made it in the movies or on TV? It could be me, or even you – who knows!'

Lalee watched her as she looked at herself critically in the mirror. Behind Chanda, Lalee could see cut-outs of various Bollywood heroines pasted on the stained walls. Madhuri Dixit in a pointy bra, Kareena Kapoor in a red dress, Priyanka Chopra in a wet yellow saree. Other than calendar gods and goddesses, the most popular item of home decoration in The Blue Lotus were these glamour heroines, the textured, uneven walls, distorting their bodies

They both heard a soft whimper and an indistinct thump from above.

'I hope it's not too bad,' said Chanda.

'What do you mean? What's happening over there?'

'Go see for yourself – I'm not saying anything. And anyway, I don't like trouble; what's it to you or me?'

She stared intently at the mirror, drawing an exaggerated line around her lips, refusing even to meet Lalee's gaze.

Lalee's ears tried to pick out the voices from the background clamour of The Blue Lotus. They sounded familiar.

She took two steps at a time and stopped at the landing on the second floor, catching her breath. From where she stood, she could hear a man's voice, rather thin, but what it lacked in robustness it made up for with vindictive rage. It was Chintu. He was calling his invisible target a multitude of names, though most of them were variations on the theme of prostitute. *It's amazing,* thought Lalee, *how many synonyms one language could have devised and seemed to need for women who sell their bodies for money. We are an expletive – a whole population of women connected only by their livelihood reduced to a single word of offence. At least we do what we do, but the ones who don't aren't spared either. At one time or another, every woman is turned into a profanity.* A soft whimpering pierced her train of thought and she ascended the last few steps quietly, with caution.

Chintu, short and squarish, was standing in the middle of the room with what looked like a whip in his hand, and Amina was whimpering a little distance away from him, with her forehead resting on the corner of the wall. She was in her bra and a pair of leggings. Her hair was all over the place, and she was breathing huge gulps of air between grunts of pain. Once Lalee's eyes adjusted to the dark room, she saw that what he was holding was not a whip but his own belt. It was fitted with a large buckle and the girl's back was covered in raised vertical welts. As she stood motionless taking in the scene, unobserved by the other two, Chintu rushed towards the cowering girl, shouting and grabbing her by the hair, and moved as if to knock her forehead against the wall. Lalee rushed at Chintu and fell with all her weight on him, knocking him to the floor. He pushed her, making her slide backwards on the smooth cement floor. Then out of an instantaneous animal rage, Lalee charged once more at Chintu, scratching, hitting, kicking all at once.

It was impossible to say how long it lasted. To Lalee it felt like the fraction of a second. A deep, familiar voice said suddenly, out of nowhere, 'Not the face, Chintu, never the face. You should know better.'

Both Lalee and Chintu froze in an instant, as if they were no more than bickering alley cats on whom a bucket of ice-cold water had been poured. The rage drained out of Lalee; her vision, which had narrowed in anger as it focused on Chintu, widened. She saw Shefali Madam entering the room through a door on the left, pushing aside the shiny curtains.

She clicked her tongue and shook her head, talking in a soft, low voice like she was reprimanding Chintu for leaving the lights on too long.

'How many times do I have to tell you?'

She walked over to the other side where Chintu was still fuming, barely taking his eyes off Lalee, and sat down heavily on a plastic chair.

Lalee had never once heard her raise her voice, but neither had she seen Shefali Madam been contradicted or disobeyed. She never raised a hand herself, but she was the cause of violence in others. And yet, some of the girls never left her side. She drew as much respect as dread, and from some, a feral loyalty.

Chintu rolled up his belt and, without another word, walked out of the room. Lalee heard his footsteps thudding down the stairs and a loud bang as a door shut behind him.

Shefali Madam was holding a small box in her left hand. It was a fine brass thing, studded with a number of semi-precious stones all around. She placed the box on her lap and opened it. Inside, betel leaves were neatly arrayed, each fatly wrapped into a conical shape. She picked one up and, with great ceremony, popped it into her mouth. After a minute, she spoke to the girl still cowering by the wall.

'Freshen up. You need to get ready for the evening.'

Amina, Lalee noticed, had stopped crying entirely as soon as Shefali Madam had entered the room. She was now crouching in the corner, staring at the older woman seated on the chair. She wiped her nose with the back of her hand and half crawled, half dragged herself forward. Lalee saw her scrambling out of the room. She waited until Amina's footsteps had faded in the distance.

'What's going on?'

Shefali Madam chewed thoughtfully for a moment, looking past Lalee.

'He's still coming? For the money?'

Lalee stopped, looking at Shefali Madam. The older woman laughed.

'That was what the loan is for, isn't it? You girls never learn. You know how much I paid for you, twenty years ago? Two thousand rupees – not a lot these days, but enough for them. And you'll still give them your money?'

Lalee sputtered, tripping over responses and comebacks. Madam's faint, ironic smile put a stop to that. Lalee settled on sullen silence, looking away from Shefali Madam. After a few quiet minutes that stretched uncomfortably between them, Madam spoke again.

'It's never good, Lalee, when outsiders get involved. It's about us, you realize? Just us. No one else cares. We're best left to our own devices; the less people from the outside get involved in our affairs the better it is for us. Anyway, you won't get that loan. The bank is in no position to give you any money. If you want to, get ready – there are some good clients lined up. The mem will accompany you, but you may have to go away for some time.'

'Go away where?'

'You'll find out. First a hotel, then somewhere nice, for a few nights. You know how doctors make house calls? Think of yourself as a doctor. House calls are worth more money.'

Shefali Madam got up from the chair, pushing her plump body forward. Lalee shouted at Shefali Madam's back, hearing her voice getting shriller, and hating how this woman could still throw her off-kilter.

'What's wrong with Amina? Why use your pet monkey to beat her up?'

Shefali Madam looked back at her, smiled and walked slowly away, like she had all the time in the world.

Lalee fumed, alone and ineffectively in the dark room. She kicked the chair Madam had been sitting in, punching the seat that was still warm. She collapsed on her haunches, remembering Madam's face from a long time ago. She'd come to Madam's room one afternoon, a blood-soaked underwear in her hand, inconsolable. She was afraid the men from the night before, the ones Madam sent to her every few hours, had done something to her, broken something badly inside her and now she was bleeding. Madam had smiled – the same smile that could still reach its hand inside of her somewhere she couldn't reach and twist, until she was burning inside. Shefali Madam folded a piece of cloth. Showed her how Lalee would need to fold such pieces of cloth for the next several years until she could afford cheap sanitary napkins. And that night, she'd sold Lalee to someone who liked bleeding women.

# 19

SHE COULD TAKE THE LIFT, BUT DEEPA DECIDED TO WALK the six flights of stairs. Halfway up the fourth flight, Deepa stopped, heaving slightly, watching two large cockroaches scramble across the floor and disappear into a crack she had never noticed before. The book launch she had just attended was predictable. A few well-known faces sat in distant corners, enveloped in cloaks of sullen gloom, while the fame-hopefuls fawned over the famous authors, the star editors and anyone else who would talk to them. Their eagerness, their misplaced desperation, their oversensitivity to imagined slights, exhausted Deepa. Still, there were obligations she needed to fulfil. Apparently, the book was based on a real crime, a fictionalized account of a much-publicized murder of a young woman and child a few years ago. Deepa bought a copy dutifully, though she had no intention of reading it and wondered when, if ever, the case would be solved. She felt the corners of her mouth tug in an approximation of a smile. Real crime was about waiting. She had lodged endless FIRs in her time, and she could write lengthy books about the waiting, the slow drip of days and weeks and months and years that went by before anyone, anything moved. People who had never set foot inside a police station, people who treated police stations the way they treated leprosy clinics, imagined that the system jumped up and launched into investigations. In reality, the days stretched out into the distance, reaching an inconclusive horizon.

Deepa put the latchkey in the door and leaned against it. She heard the faint strains of John Coltrane, and a wisp of light breaking through the crack under the door. She practised her breathing, in and out, in and out, pressing her face against the uneven surface of the carved wood. This was Vishal's door. Twenty years ago, when they had received this apartment from Vishal's parents as a wedding present, he had declared in his usual, voluble way that he was going to rip the standard, non-descript door out and put in a Burmese piece. Deepa's new in-laws forbore from making a comment. Breeding, Deepa remembered thinking at that time, breeding and money. The sheer callousness of not caring, in that well-mannered, shaggy way Vishal had, of all things material. For as long as they had been married, Deepa had thought of that moment as the defining experience of her entry to that family-by-marriage.

She turned the key and walked in. A loud, hearty voice boomed from the kitchen, drowning out the Coltrane flowing pitch-perfect from unobtrusive Bose speakers hidden like Easter eggs throughout the flat. 'Begum,' Vishal called out, stressing the last syllable with an unnecessary 'h', the way he did when he was feeling particularly romantic. 'Come in here and look at what your husband's doing.' Deepa walked into a kitchen sizzling and hissing with whatever Vishal was cooking, and the man emerged, as always, like a small hillock, from a smother of smoke. Holding up his spatula like a spear, he squashed Deepa against his torso with his other hand, which held a burning cigar.

'Did you burn something?' Deepa asked.

'No, why? Do you smell burning?' Deepa shook her head. Vishal reached out to grab his e-cigarette, blowing out a huge cloud of smoke, carefully away from Deepa. White tendrils split around Vishal and flowed towards her nonetheless.

'Never mind,' Deepa smiled. 'How can you smoke both things at the same time?'

Vishal didn't reply, concentrating on flipping the searing meat on the frying pan and harmonizing with Coltrane.

Deepa went to her study. She left the door open. There was a certain comfort to the sounds Vishal made, ambling through the rooms, cooking bizarre things, singing to himself. In twenty years, Deepa had never allowed herself to admit to that comfort. It always felt like a thing she had stolen, something she had no right to in the world. But she felt the shape of that comfort, the steady faith that held two people together. She turned on the table lamp, standing sentinel next to her desk. Vishal seldom entered this room and never in her absence. She ran a finger across the rough surface of the old desk, the single thing she had brought with her to this house. In the second drawer, there was an envelope, one she didn't open often. She took it out and undid the twine around it, fingers shaking slightly. She laid out the photographs on the desk, one after the other. Sathi, 26. Protima-di, 52. Sonal, 43. Tezima, 23, Mohamaya, 28. Dead woman, she had seen, eaten with, laughed, argued and raged with. She bent over the pictures, finding the chair with one unsteady hand.

Vishal thought of knocking on the door, saw her and

withdrew his hand. Deepa heard soft footfalls on the floor and reached out. Vishal placed the cut-glass tumbler on her desk, softly, as if he was at a shrine. Deepa leaned over, clutching his coarse kurta, bending sideways, looking for the familiar, everyday bulk of comfort.

After a while, Deepa pressed the cold tumbler to her cheek, the square heft of ice cubes still intact in two inches of the amber liquid. 'Shouldn't have married a, you know, social worker.'

'Shouldn't have married a Parsi,' Vishal boomed through the jungle of his beard. Between the shaggy hair, the unkempt eyebrows and now this latest, a giant bushy beard, all Deepa could see were a pair of gleaming leprechaun eyes, unchanged after two decades. 'You know what they say – they're all a little mad.'

'A little, huh?' Deepa raised her eyebrows.

Vishal smiled at her, sinking back in his old-fashioned rocking chair.

'It's not a war of narratives,' he said, after a while.

Deepa didn't say anything.

'Your experience is no less valid. You're allowed to have the courage of your convictions.'

'Do you know what she said to me? The first time I met her?' Deepa said, her voice creeping around the low bass of the music. 'She explained to me the difference between equity mutual funds and debt mutual funds,' Deepa smiled, closing her eyes, rolling the tumbler over her forehead. 'It was at some point of the index funds and exchange-traded fund bit that she reminded me that I was staring at her, and might like to close my mouth. She could be funny like that, Maya. She always had a plan.'

Vishal knew how to quietly listen. Deepa went on, 'She never told me where she was from, how she got there – eventually they all do, that story comes out. Of course I didn't press her, but that was odd, and I kind of admired her integrity, I suppose. There was something different about her, but she was one of us. I still think it was my fault.' She opened her eyes for a minute and didn't need to tell Vishal to not interrupt her with a refutation.

'I know it was my responsibility, and what happened is my failure,' Deepa continued, closing her eyes once more and leaning back on the thick cushions. 'It was her choice, and I who go on and on about choice couldn't tell her what to choose. Still, it shouldn't have been her. It shouldn't have been any one of them.'

'You cannot protect them – it's not your job,' Vishal said in a calm voice, each word following the other slowly, deliberately.

'Should be someone's job,' Deepa replied quietly. 'Someone. One godforsaken person – God, Devil, religion – someone, something. Who's looking out?' After a while, when Coltrane had gone silent, Deepa spoke again. 'How do you think Malini will feel when she knows it was me? What equals that scale of betrayal?'

Vishal heaved himself out of the rocking chair, shuffled towards his wife and kneeled down. Deepa placed a hand on the back of his neck. He leaned forward and touched the cold tip of his nose to her collarbone. Deepa ran her hand through the thicket of his hair, the heat from his chest swirling around in the cold air of the AC. 'Come, eat dinner,' he whispered.

Deepa nodded, squeezing her eyes desperately against Vishal's dishevelled hair.

# 20

SAMSHER SINGH WAS FEELING RATHER SICK TO HIS stomach but heroically refrained from retching, in the interest of maintaining his dignity in front of his subordinates. The truth was that Samsher had never actually been part of a murder case before. He had seen dead people, road accidents, death by lynching, but he had never actually seen a mangled body with its mandatory post-mortem stitches frozen solid in the cold trays of the morgue. To make matters worse, it was the naked body of a twenty-three-year-old woman. Her naked torso lay in front of him, taut and cold, erotic and revolting. Samsher, not used to dealing with unsettling emotions, felt at once aroused and nauseated. He was going to have a few nightmares, there was no doubt about it. He walked out of the cold room into the relatively fresh air of the porch outside the building and drew great gulps of air to forget the stench of death and formaldehyde. Even so, he suspected the phantom smell would haunt him for some time to come. Samsher realized that a young man, a morgue personnel, was looking at him. He turned around and attempted to make his voice grave and important.

The badge on the man's lab coat read 'Chatterjee'. He was wiping his hands with a small hand towel with a cool, disaffected calm. Singh decided to go for patronizing familiarity.

'So, you have had the body for a while?'

The morgue technician tucked the towel into his side pocket and left it hanging.

'No, not really, compared to the number of unclaimed, unidentified bodies we get here. She's only been here a week and a few days, at most.'

'Did you do the ... thing?' Samsher moved his middle and forefingers mimicking scissors.

The man laughed as though he expected nothing more than such ignorance from a policeman.

'Haha, no, I just write up the reports. Doctor's assistant. But I can give you her file if you want.'

Samsher nodded.

'Just tell me what you found, that's all.'

'Well, the cause of death seems to be a collapse of the respiratory system once the jugular was ruptured because of the acid. Of course, then the bottle was thrust into her neck. I would suppose the acid was aimed at her face though a large amount of it also fell on the neck and burned the flesh. But there was also a bump on the head. I think she might have lost consciousness before the acid was splashed. There are also signs of asphyxiation. Though that was not the final cause of death.'

Samsher tried to take it all in. He suspected that Chatterjee was throwing in more medical jargon than was necessary. After some thought he said, 'That would explain why she didn't cry out sooner. I mean that place is as full as a slum. People everywhere. There's no way that someone wouldn't hear her scream. Especially since there are at least ten other girls living on the first and second floor of that house. If she was indeed strangled, the attacker would splash some of that acid on his own hand, wouldn't he?'

'Not necessarily. He could have strangled her first and then thrown the acid.'

Samsher sighed. It would be a case of interrogating the whole village to find one thief. No wonder Indian police investigations didn't go very far. Oh he had seen the Indian shows too – *Police Patrol* and that kind of stuff. It was more fiction than reality. Or maybe if he met any of those superhero cops in real life someday he could find out the truth behind it all. It all seemed very far-fetched to him.

On the ride back, Samsher was unusually quiet. Constable Ghosh knew better than to disturb his boss at such times. Eventually, Samsher said, 'It's very unpleasant, no, Balok-da?'

'It's a dog's job, syaar. We are the washermen's dogs as the saying goes, we belong neither at home, nor at the washing ghats.'

Samsher nodded. It was a saying his late father was fond of repeating.

'Did she have a babu?'

'They all do. I don't know how they can be so stupid. Every girl there will hand over her money and all her savings to the first asshole that promises to marry them, if you excuse my language, syaar. Even those that have been cheated before. It's such an obvious con and one that has happened to almost all of them, I don't know how they keep falling for it over and over.'

'You think it was the babu? Seven times out of ten it tends to be.'

Balok Ghosh shook his head. He was tempted to add, 'When it's a housewife, it's the husband or the in-laws ten times out of ten.'

'Ah, syaar, they whack the girls about a little bit all the time, and still the bitches give them money and do their bidding. Now who's going to say whether there was a problem or not? There's always a problem with these people. This isn't the first and it won't be the last of its kind in that place, or anywhere, syaar.'

It seemed for a moment that Samsher was going to say something in reply, but instead he paused thoughtfully for a moment, before saying,

'But the media's all over it now, and soon someone from upstairs will put pressure on us. We can't sit and do nothing. Who's the guy?'

'Salman Khan, syaar.'

'What? The film star?'

'Arrey, no, no, syaar, Pappu Sheikh. Man's a bit of a peacock and a big fan of the actor, dresses like him, talks like him – that sort of thing. So people call him Salman Khan, Sallu Bhai.'

Before the police car turned the corner and entered the ever-present traffic jam at the Sovabazar five-lane crossroads, Samsher asked a question Balok Ghosh wasn't prepared for.

'What's her name?'

Balok Ghosh didn't know the answer. He reached over to the backseat of the car and pulled out the brown-paper folder that had been handed over to him at the police morgue. He untied the string knot and took out the first sheaf of papers.

'Mohamaya, syaar, Mohamaya Mondol.'

# 21

THE FRYING PAN WAS ENORMOUS. SLICK WITH OIL AND shining in odd places like a softly melting rainbow was slithering on its surface. Tilu watched as the man wiped his forehead with his left hand. Bhoga said this was the best mixed chowmein in the area, overruling Tilu's more modest plans of eating his midday meal at a rice-and-curry hotel.

'Syaar,' Bhoga said, letting his eyes wander around the street, holding his gaze on a woman walking by, hurrying after a slowing bus. 'The market is hot right now. Don't take anything less than a thousand for your next one. The boss will try to get it on the cheap. I'm telling you now.'

Tilu looked at the sky, at the sagging electrical wires that hung so close to his head.

'Let's see,' he said. 'I'm planning something big right now.'

Bhoga turned and looked at Tilu, his eyes wide with excitement. 'Is it a different kind of choti, syaar? You can do it, syaar. This sister-in-law stuff is steady, but I think you can do better. Maybe an NRI sister-in-law? Just picture it, syaar, husband away, maybe in the Navy …'

Tilu looked at Bhoga, his most dependable reader, his

number one fan. Bhoga didn't know how old he was. He was shorter than Tilu, perhaps by a hair's breadth, but it was a thing that went a long way in endearing him to Tilu. In a world where absolutely everyone was taller than him, Tilu felt a special kinship with those shorter than him. Bhoga sold ayurvedic medicine on the local trains, more specifically on the Shonarpur local that travelled daily between Kolkata and the suburbs, before joining the troops at Amulyaratan Chakladar's printing business on College Street. The recipe for the cure for all arthritic pain was revealed to his great-grandfather in a particularly fortuitous dream, and Bhoga, like his father and his grandfather, had hawked the remedy to suspecting and unsuspecting daily passengers. Why he had given up that peripatetic life to sleep in Chakladar's windowless warehouse was a mystery to Tilu, and Bhoga had never clarified either. But if there was a gun to Tilu's head, he would say this young boy was about the only friend he had in this world.

The man brandished half an onion and held a naked blade in his right hand. He made quick successive horizontal slices on the onion's curved purple back, alternated that with deep vertical cuts and then collected the finely minced bits with one undermining slice, halving the onion. He added this to a pool of translucent oil in the middle of the gigantic pan. He added shredded cabbage with his left hand and stirred them about.

'I'm on the last one. Only five pages in.'

Tilu looked like he was miles away. *Writerly people*, thought Bhoga, *they could see the universe in a drop of water*. In his short time as a publisher's assistant, he had seen many writers. But none of them had quite the right temperament, not quite like Tilu babu did. The man had taught him all he knew about women. Not to mention the new words that he had to look up in newly printed Bengali dictionaries languishing in a dark corner of the Ma Tara Publishing Works godown, conveniently placed next to his damp, lumpy mattress.

'Which one?' Tilu asked, and then added anxiously, because no writer could resist that question, 'Do you like it?'

'My favourite is the first one, syaar. You know that part when she curves her finger slightly upwards like this and she—'

'Yes, yes, I know which one you mean,' Tilu said quickly.

'Nice, syaar, scientific. I like to know things like that. Might be useful someday.' Bhoga frowned slightly, 'But syaar, if you don't mind, I didn't like the third one, syaar.'

'*After the Bath*?'

'Yes, too many trees and country roads and lanterns. I mean I like description. I get it, because I work in publishing and I know about such things, and I love your description. But if you give me a book called *After the Bath*, I ask myself, what will you be describing?' Bhoga upturned his palm in a gesture of reasonable debate, 'What does the reader expect you to describe? If you take my advice,' he said with some importance, 'I don't like her moans of pleasure drowned out by the sound of jackals. I don't care how endangered they are.'

'The next book,' Tilu said conspiratorially, lowering his voice, 'is going to be something else.'

Bhoga took off his sunglasses and stared intently at Tilu. He had bought the sunglasses at night, from a footpath stall near New Market. In the morning he noticed that one lens was dark blue and the other bottle green. Bhoga meant to go back and give the man a well-deserved yelling, but eventually decided to pass it off as avant garde fashion, if anyone asked.

'It's about Job Charnock. Do you know about him?'

Bhoga shook his head. Tilu's face fell, but that was the reason he was writing, after all. Edification of the masses. A good book teaches as well as entertains.

'He founded Kolkata,' Tilu said, watching the noodle-seller's hands move through the pile of tangled, white strings, separating them with a long iron spike and a spatula. They rained on the hot pan, sizzling softly in the nameless, translucent oil.

'It is about ... about ...' Tilu gestured wildly, spreading his hands towards the sky, the sagging electrical wires, the lonesome starving mongrel sniffing a little distance away. 'About all of this, before this was all ... this. A glorious age. Do you know what glorious means?'

Bhoga shook his head from side to side, staring at Tilu like a man hypnotized.

'We were great once. This place was once the City of Gardens. Job Charnock, the sahib, madly in love with a native woman is roaming the jungles of Calcutta. He's an explorer.'

'What's an explorer?'

Tilu Shau had to think a little bit about this. He had assumed that anyone reading an adventure series would have a pretty good idea of what an explorer was. 'A person who sort of goes from one place to another, exploring.'

Nothing dawned on Bhoga's face.

'A place like ... like ...' Tilu tried to think of a most exotic, adventurous land, 'like Thailand.' He tried desperately to invent an extemporary adventure for his audience of one. 'Say, he goes to Thailand and gets mixed up with an international gang stealing the king's jewels ... something like that,' he finished lamely.

'You mean the king's ... jewels?' Bhoga pointed to a particular area of his anatomy. 'No, no, jewels like diamonds and rubies.'

'Aw,' said Bhoga, clearly not impressed. 'Everyone goes to Thailand these days.' 'Okay, Africa then.' To both Tilu and Bhoga, Africa was one giant forest. 'So you mean to say there's an actual job like that? People become explorers? Like dentists and accountants?'

'No, no,' said Tilu, shaking his hands impatiently. 'If it was a job it wouldn't be special. Some people are like that – adventurous.'

'Okay, so where is Job sahib going? Thailand or Africa?'

'Nowhere, he's right here, in Calcutta. Calcutta was like Africa at that time. Everywhere a dacoit, a Thug, a Royal Bengal tiger!' Tilu flung a hand at Bhoga in his enthusiasm, nearly knocking the sunglasses off his hands.

To appease his visibly disappointed devotee, he hastily added, 'It's a historical book, Bhoga. It takes place in the first half of the nineteenth century. The British have settled in but the city is still rife with dacoits and Thugs. Job must find the Rajah of Munsigarh's priceless diamond before it is lost forever.'

The chowmein man shoved two melamine plates at them. Egg chowmein, with extra onions and chillies. Bhoga wolfed down his food, while Tilu could hardly eat, transported as he was to a time when everything around him was a swampy, dengue-carrying jungle.

Walking back at a leisurely pace, so that he could delay going back to work as much as possible, Bhoga said to Tilu, 'I saw a Royal Bengal tiger once. In Alipore zoo. Fucking tiger, oh sorry, writer saab, the tiger was drugged. Wasn't worth it.'

But writer saab was in his own world. Bhoga liked this man. He had read many erotic books. Certainly all of the ones that passed through the Ma Tara Printing Works press, and even some that he had bought or traded. When all was said and done and he'd washed the stuff off, saving his pants so he didn't have to wash them too frequently, this man, this writer saab, managed to touch his heart. It was sex, yes, and Bhoga had learned a lot. But *Monsoon Has Come, Sister-in-Law* had made him bawl like an infant. The ganja was good that night, and he had found a half-full bottle of Chakladar's Bangla. He had cried and cried – ah, accursed love. Writer saab had a magic pen. But like all good writers, they'll try to do something inadvisable, like writing some kind of 'worthy' book, like it was some kind of a magic genie that would come out if you rubbed hard enough. Still, it was best to let them get on with the foolhardiness. In time, writer saab would be back to writing the Sister-in-law series, and all would be well with the world.

Bhoga smiled encouragingly, 'If Chakladar babu agrees to do it then you can have it out in time for the Kolkata book fair. You know Ma Tara always has a stall next to the Bijoli Grill snack car, and their fish fry is the best, syaar, best. Don't know if it is all the extra dust from the fairground, but it never tastes that good outside the book fair. Except during Durga Puja, of course, but then I find that the mix chowmein is best. During Puja they usually stint the meat in chops and cutlet. Why should a man eat a fish fry with only a sliver of fish, I ask you—'

'Yes, yes,' Tilu stemmed Bhoga's flow anxiously, pushed back his glasses with the knuckle of his index finger and asked, 'but which book of mine were you referring to?'

'What?' Bhoga blinked.

'Er … earlier you said you liked my book. Which one?'

'Why, the Sister-in-law series, of course, syaar. Jackals outside the window. Less countryside, more sister-in-law – that's my advice.'

When they arrived at the by-lane off College Street where Ma Tara Printing Works was located, they saw a very hot and bothered Amulyaratan Chakladar shouting invectives at a sweating boy who was currently raising a garishly printed flex sign over the shopfront bearing the company name. Chakladar was overseeing matters with his usual bad humour. Tilu stood next to the old man and watched the proceedings with interest but Chakladar was so busy supervising matters that he did not register Tilu's presence for a few minutes.

At last when he looked at Tilu, his face contorted in vague disgust, 'Awh, it's you, go inside.'

Tilu walked into a dingy room, shaded pleasantly from the glaring sun outside. Small piles of books lay against the walls tied crossways with twine. Tilu stood in front of his latest novella in the Sister-in-law series, stacked in high piles. The cover showed a large, unnaturally fair woman baying at a full moon. Her long, flowing, dark hair covered a portion of her ample bottom, a saree of some sort was slipping from her shoulders revealing a rather oversized, biologically inaccurate side-boob. Her red mouth was open, chin tilted towards the moon. It would be hard to say whether she was in ecstasy or in the process of transforming into a werewolf, but the code 'sister-in-law' was enough for the discerning reader. A small sigh escaped Tilu Shau. If only Lalee could see his creation. It was a pity that these novellas never carried the author's name.

'Marvellous cover, no, syaar?' Bhoga said loudly.

'A little too much?' Tilu said tentatively. He felt, perhaps unjustly, that the artist had tried to outdo him.

'What? No! These days you have to grab the attention of the customer, syaar – too many people in the market. On this street alone there are at least four to six people in the erotic novel business. We're lucky to have this artist. He's pure gold.'

Chakladar joined them with his customary sour face. He glanced casually at the two and mumbled, 'Don't know what the world is coming to these days – all he does is put up one blasted banner above my door and asks for 300 rupees. Says it's the going rate. They bleed you night and day, I tell you …' and so mumbling, he went inside. In a moment, he motioned towards Tilu to follow him in. He looked irritable as he tried to open a heavy wooden box with an equally old key. 'So you want the money for the last instalment, I guess? Well, wait here a moment while I settle with the flex banner thugs first.' Chakladar took a bundle of 100-rupee notes bound together by a rubber band from the cash box, locked it most carefully once again and hurried out of the dingy counter that served as his front office.

Tilu liked sitting in this room, looking around at the books that lay haphazardly around him. When it was quiet, which it rarely was, he could hear the hum of the printing machine, located in the basement. He felt carefully excited about this new book. It felt good to talk to Bhoga; he imagined Bhoga with the manuscript, shivering with excitement when Job fought a hundred Thugs in the dark jungle of Chowringhee. And that part where Job is driven nearly mad because the evil Brahmin pundits would not let him marry the Bengali Hindu widow he had lost his heart to. Oh, the anguish! Tilu shivered slightly, shaking softly with emotion. Perhaps she could be modelled on Lalee. But the thought of Lalee made him a little melancholic once again.

'Want to see something, syaar?' Bhoga whispered now, looking sideways to make sure Chakladar was out of earshot. 'They're doing something amazing with computers these days. You can ask the boss to make your cover on the computers next time.'

Tilu followed Bhoga into an adjoining room, much smaller and darker than the room he usually waited in. Two figures were sitting in a corner. A young man, around Bhoga's age, was peering into a computer in front of him. The screen flickered and Tilu couldn't see what was on it from where he stood. A man in flashy clothes stood on the side, giving orders and directing his younger cohort who pressed buttons Tilu couldn't see. Taking out a handkerchief of the most garish green, the older man began wiping his brow.

'Ai Bablu,' Bhoga yelled, as the young man at the computer looked up. 'Show writer saab what you're doing.' Bhoga pushed Tilu towards them, placing an encouraging hand on his back. 'Go, see, writer saab – you can get Bablu to do your book cover next time.'

Tilu peered at the screen. Rows upon rows of women were laid side by side on the flickering screen, their faces splotched by misbehaving pixels. Kolkata Call Girls Escort High Class Russian Foreigners: the words flashed repeatedly across the screen. Tilu looked at the faces.

'You can ask for anything from the high class call girls and be ready to be served by same in return. Your fantasy is exquisitely fulfilled by Our High Class Escorts all inclusive. Don't be lonely anymore in the City of Joy; nothing can get between you and the girl of your dreams.'

The young man in front of the computer smiled at him and obligingly scrolled through the pictures slowly. Names appeared next to the women on the screen: Pamela, Olivia, Jasmine, Lovely, Missha and there, in a corner, was Lalee. Tilu looked blankly at the man next to him. It took a moment for him to realize that he had met this man before. It was Rambo Maity. Tilu had seen him hovering around Shonagachhi, coming and going out of The Blue Lotus.

'High quality, ah,' Rambo smirked at him, and then gave him a once-over. As a pimp and sometimes a tout, he prided himself on his ability to tell the measure of a man, the rich and the powerful from the craven and the poor. Tilu depressed him. He reminded Rambo too much of his early days of struggle and grovelling, finding pauper clients like Tilu.

Tilu was staring at the screen. The other women were a blur for him, even if some of them looked familiar or much too young. Tilu looked only at Lalee. The screen bore a different name, and some numbers were printed neatly below it: One hour = 15,000 ruppes; two–three hours = 20,000 rupees; overnight = 30,000 rupees.

'Okay, print fifty pieces for me, just the top ones. The rest can be on the website, no problem. I'll wait outside,' Rambo turned and started walking away.

'Wait,' Tilu wailed. 'I know that girl.'

Rambo stopped outside, sat on a table and pulled out a

packet of India Kings from his pocket. Tilu almost ran towards him.

'That girl in there ... why ... how ...'

Rambo smiled. At a distance, Chakladar was walking briskly towards them, shouting at an invisible target. Bablu came out with something in his hand. 'Mock-up, Rambo-da; looks fine, no?'

'There, and that'll be three thousand,' said Chakladar as Bablu put the catalogue in front of Tilu and Rambo.

'What? Three thousand?' exclaimed Rambo. 'What for?'

And as the two men haggled with each other over price and exclaimed how each was trying to take advantage of the other's innate innocence, Tilu saw lying on the dirty countertop the image of a woman he thought he knew so well. It was Lalee, unmistakably Lalee, even if printed letters said a different name. He took another long look at the man who was haggling with Chakladar now. Lalee was getting further away from him. Tilu's heart sank. He reached for the photos, picking them up from between the two men who were still trying to win at the game of outrage. Rambo stopped remonstrating with the old man. He held up a hand and turned towards Tilu. He snatched the photos out of Tilu's hand.

'You're a strange one,' Rambo nearly yelled. 'Why do you touch things that don't belong to you?'

Chakladar's reply came unsolicited, 'Ah, might be a customer. Or is serving the common man beneath you now?'

Rambo trained an annoyed look at the old publisher's face. Chakladar had walked over to Tilu, put on his glasses and peered at the photo. 'Bit dark, no?' Chakladar asked.

Rambo felt extremely irritated with both of them. 'She's

not available,' he said and put the photo away in his folder. He looked at Chakladar and said, 'Listen, charge whatever you want, but just do it, okay? I don't have time for this.'

Tilu felt angry. The unfamiliar emotion ricocheted around in his small chest and fizzled out as unpredictably as it had arrived. He was affronted by Rambo's seeming familiarity with Lalee, as if he, Tilu Shau, had not made love to this woman for years, left on her bed the better part of his meagre earnings. This man, this peacock, was carrying around Lalee's photograph as if she was his secret lover. Ugly suspicions began to assail Tilu. Who was this man? Did he and Lalee have a special relationship? Was he something more than her pimp? His heart skipped a beat. This flashy man, still young, could he be her lover, her babu? No, she wouldn't do that, Tilu tried to convince himself. She wasn't that kind of a person. She never trusted anyone and whenever Tilu had tried to wheedle personal information out of her, tried to learn if she had a lover, Lalee had always dismissed the questions. She had no patience with that particular breed of Shonagachhi men who lived on their women's earnings. She wouldn't take a babu – Tilu desperately tried to hold on to that belief. But someday, he'd be the only man for Lalee.

He picked up the catalogue once more. He turned it over, and there again was Lalee. A different photo this time, in which she was wearing a long oversized white shirt, the buttons done up in a haphazard way so that much of her chest was exposed without actually showing her breasts and the shirt flagged asymmetrically on her thighs. She certainly was very dark, and the white shirt she wore like a shroud only accentuated her skin tone. Her legs were lean, and her hair fell to her thighs. She was looking at the camera with a rather supercilious half-smile upon her lips. Much of her sexiness seemed fake, but there was something sincere about the way she was gazing at the lens, a challenge in her eyes, or so he imagined. A sliver of sunlight fell on the picture, and Tilu had to avert his eyes. She seemed so distant, so far away from Tilu Shau and his world. He wanted to touch her, to feel his skin against hers. If she saw him again, he would just want to lie down next to her, sleep with her through the night and wake up to her face in the morning.

Rambo walked back into the room and saw Tilu holding another photograph. Rambo wagged a finger under Tilu's nose and said in a low, gruff voice, 'She's not available. Get the fucking point, okay? Or I'll make it in a way you won't like. I've told you once.'

An unfamiliar defiance gripped Tilu's shrivelled heart. 'Why?' he demanded, rising up from the chair, drawing himself up as high as he could. 'Is she your lover or what?'

Rambo breathed out. He pressed his temples with his knuckles and closed his eyes. He lowered his voice further and brought his face close to Tilu's. 'Do you know a place called Nandankanan?' Tilu shook his head. 'Yeah, high-level stuff, understand? You don't want to get involved with that. You want a girl, I can give you a hundred. I'll leave you my number and you can call me anytime. But this one is not available. She'll be gone before you know it – girls like that go on foreign trips. See how many foreigner girls I have here? Besides,' Rambo laughed, 'you saw her new rate? I don't care if she said "I love you"; you can't afford her now.'

Tilu sat down, pale-faced and empty-eyed, his brain still

trying to make sense of what he had heard. Rambo pulled the catalogue out of his unresisting hands and walked out of Ma Tara Printing Works. A second too late, Tilu ran outside frantically searching for the flashy, distasteful man, his head spinning with questions. But the grand chaos of College Street had already swallowed up Rambo Maity.

# 22

THE PHONE BEGAN TO RING. CHINMOY NASKAR, WHO WAS sitting at his desk frowning, wondering how to spell suo moto cognizance, answered and immediately stood to attention. His first instinct was to salute, a fine military art he had never mastered. Then, realizing that his telephonic interlocutor could not possibly see this mark of deference, squeaked in a high-pitched voice, 'Yes, sir, right now, sir, please hold, sir.' Covering the mouthpiece with one hand, he motioned towards Samsher Singh and began mouthing something that Samsher did not understand. So Naskar gestured frantically towards the phone on Samsher's desk until he picked it up.

'Deputy Commissioner of Police (North) speaking. I have just had a call from the Chief Minister's Office. Have you seen today's papers, man?' A male voice barked on the phone.

'No, sir, I mean I just arrived sir, it's very early … I was just going to …'

'What? It's because of your lackadaisical attitude that the media gets to dump this sort of shit on us, don't you realize? Take a look at the papers.'

Samsher was fumbling through the junk on his desk, trying

to find the day's newspaper with his free hand. When he finally opened it to the second page, he found on its lower half a headline announcing that in protest of a recent murder, a candlelight march was going to take place in Shonagachhi. A sizeable photo of several women gathered around a makeshift dais listening to someone speaking into the microphone accompanied the story. An old woman was holding up a placard with the words 'Stop the Slaughter'.

*Fucking English drama*, Samsher thought. *Who came and wrote the placards in English? Drama for the TV cameras.*

The voice carried on, 'Of course the media will jump at it. Would those jackals let such a golden opportunity pass? The police force is the villain in everyone's story. Anyway, this won't just end here, you hear me? If they are going ahead with this candlelight march, there'll be more protest marches and you can be sure they will get full coverage in the media. They will generate round-the-clock interest in this thing. Already five overnight experts were debating the case hotly on primetime news, didn't you see that? One of those rabid feminazis will be present, I expect.' The man continued, 'Now look here, I don't want the police to appear like an army of chumps. It won't just be about this murder, they will drag human trafficking, sex rackets, police complicity, bribery and everything else into it.'

'But sir, you know very well that whenever we have any trafficking information we crack down on it and organize rescue missions …' Samsher began to protest but even he couldn't bring himself to deny the charge of bribery. It would be too bold-faced a lie.

'Save it,' the DCP said curtly. 'You personally may not be mixed up in all that, officer, but the media's portrayal of the police in that particular story is hardly going to be sympathetic. Anyway, I want you and your men to make a show of effort. Okay? What have you done so far?'

Samsher suddenly felt he was on firmer ground. 'We took down an FIR, sir,' he said. 'Er … it is about the murder of the girl in Shonagachhi, right, sir?'

'Of course it is. Don't be such an imbecile. Read the newspaper, man. Two or three high-profile NGOs have got behind this incident. One of those has its headquarters in Delhi and some international visibility as well. They are trying to give it as much media coverage as possible. Once there is public interest in the matter, things won't remain buried, you'll see. So as long as there is scrutiny and limelight on the issue I want the police force to show initiative and get some positive press.'

'Er, does that mean we have to make an investigation, sir?' asked Samsher.

'Of course! Are you stupid or what? At the very least there needs to be some appearance of the police making an investigation. Consider myself personally involved in the matter, Singh. The Crime Branch will also get involved. We can't have negative media feedback again so soon after the Park Street rape case. You understand?'

'Yes, sir, of course, you don't have to worry about anything.'

'See to it, Singh.' The DCP hung up.

# 23

'ANYONE WHO EVER FED YOU WILL HAVE THEIR PRICE sooner OR later,' Lalee's father used to say. Lalee marvelled at these strange snatches of her old life coming back to haunt her in odd corners.

It was twenty to nine. Beggars and second-hand booksellers lined the pavement outside The Park hotel. Lalee stared at a long black car entering the hotel's short driveway. Behind the dark windows of the car she saw a woman, her face heavily made-up and beautiful, glance at her critically and then look away, like she was nothing of importance. Lalee faltered. Sonia was waving away the car that had dropped them both close to the hotel. She gestured to a corner and walked towards it, took a hand-rolled cigarette out of her bag and began rooting for a lighter. She noticed Lalee staring and said, 'Helps to calm me down, dear, don't worry about it.'

Lalee looked around, feeling slightly lost in the steady stream of people. The way the woman in the car had looked away, exposing her for what she was. Lalee avoided the relentless urging of street urchins to buy something or the other and walked over to the hole-in-the-wall booth next to the hotel's entrance and ordered a double egg roll.

'What are you doing, darling?' Sonia yelled. 'They'll have plenty of food in there for you.' Lalee pretended not to hear her.

A young boy on the other side of the counter said, 'Fifty,' and extended his hand. 'Fifty? That's robbery – fifty for a double egg roll? It was twenty only yesterday,' Lalee protested. The boy ignored her and stared into the distance. Lalee continued, 'You can charge these Park Street prices to other people, young man. I know—' The boy interrupted, 'Arrey madam, if you want to eat, you eat, otherwise don't, okay? I've got a long line here. This is the best kathi roll shop in Calcutta. We don't use potato filling, our double mutton roll is world-famous.' He looked away, grumbling.

Lalee wrapped her arms around herself. She had seldom been out of Shonagachhi, much less to a fancy hotel in the posh part of the town. She didn't know where she fit in. If nothing, she could still feed herself. She wouldn't go hungry tonight or any other night if she could help it. She handed over ₹50 to the impatient young vendor.

She watched a sweating man in the back of the booth flip the flattened oily dough up in the air and froth the egg mixture before frying them together.

Lalee saw Sonia squash her half-smoked cigarette under her long, red heels, spray her mouth with a small bottle, wince, hunt for a bottle of perfume in her handbag and train it on herself like she was taking a bath. Lalee ground her teeth watching this wastefulness. She had bought a single bottle of perfume, a long time ago – it was called The Blue Lady. A white silhouette of a woman in a hat decorated the paper box, and a blue ribbon was tied around the bottle. Lalee had saved both, carefully returning the bottle in its box for years, always wondering if the occasion had warranted the expenditure. To be rich, she knew, was to have the luxury of wastefulness.

Sonia opened a side door and stepped onto the black-and-white floor. A couple sharing a dessert at the table closest to the door looked up at her. The girl averted her eyes, feigning nonchalance, as if Sonia was nothing to be looked at. The man, however, watched her as she walked away, even turning his head as she passed his field of vision. Lalee noticed it all, allowing herself a smirk as she walked past the couple. Almost unconsciously, she tugged at her dress. It was a sleeveless, sparkly black thing that rode up her thighs every time she breathed. Sonia had pulled it out of her own suitcase and thrown it across the bed carelessly at Lalee. She had never seen Sonia wearing it, but she could imagine how it would fall perfectly over her breasts, her emaciated, doll-like waist and hide just enough of her milky-white thighs. On Lalee, the dress emphasized her drooping breasts and bulged outwards around her stomach. She ran a hand through her hair. At least she had washed it, even if it curled up in odd places and stuck out near her ears. She dropped her hair over her breasts, straightened her back and followed Sonia.

Sonia walked with the self-possession of a woman who had never had to feel out of place anywhere. White chairs, shaped liked hollowed out eggs, lined the mirrored lobby. Rambo swung into view, swivelling around in his own chair, like a child on a merry-go-round. Sonia walked over to him, bent down and planted a dainty kiss on his cheek. Rambo grinned with all his teeth. Lalee winced inside. She had a bone-deep distaste for Rambo that she could not explain. He was wearing his usual gold-rimmed aviators, a garish silk shirt and shiny, pointed shoes. Lalee watched them conferring, occasional laughs bursting out of their bubble. She looked around herself, as the staff, decked up in black suits with small walkie-talkies in their hands, politely ignored her. She wondered if she should ask them where the toilets were, but the studied way in which they avoided eye contact with her told her that they knew exactly what she was, like her address was printed on every inch of her skin. She walked away, partly to walk off the anger that was beginning to clench her fists, and partly out of a misplaced determination to find her own way to the toilets, as if she had something to prove, as if anyone cared if she proved it. She followed a group of giggling girls into a hidden corridor, standing behind them as they talked to each other in English, exchanging jokes and laughing loudly. She waited outside for her turn. When she entered the restroom, she was all alone. A couch sat in a corner, flattering lights hung over the spotless mirrors, casting a soft glow on the dark granite washbasins with soaps and moisturizers around them. A tall areca palm in a golden pot languished in a corner next to the couch. Lalee surveyed her face, took a deep breath, clutching the corner of the washbasin. She couldn't bear to look at the mirror, its spotless surface too exposing, too confronting for her to endure. She closed her eyes, breathed, until someone tapped on her shoulder and said in an impatient voice, 'Come along now. The customers are waiting.'

Lalee followed Sonia like a woman navigating by starlight. The lighted foyer seemed like a pit waiting to swallow her whole, every stare saying, 'I know what you are.' She tried to keep her eyes on Sonia's conspicuous blonde hair, her white limbs moving through a sea of unknowable brown faces. Lalee found herself facing a dimly lit room, tables parked in their own cocoon of lights, oblivious to the world around them, as the liveried waiters flitted through them like bees. Sonia walked up to two men dominating a large table in a corner, seated on a plush brown leather couch. She leaned down, put her arms across a fat middle-aged man, brought her lips close to his ears and whispered something. They both laughed. Sonia straightened up, gestured towards Lalee and said, 'This is my friend.' Lalee smiled and sat next to the quiet man on the couch. Sonia slid down next to the fat man, like a discarded coat and clung to his arm. A bowl of cold fries lay on the table. Lalee toyed with the idea of reaching out for them, actually putting one in her mouth, but refrained. The sight of the limp fries was as distasteful as that of the men around her.

A bottle of wine with a white cloth draped around its neck had been propped up in a metal bucket. Despite the chilly air-conditioned room, droplets of condensation trickled down its dark back. Lalee ran a finger down the cold, sweaty glass of the bottle. The man next to her cleared his throat. Lalee withdrew her hand and turned to face him, smile at the ready. The man was wearing a light-blue collared shirt and dark pants. He was twirling the ice in a tumbler half-full with a dark liquid. Lalee noticed the several rings on his fingers, astrological stones set in gold and silver. Lalee guessed he was about thirty-five, but he looked older. His clothes were quite ordinary, he wore glasses and his thinning hair was parted to the left. He looked at Lalee and smiled, pushing his glasses to the bridge of his nose. He looked like a lackey. The man on the other side, the fat one still whispering in Sonia's ears, seemed to be the boss. Lalee felt a sudden panic rising up her chest. Sonia had the better customer, while she had been saddled with the less lucrative option.

The smell of stale leftovers wafted towards Lalee. She wondered why people ordered food, at an expensive place no less, if they were not going to eat it. The roll she had eaten before hadn't been enough. She wondered if someone would order more food.

'Maity, come,' said the fat man, peeking out from behind Sonia's blond hair. Lalee looked around and found Rambo smiling ingratiatingly from behind a tall areca. The fat man sat up straighter and Sonia moved away from him instinctively. He gestured expansively towards the couch. Lalee didn't miss the lost expression on Rambo's face. He looked at the man, smiled nervously and ducked out. In a few minutes, Rambo came back lugging a heavy-looking chair behind him. He sat down, smiling widely. No one spoke for a few seconds. Then the fat man said to Rambo, 'On time, eh? And you've got us both black and white – nice contrast.' He laughed at his own joke.

Sonia looked away from him, her smile freezing up just for a second. Lalee was watching the man – he was middle-aged, maybe in his fifties, quite a bit older than his friend. He wasn't actually fat, but rather portly, with a roundish face. He spoke softly to Rambo, and with authority. He was clearly used to being obeyed and didn't need to raise his voice. He was wearing a non-descript shirt, sleeves folded up to his elbows as though he was getting ready to do some heavy digging, but an expensive-looking chrome watch dangled from his left wrist.

Sonia had slipped into his arms like a rabbit in a hutch. It occurred to Lalee that Sonia was almost water-like. In the presence of any male, she seemed to be able to drape herself or mould her body around theirs. Lalee found herself wondering how good Sonia was as an escort, how much better than her and whether she was one of those elastic ladies who could touch the back of their own heads with their feet.

Sonia reached for the bottle in front of her, 'Ooh Cava,' she announced. Magically, a young man in a white shirt, black waistcoat and bowtie appeared out of nowhere to place two wine glasses in front of her and Lalee. The younger man at the table, Lalee noticed, did not look up from his whiskey.

'One large rum,' Rambo told the waiter.

'Would you like it with some Coke, sir?'

'No, just ice. On the rocks.'

The older gentleman untangled his arm from Sonia's and pushed a basket of French fries towards Lalee, 'You can call me Mr Ghosh. Lalee, wasn't it?'

'Yes, er … thanks,' Lalee said. So far, she had not been in her best form. Mr Ghosh waved a hand and another waiter materialized to fill the wine glasses, and just as he was done, the previous waiter returned with Rambo's rum. 'This is my associate, Shamik. A bright boy – I'm sure one of you ladies will have a great time with him tonight,' Mr Ghosh said as Shamik looked up from his drink and winked at Lalee.

'All arrangements made, Maity?' enquired Mr Ghosh.

'Yes, sir. Of course. With us, you never have to worry about service, sir. It's all been taken care of. First class all the way,' Rambo replied deferentially.

'Capital. And now perhaps you can go finish your drink

somewhere else, among your friends, Maity,' said Mr Ghosh without missing a beat.

Rambo blinked twice, which, in the circumstances, was a commendable short space of time for him to change mental gears.

'Of course, sir, of course. And I'll see you later, sir?' The question mark hung in the air like the greasy upturned hands of pimps everywhere. But since no one was paying him any attention anymore, least of all Mr Ghosh, who had swatted Rambo out of his universe, he only paused for a second before leaving the party.

Lalee noticed Rambo flashing her a thumbs up just as he disappeared into the shadows.

# 24

RAMBO STEPPED OUTSIDE THE HOTEL FOR A SMOKE. HE had been experimenting with brands. He tried getting used to Marlboro first but the white was as good as smoking air and the red tasted as foul as the cheapest local roll-up. Then he tried Camel, but whether it was the picture of the camel on the pack he couldn't tell, but it tasted like camel shit to him. At the moment he was trying out India Kings, and this vanity patriotism was so far passing muster. He had noticed that ever since he had started making a bit of money, his body had become sensitive. It complained a little more loudly about uncomfortable temperatures, smells, unsavoury tastes and so on – a luxury he hadn't been able to afford earlier. Being rich, by Rambo's estimation, was a wholesome existential experience, as in it affected one's entire physical, emotional and spiritual existences. He lit an extra-long, special-filter, unique-blend India Kings stick with a dragon-shaped lighter which not only breathed fire but also played 'London Bridge is falling down, falling down, falling down, London Bridge is …' while doing so. Rambo Maity blew a perfect ring and strolled towards the paan shop a few feet away.

Normal people, reflected Rambo – if they thought about it at all – thought of the city as having designated red-light areas, and these were the well-known whore pits that those normal people avoided, denied, visited or went on a dare to. But for someone like him, the entire city was something that happened between whore pits, which were indeed more numerous and proliferating than those normal people knew or suspected. Whores go everywhere. It was something Sonia had said to him, 'My dear Rambo, whores go everrrywhere,' she had purred, rolling out the 'r'. He smiled at that memory. He'd repeated that sentence to others. It was a good catchphrase, true too. For example, the footpath he was standing on wasn't so much a Park Street pavement on which many reputable restaurants and watering holes opened their doors, but a sort of hallway for the giant red-light area that Rambo knew it to be.

Rambo walked slowly up the pavement towards Mirza Ghalib Street, avoiding potholes and nagging children who begged him to buy bubblegum, incense and cheap geegaws that he neither needed nor cared about. He stopped in front of a small paan shop on the pavement. The paan shop did very good business as such establishments on Park Street tend to do; the dressed and prepared betel leaves were more expensive by half than anywhere else in the city and were stuffed with a large number of artificially coloured, flavoured, violently sweetened plasticky goop. Rambo liked this shop. The paanwallah knew him too; they were to the Park Street pavements what old butlers are to society houses, or knowing concierges to iconic New York hotels. This particular one, located just outside Karnani Mansions, was a regular haunt of

Rambo's, as it was of every other middling pimp who wasn't totally down and out.

Lakshmi Pandey, the shop owner as well as the Karnani Mansions recording angel, greeted Rambo with a broad smile. He started assembling a sweet betel leaf with all the aplomb of a miracle worker. In a minute he looked up and Pandey's smile broadened even further than it had for Rambo.

He boomed, 'Oh, aaiye, aaiye, Officer saab. You have forgotten your old servant.'

Rambo Maity was sucking pleasurably on his cigarette and gazing thoughtfully into the dark bowels of Karnani Mansions. Now he turned around to look at Pandey's new favourite customer.

Samsher Singh was sitting in a police jeep next to a slightly plump, bald man with a drooping moustache, who Rambo instantly recognized as the inspector-in-charge at the Park Street police station. Rambo knew him as Inspector Bose, his first name having momentarily escaped him. Behind them was old Constable Balok Ghosh.

'Ah, Maity,' Samsher said sourly.

'So, Maity,' began the Park Street inspector, who was in better spirits than his colleague, 'long time no see, eh? You've been doing well, I hear? My boys no longer need to bring you in kicking and screaming? Oh have you reduced our workload by half, haha, but it's not good to forget old friends. You should drop by sometime, tell us what's happening. Otherwise we'll have to find out on our own and that's too much work. Ha, ha, ha, a waste of civic resources and the public's hard-earned money. What do you say?'

Rambo never liked Inspector Bose. It was more than a

matter of being adversaries in the game of cops and criminals. Rambo knew many cops – they were his compatriots, clients, friends. But there was a sliminess to Inspector Bose that Rambo knew and loathed. He'd known men like him, and they always floated on top of foetid ponds like all rotting things. He faked a smile and said, 'I'm your humble servant. Anything I can do to help I'll always …'

A sulky Samsher interrupted Rambo, 'Oh stop, you only talk when your ass needs saving. The important thing that people tend to forget about lock-ups is that no one can get in. That's way more important than not getting out,' he looked pointedly at Rambo as he said, 'for some people.'

Rambo wondered what had happened to put Samsher in such a foul mood.

'Anyway, what are you doing here?' Singh barked, and then nodded towards Pandey who was sending a young boy towards the police jeep with a couple of paans and a packet of Gold Flake cigarettes, 'Two Pepsis, Pandey, it's too bloody hot.'

'Just some business, sir, just some business, a poor man's got to eat,' Rambo said.

'Well, go eat somewhere else – we're shutting down this Karnani Mansions business.'

'Mairi, you guys won't leave anything untouched,' said Inspector Bose. 'A historical street, an icon of our great city, but you people have to taint that as well.'

'Sir,' began Rambo, 'Park Street business was on even before I was born, sir, and will continue long after I'm gone. It is what it is, sir, we didn't really …'

The inspector waved at Karnani Mansions, pushing a paan in his mouth, 'You people are worse than rats. I mean these are fucking old buildings, some dead white British fuck probably built it. Well, thanks very much, but what do you people do? Make a sex racket. You see a room, you make a sex racket. I mean, man, it's terrible. We sealed a room, and what happened, eh Balok-da, tell him what happened.' He drank his cola with a white straw.

Constable Balok Ghosh, who was sitting in the back of the jeep with an extremely old and rusty rifle, said, 'What to say, sir? He knows, of course. These guys know everything.'

'I bet he does. Sala, we sealed a room because one of your colleagues had a tidy business going and the neighbours were complaining. Turns out that the madam somehow got a court order to reopen the room. The residents posted private security guards on each floor to stop the pimps and johns, but somebody bribed the guards to look the other way when customers came. They made a rule to close the doors of the building at eight p.m.' He waved at the direction of the building, 'And now, sala, customers are going through that corridor, climbing up that wall, sliding through a broken window and getting up on that cornice to get into the flat,' and paused for a long, noisy cola intake.

'Which cornice?' Rambo asked, turning around.

'Arrey, that one over Mocambo.'

'Really?' wondered Rambo admiringly. Mocambo was one of the most well-known, if old, eating establishments in Calcutta.

'Yes, so now, not only are the residents complaining but also the owners of Mocambo and people who come to eat there. You know what a long queue there usually is for the restaurant? They all see people hop on and off above them. Imagine.' 'Sir,' Balok Ghosh coughed, 'if you forgive my speaking out of turn, I want to say something.'

'Of course, of course, we're a democracy – go on,' said Inspector Bose.

'These neighbours, sir, I mean they have some nerve. Complaining even though half of them are the ones running the sex rackets.'

'Now, now, Balok-da, you cannot go maligning people,' Bose interrupted him, 'or you'll have a defamation case against you. I have seen perfectly legitimate families living in there, old families, old grandmothers even.'

'Yes, sir, living here for generations, and how much rent do they pay? Not more than 200. While in the whole city you won't find a family apartment for less than 7,000–8,000 at least.' Balok Ghosh was only just warming up. The injustices heaved upon the toiling poor while the idle rich lived in grand mansions in Park Street burned holes in his heart. It gave him some comfort to know that the mansion they lived in for next to nothing was a crumbling, dark and dingy, rat-infested edifice, very well known to a certain type of populace as a sex den. He felt they shouldn't complain so much. After all, they weren't paying the rent he was.

'That's true,' said Bose, 'but the owners are sitting on millions, millions, I tell you.'

Rambo wanted to edge away but couldn't find a polite way of doing so. He dithered a bit and stayed. Samsher Singh sat with his head turned away from them, watching the people across the road. He hadn't said anything during this long exchange and Rambo wondered why Singh was here at all. Park Street fell under Inspector Bose's jurisdiction, but Singh's kingdom was further away to the north. Rambo knew they were friends, as men of slightly questionable integrity doing a dirty job in the same city could be friends, but he didn't think Samsher Singh would be officially involved in any investigations the Park Street station might be conducting. It was more likely that they had come for a shared whiskey or two at Oly Pub.

On an impulse, Rambo asked, 'So what are you doing here, sir?'

'Oh, Oho ho ho ho!' exclaimed Inspector Bose gleefully, his eyes shining with petty malice. 'We're being questioned, are we? Eh Maity? Think these streets belong to you? Too big for your boots, boy, too big for your boots. We go through five like you on a daily basis down at the station.'

'Of course, sir, of course,' Rambo affected great innocence, and watched Bose bask in his obeisance. 'I would never dream of giving offence, I only meant …'

'Reconnoitering. Know what that means, Maity?'

Samsher looked up from his smartphone and made a tutting sound, frowning at his friend. Bose waved a hand in dismissal.

'Hah, big secret, he might as well find out. If he tells a few of his chums, we'll have less people to scare and chase away. I get a nasty pain in my hip when it rains a bit; I can't be running around.'

'You should see this old baba my mother found,' Samsher said off-handedly. 'He makes herbal medicine. People come to him from all over the place.'

'You know some of these babas have this really potent stuff,' Bose responded with enthusiasm. 'Afghanistani, old herbal magic. If you take a little bit, your penis stands up for five hours, sometimes twelve. Just like the Eiffel Tower.'

'What? Where do you get this bullshit from?' Samsher cut in.

But Bose went on, undeterred, 'Arrey, I know. These sex babas come from the Middle East. I got a tip, but naturally I ignored it. All sorts of nutcases roaming around everywhere and all these fuckers have a mobile phone. Nothing to do? Give the police an anonymous phone call. Sala, if I ever lay my hands on one of those bastards I'll work him like … anyway, I ignored it, but then I got a call from the head office; they thought it was a good idea to go around once and shake up this baba. I wanted to see what the hoopla was about, so I went. He'd taken two rooms in a shitty hotel in Dharmatala. Can't remember the name at the moment, but,' Bose paused for effect, and looked at his audience. 'Arms dealer,' he slapped the car's dashboard in triumph, 'with a side order of pure A-grade Afghan heroin.'

'But that's in Dharmatala, not here,' said Rambo.

'Arrey, that's just side information, not relevant. We have orders, understand, Rambo? We have to make this city safer, save these iconic streets,' Bose pointed a forefinger at the lighted shopfronts of Park Street, 'from becoming another Shonagachhi.'

At this, Samsher Singh visibly bridled. Then, looking at Rambo, he launched into a harangue, 'Know what's been happening on your own streets, Maity? I told you the other day, be straight with me, but don't know why I bother. Everyone knows you guys are the worst sort of double-crossers.'

'Sir, I've never …'

Samsher held up a hand, 'Forget it. There's a candlelight vigil in Shonagachhi soon. And you didn't think it was necessary to mention it to me, eh? Good thing I have backup informers. Not that any of you shitters are reliable in the least.'

'What?' Rambo said, quite at sea now.

'Heh,' said Inspector Bose and spat out a large blob of red betel juice which splattered on the asphalt. 'Didn't know, eh? Rambo Maity, the enlightened whores of Shonagachhi will be marching on the streets with candles in their hands in protest of the murder of that girl. How did that happen again?' he enquired of Samsher.

'Acid,' he murmured in reply.

'Awh, old-fashioned. It's like the nineties again. Remember, Singh? Every two months there was an acid attack. All jilted lovers, broken-affair cases.'

'What would you know?' Samsher said sulkily. 'You got the posh station, you have rich businessmen and glamorous call girls. Good perks, good connections when you want a recommendation for your nephew's admission to St Xavier's College. On my streets, some bitch gets murdered every month.' He might have gone on had Inspector Bose not interrupted again.

'That's what you think. I've got problems. You know that rape case that happened last month?'

'Which one? There are so many I can't keep track.'

'Arrey, the one we got all involved in. I tell you, this woman won't back down. We didn't want to take the FIR at first, naturally. Some Anglo-Indian chick came to a nightclub and got into a car with some men, and now she says it's rape. Who'll believe her? Of course, we dismissed the whole thing, but she threatened to go to the press, so we had no choice but to take down the complaint.'

'Yes, so what?'

'I wish it had ended there. But no, she'll fight the case, she says. She says they gang-raped her, but the people she's incriminating are powerful, so it's already getting media attention and all. She's even got two daughters.'

'What was a mother of two doing at a Park Street nightclub with men anyway?' murmured Samsher from his seat.

'Exactly what I want to ask. You know what the local MP said?'

'No. What did he say?'

'She. She said that it was a misunderstanding between a lady and her client.'

*Ah*, thought Rambo. *Prostitutes normally don't insist on filing FIRs or pressing charges.*

Inspector Bose lit a cigarette, offered the packet to Samsher and took out his phone. With his cigarette dangling from one corner of his mouth, he said to Rambo, 'Wait a minute, I think there's a picture of her somewhere. Ah, there it is.' Rambo walked to the other side of the jeep to take a look at Inspector Bose's phone, deftly avoiding the blob of betel juice on the street.

'No, don't think I've seen her. But then I can't know everybody. There are new girls coming every day.'

'Coming?' Samsher gave him a sharp look.

Rambo started. There are some things you didn't speak of openly. It's not that the police didn't know. Without their knowledge, half the things that happened in the trade could not happen. But you didn't talk about them all the same. Except with the ones who were, so to speak, actively involved in the goings-on. Rambo quickly steered the conversation in a different direction.

'No, if you ask me, she doesn't look like one of the girls.' Thankfully, Samsher let it go.

'So after that stupid MP made that comment the feminists are up in arms, as is the victim herself,' Bose continued. 'Man, I tell you, a rape victim but she's not trying to hide or forget it or anything. It's like she actively wants people to know what happened. Never seen such a thing. And of course, the media and the "lesbians' lib",' and here Bose laughed at his own joke, 'are capitalizing on it. Pushing her forward, egging her on and we're the ones under pressure to at least try to catch these people. Apparently, there's CCTV footage as well.'

As soon as Rambo had walked over to Inspector Bose, he discovered the source of his chattiness: he was plainly stinking of whiskey. Rambo knew Bose's brand was Royal Challenge. You had to be loyal to something, even if it was only a brand.

Bose carried on, 'No shame, no, sir. She won't back down. Nothing left of modesty …'

Samsher said something that Rambo didn't catch. 'What?'

'I said, if she's the one hiding, surely there's something wrong with that.'

Bose blinked a couple times. 'What do you mean?'

'I mean, she gets raped and tortured, and then she has to hide away – that doesn't make sense.' He took a look at his colleague's face before continuing, 'Yes, yes, I know what you mean, that's what happens, but logically speaking, if it's those guys who committed the crime and have an FIR filed against them, they should do the hiding, no?'

Bose stared at Samsher and then burst into laughter. 'Did you hear that, Balok-da? Your sir's gone mad. He'll join the lesbian liberation movement any time now. Be careful or you'll lose your boss. He'll run around Shonagachhi trying to rescue every girl standing on the street, and where will you lot be then, eh? No more income. You'll have to finally live on your salaries.' Inspector Bose laughed alone.

# 25

LALEE HAD NEVER SEEN A ROOM LIKE THIS. A GIANT BED sat in the middle, laid out in cream and muted gold, so very elegant that its colours seemed to whisper. Two chairs and a large wooden table were arranged in front of a glass wall, and a semi-glittering city lay beyond it. She walked straight towards it and looked down at Park Street. Shop signs and traffic lights and dark ochre cabs lined the street. She felt like a ghost, standing at a remove from a darkly painted city.

Mr Ghosh took off his shoes, walked over to the desk and poured himself a glass of whiskey. Lalee turned around. A cut-glass tumbler stood next to the bottle, a paper coaster on top, a shiny steel container next to it filled with big chunks of ice. Mr Ghosh pushed one of the glasses towards Lalee.

'Can't abide those tiny, fiddly bottles. So annoying,' he said. 'At least they know what I like here.'

Lalee sat down on the bed and felt it sink pleasantly, curling around her like an invitation. The mattress was thick, neither too soft nor too hard, and the sheets made of the softest cotton. She ran her hands over the luxurious fabric. A duvet had been folded and its ends tucked underneath the giant mattress. She couldn't fathom the reason for this. It looked like it would need to be pulled off the bed to be used. Mr Ghosh sipped his drink and looked at her without blinking. She got up and began to take her dress off.

Mr Ghosh walked to the other side of the room and sat on the armchair in the corner. There was a tall standing lamp beside it. The yellow light reflected off his glasses. He gave Lalee a wan smile.

'What's your hurry? We're going to be here for a while.' He gestured towards the glass he had left on the desk for Lalee. 'I hope whiskey's acceptable? I've been told the ladies don't like it, but I don't consider anything else worth drinking.' Lalee, her dress halfway over her head, couldn't decide if she should take it off or pull it down. As she hesitated, Mr Ghosh chuckled softly.She smoothed her dress and picked up the glass. She was still standing and sipping her drink when Mr Ghosh said, 'Relax, there's no need to be so formal.'

She sat down on the bed.

'I hate hurrying,' said Mr Ghosh. 'The very rich and the atrociously poor, they can go at whatever pace they like. It's men like me who run around hustling for one thing or another.'

Lalee doubted that Mr Ghosh had to hustle very much – he had the bearing of a rich man. His clothes were not flashy, he was short and pot-bellied, but he exuded a quiet confidence. As though he knew his place in the world, and had nothing to prove to anyone. Lalee hadn't met a lot of men like that. In her decades in Shonagachhi, she had met desperate men, poor men, rough men and men who boasted about power, but she hadn't met truly powerful men. They were there, all the same, in someone else's bed, with someone like Sonia or Mohamaya.

She smiled and willed herself to look interested. All men liked women to listen to them, to show some interest. She'd learned that long ago.

Mr Ghosh sipped his whiskey, put down the glass neatly on a coaster, careful not to leave a stain on the table. Then he said, 'So, what's your story?'

Lalee felt her body tensing up, but she didn't allow it to affect the smile on her face. There was always someone like this, someone who wanted to know her 'story'. She could see the satisfaction written on their faces, the satisfaction of having done a good thing, of having listened to a fallen woman tell her story and sympathizing with her plight. She had a way to deal with such entitlement when a simple refusal would not do. She had many stories, some of them hers, some that could just as easily have been hers. She told them to the soft-eyed johns and the earnest social workers, all of whom wanted to know her 'story'.

'What do you mean my story?' she asked, sipping her whiskey.

'Who you are, what's your real name, how you came to this … life.' He raised his glass a little towards Lalee.

'I think it would spoil the mood,' Lalee said. 'Most gentlemen prefer to get on with other activities.'

Mr Ghosh chuckled again, undid his belt and pulled his shirt out of his pants. Lalee thought that was her cue to approach him. But Mr Ghosh got comfortable in his chair and picked up his glass again. 'Continue,' he said.

'My real name is Jigri.' Lalee watched Mr Ghosh raise an eyebrow.

'I'm from a small village in Jharkhand. I was ... brought here as a child.'

'Who brought you here?' Mr Ghosh asked.

Lalee paused, trying to look for either empathy or arousal in Mr Ghosh's face. Social workers and journalists asked that question for one reason, johns asked it for another. The prostitute's story was no less a part of the erotic experience. Those johns sat there absorbing Lalee's words and Lalee imagined them emotionally masturbating. She couldn't put Mr Ghosh's empty, expressionless face in either category. She wondered if he was different, better even. 'What will you do with my story? Will you write a newspaper article on me?' Lalee laughed awkwardly, unsure if she had stalled Mr Ghosh's unwelcome curiosity.

He merely smiled, signalling for Lalee to continue.

Lalee moved to the other side of the bed, closer to Mr Ghosh.

'Tell me,' he murmured, taking a few strands of Lalee's dark hair in his fingers and examining them, as though it was of some scientific significance.

'Well, it's not so different from the stories of the girls who end up in Shonagachhi. I was born in a small village, and my father was a farmer. I was the eldest. I had three sisters and one brother, all very young when my father killed himself.'

'Why?' Mr Ghosh frowned.

'The usual. We had a drought, my father borrowed money from the moneylender, the next year there was a drought again, my father borrowed more money and it all added up until there was no way for him to pay any of it back, or feed us, for that matter.' She drew her breath slowly. 'I remember starving, I remember hunger.'

Mr Ghosh took another sip, his forehead furrowing in concentration.

Lalee paused for an appropriate second before continuing, 'After he died, my mother sent me to live with my aunt in this city, to find work, perhaps as a maid in someone's house. I had never seen this aunt before. One day, she told me we were going to visit some relatives who would help me find work and brought me to Shonagachhi. She left me there and said she'd be back in the evening to pick me up.'

'Then?' Mr Ghosh urged.

'Evening turned to night but she never came,' Lalee went on – she had the story down pat. 'I waited all night and cried all of the next day. The people in the house that she brought me to, a woman of about forty and a couple of young girls – they were nice to me at first, they told me my aunt had sold me for 5,000 rupees and that the money would go to my family, feed my brother and sisters, and that perhaps my brother would go to school and have a respectable job someday. They explained to me that it was for the best. But when I didn't stop crying, they beat me. Never in the face or the thighs or the stomach – there are rules about beatings in brothels. They'd cane me on my shins and calves, sometimes on my back.'

She stopped, but Mr Ghosh didn't say anything. He went and poured himself some more whiskey even though he hadn't finished what was left in his glass. 'And?' he asked softly.

'At first I didn't know what was happening. It took some time, I was young, but it wasn't very hard to figure things out. In the beginning I would cry, I would beg those men who came for me to leave me, to not touch me. They'd laugh if they were a good sort, but mostly they'd hit me. They were desperate men. Boatmen, truckers, labourers, men who lived by strength or cunning and they'd paid with money I imagine wasn't easy for them to come by either. They were not about to let me go.'

Mr Ghosh took her glass and poured some more whiskey in it. Even though Lalee had hardly had time to sip her drink, the two gulps she had taken previously were big ones and the glass was half empty.

'Go on,' Mr. Ghosh urged, pushing the glass once again towards Lalee. Lalee smiled to herself. Yes, he was definitely that kind of customer.

'One night, business was slow and I saw my madam, passed out drunk in front of the TV,' said Lalee. 'None of the other girls were paying me any attention, so I just got out of the door and ran and ran. I had no idea where I was going – I just ran as fast as I could. It was winter and quite late. Then I saw a traffic policeman sitting inside a police booth. I ran to him and told him everything and asked him to help me. He said he would take me to the police station and get me help.'

'And?' Mr Ghosh prompted her again, 'You escaped?'

Lalee laughed, 'No. What do you think they did? He and a constable. I was there all night, in the backroom.' Lalee looked away, 'In the morning, I came back to the brothel, to madam.'

'Did she hit you?'

'No, she didn't. She wasn't a bad person. She fed me and taught me things, she protected me, in her own way. She just said she had a bad hangover and never asked me what had happened.'

'That sounds strange,' said Mr Ghosh.

'Do you think I was the first of her girls who'd tried to run away? A lot of girls try that sort of thing. When they see what's outside, they come back.' Lalee picked up her glass decidedly. 'Some of them even go home, but their family won't accept them anymore. Some are more intelligent and don't waste any energy trying to escape, at least not quite as simply as running away.'

She smiled at him, suggesting her story had come to an end, and laid a hand on his thigh. This time Mr Ghosh didn't object, though he periodically broke apart to have a sip of his whiskey. At first, Lalee tried to keep him in bed, provocatively insisting on his attention, but before long, she gave in to the disjointed, fragmented nature of their encounter. She found him to be a decent lover even if he was dispassionate, treating Lalee like a curiosity, an object he was scrutinizing for a while, but it mattered so little in the scheme of things. She did notice, however, that whenever she tried to take control, Mr Ghosh seemed to find it amusing and would let her carry on for a short while like a man tolerating the antics of a pet, but he eventually subdued her, sometimes with some impatience. After a few rounds of these tussles, Lalee gave in, becoming entirely compliant, reciprocating and malleable.

Afterwards, as Mr Ghosh snored on his back, Lalee sat beside him with her legs sprawled in front of her. She thought of the long road that had taken her to where she was in that very moment. At one time she would have thought it impossible that she would spend a night in a place like this. How much would such a room cost per night? Ten thousand? Fifteen? She looked at the quiet, middle-aged man passed out on the bed, his chest heaving softly under the covers and tried to imagine having that kind of money to spend on a night of fun. Most of the girls she knew didn't earn that much in a month. She wondered how much Mohamaya had earned, if she had ever been inside an expensive hotel room, and if she missed her children when she found herself in front of plentiful plates of food. Ever since the murder, her thoughts kept turning towards this young woman she had hardly known, and each time she felt angry. No one knew better than her that it could have been anybody. It could have been her instead of Mohamaya. To the rest of the world, the whores of Shonagachhi and of such other shanty meat markets were interchangeable. But what did that matter. The more one got used to money, what you could buy with it became meaningless.

She slipped silently to the floor, taking care to replace the sheets on Mr Ghosh's broad back. His glasses were placed precariously on the edge of the bed. Lalee picked them up carefully and put them on the bedside table. She poured herself a larger drink this time. Mr Ghosh turned in his sleep with a muffled sound.

She tiptoed to the giant glass wall, sat down and hugged her knees, rested her chin on them and watched the street below. For as long as she had been in this city, she had thought of Park Street as an almost mythical place of gaiety and opulence. Even the prostitutes here had better clothes, hair, money and English names. Now at this hour the street below looked ramshackle. From the fifth floor, Lalee had a good view of the bedraggled old colonial buildings that people who came to wine and dine in Park Street forgot to look up at.

Underneath, the well-lit shopfronts and posh restaurants had downed their shutters and long gone home. On the pavements, homeless people were curling up into tight balls, wrapping themselves with newspapers and shawls. Yellow taxis crawled by looking for passengers, few and far between, the drivers milling around after parking their cabs on the side of the streets as drunks and partygoers emerged intermittently from the Park.

# 26

THE DOOR WAS ALWAYS OPEN. VISHAL DIDN'T KNOCK; HE SIMPLY walked in. The apartment looked the same as usual. He wondered whether it would have looked different to him if he had ever moved far away enough, to study or to find a job – like so many had – in a city where there were never enough jobs for the upwardly mobile. Would he have returned a changed man, if he left the city that he grew up in, only two buildings down from his childhood home, having developed a pair of eyes that took in the cobwebs, and the jaundiced light that shone on the antique furniture?

His mother and her friends – Mrs Barwani, Mistry, Edulji and D'souza – were gathered around the little coffee table that was still standing on its three legs as it had done since before he was born, fidgeting with their cards. He remembered long afternoons turning into even longer twilights and evenings as they played for laughably small stakes, a pittance compared to the smallest rings on their fingers. It took him a while to realize that it was the pleasure of the game and its leisurely unfolding that mattered, not what money was won or lost. These were women of leisure who had never had to work for a living, but their days were full of presiding over countless committees, organizing exhibitions, club events and charity drives and in general, Making Things Happen.

'How're you, Ma? No time for Atash Adaran these days?'

'Oh hush,' his mother said, waving a hand half-heartedly at him, barely looking away from her cards. 'I'm a trustee of the temple, I've got all the time in the world for it. Isn't Deepa's thingie on TV today?'

Vishal nodded, doubting his mother would see it.

'Put it on then, go on. Papaji is sleeping and I doubt he would wake up for a big clock.'

Vishal went to the kitchen, emptying the grocery bags he had brought into its dark and unknowable crevices. Like everything in this house's universe, it was antique, valuable to a museum of early technology and meticulously maintained. He liked stuffing it with exotic and expensive things he specially arranged to be imported, collected or otherwise obtained. He liked to imagine that Ma Currimbhoy appreciated such efforts, even if she never said so.

He walked back into the living room, flopped down to the squishy depth of the sofa and turned on the TV, adjusting the harsh volume to a tolerable level.

'Oh please,' snorted Vidya Dehejia on screen. 'All of those brothels – Blue Lotus and … and ... Nanda Ranir Bari – they all have a tehkhana where they hide the underage girls during the raids.'

'Okay, Ms Dehejia, so you're saying that these brothels have a high rate of trafficked minor girls in the trade?'

'Absolutely. Anyone saying otherwise is lying. But of course, you need to ask: Who is making them? Trafficking is a global phenomenon and let's just say many people stand to benefit from it, even those who declare they want to end it.'

'I believe,' smiled the television anchor with the self-satisfied smile of a shark, 'that's a direct challenge to you, Ms Marhatta.'

'The Self-regulatory Board of the Collective has worked very hard since 1995 to make sure that no woman who works in Shonagachhi is there due to coercion or is a minor. With these raids you are delegitimizing their profession, their right to unionize and fight for their labour rights. They have spent years and very hard-earned resources getting bone scans and talking to every last woman making sure that they are of legal age and are there by choice.'

'Choice!' Vidya Dehejia burst out. 'It's easy to talk about choice when you're sitting in an AC room cocooned in all your privilege. These women do not have a choice. I repeat, they do not have a choice. This is not a life any one of them would have chosen. And that is why we need the raid-rescue-rehabilitation model. Find them, save them and help them find another way in life, and that is what the Nari Shakti Vahini is doing.'

A roar of claps and hoots went up. The camera turned on the audience in the studio, flinging their hands up in the air. 'Rescue and rehabilitate,' they chanted. The television anchor smiled, and made a show of quieting the uproar.

'It's clear what the public believes, Ms Marhatta. Please tell us what you think.'

'Sure, that all sounds grand when you put it that way – it's all jingoism at the end of the day.'

'Jingoism! Really?' Dehejia exclaimed.

The anchor gestured to her to simmer down.

'Yes,' Deepa continued. 'Choice in this context is a lot more complicated. Yes, a lot of them wouldn't have "chosen" this.' She air-quoted the last words. 'But this is their home. This is where they have made a life, had children, had marriages even, fed themselves and their families. These rooms are the only places over which they have any control and the repeated raids are nothing but an oppressive state machinery—'

The anchor cut her off mid-sentence as the crowd started getting louder. Vidya Dehejia took the opportunity to pick up her microphone and yell, 'See, this is what I mean. These people want the battered women of Shonagachhi to stay there so they can look forward to more murder and sexual slavery – and, for some among us, playing the part of saviours is more important than saving anyone'

The cameras panned on the anchor's face as the audience in the auditorium got to their feet. 'Not one more!' they chanted and some of them held up placards saying #NotOneMore and #JusticeForMaya. Vidya Dehejia resolutely refused to make eye contact with Deepa. She stood up and walked off the stage as the anchor said with sincere joy and enthusiasm, 'That's our debate on rehabilitation of sex workers in today's society. You've heard their arguments, now you decide. Send an SMS to the number on the screen and tell us what you think: Should we rescue the women who truly need our help or should we "respect their choice"? Call the toll-free number on your screens—'

Vishal turned off the TV.

'You're staying for dinner, beta?' his mother asked, looking up from her game.

'Play the ace, Ma – you won't take it with you when you go, you know.'

His mother frowned slightly and concentrated on the cards. The other women were talking among themselves, pushing up bifocals and rearranging the fan of cards, held at an arm's length from the spectacles.

'Come over for dinner on Saturday, beta?' Vishal's mother called out. 'I'll tell Papa.'

'Why? You're planning to set me up with a third cousin again or what?'

His mother threw a cushion at him. 'Bring Deepa, of course,' she said and returned to her cards.

He waved and shut the door after him.

# 27

IN THE ADHESIVE HAZE BETWEEN SLEEPING AND WAKING, Lalee heard several impatient knocks on the door. It took her a few moments to realize where she was. Debris from the night before was strewn around her. A crisp, newly minted 2,000-rupee note lay next to her on the covers. There was no sign of Mr Ghosh.

Her discarded clothes, her panties, bra and cheap handbag, with the fake leather peeling in small black crumbs, looked out of place in the grand room. She draped a bathrobe around herself that she'd been secretly elated to find hanging in the hotel closet the night before. There were soft murmurs and laughing outside. She unlocked the door, apprehensive, fumbling with the complicated mechanism. Outside, two women stood talking to each other with a trolley between them.

'Housekeeping, madam,' one of them said, eyeing her up and down.

Lalee didn't understand what she meant and stood there without replying. The other woman pointed at the room and said, 'Change bedsheets, clean bathroom.' Lalee noticed that they exchanged a look between themselves, the taller woman smirking slyly and turning away.

*They know what I am*, Lalee thought, feeling small in this unfamiliar territory. There was contempt in the women's eyes. Lalee would know it anywhere. Something hardened inside her. She would not be thrown out.

'Come later,' she spat at them in English and closed the door.

Lalee dug through her handbag for her phone. There were two missed calls from Rambo and one from Shefali Madam. She pushed aside the heavy white and gold drapes from the clear glass wall. Layered behind the thick drapes, diaphanous white curtains moved gently in the circulating processed air of the room, bathing it in soft unearthly light. Lalee could see the choking traffic on the street but only heard the soft hum of the AC. It felt peaceful. She opened closets and drawers and rooted through the bathroom vanity wondering if she could take the small items – shampoo bottles, plastic toothbrush, the soft, white towel-like slippers. She wondered if she would get into trouble for stealing. If the women outside her door would notice the theft and chase after her. She left the things where they were, glancing at the bathtub she would never use.

Her phone was ringing – it was Madam. Lalee toyed with the idea of not picking up, of locking herself in this beautiful soundless room and wrangle a few more minutes of peace and respite before dragging herself back to reality again. But she answered her phone anyway – if she did get into trouble, the only one she could turn to was Shefali Madam.

'Busy morning?' Madam asked.

'No,' Lalee replied. 'Just woke up late.'

'Well, that's good. Get your things together and go downstairs. Chintu will meet you in the hotel lobby.'

'Lobby?' Lalee repeated.

'Yes,' Madam replied with the confidence of a woman who had herself once been stupefied by the term. 'It's the big room inside the main door of the hotel. You can sit and wait there. No one will say anything.'

'When will he arrive?'

'He has ... a few arrangements to make. He'll be there when he is done. Now get out of the room. Your rate won't pay for another night in that hotel.'

Lalee suspected it would. Mr Ghosh was a rich customer and Shefali Madam knew what to do with the type. She didn't mention the new note she had found on the bed and allowed herself a small amount of gratitude for Mr Ghosh – this tip was a lot more than her rate in Shonagachhi.

She spotted Sonia sashaying down the lobby towards her. Sonia blended perfectly with the muted gold-beige interior of the hotel, reflected in an infinity on the mirrors lining the walls. Lalee looked around for Chintu. In the years Lalee had known him, she had seen him lay out unruly johns and working girls alike, carried out every one of Madam's commands without a question or thought. Lalee hated him with all she had, but Chintu was the one who had stood between her and a john with a knife, a john who might have knocked her teeth out or choked her within an inch of her life in the name of pleasure. Newspapers were full of reports of stray dogs tortured, flayed and set alight for the sake of someone's pleasure and everytime, Lalee knew the exact impulse that drove people to seek that particular kind of gratification. She'd seen it more times than she wanted to remember in a customer's eyes, in the eyes of that customer's friends when they came in a group. Sometimes, Chintu was the only thing standing between them and her. It was a complicated algebra; it was the algebra of need in Shonagachhi.

But she wasn't in Shonagachhi now, Chintu was nowhere to be seen and Sonia was descending upon her like a shark chasing a scent.

'Come along, my lovely, the car is here. You had a good night? I had a lovely one.'

Sonia was already walking towards the door. Lalee remained seated. 'I have to wait for Chintu,' she said. 'Madam called me.'

'Chintu is here already, waiting outside in the car. *Mere saath chalo*,' Sonia spoke slowly, gesturing for Lalee to move.

Lalee felt annoyed that Sonia seemed to know what was going on but she didn't. But it was impossible to stay in the hotel lobby – people were already glancing at her, knowing as she did that she didn't belong in such a place.

She trailed after Sonia, feeling a surge of anger towards Madam and Chintu for keeping her off balance. Not for the first time she began to think that it may have been a mistake to accept Madam's offer. But it wasn't a choice. She had a debt to Madam in more ways than one. Maybe 'upstairs' could become a means of escape, or at least a better way of surviving.

Sonia pulled out a pair of giant sunglasses from a stiff, pale leather handbag dangling elegantly from her arm. Next to her, Lalee felt more legitimate, somehow more deserving of the space she was taking up. A black car pulled up in front of them with Chintu in the driver's seat. Sonia walked around to the front and said, 'Get in.'

Lalee found Rambo Maity occupying most of the backseat. Next to him, two girls, barely twelve, were huddled in a corner, one sitting on the lap of the other. They looked frightened and half-starved. Lalee knew instantly what that meant. Shonagachhi swallowed and spat out girls like them every day. She'd been one such girl a long time ago. But Lalee was an entirely different animal now. Her hide had thickened, her claws were sharp such that she could tear her way through Shonagachhi to survive. But her stomach sank when she saw these two girls' faces.

Lalee realized they were twins. Both quite comely girls, under the grime and the matted hair. She felt nauseous, knowing full well what lay in store for them. Sonia turned on the radio from the passenger seat. Chintu, as usual, said nothing.

Something forceful rose up in Lalee, like a surge of anger she had come to know well. She turned savagely towards Rambo and hissed, 'What is all this? Why are you here and where are you taking these girls?'

Rambo backed away from her in mock terror. 'Arrey madam, slow down. They're going where you are going. Shefali Madam's orders.'

'Tell me what's going on now, Maity. I'll scratch your balls off if you don't. Where the hell are we going?'

Sonia, her face half covered in dark glasses, turned towards the backseat passengers and said, 'Calm down. You'll soon find out. You passed the test last night. Congratulations.'

As her unease grew stronger, Lalee screamed, 'Let me out right now!' She tried to open the door but it was locked and would not budge.

Chintu sighed loudly from the driver's seat. Sonia opened a window and lit a cigarette, the smoke slowly mixing with the burning midsummer air that came rolling in. The two girls in the back began to cough but Sonia carried on smoking.

In her frustration, Lalee shoved Rambo and swiped at him. Rambo took off his gold-rimmed aviators and grabbed her wrists in one strong grip.

'Shut it, okay?' he growled at her. Lalee noticed he had a black eye. 'You agreed to Madam's terms. This is the next step. Madam is sending you to do a job.'

'She would have told me what job it was,' Lalee said, desperately trying to hang on to her anger to stave off the sinking feeling of uncertainty and dread.

'Would she have?' Rambo laughed. 'Settle down – you're onto big money now. Madam has a big job coming up and she's putting her best girls on it. You'll be in the VIP seats soon, that is, if you can behave yourself. Your two-bit whore ways won't fly where you are going. They might just get you killed.'

Lalee wanted to slap him, but her wrists were still firmly in Rambo's grip. Rambo leaned towards her and whispered, 'I'm not allowed to touch your face, otherwise you'd be missing a tooth already.'

Lalee looked at the two cowering girls trying to fade into a corner of the car. They stared at Lalee and Rambo, frozen on the edge of terror. Lalee freed her hands from Rambo's clutches and leaned back on the seat. The car was calm and chilly; Sonia had put the air conditioner as low as it would go. Lalee felt an involuntary shiver and closed her eyes.

'Just tell me,' she tried one last time.

'A holy place,' Sonia said distantly, exhaling a cloud of smoke. 'The kind you Indians like so much. And then, we're going away. Far, far away.'

# 28

MALINI WAS SITTING CROSS-LEGGED ON THE FLOOR, LIKE THE eye of a storm of paperwork. Heavy folders fat with sheaves of paper lay about her, as did cardboard boxes. She had a wad of papers on her lap and was peering at them through her bifocals.

After watching her wordlessly for a while, Deepa said, 'Leave it be, for now Malini. It's late, we should go and get something to eat.'

Malini mumbled something; her attention was clearly elsewhere. Deepa tried again. 'We can come back and give it another try. Let's go have dinner now and then maybe visit the girls at the police station. Maybe we can fill up a flask for them at Manik-da's teashop.'

Malini looked up at her. 'It's hopeless, Deepa-di. We used to do four to five lakh rupees a day. After the notebandi, we were lucky if the day's deposits reached 40,000. We still haven't recovered from the shock. You remember how it was last November?'

Deepa nodded. Their ongoing projects were entirely overshadowed by the financial fallout of a country of primarily cash users suddenly realizing the notes in their hands were less useful than yesterday's newspaper. She didn't want to bring that up. Instead, she said, 'The first two days were good though, Malini. After they announced that ban and we asked the girls to take the banned notes anyway, we did make nearly five and a half lakhs in two days.'

Too late – Deepa remembered what had happened to the money. Hundreds of lakhs worth of banned notes now sat uselessly in the coffers of small co-operatives like the one run by sex workers, or those by farmers in rural heartlands. Not all of it could be exchanged in the limited timeframe. Not all of it could be recovered. Bank notes in mattresses, old socks, hidden carefully under little idols of gods and goddesses. Secreted by abused housewives, hiding money from patriarchs who drank too much and pulled a punch too often. Stowed away by sex workers to pay off old trafficking debts to pimps, touts and the police. There wasn't time enough in the whole world to change all those crumpled notes, made dirty with sweat and fear, even if those people could find a bank, could stand in a line two miles long and could persuade overworked and unsympathetic government employees to be kind to them.

An industry worth a few hundred billion dollars, built off the backs of women, girls and trans people, and what did they have to show for it.

She realized Malini was saying something.

'... have to do something, Deepa-di – this can't go on. Forget loans, we don't even have enough for the girls to withdraw money. Most of them are running out of their savings. Already some of them are having to stop insisting on condoms. The customer just goes next door. Everyone is strapped for cash.'

'We need to think first about the girls who have debts.'

Malini got up and started pacing around the room.

'Some of them, such as Sonal, have had to borrow again from the owners. Some of them will never be able to pay off those debts. They'll just get sold off again, or worse.'

Malini paused for a moment and looked directly at Deepa, who lowered her eyes, got up from the floor and picked up her large, fat-bellied handbag.

'Have you heard anything, Deepa-di?'

Deepa shook her head, not meeting Malini's gaze. Malini persisted, rooted to her spot.

'The owners haven't got their payments, I know it – I keep hearing rumours. The girls haven't made enough to make their monthly payments and if those bloodsuckers don't get their debt paid off, they'll start making desperate deals, or will be trafficked again.'

Deepa nodded, opening her bag and looking for something, avoiding the searching apprehension in Malini's eyes.

At the sound of a sudden commotion outside, both women ran to the verandah. Malini didn't bother with her shoes while Deepa struggled uselessly with the straps of her sandals. Two police vans and three unmarked cars were rushing down the narrow lane, scattering people in their way.

Three female constables were dragging some girls through the front door of The Blue Lotus. Deepa realized that the faces were familiar; she tried hard to recall their names. The raids were so commonplace that the police officer didn't bother to explain their presence. The duty officer – from what Deepa could tell – was standing off to a side, stone-faced, barking orders at his subordinates to round up the underage girls. Deepa spotted a plump, imperial-looking woman in a bright pink saree, with her hands folded across her chest, one of the organizers of Nari Shakti Vahini. She turned towards Deepa and offered a sardonic smile that stung even from a distance. 'This is the fallout.' Deepa shook her head just slightly. The state machinery springing into action to save other innocents under the glare of a highly-publicized murder in the only way they knew how – responding with force and censure. Malini was talking to the officer, hands gathered, head slightly bowed, explaining with a slight tremor in her voice that the Collective checked all the girls' bone scans to make sure that they weren't underage. The officer didn't even look at her. He barked something at Malini. Deepa placed a hand on Malini's shoulders. She watched as the bodies brushed past her. She felt the shoves, the close contact with skin and the shouts that erupted but for all their immediacy, they still seemed to happen in a different universe, where she was only a bystander. A man in a khaki uniform walked towards Deepa, leaving a trail of hard-faced policewomen in khaki sarees dragging some of the recalcitrant girls by their hair, twisting their arms behind their backs. Deepa found herself wondering, inopportunely, how these policewomen manufactured this deep and abiding hatred for women they had never met. Was geographical location and accidents of birth and circumstances reason enough? Deepa had encountered many kinds of hatred, but nothing, she thought, surpassed what respectable, middle-class women held in their hearts for prostitutes.

The policeman ignored Malini and stopped in front of Deepa.

'Here, madam, we're doing what you all asked us to do. Rescuing these poor children from a terrible life and monsters,' he laughed, baring paan-stained teeth.

Deepa looked closely at him. A name tag on his chest said 'Bose', a pack of India Kings cigarettes peeked out of a pocket, his bald head rising like a dome as rivulets of sweat streamed down his body.

'What happened, madam? Your friend here,' he turned around and pointed at Malini, 'is creating difficulties. We will help these girls. They will be taken away to our rescue centers. They get sewing machines and lots of training, you know. You blame the police saying we don't do anything, but you don't like it when we work.' Bose spat on the ground, and looked up at Deepa, grinning.

Deepa stopped herself from saying all that she wanted to say. She wanted to shout at him to look around himself and realize how he was uprooting these women from their homes. From a hapless, stitched-together family, a refuge, a chance at earning money that they never could have. Not only that, but this raid was another bomb detonated in the heart of the Sex Workers' Collective, delegitimizing their rights as workers, their unionization, their daily, indefatigable effort to ensure safety and consent for the women who worked here. The futility of this tirade in the face of Bose's idiot, bigoted, bog-like mind struck Deepa like a fist. The air left her lungs. Before Bose or Malini could say anything more, she threw a look at Malini and ran. Her phone was at the Collective's office, inside her bag where she had left it. If she could contact some of the human rights lawyers who volunteered their services, maybe she could trace some of the girls quickly, stem the flood of their scatter across the crevices of this city, homeless and unsafe. And so she ran, leaving Malini barely afloat, like a tiny island, in a sea of khaki uniforms.

# 29

WHEN LALEE WOKE UP WITH A START, THE SKY WAS BEGINNING to darken. A murder of crows was cawing loudly as the car stopped in front of a large ornate iron gate. Iron flowers painted golden twined the long black grilles. Above the gate, an arch bore the legendary name Nandankanan. On the walls around the gate, sizeable posters bearing the face of Maharaj plastered the walls.

Lalee's stomach twisted; she felt as if she was about to free fall from a great height. She turned around to face Rambo, pulled her arm back and slapped him as hard as she could. Then she shook some life back into her hands. Rambo stared at her, shocked, and then rage filled his face. Lalee could see that in any other circumstance Rambo would have hauled her one, but for some reason only he knew, Rambo was exerting considerable self-control. He settled for growling at her, 'What was that for, cunt?'

'You drugged me,' Lalee yelled, waking the two sleepy girls still huddling in a corner, blinking in the dim light.

'You drugged me – how dare you?' Lalee yelled again. 'That water you gave me, was that it?' Then she laughed. 'Fucking you and fucking Shefali Madam. If this was such a straightforward job, how come you have to drug us to bring us here?'

Even as she was yelling at Rambo, Lalee noticed that Sonia was wide awake. She was silent, staring at the distance with her windows rolled down, smoking another cigarette. Her face was impossible to read, averted from Lalee and the others in the car. Sonia didn't look drugged, instead her face was concentrated in a frown, tension wafting from her along with blue curls of smoke.

Chintu blew the horn a couple of times and looked at the back seat of the car, eyeing Rambo and Lalee. Rambo rubbed his cheek a couple of times and leaned back, closing his eyes as if to calm himself. Lalee could feel a tight weave of apprehension settle in the car and sat up straighter on the edge of the seat.

A couple of men, decked out in black uniforms with red waist bands, carrying large rifles, strolled up to the gate. One of them unlocked the iron gate, which opened with a loud screech – the only sound except the passing trucks on the highway and the cacophony of birds in the dusk. The guard stooped down to look at Chintu and Sonia, nodded at his colleague and both the gates opened wide for the car to pass.

Lalee kept her eyes peeled on the narrow dirt road as the car slowly made its way into the compound. There were more guards, she noticed, walking in groups around the gate and the perimeter, sometimes sharing a cup of tea and food. But each of them had a rifle slung from their shoulders. She had never seen that many men with guns in her life.

'What is this place?' she asked Rambo, Sonia and Chintu, not caring who would answer her, as long as someone did.

Chintu kept driving. Sonia threw her cigarette outside the gates and continued staring ahead. Only Rambo opened his eyes and sighed quietly.

'What is this place?' Lalee repeated, panic lacing her voice.

'This is not the time to ask questions,' Rambo said in a low voice, which merged with the background hum of the car's AC, now cranked up to maximum. 'Don't do anything rash, and always, always follow instructions,' Rambo said and tried to smile at Lalee.

His smile looked like that of a man headed for the gallows. Lalee wasn't certain if Rambo had been coerced to come to this place – whatever it was – as she had been. Surely, unlike her, he had chosen this for some kind of gain. Rambo, a veteran of the rough streets that Lalee herself knew so well, wouldn't have been careless enough to get himself into a difficult situation. Only, Lalee thought, he would. His greed surpassed his common sense. For enough money, Rambo would do anything.

Chintu stopped the car in the farthest corner of a big parking lot. It was nearly full with cars ranging from modest to large to expensive. Two women, accompanied by two guards, slowly walked towards them. Rambo leaned over to the twins' side and unlocked the door, urging them to get out. Sonia, Lalee noticed, was already out and stretching her legs. Her skinny jeans and tank top looked out of place as the two women clad entirely in white long-sleeved blouses and the ends of their sarees covering their hair, reached them. One of the women kept her eyes trained on the ground. The other handed out thin red shawls to Lalee, Sonia and the twin girls.

Sonia tried to refuse the shawl, complaining about the heat, but the woman in white thrust it on her all the same.

Chintu never left the car. Lalee waited nervously, hoping he would take them back, not daring to stray too far from the car. But when Chintu started backing out of the lot, panic set in. He was the last remaining tie with the outside world, and Lalee had never imagined that she would feel so lost and forlorn at the sight of someone like Chintu driving away from her. For a moment she contemplated running after the still slow-moving car, waving her hands like a madwoman, refusing to be abandoned. As if she had read Lalee's mind, Sonia looked at Lalee and shook her head. The brash ease that Lalee had begun to associate with Sonia had dropped off her like she had abandoned an act. She was composed, unlike Lalee's own panicked state. Lalee looked around herself. The two accompanying guards hovered in the background; their presence seemed like a formality, not a threat. But the high walls surrounding them gave Lalee pause. The parking lot was very close to the walls and the trees that proliferated the rest of the compound had been cleared for the concrete parking space.

The woman who had handed them the red shawls, unfolded one and wrapped it around one of the girls. They were still holding hands, shrinking against each other. One by one, they all found red shawls around themselves, except Rambo, and the two women with the two guards escorted the women towards the main square.

From the outside, it looked like a big temple. Conical spires topped with tridents and colorful flags sprouted towards the sky. A series of thick columns supported the long corridor where a sea of shoes and slippers lay in disarray. Lalee, Sonia and the girls were ushered to the back of the congregation. In the distance, Lalee could see Maharaj sitting on a red velvet throne, adorned with garlands of roses, marigolds and tuberoses. A large screen hung over the auditorium showing a close-up of the man on the throne, smiling and tapping his feet to the beats of the music. Large speakers blared chants set to rhythmic beats as people – a sea of them – clapped their hands, chanted and swayed to the music.

Lalee instinctively reached out to hold the twins. Sonia stood by them with her arms crossed across her chest, impressively tall. Lalee noticed Sonia was frowning. When Lalee agreed to Shefali Madam's offer, she hadn't dreamt of ending up in a religious commune. When she had thought about her destiny at all, it was hotel rooms and rich clients that she envisioned. She had heard that highly paid escorts accompanied rich johns to nightclubs and events, even travelled by air for short holidays. She knew these things were true, but she never thought they would happen to her. When Shefali Madam asked her to work upstairs, she hadn't quite dared to dream that far, but she thought … about possibilities, about what life could become and that distant horizon getting a little closer to her reach.

Instead, she now stood with two scared young girls and an aloof white woman in a multitude of sweating people, in a room festering with the heat of bodies, dust from a hundred shoes, the stench of quietly rotting flowers and the smog of incense. She brushed the sweat off her forehead and watched the hulking bearded man on the screen stand up and spread his hands wide, throw his head back and smile at the universe.

Ten young ladies in all-white sarees, long blouses and head coverings – just like the two women who had escorted Lalee to the hall – walked up to the raised platform around the red velvet throne, carrying large brass plates with offerings that Lalee couldn't quite make out on the big pixellated screen.

The women proceeded to rub something on the arms and feet of Maharaj, as he looked on benignly. Flowers were laid at his feet; the women lit ten lamps and circled their guru with hands bearing firelight.

Lalee felt a prod on the small of her back. The escorts on either side of her indicated that she should bow her head and join her hands together in reverence. Lalee looked at their impassive, expressionless faces and chose not to argue, bowing her head and loosely joining her hands together. In front of her, a bent old woman was crying and wiping her tears with the palm of her hand at the same time. Even through the music, Lalee could hear the old woman repeating over and over again, 'Bring my son back to me, Maharaj, he's my only son, make that bitch pay, give me my son again. That witch enchanted him and now he belongs to them, Maharaj, Maharaj, Maharaj ...'

A shiver ran down Lalee's back. The sincerity in the woman's voice, the passion, the prayer, the curse, began to numb her limbs. She struggled for air, the room seemed to become smaller, the press of bodies around began to feel oppressive, and Lalee thought she was going to drown under their combined weight.

She clawed her way outside, elbowing some and shoving others. Outside, the evening had turned to night. The trees in the distance absorbed the dim glow coming from the stray lamps around the hall, the shadowy figures of armed guards flitting in and out of the light. Lalee gulped big puffs of air, collapsed on her knees and retched on the hallowed grounds of Maharaj's temple.

# 30

SAMSHER SINGH WAS SITTING ON A MOULDED PLASTIC chair and sipping a cup of tea. Shefali Madam was sitting in another of those chairs across from him, surrounded by three women of varying shapes and sizes who stood guard around her. Samsher felt a tingle flow down his right arm, and his mother's face flashed in front of his eyes. He felt a vague sense of disgust when he was climbing up the stairs to Shefali Madam's private room, stepping on the dirty, blackened stairs lined with porcelain tiles, each of which bore the face of a different god. Old paan stains ran down the walls in thin, dark brown rivulets, reminding Samsher of dried-up blood. He felt the same disgust now as his lips lowered into the cup of hot, milky tea, and he looked at the girls around Shefali Madam from the corner of his eyes, noticing their breasts, the angle of their hips.

He tried to shake the unease, something that crawled like an invisible spider up his spine, towards the back of his neck. Bose had conducted a raid not two days ago, arrested about fifty girls of all ages, so this was a sensitive time for a man in uniform to come asking for a favour. Samsher cleared his throat, as if he was going to say something. One of the younger girls who looked visibly startled took a small step back. Samsher liked that; it made him feel better. Though it did nothing to take away from the bitterness he had been carrying around for the last two days. He had been overlooked while Bose was put in charge of such a high-profile raid when media was on high alert. Sala, the DCP would call him up when he needed to punch down, but the real footage went to fucking Bose. Couldn't the DCP have asked him? It was his jurisdiction after all, he had a relationship with these people. But he would show them; this murder case could finally be his ticket. He didn't want much, just a picture in the papers. His wife's face came to mind. She'd be proud, to say nothing of Ma … oh the things she would have to tell the neighbours then …

Samsher looked up and was confronted by Shefali Madam's eyes, which were looking directly at him. The calm control of her manner affronted Samsher. A man as large as him, in the Kolkata Police uniform, ought to be the one in charge. But a short, plump, well-built woman in her late forties with paan stuffed into her face seemed to be steering the conversation.

Shefali Madam was the soul of politeness. She had welcomed the police officer with no less grandeur than the famous nautch girls of olden days would have welcomed the incumbent nawab and brought forth the finest blooms of courtesanhood for his pleasure. Initially gratified, Samsher began to wonder if she was mocking him. She had ordered both tea and paan for him and was now sitting across from him with an expression of old-world hospitality. But since she made no move to open the conversation, Samsher Singh cleared his throat, 'We are here, madam, about the death of one of your girls.'

Not a muscle moved in Shefali Madam's face. It was as if Samsher Singh had mentioned something about the weather.

Somewhat irritated by this silence, Samsher continued, 'You know the news channels are sitting on your doorsteps? This candlelight march has been on the news, you know, right? The media's going to lap this one up.' He shook his head. 'So you've got to talk to us.' He returned his cup to the saucer with a clink.

Shefali Madam made an expansive gesture with her hands. 'My dear Officer saab, we have no problem talking to you. Two days ago your friend was here, took away some of my girls.' She laughed. 'He said they were rescuing my girls. Though when my rescued girls run away from your centres, they tell me they are put in cages like poultry chicken.' Madam looked straight at Samsher, enjoying the discomfort plainly visible of his face. 'My rescued girls come back to the same dustbin you scrunch up your nose at. But Officer saab, the stories I could tell you. The men in uniform who come in the jeep to do a raid, and when those same men come back in the cover of night, wearing fresh pyjama-panjabi, drinking a little bit …' she chortled.

Samsher cleared his throat again. He didn't exactly know what he was going to ask this woman, but he wanted her to stop talking. He had some vague idea, if any at all, that as soon as he started the interview, big nuggets of startling information would start dropping out of nowhere and all would be clear. Instead, he was coming up against the implacable facade of the matriarch of the brothel. He fell back on certainties. 'What time was the crime committed?'

'We assumed it was midnight. One of my girls went downstairs around that time to ... solicit. She had to cross Mohamaya's room to go out the door and it was then that she saw the poor girl lying on the floor.'

'There were no screams, no one heard anything when it actually happened?'

'No. There is always some loud music playing up here. At night, we have to make ourselves heard and visible, you understand? Competition is very stiff around here, as you know, and the girls are always chattering and shouting among themselves, talking with the customers. Plus, we have children, pimps, babus and servants in the mix. So it is difficult to hear anything. But yes,' she paused, 'it is strange that we did not hear her at all.' She smiled at him. 'But I was hoping you could explain that to us. After all, you must know a lot more about such things than we do.'

Samsher Singh sidelined this trap and went ahead, 'So no one heard anything till this girl discovered the body. Who is this girl; is she here? I would like to speak to her.'

Madam motioned silently to one of the women and she disappeared through a door. She emerged moments later with a younger girl with swollen red eyes and dishevelled hair. She stood awkwardly before the two policemen, glancing with fear at Madam.

Madam said, 'This is the girl who discovered the body.'

'You knew the girl who was killed?' asked Samsher. The girl looked at Shefali Madam again and quietly nodded. 'What's your name?'

'Amina Bibi,' she said in a whisper, staring at her own feet. 'What time did you discover the body?'

She looked at Madam again which irritated Samsher but he forbore from making any comment. 'I don't know,' she said at last. 'It was around midnight. I had just finished with one customer and gone down for the next shift.'

'Okay,' said Samsher, 'did you know the girl? The one who died, that is. What's her name again?'

'Mohamaya. Her name was Mohamaya.'

'Yes, yes, that,' he said. 'So you knew her well?'

'We were friends,' said the girl, still not looking up.

Shefali Madam clicked her tongue and the girl darted furtive looks at her. Samsher feared that the presence of the madam was influencing his witness. He thought of asking for some privacy but was sure that Shefali Madam and her informants would be somewhere close by listening in. It wasn't worth the trouble.

'So when you went there,' he continued, 'what did you see?'

'I was just going out when I saw her lying on the floor. I just went in to check' – big blobs of tears were dropping on the floor like rain – 'and she was lying there, dead. Half her face ... just wasn't there. And her throat ... it was ...' she stopped and shut her eyes.

'Yes, yes. You don't have to go into all that,' Samsher mumbled awkwardly. She couldn't have been more than nineteen or twenty-one, he noticed. A slight girl with large eyes; something about her reminded him of a village belle. His sentimental heart softened. He said kindly, 'Where did the acid come from?'

'I don't know,' she wiped her nose with the back of her

hand, 'it was just the stuff to clean toilets with. We all have a bottle in the bathroom or in the washing areas to clean moss and dirt and unblock the drains.'

'Do you do it yourself? Did you buy a bottle recently?'

'No, here,' she indicated Shefali Madam, 'we have a servant to do that kind of thing, but Mohamaya … well she had recently started on her own.'

'But she was still under your roof,' Samsher turned to Madam.

Again she made that expansive gesture with her hands. 'I like to keep my girls close, Officer saab,' Shefali Madam said. 'Especially the ones who haven't seen Shonagachhi without my protection. I'm their mother and father and friend. I'm all they have got; I have to look out for them.'

'Yes,' said Singh sourly, 'and yet she died under your roof.'

'Just roof, officer, just my roof, not my protection,' the older woman said. 'You're forgetting that she was only renting the room from me. She wasn't any longer one of my girls. She had paid herself off, bought herself from me. And she started on her own, well or at least so she thought,' she said enigmatically.

'What do you mean?'

'Oh these girls, sir, what can I tell you about these girls,' she said laconically. 'Every one of them is a romantic fool. Too many Hindi movies, you see. They watch Kareena and Katrina and Priyanka and Deepika fall in love with a dashing hero on screen, marry him and live happily ever after and they think that's exactly what's going to happen with them.' She clicked her tongue, as though commenting on a minor character flaw. 'They've all got their self-styled heroes over here. Especially the ones who make a bit of money – the girls who make the money, that is. The gender roles over here,' she shrugged, 'are a little bit skewed than what you might be used to.'

'So she had a lover?' asked Singh.

'A babu, Officer saab, a babu. The unofficial "husband". Only as is usual with girls like Mohamaya, it was not a denewala babu, just a lenewala babu. The kind who takes, officer, not the kind who gives.'

'So who was this guy? You know him surely?' Singh asked, even though he already had that information.

'A young worthless streak of nothing called Salman Khan,' Shefali Madam burst out laughing raucously. 'Imagine that. I tell you, Officer, every day in this life is straight out of a Hindi film.'

Discomfited by the woman's ease and lack of apprehension at the presence of police investigating a murder that happened under her roof, Samsher said, 'And what can you tell me about him?'

'Nothing good,' she said. 'One of the many parasites that find their perfect wombs here in Shonagachhi. Although,' she shifted her weight in the unyielding plastic chair and gave Samsher an appraising stare, 'he has enterprise. There's a certain gentleman – and I think you're acquainted with him – a Mr Rambo Maity. Well, this Salman Khan, Mohamaya's babu, was known to have collaborated with our Mr Maity.'

Samsher remained silent, not one flicker crossed his face. Madam on the other hand simply looked satisfied with herself, neither urging, nor waiting for an answer. Both people baited the other to react, for the trade of information to begin.

Shefali Madam won in the end as Samsher finally gave in, 'What kind of collaboration?'

Madam smiled, 'I'm just a woman, Officer saab, but in this trade, information is everything. I hear Rambo Maity has been doing very well recently. I also heard that Mohamaya's Salman Khan knew Maity really well. They often went around together.'

'What do you mean?' probed Samsher.

Madam shrugged. 'Officer saab, you seem to think that I have supernatural powers. I'm not the prime minister of the country.' She smiled. 'I can only tell you so much. There are a thousand ways to make money in this city. In Shonagachhi, there's ten thousand ways.' She laughed heartily, as if something quite hilarious had occurred to her. But Samsher felt annoyed. He felt he was being got at in some way, but he didn't know how.

'Was the girl involved in this? I mean the girl who was killed? Was she involved in Rambo's … er … scheme?'

Shefali Madam would have sighed openly if she could; it had taken her a solid fifteen minutes to lead Samsher to a conclusion she hoped had been staring him in the face.

He was finding it hard to hide his excitement at having found a solid lead at last. 'Do you have any information on this girl? What she was doing with Rambo and his lot?'

Before Madam could say anything, the girl who had been brought to bear witness in front of Samsher gave a frightened yelp, which she then cut short by covering her mouth with her hand.

Samsher turned towards her and said in the most intimidating tone he could muster, 'So what do *you* know?'

She looked between the towering policeman and the seated madam like a deer caught in headlights. Shefali

Madam's expression was unreadable. If she was looking for encouragement or censure, none of those were available. Withering under Singh's glare, she blurted out, 'He told her it would be a good idea, sir. It'd make her a lot more money than the customers, sir, and it was all … religious. It would make her pure, like a real woman, not like ... us. They would find her a good husband, if she went with them.'

'What are you talking about?' Samsher barked at her. 'What do you mean religious? Where is this husband?'

'She didn't want to, sir. She didn't, she told me. See, Mohamaya had two kids. The boy is older; they have just admitted him to a boarding school. They don't know what she does … what she did … her parents didn't know. She was afraid that someone would see her here so if she could say that she was in …'

Samsher looked from one face to the other, pulling his officer-in-charge face to intimidate them both. He also felt confused; this story seemed to be getting away from him. 'What husband? Which place?' Samsher barked at the girl.

Shefali Madam's face froze into a smile. 'Girls run away all the time, Officer saab. You can't conduct an investigation every time.' She paused and then said, 'And since you have found out everything we know, and we know so little about this thing, it's shameful … well, since you can see that nothing here is wrong, perhaps you will let the girl go get ready for the evening. Police presence in the brothel isn't exactly good for business. We are working girls, you understand? We neither have a salary, nor a pension fund.' She flashed him another bright smile. 'Plus she'll need to recover from this interrogation, poor thing.' Madam gestured towards the girl and she walked out of the room as fast as she could.

The finality of Shefali Madam's last gesture made it clear that the interview was over. And though Samsher Singh knew extremely well that he could not only drag the woman and her minions to the station right now, but arrest her and the whole lot too, he also realized that doing so wouldn't help him solve the problem. Besides, he had a target now. He felt that if he could lay his hands on the dead girl's babu, he would solve the murder. And since springing into action suited his temperament better than patiently manipulating more information out of this lot, he decided to leave.

# 31

OUTSIDE THE BLUE LOTUS, WHERE HIS SUBORDINATE WAS having a surreptitious bidi and a cup of milky tea, Samsher said to Constable Balok Ghosh, 'I don't like it, Balok-da. I think they are hiding something. They will clam up against us, against any outsiders, Balok-da. They don't like us interfering in their affairs, even if it is murder.'

Since Balok Ghosh secretly nursed the opinion that this was a much better alternative than the state wasting its valuable time and resources chasing down a whore-killer, he refrained from commenting. After a while though, he felt inclined to part with some information that he had gathered when he had been left alone to talk to the people who got everywhere and saw everything – the servants, the paanwallah, the pimps and the hangers-on. 'There's something else, sir,' he said, measuring his words.

'What?' Samsher asked in the safe knowledge that Balok Ghosh had an ear very close to the ground. What pimps and servants and pickpockets would not say to an officer, they would say to a quiet constable.

'That girl who discovered the dead body, she was the one

who told the NGO. I hear things, sir, but not everything. They don't know everything but Biswas on the kiosk heard from some other pimp who does some flying business for that madam.'

'I wish I knew what she said to them,' Samsher wondered quietly.

Balok remained impassive. 'More than she told us, sir, I think some sex trafficking routes might be involved. Who knows, sir? But, do you think Rambo Maity would be alone in this? He's a flounder, always at the bottom of any pyramid. I would think, sir, that it's only the tip of the iceberg. He's got himself into something big. You know what is happening in a few days, sir, don't you?'

Samsher Singh turned towards his constable. 'The march? Yes. But that's just a media trick – what of it?'

Balok had to work slightly hard to suppress his sigh. 'No, sir. There's a big boat-load of fresh girls coming. The NGO knows and they've got informers everywhere to sift out the underage girls, but the people who are bringing in the girls? Oh maybe they are hoping the candlelight march will provide a good distraction.'

Samsher turned this over in his mind. *Yes, it made more sense*, he thought. 'But, that woman there, surely she would not take this risk? Because of that blasted murder now the news vans are here all the time, and a raid happened only two days ago. And I just don't see,' Samsher vented, 'how of all people, Rambo Maity is involved in this mess!'

'Best time for it, sir, when everyone is looking the other way.' Balok Ghosh stopped.

Samsher Singh was thinking aloud, 'If the NGOs did have

something on trafficking, they wouldn't come to us … no, they wouldn't. But the media is quiet about it. Maybe it hasn't gone to them yet?'

Balok replied, 'Most of the raids reveal nothing, sir, because both parties know when and where it is going to happen. The real goods are never where they are said to be. But if the media caught on to the racket and had evidence, if the NGOs could find that then it'd be a very high-profile raid, sir. And who knows what one will find. It'd be the proverbial finding a snake when you thought you were digging for a worm. All in all, it's either arsehole or lunchtime.' Balok Ghosh spat on the ground and shook his head, 'No, sir. If you ask me, that is not the main problem. Everyone knows about trafficking.' He gave his commanding officer a sheepish glance. It was bad etiquette to talk about bribes and cuts in front of a superior officer; everyone partook in it, but one didn't talk about it. He continued, trying to lead Samsher into a more fruitful line of investigation. 'But the people, the really high-ups. People who traffic in girls, abduct or con them into this life, they come here, sir. They meet here, they deliver goods here, they talk about these plans. Can you imagine what the NGOs working here would give to get that kind of information, and I mean evidence, on tape?'

'So you are trying to say,' said Samsher in wide-eyed wonder, 'that Rambo Maity is working to expose the sex trade? Maybe he is in league with the NGOs, eh? Trying to bring them to justice?'

Balok Ghosh felt what Shefali Madam had sensed not so long ago. He sighed inwardly and said in a level tone, 'No, sir. I highly doubt that, sir. I just think that Rambo Maity does not realize what hornet's nest he has kicked. Especially, sir,' he lowered his voice, 'if that girl we saw today has already gone to the NGOs with this information, and maybe, even tapes.' He did not add that he had heard from one or two reliable sources – sources so lowly and unobtrusive that no one would think of asking them – that one such video, a discreet recording on a phone, was already in existence. Information like that was valuable, and dangerous. Balok had no intention of giving it away for free.

Samsher Singh stood stock-still. He felt he had been a massive fool. He turned around and began walking purposefully back to the purple house he had just left. Several girls were crowding the doorway, their faces arrayed in cheap make-up, awaiting their turn.

'I need to get in right now,' Singh said with much more force than necessary. The girls nonchalantly stepped away. They had known and bribed too many policemen to be scared of them any longer. One girl, wearing dark plum lipstick and a tight T-shirt with the Facebook logo on it ran up a flight of stairs, presumably to inform the matriarch.

Samsher Singh pushed past the women and looked around the first room he entered. His confidence was somewhat hampered when he realized that he didn't actually know which room the murder had taken place in. He leaned towards Balok Ghosh and whispered something. The constable nodded and Samsher straightened up.

He noticed the green walls, the pictures of the leading ladies of popular Bollywood movies lining them, the big bed in the middle of the room and a shelf full of odds and ends. There wasn't much else to see. He looked at Balok and asked, 'Here?' pointing to the only available space on the floor.

The constable nodded and Samsher kneeled down in front of the bed as if his eyes alone could perform the forensic search that this crime scene was yet to receive. He knew it was useless even as he conducted the search. How many customers had passed through this room since the thing happened? How many girls would have used this bed, this room since then? Everything had been cleared away, every trace of the girl wiped to make room for the next hour and its patrons. Samsher felt hopeless. The surge of confidence he had felt just moments ago dropped in an instant. It was so stupid to not have searched this space. If any camera, any evidence had been hidden here, it would have been taken away or destroyed long ago. But who knew that he would in fact be asked to investigate the case? Whoever investigated the death of a whore?

Shefali Madam entered the room. There was no sign of displeasure on her face, as usual. She smiled a welcoming smile at the two policemen and said, 'Oh I must have seen someone's lucky face when I woke up today. Officer saab likes us so much that he simply won't leave us be. Shall I offer you some of my finest, Officer saab? How do you like them?'

Samsher Singh made no response to this offer. In a brisk voice he said, 'I need to conduct a thorough search of this room.'

Shefali Madam remained unperturbed. 'If you must, you must, sir. Our survival here is due to your charity. Consider me at your disposal.' He began a haphazard search of the room in which blustering around played a far greater role than observation. Balok Ghosh made some motions to appease his senior but much preferred to stand passively in one corner, knowing fully well the futility of such a search. From time to time, Samsher would fling questions at Madam. 'Where was she found?' *At the foot of the bed.* 'Where was the bottle of acid lying?' *Next to her, broken in half.* 'What did you do with it?' *It was thrown away.*

In less than twenty minutes, Samsher had proved to both himself and the bystanders that searching a crime scene days after a murder was merely a waste of time. He felt he could do something more but couldn't for the life of him think what that something was. With a grave face, he said, 'I need to see that girl once again. I don't think we have heard everything.'

Shefali Madam said, 'Sir, I assure you, she doesn't know anything more. Besides, I have just given her some painkillers and a sleeping pill. Poor thing has been feeling traumatized since the murder and talking to you today has only made things harder for her. So, if you don't mind, I'll send her over tomorrow, if you please. And now, if you are quite done, could I have my room back? There's a long queue forming at the door.'

Walking out once more, Samsher Singh nursed the suspicion that he was overlooking something that was obvious and staring him in the face. He didn't know what he could do, except chase down the girl's babu, who he felt quite sure was her murderer as well. If this was indeed about the sex-trafficking business, it was much beyond the grasp of Samsher Singh. Far bigger men than him with far more power and money were sitting at the helm of that business. He couldn't do anything, he knew even before getting started. He hadn't joined the police force to clean up the city, or to right all wrongs. In movies they showed that kind of thing, but he hadn't met a single man in the police force who actually joined with that sort of ambition. Once in a while such men would appear. The whole station would be wary of such people, and they were inevitably handed unwelcome transfers. He didn't want to be a hero. He liked the films where the hero was a good cop, and there had been many of them. Once he even took his wife to a 'first day first show', braving the torrid storm of his mother's moods for weeks, but he had no desire to be like them. He wanted to grow old, buy a flat in south Calcutta and accept a decent amount of bribes. He didn't want to die.

# 32

LALEE SAT ON THE EDGE OF HER SINGLE BED, STARING AT THE mint-coloured walls and the single picture of Maharaj raising his hands in benediction that dominated the room. She knew that it had been a few days, but exactly how many of them had passed, Lalee wasn't sure. After the intensity, anger and exhaustion of the first forty-eight hours, the days began to bleed into one another. Lalee catalogued the minutiae of the place, keenly watching feverishly small events, committing to memory insignificant details, while the big pictures of why and where slid past her.

The place worked like clockwork. On the first night, the four of them, including Sonia, had been herded to a small dormitory, tucked away in one corner of the compound. Their escorts made it clear that they would shower and change into the loose white robes provided by the sevikas before they retired to their rooms. Across their dormitory, women clad in white, heads covered in long white cloth, moved rigidly in front of her, never making eye contact. Lalee noticed that they came out at certain times, headed to a large dining room for their communal meal, while dinner for her and the two young girls would be brought to them in clean steel plates. It was always a modest meal, left covered outside their rooms, as if the three of them were contagious, diseased bodies that carried the plague in the folds of their flesh. Lalee understood the nature of this contagion, this invisible leprosy. She had seen the extent of its invisible fingers, long and insidious, scratching at the people it had made untouchable, sub-human. Her mother used to dump uneaten food by the river, on the soft loam, where men marked by those invisible fingers came in search of food when the rains had forgotten the way to their village. Every time Lalee picked up those shining steel plates, compartmentalized in eccentric cavities for daal and vegetables and a pickle, Lalee felt the plague's scratch. But she needed the food and the shower and there was no one to argue with.

There were four single beds laid side by side in the room. Sonia had settled on the corner one, Lalee decided to take the middle one and let the two young girls have the other corner to themselves. After the shower washed off the grime on the twin girls' face and smoothed out their matted hair, Lalee realized they were quite nice-looking, and younger than she had first assumed. One of them had refused to touch her meal, curled on her side of the bed, whimpering quietly. Her sister had kept a hand on her waist, sitting still next to her.

'What are your names?' Lalee whispered.

The girl who was sitting quietly and comforting her sister ran a tongue over her dry lips. 'I'm Durga and she is Lakshmi,' she nodded at her sister.

'Did Shefali Madam send you here? Were you working for her?' Lalee asked, keeping her voice soft so as to not scare the girls. She was curious; she'd never seen the girls at The Blue

Lotus. There were young girls there, but for a long time she hadn't seen girls this young under Shefali Madam's roof.

Durga slowly shook her head. 'That man ... he brought us here.'

Lalee asked, 'Which one?'

'The one who was sitting next to us, with the sunglasses.'

'Oh, Rambo,' Lalee said and Durga nodded her head slowly.

'How did he get you?'

'At Sealdah station.'

'What were you doing there? Where are your parents?'

Durga shook her head and glanced at her hands gathered in her lap. Her sister Lakshmi turned on her side and blinked at Lalee. She said in a voice still gruff from crying, 'No parents. That man told us he would give us work and food and a place to stay if we came with him. He took us to another place, in Calcutta – I don't know where – and we lived there for two months.'

Durga added, as if taking a cue from her sister, 'He would send us ... men. Sometimes we were together, me and Lakshmi, and sometimes we did it separately. First time, it was horrible.' She closed her eyes and scrunched her hands into tight fists and shuddered softly. They both fell silent, leaving Lalee to wonder if she should say anything further.

Unbidden, Durga went on, 'He said the seal must not be broken, otherwise they won't want us anymore. But we still have to pay our way, so he sent the men. They were allowed to do some things ... everything, except breaking the seal.'

In the last few days Lalee had told herself that it was just another job. She'd wanted to move on from Shonagachhi with clients like Mr Ghosh. In feverish, desperate dreams, she'd dreamt of 'foreign' holidays – a picture stitched together from idiosyncratic scraps from Hollywood cinema, and held together by a tenuous thread of make-believe. An apartment, some money and a regular babu, who paid well and by whom Lalee would do right. When she closed her eyes she could almost touch the two bedside lamps beside an imaginary bed, neatly made, covered in new bedsheets that smelled clean; she could smell expensive creams that would make her skin softer, three shades lighter. Her grandmother used to tell the story of a girl who swam in a magical lake, and when she came out again, she had transformed into the most beautiful woman. When a king on a hunt saw her, he married her, taking her back with him to a life of exquisite riches. Without knowing and with wilful ignorance, she had made her own magical lake out of Rambo and Shefali Madam, the upstairs quarters and Mr Ghosh, and that strange, air-conditioned, softly fragrant room in a Park Street hotel and Sonia, whom she had followed like a mirage, an advertisement, like a drunk follows the ethereal lottery ticket.

Sonia. Lalee felt a sudden tide of hatred. She came and went as she pleased, that invisible plague that marked their hides sliding off her skin with an ease Lalee envied. Where did she go? Was Rambo still here? What did Sonia know? This was still a job, Lalee told herself over and over again. Maybe it wasn't straightforward, but it was better than believing that she had been ferried here and imprisoned. Religious men had always found space within the scriptures for sinning. Either she was here to do a job for money, or she was a victim. She didn't know what she could believe.

Lalee found the cold, oblong square next to her pillow. She

pressed a button and the phone lit up. She checked the app Rambo had installed on the screen; it showed a number that Lalee found hard to believe. If that was money, where did it live? If that was money and it was hers, she was no victim; this was a job and when it was done, she could go back to a life she knew, chisel out another life she wanted. If that was really money and it was hers, she wanted to have it in her hand. But not the pale yellow 500-rupee notes. Lalee shuddered. Notes that were merely paper now … and parts of her broke inside. If she had a stack of 500-rupee notes now she would scatter them from the balcony of The Blue Lotus, she would set fire to them, she would light them up like a cigarette just for the freedom and the heartbreak of it. The light went off on the mobile phone and Lalee pressed the button again, staring at the numbers so neatly arranged on the screen. She could give that money to her brother, she would have to learn how she could get the money out of the screen and into her hands. She could ask Maya. Lalee paused. Yes, Maya knew of these things. Maya with her swollen, blue face and gash of red on her neck. Did Maya also think she had found a magical lake?

The girls were sleeping now. Durga was curled up beside her sister, her hand still resting crookedly on her waist. Lalee watched them, curling themselves into broken fetal positions to fit their inconvenient bodies on one narrow iron bed. If they had come to do a job and no more, what were the girls doing *here*? And if they too were here to do the same job as her, what was it that Lalee was expected to do?

# 33

RAMBO WALKED TOWARDS A COPSE OF TREES, AWAY FROM the lights of the dormitory where acolytes were still milling around. Even though the giant archway in the entrance proclaimed the legend Nandankanan in iron letters, most people called this the palace. Rambo secretly considered the Maharaj a pompous man, though he would never let that thought pass through his lips. These people terrified him – from that peasant Chintu to Shefali Madam and the all-powerful Maharaj.

They were the sharks, he was a lowly poisonless snake that sometimes got tangled up in the fishing net, no use to anyone else. Rambo knew what he was. But then again, there are the sharks, and there are people who know all about the sharks. There is always someone who'll sell you information.

Some people bought lottery tickets, gambling on a chance. Rambo bought some information. He took a chance.

There was money to be made. Money was wafting through the air. More so now that you didn't even need banknotes or cheques or anything that in his long, hustling life had meant actual money. Sonia had said they were zeroes and ones.

Imagine that. Rambo wished he had a friend, a real friend that he could say anything to without fear and without the chance of betrayal. He'd have said to that imaginary person, 'Zeroes and ones, brother, and they're all around you, passing overhead just like electric … zzzz … passing overhead just like that.' Like radio waves, Sonia had said.

He knew better than anyone that none of these people would give him another thought, if he had to be left by the wayside, or indeed, silenced for good. But he'd never even been in the vicinity of such money as he could make in this venture. Some sacrifices had to be made. He was out of his depth; all he hoped for was to make enough money for a short while and then disappear somewhere, away from these dangerous people. Maybe he'd move to Bombay, find some good-looking girls desperate to make it in the movies and then, well, then it'd be a whole other gamble.

Somewhere here were wads of cash, gold, jewels, cheques. Rambo's limited imagination ran short at this point. Would it be a black bag full of the shiny coldness of diamonds, glinting in the soft, bifurcated light like they do in the movies? Or maybe solid gold idols like in spy movies. Rambo liked thinking about it. Shefali Madam must know about it too. Thieves had no honour among themselves. These girls he was supposed to transport – how many would they have to transport for the price of one diamond, or just one small bag full of unmarked notes? Sonia's plan was good. She was a smart girl. His mother's astrologer had always said that his destiny would come to him through his wife. And already, she was bringing him luck, money and the gamble of a lifetime. Who'd have thought a boy from the slums like him would end up with a memsahib? From here they would flee, who knew where. Sonia had dropped hints, but never been specific – to Bangkok, to Hong Kong and then to snow-covered Russia. He dreamt of white hills and wooden huts awaiting their life together.

He found a spot behind a thicket of bamboo trees, well away from prying eyes. He sat on his haunches and took out his cellphone. It was still ten minutes to the appointed time for the phone call, but his heart was beating fast. A swarm of mosquitoes was methodically attacking him everywhere. He was trying to swat as many as possible in the dim light of his cellphone and waiting anxiously for the call. The phone started vibrating. Rambo took a second to compose himself before answering. Then he pressed the button.

'Hallo,' he said, voice trembling. 'I can supply the ... product. Yes, yes. Just as requested. Virgin, young. Seal unbroken. No need to worry about that. We checked thoroughly. We can supply in a few days, no problem.' Rambo risked a smile. 'Don't worry about it, sir – satisfaction guaranteed.'

He had picked up the last phrase from a mattress ad he had seen somewhere recently. A sexy woman sat invitingly on a giant white mattress, quietly promising to fulfil every one of the beholder's fantasy. Rambo liked the ad, especially the part that said 'Satisfaction guaranteed', Maybe it could be the new motto of his business. He felt good; this might be a success after all. He had filled his head with unnamed fears, and what for? Ultimately, he knew what he was doing. He had the girls. Healthy, young, unspoilt. He cleared his throat and whispered, 'They don't make them like this in the city anymore, genuine village girls, and ... they're twins.' He paused for a second, waiting for a response from the other side. When he heard the quick drawing of breath and guarded interest, he knew he had hit the mark. 'That'll cost extra, as you know.'

When Rambo Maity looked up, his heart stopped for half a second. He followed the sandled feet and the trousered legs up all the way to where the moonlight reflected off the man's glasses. He smiled at Rambo.

'All good?' the man asked in soft, gentle tones. Like a man at a relative's sick bed.

'Yes, sir, yes.' Rambo said.

'Wonderful,' the man smiled broadly, offering a hand to Rambo. 'That is wonderful,' he repeated.

Rambo took the outstretched hand and pulled himself up, smiling nervously. He had seen this man around frequently in the last few days. Almost ubiquitous at The Blue Lotus. He stood out in his sober clothing, spectacles and his always courteous manner of speech. He unsettled Rambo Maity.

'I don't know your name,' Rambo said.

'Oh, don't you? I'm sorry. You can call me "manager" – everyone around here calls me that.'

Rambo didn't say anything. It made sense, there was always a man like that, nameless, but the one who organized – not the king but the kingmaker and more dangerous than anyone.

'How was the phone call? Everything ready to go?'

Rambo had to remind himself that he wasn't doing anything he wasn't supposed to. The deal had been arranged by him, under orders from Shefali Madam. But that the girls had to be delivered here, held, and then exported from this place meant that the Maharaj couldn't be in the dark about it. Surely, he knew. Surely this mild-mannered manager, who scared Rambo more than anyone else, knew. Rambo had to remind himself that he was merely a very small cog in the wheel.

'Yes ... yes,' Rambo replied. 'Yes, the party wants us to send the girls in.'

'Mr Maity,' the manager interrupted. 'I don't need to know. It is, after all, between you and your Madam. We have an agreement. And not knowing certain things is a part of the deal.'

Rambo fell silent. He didn't know how to navigate this new world of secrecy. He concentrated on the path ahead. Moonlight flooded the thickets of trees and bushes, throwing everything into sharp relief. Their footfalls heavy on the dry undergrowth, Rambo tried to reassure himself. He would be safe, he would get out of this, he would be rich.

'This heat has been unbearable,' the manager said. 'Even this far away from the city, it's hardly any better. Usually we get a sea breeze in the evening, since we are a lot closer to Diamond Harbour than Calcutta proper, but it seems to get worse everywhere. I hope it rains soon.'

Rambo thought to himself: *Yes, it indeed was far away from the city*. A sudden and unfamiliar dread gripped Rambo and stopped him in his tracks. *He was far away from the city.* He was a street kid, a boy who learned how to slice hip pockets and ladies' purses with a half-broken razor blade before he could sign his name on a piece of paper. The street brought him up; it took a clueless, hapless boy and pulled him up by the bootstraps. He learned guile, he learned to cheat, steal and defraud. On the streets of the city, Rambo knew who he was. Here in this endless garden, ruled by an all-powerful madman, closer to the sea than the city, Rambo was afloat, dog-paddling his way in search of shore.

# 34

MALINI WOULD BE WAITING FOR HER OUTSIDE BAPPA'S TEA stall. Deepa hurried, walking briskly, careful not to run. It was difficult to park here and most days she took a taxi. Today, Vishal had dropped her. She hadn't said a word to him in all the time they spent moving slowly and stopping jerkily at the many jams and unending traffic lights. And now, she could see Malini, standing outside The Blue Lotus, frowning distractedly in the distance.

They walked down the corridors without saying much to each other, except the names of the girls who lived in the rooms, the ones they knew, checking them off on a list, noting a single word next to them: 'missing'. They made their way inside a room that used to be Nimmi's. Malini looked it up, printed neatly in her rotund Bangla script, each letter woven into the other like an intricate painting, and hovered around her name with the ballpoint poised next to it.

'Where are the kids? Did they take them as well?'

Deepa shrugged, looking around the room. Two limes and a few green chillies stood still on the floor, stamped upon with the tread of a dirty boot. Nimmi must have just finished lunch, or maybe she had felt lazy and didn't finish the washing up. An aluminium pot in the corner of the room was growing fuzzy with mould, even though the food had been neatly scraped away.

Some of the rooms were locked up, with heavy iron locks hanging from the doors. A few of the rooms already had new occupants. Shonagachhi had one of the highest real-estate prices in Calcutta, disproportionately so, and an empty room was not left behind for long.

'They have condoms in their handbag, they have some money, they'll call when they are ready and they'll come back,' Malini said, but Deepa wasn't sure if she was talking to herself. She merely nodded.

'The older ones know it is routine. This is what they do, this atyachaar.' Malini jerked her head forward, indicating some invisible uniformed lawman outside the window. 'They come here, breaking up our shongshaar, this home we have created with our blood and sweat. What right do they have?' Malini was shaking, Deepa noticed, clenching her hands into fists. 'This is their home,' Malini nearly shouted.

Yes, it was. Deepa knew. What is a home except something you have carved out with your bare skin, claws and teeth? This was the only home most of them would have ever known, the only place where there was friendship and love, and someone to check in on you when you lay burning up in a fever. Two decades ago when she first set foot in Shonagachhhi, she was horrified. She wanted to rescue them all – the women, the pubescent girls, the children who stared wide-eyed at her. And then she had learned, over the years, from every anecdote, every story, told as often laughingly as with tears or with a level voice, that this was the only place where they could live with something almost approaching dignity, and yes, pride, and that this was home and that it belonged to them, not the husbands or the fathers or the pimps or the no-one-at-alls of the world, but them. A mangled, tenuous dignity, one with tread marks all over it, but sometimes even that is a lot. 'Amina,' Malini said, frowning over the notebook in her hand, 'I haven't seen her in a while, but we don't know if they took her during the raid … and Lalee.' Deepa looked up at her. 'They're not here,' Malini confirmed.

Deepa realized she was staring at Malini, and the seconds in which she could have replied normally, in the natural rhythm of conversation, had sped past her. How much did Malini know? She would have to tell Malini at some point, but Deepa never wanted to. She wondered if Malini realized how, just a few months earlier, they had had a similar conversation about Maya. Maya had suddenly disappeared from Shonagachhi for a few weeks, when a neat, new lock had dangled primly from her door. Although, there hadn't been a raid then, and Maya's easy self-assurance, her relative affluence had given Malini more confidence. The rumour they had carefully circulated before Maya's temporary exit was that she was exploring options as an escort, a companion to important, rich men, who could afford an apartment in the heartland of Calcutta. Deepa hadn't told Malini anything then, but that omission never sat easily with her. And after Maya died, that omission mushroomed into treachery. How could Deepa tell Malini where Maya used to go, and where Deepa knew Lalee now was. Amina's name gave Deepa temporary pause. Amina at least was not supposed to go with Lalee and Sonia, but who knew where the girls scattered when these periodic raids tore through these narrow streets like seasonal cyclones. Maybe she was in those windowless rooms that the authorities called rehabilitation centres, being taught sewing or pickle-making against her will. Maybe Amina was in a street corner somewhere, plying her trade among passersby. There were other options too, but Deepa didn't want to think of them right now. 'In the next few days, I'll go to the police, see where they have taken the girls. I'll bring Kamalesh too – we'll need some lawyers.'

Malini didn't say anything, still frowning over the clipboard clutched tightly in her hand. Now they worked as collaborators, but a decade and a half ago when Deepa was a young, inexperienced adult educator and Malini had come to her classes meticulously, never missing a day, been the first of her class to become a peer-educator for the women of Shonagachhi, Malini had looked up to Deepa as an unlikely hero. Deepa didn't want to fail Malini.

What could she say to her, at this time and in this place? In 1997, some five thousand women, men and intersex persons who sold sex for money, gathered in this very city to attend a nationwide conference organized by this Sex Workers' Collective, the first of its kind in this country. In difficult moments, Deepa closed her eyes and tried to remember that heady time, the smell and press of bodies, the sweat, the hope, the sloganeering and the shoulders pushing together, pushing forward, side by side. And what was she then? Just some impressionable, idealistic privileged girl who had graduated with first division from her sheltered Loreto College just a few years ago. But she had been there, she had felt the throbbing beat of a thousand hearts in her own bloodstream. Her blood had boiled, and her heart had burst with inexorable, ferocious love. Wasn't she looking for that same throbbing, that same connection every time she had walked in a march, or joined a candlelight vigil? On that day they had asked a question, why couldn't prostitutes, disbursing a service for money, demand the rights of workers, demand human rights? They had asked why workers in similarly exploitative industries could demand rights and to better their life through work, but prostitutes couldn't. Why couldn't adult citizens of a democratic nation sell sex and demand legally protected labour rights as workers, and improve their quality of life?

There had been victories. Where powerful structures had failed, grassroots organizations like the Collective drastically slowed the spread of HIV. There were crushing failures. There were dead girls and women disappearing into the night. In time, Deepa understood the invisible structures that stood rigid defining the limits of her work. And when girls like Maya, because they were smart investments, came under the radar of those invisible structures, the temptation to break those walls was too great and too reckless. Deepa wouldn't know if she had done the right thing by Maya. Maybe if she hadn't got involved, Maya would still be alive today. But fifteen years ago, a woman wrote an anonymous letter from an unknown location and addressed it to the then prime minister. *Maharaj embraced me and said he loved me from the core of his heart, he wanted to make love to me, he owned my body, my spirit and my soul.* That letter trickled slowly, through crevices, pooling in pot holes of bureaucracy, finding its way to a chief minister, the home minister, the Central Bureau of Investigation and then the high court. This anonymous woman wasn't alone; women like her who had either voluntarily or otherwise dedicated their life to one holy man in his fortress, were repeatedly raped, threatened and intimidated over years. Deepa knew that the holy man's consorts frequently came from Shonagachhi, and that some of those consorts were never seen again. It took fifteen years, but the CBI investigators were closing in, and girls like Maya had a part to play in that. Deepa had to wait, she had to play this close to her chest, especially now that Maya was dead. Some of the women who had escaped from the commune were in deep hideouts, as were the two other girls who had gone with Maya, a journalist had been murdered, and Deepa's contact in the CBI was certain that violent riots would break out as soon as they made a move against the Maharaj. She wondered if she would see Lalee again, and still it was a victory – one letter, written by a desperate anonymous woman, would bring down a supremely powerful man. All this she couldn't share with Malini, especially since she could not, would not, absolve herself of Maya's death.

'It's the raid,' Deepa said, rooting furiously through her handbag needlessly. 'You know what they do; Lalee and Amina are probably hiding unless the police took them. They'll be back in a few weeks when things have settled down.'

Malini didn't say anything, and they continued their survey without another word about the missing girls.

# 35

LALEE AND SONIA STOOD AT THE BACK AMIDST A SEA OF worshippers who sat on the floor, their hands joined in supplication. Lalee noticed how easy Sonia seemed in her white, sack-like clothing, so eerily at ease, smiling up at the small windows of the large hall, refracting the shards of sunlight through her long, blond hair. Maharaj sat on the velvet throne. From where Lalee was seated, he was a distant, carmine shape. A large screen on the left-hand side broadcast Maharaj's every gesture in high definition. He smiled at them benevolently, head slightly tipped on the side as if to show affection to a band of children. An army of men and women dressed in white kurtas and white saris moved purposefully between the throne and the devotees, efficient and humourless.

'Joy,' the man on the throne said, in a deep baritone that echoed around the hall from invisible speakers. 'What does it mean to be joyful?' Lalee noticed that he posed it as a statement, not a question. He tilted his head from one side to the other, glancing intimately at the people gathered in front of him, a smile lingered on his lips, as if he alone was privy to a great and secret joke.

'To find the purpose of one's life is joy,' He announced and then paused, nodding and smiling as everyone took in the apparent profundity of his words. 'The farmer toils in his field, the smith toils at his anvil, the doctor serves the ill – this brings them purpose and, therefore, joy. Without purpose, their lives would be barren as a sickle that is no longer wielded.'

Lalee thought that although she didn't know much about doctors, she knew enough about farmers and smiths to recognize that their work wasn't always joyful. Most times it was a desperate bid at survival, often a failing, fledgling bid that had the whole world stacked against it.

'How do we find purpose, if purpose is what brings us joy and gives meaning to our life?' he nodded his head one way and another, like a child playing a trick. 'Purpose comes to us through surrender. The great consciousness under whose rule the universe spins, the Brahman, demands that we surrender to his will if we are ever to achieve fulfilment in our earthly lives.'

He wasn't a fat man, but a man built on a larger scale. Lalee noticed the cast of his broad shoulders, the expansive chest, the coarse black hair peeking through the mess of gold chains and rudraksha beads under his red robe. He seemed to radiate a force field. The women and the children at his feet hung on his every word. Lalee felt the power of his deep bass voice in a place at the back of her neck, as if a command and a confidence were being entrusted to her alone among the dozens that were there. She spotted a young woman clutching her children on either knee, sitting cross-legged on the floor not far from her. She turned to a woman next to her and gave her a brief smile, a sheen of pride evident in the woman's face.

The crowd began to chant 'Hare Krishna, hare Krishna, hare Rama, hare hare' in a fierce unison that reverberated through the hall. Lalee looked upwards at the ceiling above her, wondering what she and Sonia were doing there. She came dangerously close to asking why Durga and Lakshmi were in that place, but she stopped herself. She closed her eyes and thought about the time they performed Kartik puja in the small courtyard at The Blue Lotus. The officiating priest had been one girl's long-term babu. They'd spend the morning and the long noon chopping fruits, stringing garlands and painting the floors in intricate patterns. Lalee thought of The Blue Lotus with a fondness that surprised her, her old room with its dirty, dark pink walls, its small alcove with small figurines of gods where she kept stray change in a small basket and the thick columns that surrounded the rooms around the courtyard disappearing into the upper floors, which in turn had long rectangular verandahs with cast-iron railings. Some girls leaned on the railings, watching the festivities, others herded pimps and johns to their rooms. Each floor sat on top of the other like stacked boxes, with the rectangular courtyard holding them all in one place. Lalee remembered the first time she had looked up from that courtyard, and how grand the whole building had seemed, even with its peeling paint, broken window slats and innumerable odours. The mesh netting that surrounded some of the higher floors hadn't been there then. That was a later addition, installed after a girl was found face down in the courtyard one morning, with her skull cracked in half.

Last night she had called Amina. The girl sounded breathless, as if she was whispering into the phone. There had been a raid at The Blue Lotus and some other nearby houses.

Lalee sighed. It was a cycle, this constant intrusion of the police into what they considered their homes, which left them either homeless on the streets plying their trade in even more unpredictable circumstances or caged in the name of rescue. Lalee felt a momentary sense of relief; at least she had avoided the raid. And still there was something amiss here. It had been who knows how many days since she had been brought to this place, but she was yet to see a client. Rambo's phone would be switched off every time Lalee reached out to give him a piece of her mind, to shed that nagging anger that tracked her like a hunter since she had woken up half drugged in this unfamiliar place. Money had been transferred to her account. The numbers on the screen went up by a whole ₹20,000 and Lalee could hardly believe it. She wanted to ask Sonia, but she didn't want to show Sonia the money. It was a hard habit to break, the secretiveness over money.

Sooner or later that call would come. Maybe for this large hairy man on the stage. Lalee shook her head and smiled to herself. Maybe these were the big customers Rambo was bragging about. When her brother came asking for money, Lalee didn't know how she would pay him, but if those numbers on her screen really was money, then she could do a lot more.

A couple of months earlier, she had seen a face in her speckled square mirror. It had a harshness about the mouth, a cold set to the eyes, the hair was coarse and stuck out like an argument. She didn't know how old she really was. Her parents, uninterested and dismayed with the four girls they had produced before her, never bothered to keep score. Lalee suspected she was south of thirty, and just like the world, she didn't expect her body to be forgiving. Shonagachhi was a precarious place for ageing women. They either became madams, a handful invested themselves wholly in the Collective like Malini and thousands other died in poverty. Every few months, a new bunch of girls trickled into the neighbourhood. In the early days, she felt sad for these newcomers; they cried incessantly through the night, waited relentlessly for a lover, a father, a brother, a husband or a mother to show up and take them home. Now, each new consignment made her look in the mirror.

New brothels sprang up from time to time, employing only busty, fair and tall Punjabi, Rajasthani and Kashmiri girls. The richer clientele reputedly went to these more desirable, expensive girls.

When Chintu's back was turned and Shefali Madam was likely to turn a blind eye, Lalee had entertained Rambo's clients. At first, she did a stray job or two. These men tipped well and offered safety. Shefali Madam knew, of course, but as long as she got her share, she didn't say anything. Girls like herself were scattered in and around Kalighat at Calcutta's most famous temple, in Hatibagan, Bagbazar, Park Circus, Park Street. The map of the city pimps and dealers looked at was dotted in red. But Rambo bragged about girls like Sonia, Russian girls, Chinese girls, college students, models – the ones who wore better clothes and high heels were called out to fancy hotels as companions, call girls or escorts and danced in nightclubs – Lalee felt both intrigued and intimidated by that world. When Shefali Madam herself offered a key to it, Lalee couldn't say no.

If she was patient, Lalee told herself, closing her eyes and swaying slightly to the beat of the chants around her, she would know who the client was. She'd do a good job, get paid and be on her way. They wouldn't want a girl like her forever. She'd get out of here and, in some time, she'd be out of Shonagachhi too, maybe in an apartment in central Calcutta, near all the restaurant where she would ...

'He's a god,' the woman in front of Lalee whispered to her neighbour, breathlessly between chants, staring at the man on the throne. The man on the stage was swaying to the sounds of the collective chants, eyes closed, hands held up in the air, a blissful smile playing on his lips. Lalee realized that a primal strain of drums, cymbals and harmoniums had seamlessly begun to accompany the human voices, each entwined in the throes of the other. Everyone around Lalee was swaying to the beats, most of their eyes closed, hands in the air, lost in some otherworldly bliss inaccessible to Lalee. She looked at Sonia who smiled and winked at Lalee. The woman in front of them turned a glistening, sweat-stained face towards them both: 'He's an avatar of Krishna.' 'He is, Krishna,' said her neighbour, like a woman intoxicated. Their bodies moved like one, their chants spread its feverish tendrils like ink through water, reaching a heady, rhythmic sweaty climax.

# 36

LALEE WAITED IN THE ANTECHAMBER. SHE HAD SHOWERED as per instructions, combed her long, dark hair, draped a brand new red-and-white saree and was now kneeling as she had been asked to, facing the east.

Two women clad in white entered. They touched Lalee on her shoulders; she kept her eyes shut. After a lifetime of keeping her past behind that veil of remembrance, she thought about her mother today. The woman's life had revolved around her gods. She bathed three times a day and sat in her small prayer room dressing and bathing and feeding them. The incense and the flowers in this place had brought back those memories. When the Hare Krishnas visited their village, Lalee would run out to the street every time she heard the tinny voice of the chanters and the long draw of the harmonium. Lalee hummed that melody quietly to herself, the one the travelling devotees would chant incessantly when they came to her village. It was the most perfect thing her young life had witnessed. It didn't matter if her father was dead drunk, or if he had raised his fists on her and her mother, the travelling Krishnas would still arrive once a month, five days before every full moon. The village was always on the brink of bubbling over – almost half Muslim and half Hindu. There hadn't been a riot for more than three decades, but there was always the strained tension of a divided hamlet waiting for a sign. Those bare-chested Krishnas, in their white-and-saffron dhotis and long tilaks, would still come, sing bhajans and dance on the edge of a future riot, sharp as a knife.

Silently, the women helped Lalee to her feet. Her sari was wrapped loosely around her body, unanchored to either a blouse or a petticoat. Lalee felt more naked than she ever had, without the familiar protective barrier of cloth between her legs, or the harness of a bra. The women stood at the doorway and said their names were Rambha and Menaka, both consorts of Maharaj. They didn't say much more, except remind Lalee of thc instructions that she must follow for the purification ceremony.

Outside, the tall, serrated edges of coconut trees huddled against the moonlight like conspirators, shading her skin from the light. In the city, among the alleyways of Shonagachhi, behind the clamour of the constant negotiations, there was a moon that was a stranger to Lalee. Here, she felt the white of her sari bathed in the eerie brightness of the full moon. Somewhere close, a hasnuhana bush was in full bloom. White bulbous blooms radiated a strange greenish tinge in the still, oppressive heat. *Snakes come when the husnahana is in full bloom*, she remembered her mother saying. The world was a strange and dangerous place before the monsoon. Heat and dust and the rainclouds roiling somewhere in the distant belly of the future while snakes and other dangerous things lurked in the folds of the earth's skin in anticipation of the deluge. Lalee and her whole village would wait for those first raindrops of late June. Rain was the difference between life and death, between the dryness of starvation and the muddy, sticky loam of earth that pushed forth rice, jute, potatoes.

Lalee looked up at the full moon. It had been a long time since she had seen that familiar thing – something she had taken for granted as a village girl.

One of the women knocked on the ornate door. The other held Lalee by the arm. A male voice said, 'Come in.'

The woman pushed the heavy door forward, releasing a loud squeak from the hinges. The other one pulled Lalee inside.

A large, hairy man, naked, save for a pair of dark red silk shorts, lay on a giant four-poster bed. He paused the film he was watching on a large flat-screen television hanging from the wall. Lalee's eyes turned towards the dimly lit screen. Two naked women crowded the screen, one bent over a dark-skinned man, another one on her knees, hands tied behind her back and blindfolded. The woman's face was frozen in an unending moment of pain. Lalee couldn't tear her eyes away from her face, a familiar fear clawing its way through her throat.

The man scratched his long, bushy beard with one end of the remote control and smiled at Lalee, subjecting her to an intense gaze that travelled all over her body. In this room he looked entirely different from the gigantic auditorium where men and women worshipped him as if he were a god.

He waved a hand at the escorts who were standing on either side of Lalee. The two women left wordlessly, shutting the door behind them. The armed guard outside the door resumed his post.

Maharaj walked towards Lalee as she stiffened despite herself. She had done this a hundred thousand times and many of them had treated her a lot worse from the very beginning. She forced herself to relax her limbs as a strong enveloping hug folded her into the large man's torso. When he finally released her, Lalee realized she had been holding her breath. All day she had been thinking about the ceremony and what it would entail. It should have been a religious ceremony, a pointless metaphor of her somehow ascending from the status of a fallen woman. But in her gut, she knew what it was *really* going to be about. In this room, with the pornography on the screen and a half-finished glass of golden amber liquid next to Maharaj's hand, she knew she was right. If this was a ritual, it wasn't one she was a stranger to.

Maharaj began to laugh, without preamble or cause, without context, as if an unknowable joke had amused him greatly. He walked around Lalee and bolted the door behind her. The single sound of the iron sliding inside the clasp filled Lalee's world. She closed her eyes. Pretend this was just another john, pretend she was home, in that old room with the stained walls. This was just another man in a room with a whore and he wanted what all such men wanted to do with the bodies they owned for a short period of time. But something in the churn of her stomach, the bottomless writhing within her, told her that this wasn't the same thing.

Lalee looked around the room. The walls were panelled wtih dark wood and the giant bed with its many hangings dominated the room. A wall cabinet carved with various religious symbols displayed an array of alcohol bottles, none of which Lalee recognized. A life-size picture of Maharaj hung from one wall, his hands raised in benediction over a multitude of people. A large brass plate full of petals were laid at the feet of this colossal monstrosity. The smell of alcohol permeated the room, along with the heady, musky scent of a beast that Lalee couldn't identify. She was in the lair of an animal, where she would be a brief distraction before the inexorable devouring.

'Look around, my child,' Maharaj said from the bed in a gruff voice that startled Lalee. 'See how the stage is set,' he smiled. 'This is where you will become a purified woman.'

Lalee bowed her head, not knowing what would be an appropriate response to Maharaj's declaration.

'Bring those flowers to me,' he said.

Lalee picked up the heavy plate and brought it to the bed.

'Scatter them around me, child, and then kneel next to me. This is the part where you worship me so I can grant you purification.'

Lalee did as she was instructed, still keeping quiet. She wondered if Sonia would have to go through a similar ritual. Of course, she would have to, she told herself. A man like Maharaj would not let white flesh slip through his fingers. And that thought led elsewhere – what a man like that would do to the two young girls. She kneeled by his bedside, but he gestured for her to join him on the bed. Lalee sat on the corner, tucking her body away from his, sitting as quietly as she could. She could see the way her breasts hung limply behind the weave of her sari, and felt small, and afraid.

Maharaj pressed a button, flung the remote to a side. The frozen bodies on screen resumed their sport, writhing around each other in serpentine conjoinings. Lalee stole furtive glances at the TV. A smirk animated his face. 'Have you ever seen the temples of Khajuraho?' he asked.

Lalee shook her head.

'Their walls are carved with bodies like these, bodies engaged in the eternal sport of the flesh. People don't understand sex. We are made of sex. Even the gods. What you do – that is the essence of life. Now show me as you are.'

Maharaj put his hand on the end of her saree and tugged at it forcefully. His demand, coming so close on the heels of his sermon, caught Lalee off guard. She started slipping out of the loose cloth wrapping her body, and of the little security it provided. She noticed Maharaj watching her, his head turned away from the bodies on the screen. Lalee smiled at him. She could leverage his interest. She could survive this night.

She stood in front of him, naked and in a manner that showed off her body favourably, and lowered her eyes, reminding herself to affect modesty.

'What is your name?' Maharaj asked. The loud moans and heaving of the three actors on screen filled the room.

'Mohamaya,' Lalee replied.

She forced herself to hold her ground. What she never saw was the fist coming at her, socking her in the left eye. Maharaj looked at his knuckles, shook them and laughed. A short, quick chortle, like a child had heard the sound of tearing an insect's wings for the first time. In the first split second where the pain was an idea and not yet a reality, Lalee saw his face transform. He stared at Lalee, unblinking, the laughter disappearing almost as soon as it had come.

He propped himself up on one elbow and Lalee noticed the

large muscular arms flex like a threat. He let a few moments of silence pass, eyeing Lalee's naked body. 'I knew a Mohamaya. She also came from Shefali ji's home. Sadly, she died. But she had been purified. She died a chaste woman.'

Maharaj's voice was level, almost a monotone. Lalee hoped her face did not betray her. He could have been talking about another Mohamaya, but Lalee doubted that. Hers wasn't a common name. Mohamaya's severed throat and swollen face flashed in her mind. Lalee held the smile on her face and approached the large man now prone on the bed.

She reached her fingers gingerly towards the silken red shorts covering his crotch. It was easy to undo; Lalee pulled it delicately away from his body. She couldn't tell from his face how he really felt. It was set in an expression of amused curiosity, like lesser men watched trained monkeys perform tricks on streets. Lalee held his gaze for a moment before lowering her mouth on his crotch. She felt a hand grab her throat and drag her upwards. Maharaj was smiling at her. In a moment, he released her, and Lalee gasped for air and coughed.

'I accept you as you are, Mohamaya' Maharaj said, and Lalee understood the tone of mockery in his voice. 'You have given yourself to me, body and soul. I accept your offering.'

'I haven't given myself to you,' said Lalee. The choking had set something free within her. But she reminded herself that not all pretences could be dropped. If she survived this night and perhaps the ones that would inevitably come afterwards, she could dream of escape, of freedom, even if they never came to pass.

'When you set foot in my garden, you gave yourself to me,

just like your sisters before you,' Maharaj said, lifting Lalee's face up to face his own. His words were soft but his grip on Lalee's chin was hard, painful. She understood his words for what they were.

Lalee smiled. She touched his fingers, pulled them away from her face and moved her hands to his crotch. He jerked her hand away, holding her arms against her back, squeezed her neck with his other hand, smiled and launched his teeth at her lips.

He was holding her down, pushing from behind. Lalee tried to turn her head downwards, waiting for blood to appear between her legs, flooding the bed. She didn't know, couldn't know, if it was real. Or if it was even her blood, or Mohamaya's phantom blood that had flooded out of her in some strange alchemy. A fist clamped on her skull, held her hair by the roots and thrust repeatedly against the wooden headboard. She closed her eyes, and a little before losing consciousness, found her head pushed downwards in a sea of pillows, every breath a threat, and a gift she nearly thought impossible.

In the early hours of the morning, Lalee lay wide awake staring at the om patterns embossed on the panelling above her head. She could feel the side of her face begin to swell. She tried to move her lips, and found something like glue, or invisible stitches clamping them shut. She forced them open, overriding the panic that was spreading fast. She touched her cheek. A sharp rending pain shot through the left side of her face. She didn't make any sound but couldn't stop the tears from drenching her temples. Maharaj had pushed a handful of pills into his mouth in the small hours of the night when he was done with Lalee. Even after he had clearly passed out beside her, she didn't move a muscle, didn't breathe too hard, didn't dare to show fear or pain. Between the thickness of pillows, he whispered to her, 'I am a god. Gods kill mortals. Tonight, you can disappear. Lost in the night like smoke.' Then he laughed, with the childlike pleasure of the truly innocent.

# 37

LALEE LAY ON HER SINGLE BED, STARING AT THE WALL. Her left eye was ringed with black and the left side of her face was swollen. She couldn't stop herself from touching her face, laying a hand lightly on her cheek, trying to move and wincing in pain. A fat gecko on the mint walls came out of its hiding place behind the narrow frame of the white tube light. It sat watching a dragonfly that had settled above the light, enamoured of the glow. The gecko waited patiently, unblinking, advancing a few steps on its smooth white belly and stopping. Lalee held her breath, watching prey and predator. In its final advance, a few short breaths away from its victim, the gecko extended its neck and grabbed the dragonfly in its mouth, holding it there. The dragonfly struggled, writhing its legs, flapping its wings, but the gecko held on. It finally bit down with force and the dragonfly slowly stopped moving. Lalee closed her eyes.

When the door was unbolted in the morning, Lalee gathered the loose saree around herself, struggling to wrap the fabric twice around her bare breasts, one of them bearing a bruise and teeth marks, where the droplets of blood had dried on her skin. She slipped out of the doors, glancing at the guard who was looking away from her, face turned towards the wall next to him.

Lalee kept walking, keeping her eyes on her bare feet on the dirt alleyways and the gravel, praying she wouldn't forget the way back to the small room. She felt conscious of the gazes prickling her skin. Once or twice she looked up, locking eyes with a sevika, not an inch of their skin visible to the sun, except their face and their hands. One of them looked at her with such great sadness that Lalee had to bite her palm to keep herself from breaking down and curling into a ball on the gravel.

In the room, there was no sign of Durga and Lakshmi, or of Sonia. Lalee stared outside the window, looking at the murder of crows cawing their way in the still, heavy, stifling immovability of the summer heat, until the light dimmed into a gradual darkness.

Lalee heard soft footsteps entering the room. They paused midway through the room. Lalee didn't turn around to see who it was, and the intruder didn't turn on the light. After a few moments, Lalee felt a hand on her shoulders. She opened her eyes and saw the pale whiteness of Sonia's long fingers on her skin. Neither of them said anything. Lalee felt nothing, not even anger, and without the shelter of its reassuring hardness, she was bereft. She wondered if Sonia knew.

Sonia was looking past Lalee, through the window to the trees outside. The financial collapse of 2008 had started the drain of Uzbeki girls from Dubai to India, where intelligent handlers knew their pale skins and lithe bodies would fetch a lot of business. Sonia knew it did. Lalee would do a job for

2,000, 1,500, even 500 if times were tough; some other Indian girls like the ones Charlie featured on his website would get a lot more than that. Sonia had once thought that Maya would have made a good fit for Charlie's service. She had potential, and with a little coaching, she could also develop a certain kind of class that Charlie's customer looked for if they were willing to spend 25,000 to 50,000 on any of them. But for 'Russians' like her the money climbed steadily higher; a night could start from 70,000 to even a lakh. She wondered if Lalee knew this. Daria, her sister, did not know this. Watching Lalee now, sleeping gingerly on her side, Sonia felt exhausted. It wasn't supposed to go like this, but how it was supposed to go, Sonia didn't know. When she looked at Lalee, and those two little girls, she wanted to do something she hadn't done for ages. A long time ago – so long ago that it felt like a different life, but one that sat uncomfortably against her skin – she had a ritual. A ritual that involved smashing up glass, seeking out pointed edges of steel and blade, and testing their sharpness against her skin. It bloomed beautifully. Crusting in a few hours, crumbling in iron-rich dust as the wetness began to dry, rising in throbbing welts against the paleness of her arms, her thighs, her stomach. Sonia shuddered. After Daria, she had promised herself that she wouldn't do that. Life was too precious for this endless rehearsal of death. But as soon as those two twin girls had entered the car, Sonia's careful plan, her hothouse exit strategy, stumbled.

Sonia watched Lalee's furrowed brows, the way her forearm rested across her face, avoiding the bruises. She said, hiding herself in a sardonic smile, 'You shouldn't spoil a good rescue like this.'

Lalee opened her eyes, raising her left hand as shade against the single white tube light in the room.

Sonia laughed, 'People love a good rescue story, don't they? Maharaj here is rescuing fallen women like us.'

Lalee closed her eyes again, twisting her face in pain as she tried to turn on her side. Her absence of curiosity annoyed Sonia. There was a complacence in these girls, an unwavering faith in the workings of 'fate', a fate they were quick to blame and praise. In the beginning she was confused when they'd tell her, 'It's all our forehead,' and then someone explained to her that it was fate they were talking about. That cinema of their lives fate had written on their foreheads with invisible ink at the moment of their birth. *I'd have burned that forehead*, Sonia had said. *That's what they say when their husbands die*, they'd had told her. It filled Sonia with an anger that stung more than it hurt, inflamed her in its grand insult to human endeavour. It felt personal. Daria believed in fate, and Sonia never knew where that led her, to what hellhole, to what edge of the world from where it was so very easy to fall off the face of the earth.

'You said we were going far away. What did you mean?' Lalee whispered, and Sonia wondered if she was even aware or awake. 'What are we doing in this place?' Lalee mumbled.

Durga and Lakshmi were not in the room. Sonia found that easier. There were easier confidences among adults. Lalee could take care of herself, just as she could. She had a fleeting image of Lalee trailing behind her, looking out of place in a hotel lobby, unaware that she was being vetted by people who would lubricate her way into this commune and then a long way away.

Lalee wanted to say things, ask questions, understand, but

she couldn't frame the questions, couldn't put words around the things she wanted to know. When the man had struck her in the stomach, she had doubled over. In the blinding pain, she recognized the strategy of men like him and in her head she had smiled. *Hit me where it doesn't show*, she thought. She imagined the bruise there. First blue and then black, and gradually yellowing as it healed. The drooping ceiling fan droned on in arthritic groans as it spinned overhead. Sonia broke the silence. 'I have nothing to gain by keeping you in the dark. I'm not Rambo, I'm not Madam and I'm certainly not that crazy godman over there,' she pointed at the large picture on the wall which Lalee didn't want to see. 'I didn't have anything to gain by telling you either, but now we're are all here and there's no turning back.'

Sonia's idiosyncratic mix of Bangla, Hindi and English wasn't unintelligible, but still hard to follow for Lalee. 'Madam has a new venture,' Sonia said with a small sigh. 'I don't know who came up with it, but godman here rescues girls like you. Puts on a few sham weddings, mostly with men like Rambo and Chintu. The newspapers come and take pictures and the word gets around how he is the father to all fallen women everywhere. At some point, they developed a business plan – Madam and Maharaj. She supplies the girls, and he sends them on a trip. In a few days, we will be taken to the dock, put in a large shipping container with water and food and a pot to piss in, if we are lucky. In some time we will reach Bangkok, and there someone very much like Rambo will take over. Everyone will get paid, except us. And we will never be heard from again.'

Lalee removed the arm that was covering her eyes. She sat

up, wincing when her stomach folded over. She felt stupid, more stupid than she ever had. Her life in Shonagachhi ... was just that, like many others, she would have gladly left it behind if she had another choice. At times, especially when she was young, it had seemed worse than death. But she had kept on, and in doing so she had found a life, clawed one out, fought for it with everything she had. She had made friends, found sisters, fallen in love and broken her heart; she had been hungry and sad and happy and full. It wasn't a great life, but it was a human life. It was her life, one not granted but carved. She had worked hard at it. Now, she felt that thin, squalid piece of earth beneath her feet that she had made her own, was sinking. She couldn't comprehend the idea of being shipped off to a foreign land, against her will, and deposited into the hands of some other master. The people who traded in the skins of others, selling them like the hides of flayed animals to lie unprotesting under someone's feet. Lalee thought of the long, translucent snakeskins as they lay in the undergrowth a long time ago when she used to walk through the dark alleyways of her village. She wanted to shed her skin now, leave a husk for the hunters.

She looked up at Sonia, her eyes wide and staring, not knowing what to say next. Sonia had walked over to the other side of the room, peeked through the curtains before letting them drop again. 'The guards are patrolling outside our room,' she said. 'We are a lot of money sitting in this room.'

'This is true? We are being sent to Bangkok?'

Sonia laughed softly. 'You think your madam owes you anything? She'll make a lot more money exporting you than you'll make for her in Shonagazi. Those customers don't pay that well.'

'I could have,' Lalee heard a soft wail creep into her voice. 'If she had let me work from upstairs and I had a few big customers like that Mr Ghosh.'

Sonia chuckled, and the empty feeling in Lalee's chest quickly turned to anger. Lalee hated her for having the knowledge and the power that Lalee had been denied. She had been bought and sold, and everyone but her knew all about it.

'You haven't caught on, Lalee, have you?' Sonia said, with more warmth in her voice than Lalee had ever heard. 'There is no upstairs. It's just a place to store the exports. They don't want them to be too visible – people ask too many questions. Best to keep all the exports in one place. Surveyed by the people in the business and then delivered here, to this compound. Mr Ghosh wasn't a customer; he was there to check ... the product. They can't just send anyone. You could take that as a compliment – you're definitely export quality.'

Lalee stood up, walked towards the window, took a deep breath and slapped Sonia on the face with all the rage she had in her body. The red welt on Sonia's face bloomed like a contained fire. Sonia looked at her in open-mouthed surprise, betrayal flashing in her eyes.

'And you? Where do you fit? Why ...' Lalee said through her teeth, breathing fast and shallow. 'Why are *you* here?'

Sonia didn't say anything for a long time. The squeaks of the rusty fan whirring above them seemed only to intensify the tense silence.

'I want to leave this awful place,' Sonia said finally. And a small breath escaped both of them, the room seemed to deflate, like a great fall had been arrested.

'I know people in Bangkok. Madam knows that. She

thought I could be useful, herding you – the girls. What she doesn't know is that I will disappear from there. It's easier to go back to Europe from Thailand. And if I have to stay, I can make a lot more money there. But I am not staying with their people. After we reach, I'll be gone in a few days, if I can make some money beforehand. Escape isn't cheap. No one helps you because they want to do good things.'

'Why did you even come here?' Lalee asked, collapsing on the floor, and catching herself with a quick hand, settling on her haunches. The rage left as swiftly as it came, leaving her empty, like a little death had come and gone, without anyone noticing.

'Long story. You're not the only ones with difficult lives. We have our share too. I don't talk about it because, frankly, it's nobody's goddamn bloody business.'

'I came here for a reason,' Sonia said in a whisper even Lalee could barely hear. She sat up, facing away from Sonia in a half-hearted effort to hide her swollen face. The sound of chants pervaded the room, echoing in the vast expanse of the compound, reverberating against the dark bodies of the sentinels outside the window. In the darkness their silhouettes sat facing away from each other. Already fat mosquitoes swarmed around them, taking advantage of the still-open windows.

'Do you want to leave, Lalee?' Sonia asked.

Lalee opened her mouth to reply. But it felt dry; something sticky and white had glued the corners of her lips together, and separating them tugged at the parts of Lalee's face that she didn't have the courage to look at yet.

'No, listen, it's not as simple as that. If you leave here, you cannot go back to your Sonagazi. You know what happened to that other girl? They won't even find you, Lalee. You leave here, you have to disappear. It's a lot of work – disappearing.'

Lalee didn't understand a word Sonia said. Her English was beyond Lalee, as was her garbled Bangla. When she didn't say anything in reply, Sonia tried explaining, this time carefully enunciating in Bangla as best as she could. After a while, Lalee asked, 'How?'

Sonia shook her head impatiently.

'I will get you out of here, but then, on the outside, if we do actually make it that far, I can't help you. But for now, you just need to come with me when it is time. But think carefully.'

Lalee stared at her as if she had gone mad. 'Of course,' she said. 'Why would I want to die here?'

Sonia laughed drily. 'You won't die. You're worth a lot more alive. It won't be pleasant, but eventually they will ship you somewhere, as soon as they get paid, I suppose. And then ... and with time, I suppose you would be alright, as we all are, sooner or later.'

Lalee laughed, and an electrifying pain shot through her face and head.

'So you will come with me?' Sonia asked. 'I can't help you after we get out. You're on your own.'

Lalee said, 'Some things are worse than dying.'

'No,' Sonia said, as if considering the question. 'No. Nothing is worse than dying. We live; that's what we do.'

'I won't go without the girls,' Lalee said.

In the strange mixture of reflected street lights and the blue gloaming, Lalee saw Sonia nod her head.

*Daria knew very little*, Sonia thought. She was the nice

one, the innocent one, and to Sonia, the stupid one. Someone had offered her a loan to cover the medical costs, and in turn, Daria would take up a job as a secretary to some rich man in Dubai. Daria had her travel papers made, packed her bags and left Khwarazm. From there to Tashkent, to Almaty, Istanbul and finally to Delhi. As far as Sonia knew, Daria never reached Dubai. Sonia didn't know everything about Daria's time in India, but she knew that in the very first few months Daria's passport was taken away, she was locked in an apartment with a few other girls and made to serve six to seven clients a day. Sonia didn't know this for certain, but this version of events was repeated so many times by so many women from her country, that she was almost certain that this was a close-enough version of truth. In the last nine years that Sonia had spent in the country, she learned a lot of things: that one phone call could get a man a 'Russian' girl anywhere in Mumbai, Goa, Delhi and Punjab, and that if she was very smart and very careful, she may yet survive this place, and make some money too. Sonia had Daria's mistakes to learn from.

'My sister,' Sonia said, staring outside the window as she stood still holding its thick iron bars, 'my sister ran away with a cult. To India. She thought it would bring her peace, coming to the land of holy men and spirituality. She thought she would leave the madness behind her. I came ... to see if it was as peaceful as all that. I came to see what she left me to find.' Sonia stopped talking, still staring outside at the guards in the distance.

Lalee looked up at her. The tall, blond woman had a faraway look on her face, as if she was seeing beyond the distance of the small window and the darkness outside it. Lalee thought about the first time she had met this strange, alien creature. Sonia had told her stories, horrid and hilarious ones, about her time as a mail-order bride and the one time she came close to marrying a rich American. Lalee had felt incredibly jealous then; she couldn't imagine someone having and then giving up that opportunity. 'Did you really come here for your sister?' Lalee asked. Sonia didn't answer. Maybe she had a right to make up her own story and her reasons as much as Lalee did. Every time she'd been skewered by those innocuous words that arranged themselves into a question that probed her, hunting for a story, for a fleshy bit of human tragedy so they could invent a Lalee they needed at the moment.

The door opened behind them. Lalee saw a flash of muted white in the darkness. Two women stood by as Durga and then Lakshmi walked into the room. Lalee listened to the rustle of the sheets as the two girls got into bed. After a long moment of silence, Sonia looked at Lalee and the two girls and whispered, 'There is going to be a purification, you know. '

Lalee stared at the ceiling, watching the fan go round its endless circles as the darkness outside invaded the small room, the yellow lamps at the edge of the compound cast long shadows on the walls. She could hear intermittent horns from passing trucks, coming from a world so far away that Lalee thought she might never find it again.

'No, there won't be,' she said.

# 38

WHEN TILU REACHED MA TARA PRINTING WORKS, CHAKLADAR was still stalking about the place, haranguing his employees. Tilu quickly ducked behind a handy alleyway. His heart was racing. He wished he knew what was really going on. He tried calling Lalee but her phone was switched off. The posh bhadralok voice of the recorded message annoyed him, especially when he stayed on long enough for the message to be repeated in three different languages as if he was a special kind of polyglot idiot. But her phone was all he had to contact her. Anything may have happened to her, she might need him, she might be in danger; and Tilu Shau must be there to protect her. Tilu took out a bent cigarette from his breast pocket and lit it with a trembling hand. He felt like his hero, Job, on a mission to save an exotic princess. He couldn't tell if he was shivering from excitement or fear. He let out a breath he didn't know he was holding. He couldn't do this alone, and he didn't know anyone else he could ask for help. Bhoga would have to do. He could pay Bhoga later, but it would be best if the matter of money was never brought up.

Tilu peeked out of his corner to keep an eye on Chakladar. When he finally walked out of the shop and down onto College Street, leaving Bhoga to lock up, Tilu emerged from his hiding spot.

Bhoga, as always, was glad to see Tilu Shau.

'Syaar,' Bhoga yelled. Tilu Shau immediately turned around to see if Chakladar had noticed. He was relieved to find that Chakladar wasn't even visible in the distance anymore. He was lost to the ever-moving crowd of College Street and its many buses, trams and pedestrians. Tilu felt better. He needed to convince Bhoga one way or the other. Lalee's fate depended on it.

Tilu put a finger on his lips and shushed loudly. Bhoga blinked twice, slowly, infinitely surprised by Tilu's strange behaviour.

'I need your help,' Tilu whispered, trying to convey the urgency through facial expression.

'What?' Bhoga asked,

Tilu realized his whisper had indeed been way too quiet for a rowdy, loud place like this. Bhoga hadn't heard him. Tilu looked around to see if anyone was paying them undue attention. Satisfied that no one had followed or noticed him, Tilu dragged Bhoga by an elbow and pulled him into the shop.

'Ai, boss, what's happening?'

'Shush, I'll explain.'

Tilu took a deep breath, and tried to think of a way to put his thoughts into words.

'I'm in love with a lady,' Tilu whispered.

Bhoga's face split into a wide grin.

'Yes, boss. Now we are talking. What do you want? We follow her? Beat up her brothers? Huh? Anything for you and the missus.'

'No, no,' Tilu stopped him before Bhoga could go off track. 'She has been kidnapped, Bhoga. I need to rescue her and I need your help. Anything can happen to her without us.'

'Fuck these hooligans, syaar. How dare they lay a hand on boudi! I'll kick twenty kinds of shit out of their mother-loving assholes, syaar. Just let me get my hands on them.'

'Yes, yes,' Tilu tried to calm Bhoga down. His excitement was threatening to take over Tilu's mission. But he couldn't do this alone. Plus, his heart skipped a beat every time Bhoga called Lalee 'boudi'. That would make her Tilu's wife.

'Where have they taken boudi, syaar?'

'Oh, I don't know.'

'What?'

'No, I mean I have an idea where. But it's a dangerous place,' Tilu said.

Bhoga's face lit up. 'It doesn't matter, syaar. I am with you.'

'It's well outside the city, on the road to Diamond Harbour.'

'Do you have a car, motorbike or something? We could take the train but it's too crowded this time of the evening. Fucking daily passengers and housemaids going home from the city.'

Tilu realized he hadn't planned the mission very well. Bhoga had already pointed out a key problem that hadn't occurred to him. His face fell. Bhoga walked beside him in silence until they came to the main road and a series of loud horns and miscellaneous noises drowned out the sound of their footsteps.

'I've got a friend, syaar, very good friend. He drives a company bus, you know, for those ladies who work at the call centre at all hours of the night? It's his day off, so his bus will be in the garage and he'll be pissing himself before midnight. I can get the bus and we can drive it there. We might need to give him a bit of mallu to make things easier.'

'Mallu?' Tilu repeated, frowning.

'Uff, Cash, cash,' Bhoga explained. 'Got any?'

Tilu deflated even more. He had the 1,000 that he had wrangled out of Chakladar the other day; he'd spend about 250 out of it on food, cigarettes and the bangla he had drunk that night. There was just 750 left, but it was something.

'I've got about 500,' he whispered to Bhoga.

'Ah, that isn't much but it'll do. Wait,' Bhoga stopped in his tracks. 'It's not a 500-rupee note, is it? Because no drunk is drunk enough to take a banned note.'

'No, no,' Tilu waved his hands in dismissal. 'That asshole Chakladar tried to stick me with two of those damned banned notes, but I'm not stupid. '

They rounded the corner and reached the five-road crossing with the big black umbrellas of the K. C. Paul billboard hanging precariously above the mossy old buildings besieged by tangles of electric wires and phone lines. A green-and-yellow auto rickshaw crawled past them, nearly knocking Tilu down, blaring a recorded ad for a Banarasi saree store.

Bhoga put his hand up to hail a passing bus and hauled Tilu into it. The bus had barely slowed down, but the bus conductor, leaning out from the footrest at its door and yelling out destinations to passersby, lent a hand to steady Tilu and ushered the two men in.

'What?' Bhoga asked in the face of Tilu's glare. 'Can't get from here to Salt Lake on foot, can we? Just hang on to the railing,' and indicated the women's seating area with a sly wink. 'We'll be there in no time; Boudi will not have to wait too long.'

If Bhoga got off the bus and reneged on the plan now, Tilu realized, he'd be entirely lost. When they alighted near the extremely deserted water tank in Salt Lake, Bhoga started walking briskly through empty lots, alleyways and open fields, with Tilu in tow. Tilu could barely keep up and barked questions at Bhoga who didn't reply. When they reached a small clearing on the other side of a towed-car parking lot, Tilu knew where they were going.

Tilu had heard of Salt Lake's bangla joint but never ventured to this part of the city. There were plenty in north and central Calcutta to keep him well lubricated, and the one in Garcha served his moonshine needs when he was in that part of town. The spooky emptiness of Salt Lake after nightfall impressed Tilu. He decided to come back in the winter, the dusty, polluted air of Calcutta mixed with the winter fog would create an alluring, impenetrable aura. He wanted to walk through that smog on a lonely winter's night, perhaps with Lalee by his side, like a still from a film noir he'd once seen in Max Muller Bhavan.

'Oi Gorment,' Bhoga yelled.

A large man was lying on his back with his eyes to the skies, pointing out the stars to his comrades. A few bald and bent-over men sat on their haunches nursing plastic cups and clay mugs with clear liquid in small bottles strewn around them. Tilu knew this scene; a part of him wished he could find a glass and join the circle. Even in this sweltering heat, he could do with the liquid pungency of bangla burning his throat. But he had a job to do. His lady was in danger and she needed him. He hissed at Bhoga, 'Who is your friend? I don't see a bus anywhere.'

'There he is, Gorment, rolling on his back,' Bhoga laughed. 'We call him Gorment because he is always going on about the gorment. Very political, my friend.'

'Oh, government,' Tilu said, the penny finally dropping for him.

The fat man, Gorment, yelled back at Bhoga. 'What are you doing here, you asshole? Done licking Chakladar's you-know-what?' His braying laugh made Tilu wince.

'Fucking country is going to the dogs, sister-fucking it's way to hell, and what are you doing about it, Bhoga?'

Bhoga laughed and whispered in Tilu's ear, 'Gorment is hardcore Left Front. He doesn't like the new party. Don't say anything to set him off or we'll be here all night.'

'We need your bus, Gorment,' Bhoga shouted, walking towards the sad tableau of men under the dim yellow street lights.

'What bus? I don't have a bus,' Gorment mumbled.

Tilu's heart skipped a beat. It had taken the better part of an hour to get here. And who knew what has been happening to Lalee in the meantime? He panicked.

'What? No bus? What are we doing here then? What are we going to do?' Tilu exclaimed, the pitch of his voice rising with every word.

'Oh calm down,' Bhoga replied, without paying Tilu much attention. He sat down on the ground, next to Gorment, who was still rolling about on the dead grass.

'There is a lady in trouble. This man's missus,' he pointed to Tilu. 'She has been kidnapped,' he whispered. 'We have to go save her, so I need your bus.'

Gorment swatted at Bhoga, and missed entirely. He tried a few more times and though Bhoga was stationary, Gorment kept missing his mark. He began to slur, 'The country is going to the dogs and you only want to save a woman.'

'Look at this man,' Bhoga yelled, impressing Tilu with his vim and passion. 'The love of his life has been taken from him. What is he going to do by himself, huh? An innocent woman is in trouble and you can't bother to help us?'

Gorment started bawling. Tilu was stunned to see the big fat man quivering with grief as if someone had just died. In between gulping for air and drowning in his own snot, Gorment mewled, 'Everywhere it's the common man who is getting fucked in the arse. Fucked bloody in the arse, from dusk to dawn. Take my van, boy, take it.' He patted his shirt pocket for the keys but couldn't find them. Bhoga saw the shiny pieces of steel on the ground and picked them up before Gorment could change his mind.

Half running after Bhoga, Tilu felt both exhilarated and amazed at the way his rescue mission was going. A few hours ago he was a man alone, a man with no friends, no money and very little resources. As they left the compass of yellow street lights, walking away from the moonshine drinkers and the smell of piss, they reached the dark parking lot full of towed cars. Bands of stray mongrels patrolled the road, barking at their approach. Bhoga had a spring in his step. Tilu had always taken him to be a rather simple boy, and only called on him because he was desperate. But Bhoga had surprised him. Tilu started skipping, trying to keep up with Bhoga's long steps, even though his rubber slippers caught in the rough ground from time to time.

Bhoga stopped in front of a white van, paint chipped in places, and unlocked it. Tilu stood looking around for a bus. 'Don't bother,' Bhoga called.

'I thought we were taking a bus?' Tilu asked.

Tilu simply patted the side of the van and whistled at him to get into the passenger seat. 'This is what we call "the bus",' Bhoga clarified. They both got into the white van. Bhoga found a pair of dark sunglasses above the dashboard. He put them on, checked his reflection in the mirror, blew a whistle and said, 'Where to, boss?'

# 39

THE MARCH WAS ONLY A FEW DAYS AWAY. THE SEX WORKERS' Collective was buzzing like a hive in midsummer. Malini was standing in the long office room with her hands on her waist. Numerous women of all ages were hard at work, making posters and placards, chattering, trading gossip and telling jokes. Every year on Labour Day, the first of May, the collective led a march, and it felt to Malini like walking in a dream, a living commemoration of every long, hard-fought victory. The fight for legalization, to be seen as working political subjects who demanded their rights against persecution, was still ongoing. But there had been so many victories – having their name on voter identity cards, being able to demand that schools admit their children under their guardianship alone, and the great diminishment in HIV infections here in Shonagachhi even though many sex workers in the country still battled the disease. Malini let out a long breath. This year's march would be dedicated to Maya, urging the authorities to investigate her death. These posters carried Maya's face, her memory, her name. Malini watched as a young girl carefully outlined an M with red glitter, filling in its curves, and leaned back to check her handiwork.

Malini knew how these things went, how hard it was to organize such protests, and even then, they might come out of it empty-handed. But that wasn't the point, the police wouldn't move, and when they moved they'd do it at their glacial pace, raid and arrest innocent women instead of finding a murderer. Malini glanced at her wristwatch. She was waiting for Amina who had wanted to see her.

Malini came out and stood on the verandah, watching the road. The women were talking and giggling behind her. In a corner, Malini saw a girl waving at her. She was standing in the shadows in the narrow gap between The Blue Lotus and the beauty parlour next door. Several girls were out on the street, sitting or standing laconically, their faces painted two shades too light for their complexion. Waiting, occasionally calling out at passing men. Malini walked towards them.

She felt a wave of guilt as she looked at Amina's face in the dark gloom between the two houses. She had assumed that the police had taken Amina or she had simply fled for a few days. Now, the emaciated girl was standing in front of Malini. Amina had clearly been crying. Her swollen eyes were alert with a hunted look Malini was familiar with. She felt certain that there were other marks on her body from the beating that Malini couldn't see.

She could not stop herself. Almost running towards the girl, she slowed herself down to a brisk pace, not willing to attract attention towards them.

'I've been waiting for you,' the girl whispered, looking around herself. 'I thought you'd come out sometime. But I couldn't go to the Collective – they're watching me.'

'What happened?' Malini asked.

'Will you take this?' The girl took out a plastic bag from the folds of her kameez, hidden under her dupatta.

'What is this?' Malini asked, looking at the opaque plastic bag.

'Put it in your bag or something. Hide it in your clothes,' the girl said with some urgency. 'Are you going out? Don't leave it in the house,' she said.

'What is it, Amina? Why are you giving it to me?'

'Before Maya died, she gave this to me,' Amina said slowly. 'And this one ... is mine.' She thrust two cellphones into Malini's hands.

Malini looked at the items, bemused. The two black slabs of plastic felt innocuous in her hand. She looked up from her hand to Amina's face. Amina was looking over her shoulders, wringing her hands. A couple of girls standing outside the beauty parlour were watching them. Malini wanted to whisk this girl away, put her in a safe place and talk to her, ask her questions. She could only think of a few at the moment.

'What do you want me to do with all this?'

'Just look at it and you'll know. After Maya came back ... from there, the ashram, she showed me what happens at that place. It's all there in the videos and pictures. She said if anything happened to her, I should contact Deepa madam, but I can't with them watching me. She probably thought this was going to protect her. Maya was fighting with her babu – he wanted her to go back to that place.'

'But the cellphone? I thought that was stolen by the babu, wasn't it?'

'No, I was the first to enter the room, before you or Madam

or anyone. Mohamaya was lying on the floor but I didn't take any money,' her voice rose, pleading. 'I swear I didn't. But the phone was lying on the bed. So I took it.'

Malini looked at the two phones again turning them over in her hands.

Amina leaned towards Malini. For a stray moment, Malini felt slightly scared. There was an empty desperation in Amina's eyes that made her uncomfortable. Malini had never seen anyone jump off a bridge, but she thought that she'd just seen that look of urgency in Amina's eyes. 'You remember I went away? Three months ago?'

Malini stared at Amina's hands which were clutching her own arms tightly. She was shaking. Malini did not remember a time when Amina was away. How was she to know – there were thousands of girls in Shonagachhi. And Malini had never paid any particular attention to Amina Bibi. The slight, shy girl, seemed to blend in the background, always tagging behind the more beautiful Mohamaya. 'Yes, yes,' Malini said.

'I was there,' Amina whispered softly in Malini's ear. I was there, with Maya. They sent us both but they … sent me back here.'

'Where? Where were you?'

'In the ashram, in Nandankanan,' Amina mouthed the last word, not even daring to whisper. 'I have to go now. Please keep the phones. If they find them on me, they'll kill me … they'll kill me this time.'

Amina made a move to leave, but Malini grabbed her by the arm, defying the curious stares of the girls nearby. 'Wait. Why did they send you back? What are they doing with our girls there?'

Amina stopped, looked at Malini and laughed. Malini noticed with a growing sense of alarm the madness and devastation on her face. 'They don't export certain kinds of products, Malini di. Pregnant girls are not good for business.'

Malini looked from Amina's face down to her belly, and looked back to her face again. 'Not anymore,' Amina confirmed. 'They took care of it. That's when they brought me back.'

'And Maya?' Malini asked, now desperate in the face of a toxic mystery that threatened to drown her.

'Malini di,' Amina said, 'Maya was not like me. Maya knew what she wanted, she also had more courage than me, more ambition. She wanted to help and knew how to demand it.' She laughed. 'That did not work out for her. Now they're trying to blame things on Salman, her babu.'

'He didn't do it?' Malini asked.

For the first time in this conversation, Malini saw a normal, uncomplicated woman's face in front of her. A derisive sneer curled Amina's lips. 'That man,' she said with a confidence Malini hadn't seen before in her, 'could not find his ass without a map.' Amina jerked her head towards The Blue Lotus. 'They are using him to explain things. He wanted what every babu ever wants, and Maya only kept him around for convenience.' She looked around and added, 'I have to go, or she'll send Chintu after me.' Amina paused for breath. Her face was beginning to twist in grief, 'They'll kill me if they find this stuff. I think Madam sends some of the other girls and the servants to go through my things. I have been hiding them in new places ever since I found them. After Mohamaya died, Shefali Madam and two other girls searched her room through all hours of the night. I knew they were looking for something.

And I heard Madam talking on the phone, in Maya's room. I think a new bunch of girls are coming.'

Amina looked at Malini, who saw a drowning woman staring back at her. Malini felt oddly aware of the two phones in her hand. She had nothing else to say to Amina. Whatever words she chose would fall short. So she remained silent, but held Amina's hand. She wanted to say, 'Be safe,' and whisper warnings, advise caution, but none of that would be of use. Malini couldn't do anything for Amina. She was living in mortal fear of a danger Malini could not erase.

'Okay. I'll go through these phones, and I'll do what I can.' Malini continued after a pause, 'I'll do whatever I can, Amina, I swear on my mother's life. Hold on a little longer; don't give in to them.'

Amina wiped her eyes. 'I must go. If I'm not out on the streets with the other girls, they'll suspect something. Take care of these.'

The two of them began to walk towards the street lights. 'It'll be okay,' Malini said abruptly and struggled to believe the words herself.

She watched the skinny girl walk towards The Blue Lotus and get swallowed into the rest of the soliciting crowd. Her face, drawn and swollen, reflected the pallid glow of the halogen lamps on the street.

Malini walked back to the Collective, wrapping her left hand with a bit of her saree, affecting a nonchalance that she hadn't had to deploy since her early days at the job. In between greeting people and barking instructions at the girls still making posters, Malini wondered – if the phone contained some kind of sex videos, Maya could have just thrown them away. Why would she give them to Amina? Malini sighed. Even without any help from Amina, she knew a few things. It wasn't easy to organize a group of ambitious, petty, desperate, willful, terribly vulnerable and exquisitely fierce women into something resembling an organization. She had her ears to the ground and in the wind, ears that played a game of telephone in an endless loop that wound beyond the sagging electrical wires all across the narrow expanse of Shonagachhi. She had heard things and everything had seemed probable, but there was still nothing she knew for certain. She knew small things, that people met in Maya's room, that Shefali Madam used to visit too, that none of the other girls were allowed.

Malini walked into the Collective, carefully avoiding people and conversations. She crossed the large room with its stacks of red plastic chairs and microphones, and into the small office room, closing the door softly behind her. She pulled the curtains and sat on a stool in the corner and, turning her body towards the windows, hunched over the two phones. The phones were identical, two small black rectangles. Malini turned one of them on. The screen took a moment to light up. The wallpaper turned out to be a picture of Maya with a small boy – her son. The boy was reaching out to the camera with one chubby hand, and Malini stared at it for a moment longer than necessary. She noticed that the phone battery was fully charged. Malini looked through its contents, scrolled through some messages and wondered if it was Amina who had kept this phone charged. Some of the messages were innocent, notifications from providers and pushy salespeople, while others were only a few words long – dates, times and places, nothing else. Malini couldn't find a single personal message.

She moved on to the photos. Most of them were shots of Maya in different poses. The girl liked to take pictures of herself. In some of the photos, Maya was clad entirely in white – a white saree, white long-sleeved blouse and a white veil over her face. Malini knew from hearsay and gossip where The Blue Lotus girls went, but seeing Maya in this strange costume gave her pause.

When Malini found the cache of videos in both phones, she got up, locked the door and had to steady herself before she could watch them again. Her heart had been in her mouth when she watched them the first time, trying to make out the faces, the voices and steeling herself for the violence that she knew would come. She watched the videos over and over, looking for clues, trying to make sense of the grainy movements and the shadowy faces, until she heard Maya's voice eerily whispering at her. The screen was now dark, and Maya's face had been so close to the phone that Malini felt Maya's breath on her skin. She clenched her fist, and listened intently for what Maya had to say.

# 40

WHEN BHOGA STOPPED THE VAN OUTSIDE THE LARGE GATES of the compound, a sizeable fight was already in progress. As a couple of guys tore through each other's clothes, a uniformed guard with a rifle pushed past them, knocked one of the fighters with the stock and Tilu saw a splash of blood whir in the air before landing on the dirt. He shuddered involuntarily, locking the door on his side. Bhoga's face, on the other hand, lit up like it was Diwali. 'Uri saala,' he said.

'Come on, come on,' Tilu hissed. 'Drive us out of this. Uff baba, I would have died just now. Imagine if it was my face instead of that guy's ...'

'Let's see what the fuck-up is, boss,' Bhoga said, peering out of the window.

'Are you mad?' Tilu yelled at him.

A couple of guards strolled towards them, signalling Bhoga to get out of the car. Tilu covered his head with his hands. Bhoga quickly hit ignition and backed the car away, quickly leaving the commotion behind.

When they had put a safe enough distance between themselves and the crowd, Bhoga slowed the car down behind a handy copse of trees. Tilu craned his neck behind as far as it would go, trying to see if they were being followed. His heart was racing and he could feel the blood rushing to his ears. He clenched his hands in an effort to shake off some of the tension. 'Let's go, Bhoga, or we'll be murdered in no time. Didn't you see those rifles?'

Bhoga turned towards Tilu and said, 'You have no honour, syaar. You want to leave boudi here among these hooligans? We have come to save her and we won't leave till we have rescued her.'

'Yes, yes, of course,' Tilu mumbled, feeling ashamed of his craven instincts. 'But how?' he wailed.

Bhoga was sucking on the stem of his borrowed sunglasses thoughtfully, frowning in concentration. 'Syaar …' he said slowly, 'maybe this is our chance. While the ruckus outside is still going on, maybe we could go in. You're sure she is in there somewhere?'

Tilu hesitated. In point of fact, he had no idea where Lalee might be. He looked as far back and ahead as he could, without actually putting his head out of the window, in the not unfounded fear that a bullet could pierce his skull at any moment. The vastness of the enclosure was terrifying. Even if Lalee was inside, he had no idea how he would ever find her.

Bhoga, however, was borne on the tide of his own narrative. 'Fucking assholes,' he muttered, stiffening his own resolve. 'Kidnapping a decent woman in broad daylight. Fucking Godbotherers. I'll show your fucking God. I'll put your God where the sun don't …'

Tilu didn't have the heart to tell Bhoga that he was only vaguely sure of Lalee's whereabouts. If Bhoga left now, he would not only be all alone, but also without any means to get back to the city.

'Syaar? Syaar?' Tilu heard Bhoga say. 'Come on, syaar, no point sitting here with our fingers in our—'

'Ah, Bhoga,' Tilu said irritably. 'Your language is too crass.'

Bhoga stared at him and started laughing. 'Oh syaar! *Aar parina*, syaar, you're too funny, too funny.'

Tilu grabbed Bhoga's upraised arms with both his hands. 'Ah, shhh, Bhoga, what are you doing? Someone will hear us.'

Bhoga swallowed the rest of his laughter and they walked a few paces in silence. 'I have an idea, syaar,' Bhoga said. 'We should go there and find out what the jhamela is all about.'

Tilu stopped in his tracks. He didn't know how he could refuse. Finally he settled on: 'Maybe it would look less suspicious if only one of us went.'

Bhoga mulled this over. 'Okay. You stay here and try to find a way in. I'll walk over there and try to see what the fuss is all about.'

Bhoga spread his long stick-thin legs and disappeared into the gloom within minutes. Tilu looked around, imagining shapes in the shadows. When even his incessant fantasizing failed to produce monsters from the darkness, Tilu concentrated on finding a way inside, beyond the long concrete wall of the enclosure. He tried climbing the wall. A few jumps and failed attempts later, his weather-beaten slippers gave out. Tilu cursed his luck, took off both his slippers and tried again. This time he gripped the top of the wall, narrowly missing the barbed wire that ran across its ledge. In the minute that he could hold his weight on the top, Tilu could make out nothing in the darkness beyond. Then he heard frantic footsteps behind him and clumsily dropped to the street on all fours.

Bhoga's slippers were thudding violently on the streets. He was running as fast as he could towards Tilu. 'Syaar, run, bnara, run,' he yelled. 'Fucking Nandankanan is on fucking fire.'

Tilu didn't dare get up. Behind Bhoga, a raging fire was climbing up to the sky, blazing up the dark highway. He crawled desperately towards the car, scrabbling on his hands and feet. Bhoga covered the last few metres at a crazed pace and dragged Tilu by the scruff of his shirt behind the car.

He tried talking before he had caught his breath, 'Shit is going down, boss. Uff, my god.'

'What happened?' Tilu asked, adjusting his glasses on his nose. 'Fucking terrorists, boss. They set a car on fire.'

'Terrorists?' Tilu's heart nearly stopped.

'Figure of speech, figure of speech. They're all these followers of this Babaji. This Maharaj or something. Hah, they're not followers, more like his army.'

'Stop shouting,' Tilu hissed. 'Do you want to die here?'

'Sorry, sorry,' Bhoga said. 'Some woman ... who lives in there ... has written a letter to the media, boss. Says that this Babaji uses them for rape purposes, syaar. The whole world thinks they are holy women, serving their Maharaj. Those people outside are now going crazy, syaar. They say the media will be here soon, and the police too. They say Maharaj is running a sex ring.'

Tilu tried to make sense of the information. 'What's going to happen now?' he asked, hoping that Bhoga would not hear the heart-stopping fear in his voice.

Bhoga shook his head, 'I don't know, syaar. Things are pretty bad over there. Some of the girls' families have arrived; they say Maharaj has had people murdered when they threatened to take the girls away. All the guards and those locals out there are on patrol. They say Maharaj is their god and whoever says these dirty things about him is insulting Hindus and they will kill any man. They hit a boy with cricket bats, syaar, I didn't see him get back up.'

'What are we going to do now, Bhoga?'

Bhoga looked around them. 'They're busy now, syaar. Let's take the van and drive around, see if we can get inside and rescue boudi.'

Tilu agreed. It was better than cowering behind this rundown van, doing nothing.

Bhoga drove slowly around the perimeter of the enclosure. The crowd at the entrance was growing bigger by the hour. Bhoga backed up the car, merging into the oncoming traffic on the highway, away from the suspicious glare of the armed guards who were now front and centre.

On their second round, a tall, burly man flanked by young men holding cricket bats waved at them to stop. Bhoga slowed the car. Tilu looked at him, shocked beyond words. 'What are you doing?' he squeaked. Tilu thought he'd be lucky to be alive at the end of this mad night and here Bhoga was slowing down to oblige his future murderer. 'Ah syaar, it will look suspicious if we don't stop. Just let me do the talking.'

The burly man walked to Bhoga's side of the car. 'What's going on? Where are you going?'

Bhoga put on an expression of imbecilic innocence. 'Oh syaar, just taking my jamaibabu to our house, syaar, for Jamaishoshti.'

The man frowned, looked between Tilu and Bhoga and

said, 'What Jamaishoshti? Is this the month for Jamaishoshti, you fool?'

Bhoga allowed his face to contort into terminal confusion. The man gave them the once-over, and then waved them away, ready to flag down the car behind theirs.

Bhoga winked at Tilu, who could still hear his heart pounding in his throat. 'See? I can act, no problem.' He blew a kiss at the mirror.

'Let's just try to find Lalee,' Tilu said, looking for his handkerchief in his empty pockets, praying to any gods that might be listening that he would somehow leave here alive and with Lalee by his side.

# 41

LALEE'S HANDS WERE AROUND ONE GIRL. THE OTHER SLUNK close to her body, folding herself in half, slouching with one fist under her chin. The evening wasn't gone yet, laying its thick layers of grey and blue against the sky, fighting against the yellow of the halogen lamps. The chants from the evening aarti drifted into their room. From here, Lalee could pretend they were as unreal as the title song of a long-standing TV serial drifting from the neighbour's window. She didn't want to think of that man, the strange unguent smell of alcohol and body odour and incense festering in a sea of rotten flowers and worship. The sweating of dusty bodies, cajoling, banging together like cymbals for prayers given and, in the man, the stink of prayers received, the filth of such power, such belief. Her face pressed, squashed against the hard wood of a headboard, forced, until there were no more breaths to be taken.

'In a land far, far away …' Lalee was telling a story. 'There was a princess, all alone in the world. And in another place there were the brave brothers, one wearing red and the other in blue. Lifelong friends, in search of an adventure, of monsters to find and kill.

'The brothers set off to find the princess, travelling to the land of the monsters. They journeyed through the forest of enchantments, the land of the cannibals and arrived at a strange land. Everything was calm, and a golden light fell on all but the land was sleeping, under a spell.

'With them they had a silver wand and a golden wand. One would wake, the other would enchant into a deep sleep. In front of them was the stolen princess, sleeping the sleep of the dead. One brother said let's try the silver wand, the other brother said the golden, but already there were footsteps in the distance. The distant thudding of something that comes with warning, but no time. The monster was big, he covered the sky, loomed like monsoon, like thunder before you could see the lightning. He was that inevitable thing.'

'Who'll come to save us?' asked one of the twins and Lalee thought: *Who indeed?* It was a good thought: someone on their way, coming to save them, an army of the righteous marching behind. It was also incredibly frustrating. Waiting to be rescued. Leaving her fate in the hands of the imbeciles, the obtuse, the hesitant, and all without the benefit of the enchantment that knocked you out, pushed you into the land of the oblivious, in limbo, stretched like a dream between life and unlife.

'We're doing it our way,' Lalee whispered in their ears. 'Don't tell anyone.'

'Where will we go? When we get out of here?' Durga asked.

Lalee could remember, and invent when she couldn't. The stories always stopped at the rescue, at the marriage, but where did they go, the rescued? What would Lalee tell them? About the jail-like rehabilitation centres with their Singer sewing machines where they taught you to sew petticoats for ₹25, or some other fantasy of the rescued. Another land, the contours of which were misty, half visible through the cloud of the possible.

'No, you must have somewhere to go, when and if we choose to go,' Lalee whispered in their ears. One was sleeping, the other looked up at her. Her large, liquid eyes shining in the sharp, focusing dusk that underlined things one would miss in the broad noonday sun.

Lalee had known a home, within the plastered walls of Shonagachhi. In the home of sorts that Shefali Madam had given her. A home that was more home than the one that she had been born into. Where was that other home, a memory of something she had known a very long time ago, something that would have existed, but doesn't anymore? Because things in your head are not real, like memories and cobwebs. One must not get too close, if only to preserve. So many – an innumerable number of them – chose to stay, because there was nowhere else to go, because the home you knew was the only home you had.

*The stare of a child is a test,* Lalee thought. You can lie, you can invent, faster than you would with adults. Lalee reached out to a fantasy, a certain kind of possible that lay right behind the hopes and the fears and the freedoms of now.

'It is not visible now, but there is a place out of here. If you close your eyes, you can see it. It's right there, just a little way in the distance.'

A lie and a truth. But it was hard not to believe the lies when two small, warm bodies snaked around her, warming her back to something Lalee wasn't prepared for.

When Sonia hurried into the room and didn't stop to turn on the light switches, Lalee knew that the time had come. She clutched both girls, gripping their arms so tight that Durga let out a soft whimper. Sonia looked around the room frantically, until she saw the silhouette of Lalee's head and the halo of escaped hair around it. Lalee was sitting in a corner, the two girls lifting up their eyes at Sonia.

Sonia took one look at her, paused for a moment and came to stand in front of her, looking down at Lalee's slightly turned, bowed head. 'We need to go,' she said in an urgent whisper.

Lalee didn't move. Her whole body stiffened, her hands tensed their grip on the girls. 'We don't have a lot of time, Lalee; get a fucking move on,' Sonia whispered. The inertia Lalee had felt all day, the engulfing helplessness, was replaced with rage. It burned through her throat like hot steel, and sat in her stomach smouldering, coursing down her spine. She jerked herself upwards, twisted her long, dishevelled hair into a bun and said, 'Okay, what are you planning to do?'

Lalee followed behind Sonia, sometimes running to keep up with her. Their room was in a long corridor behind the quarters where the sevikas lived. None of them could be seen now. The lights were turned off, but the tall lamps around the courtyard painted their path in light and shade. 'Where are you going?' Lalee hissed at Sonia's back, irritated with her silence. Sonia stopped suddenly, Lalee almost colliding into her. Sonia put an arm out, signalling Lalee to stop. They slid behind a column, hiding in its shade. A couple of armed guards raced across the path in front of them, briefly illuminated by the light above them. Once they had left, Sonia poked her head out and scanned the way ahead. 'Lalee placed a hand firmly on Sonia's hand. Sonia looked up at her; Lalee shook her head. 'You need to tell me now. I'm not following after you like some dog,' she whispered. Sonia sighed, 'You have the worst timing, you know that?'

Lalee didn't reply, and she didn't take her eyes off Sonia. 'Okay, here is the short version,' said Sonia. 'One of the girls here, the ones in white they call savakees—'

'Sevikas,' Lalee corrected.

'Yeah, those. One of them wrote a letter to some minister, a tell-all letter. About what's happening here, how they have been treated. Look,' Sonia said slowly. 'This has been happening for a long time. Your NGOs know all about it. They've been waiting for this, they have their informers inside. Today your police is here to raid this place. This is our opportunity to do what we came to do. I don't have time to explain this Lalee, now can you just do as I say?'

Lalee stepped away from Sonia, uncertain. 'Can't do a job for free now, can you? It's time for you to get paid,' Sonia said and smiled at Lalee, her light eyes sparkling in the reflected light of the lamps. 'I know where that bastard keeps some cash. If we are going to get out, now is the time. You've made us waste enough time already; now can you just come along?' Sonia moved like a big cat, guiding Lalee through long corridors and stairs.

She entered a dark room. Lalee stood behind the door, holding the two girls on either side while Sonia rifled through the cabinets and furniture by the light of her phone. Footsteps rang through the grounds outside, loud in the eerie silence. Lalee could hear the uproar, the shouts coming from a long way away, while inside the compound there was only the occasional thump of footsteps. Lalee could hear her heart beating louder with each approaching footstep. She looked at Sonia, still rifling through the room, oblivious or unconcerned. She wanted to shout, to warn Sonia. Her mouth was open but no sound came out. As quickly as it came, the sounds outside subsided, fading into the distance, replaced with the sound of Lalee's shallow, rasping breath and, she realized, with the shaking of the two girls she held next to her. With her heart still in her mouth, Lalee found herself wondering how deeply Sonia was involved, and more importantly, where her loyalties lay. And what Sonia would sacrifice when push came to shove.

'It's not here. Come on,' Sonia whispered, gesturing Lalee to follow her. Running behind her once more, still holding Durga and Lakshmi who struggled to keep up with the pace, Lalee realized this wasn't only about the escape. Sonia was looking for something. Sonia was going to steal from these people. From Maharaj.

Sonia stopped outside a pair of large doors. Lalee recognized the polished woodwork, with its raised om patterns. She had spent the better part of one harrowing night staring at this woodwork. Lalee could hear her heart racing. She felt sure that if there was any treasure lying beyond those doors, Maharaj or his henchmen would not have left it unattended. Sonia was smiling. She turned towards Lalee, and the look on her face sent a shiver down Lalee's spine. In that second, Lalee wondered if this was a trap of some kind, if in some way she was the sacrifice, the twist at the end of the tale. Sonia put a hand in her pocket and pulled out a shiny metal object that glinted in the moonlight. It took a moment for Lalee to notice that it was a large key, not a knife. She let out a sigh of relief, more loudly than she had intended to. Sonia flashed her a look of annoyance and warning, putting a finger on her lips. The four of them stood still, barely breathing, trying to fade into the shadows cast by the large columns outside Maharaj's chambers. When the cries from the distant ends of the field had once again dissipated into the night air, Sonia turned the key in the lock. The door swung back, screeching faintly. The small noise evaporated into the air outside. Then Sonia stepped inside.

Lalee stood on the doorstep, The small, wooden doorsill felt like a mountain. There was no other sound in the world but the sharp ringing in her ears; nothing else to see but the large bed in front of her and the phantasm of her body being crushed by another. A hand held her's, gently, bringing her back to the moment. She looked down to see Durga's face looking up at her. Lalee stared at her face blankly, breathed out, and then stepped inside.

It was dark. One lone red bulb was glowing softly over a large altar in the corner of the room, lighting a large, golden statue of Ganesh. Lalee looked around herself, panicking, and could not believe that the room was unoccupied, especially now that Sonia was wrecking havoc, turning the room upside down, looking for something. She peered into the shadows, imagining spectral shapes in the darkness. She saw Sonia step over something large and dark. When she tried to look more closely, her heart stopped. A pair of legs lay sprawled on the floor, the torso hidden behind a large couch. Even in the gloom, Lalee knew that the thing on the floor was no longer a person, but a body. A dark splotch of liquid pooled around it. Lalee had never seen blood under red lights. The viscous, dark clumps on the floor didn't look like anything that could have come from a human body. She felt herself slip, and caught herself against the wall and looked down at her feet to see the long tread marks she'd left in the blood. Sonia moved on unperturbed, patting down drapes and looking under drawers around the altar. *She couldn't have missed it, could she?* Lalee wondered. She inched closer towards Sonia, keeping her eyes trained on the corpse, expecting it to move at any moment. Sonia pointed towards the door, signalling Lalee to keep an eye out. Lalee looked between the body, the door and Sonia, unable to decide which of them she should watch over. Beyond the small glow of light where Sonia was frantically looking through the drawers, Lalee noticed a dark shape, coming closer towards Sonia. The beginnings of a scream formed in her throat, and then she saw Rambo's face in the red light. The second stretched for what felt like an eternity, Lalee stood stock-still, unable to move or scream, waiting for something to happen. Rambo lowered his hand. He was holding something – something heavy and small. Lalee recognized it for what it was, even though she had never seen a gun before.

Rambo put his hand over his eyes and wiped his forehead. Sonia looked up at him and hissed, 'Where is it?' A flash of anger crossed Rambo's face, and Lalee's eyes flicked to the gun clenched in his hand. Rambo leaned close to Sonia and said, 'I've done my job,' and nodded his head towards the dead body on the floor. 'It's my head on the line now and time for you to do what you were supposed to do.' Sonia did not pause.

Her fingers rummaged through the idols on the altar, upturning gods and scattering flowers. 'My head is on the line as well. It's here somewhere. Where are the girls?' Sonia asked. Lalee felt a sudden panic in her chest. In all the madness, she had lost sight of Durga and Lakshmi. She felt a strong need to run away from here, find the two girls and keep them safe. A loud thud made Lalee turn back towards Sonia and Rambo. The golden Ganesh was lying on the floor, broken into smithereens. In the dim light, the statue looked solid, as if it was made of brass or some other metallic alloy, but now, it had shattered onto the floor like glass. Among the broken pieces, small bars of gold lay scattered on the floor. For a moment both Rambo and Sonia stared at them. A small sound escaped Sonia's lips. Rambo sat down on the floor, gathering as many bars as he could. Sonia was not far behind. But Lalee found herself unable to move. The two of them did not seem to realize that other people could have heard the loud thud. Lalee moved to the door and stood there like a sentinel. Sonia unfolded a small backpack from the band of her trousers. She began to put the gold bars inside it. Then she took a small bag out and filled it with more bars and threw it at Lalee. Lalee missed, unprepared. The bag landed on the floor. 'Your share,' Sonia said, and began gathering the rest. Rambo's hands moved snakelike and held Sonia's in place. 'I didn't do this for small returns, bitch,' he hissed. For a moment, Lalee waited for the inevitable fallout. But the uproar that had been in the background was crashing into the room. Both Rambo and Sonia stopped arguing. The sound of chaos increased. Screams and yells began to draw closer. Sonia stood up and jerked Lalee by the hand. 'Meet me at the spot with the girls,' Sonia said to Rambo who was still scrambling on the floor, looking under the couch and corners. He did not reply and Sonia did not wait. Sonia and Lalee began to run. Lalee could see a group of armed guards ferrying a few women in the distance, coming towards the women's quarters, where Lalee had so recently lived. The women's white sarees looked yellow in the lamplight.

Lalee ran as fast as she could. The compound, with its endless trees, stretched out as far as she could see. She felt certain that she wouldn't reach the end of the compound where the tall walls stood between her and the highway. Sounds of footfalls echoed behind her and still she did not turn her head around. Maybe the sounds were in her head, or maybe she would feel a bullet fly through her soon, and she would stop. Lalee didn't care anymore. If there were people behind her, she would rather take the bullet. What scared her more was a pair of hands clutching on to her, was it Durga or Lakshmi? Lalee didn't dare to look behind her. The small hands that held on to her filled her with dread – both for herself and for them. Hands that could drag her back to those rooms, push her into the ground, never to get back up again. She ran, seeing nothing in front but hazy points of light, blinking in the distance, moving up and down with the rhythm of her body thudding down on the ground.

She couldn't see Sonia in the distance. Lalee knew that Sonia was somewhere out there, probably being more careful than her, negotiating her way more cleverly, with more cunning than Lalee ever could muster. She clutched the small cloth bag to her chest. Lalee reached a thicket of trees, stretching from a dark circle all the way to the compound wall. A hand from the darkness shot out and grabbed Lalee around the waist.

Before the shriek could come out of her throat, Sonia's long, bony arm clapped across her mouth, nearly choking Lalee. 'Shut up, shut up,' Sonia whispered into Lalee's ears. 'Stop huffing like a horse,' Sonia held her until Lalee calmed down. 'Where's the money?' Sonia hissed. Lalee held up her hand in front of Sonia's face, the cloth bag clenched in her fist. Then, she moved the bag away, hiding it behind her back. Sonia did not comment. She tried to listen for approaching footsteps. Beyond the walls, a conflagration was rising. It was close enough to see, blazing through the shouts of the rioters and the screeching of car tires.

Sonia said quietly, 'Wait a bit; it's not safe now.' Her voice seemed too loud. Lalee peeked out from her hiding place to scan the compound. 'What now?' Lalee said, without looking at Sonia. There was no reply. When Lalee looked back, Sonia's face was full of concern. 'That damn Rambo was supposed to be here.' Lalee couldn't hold it back any more, 'What's happening? What have you and Rambo done?' Sonia replied, in a tight, low voice, 'This is not the time,' and Lalee knew that was all she would get from her. The answers would have to wait. After a minute, Sonia clenched her fist and punched the tree trunk next to her. 'Fuck this, I can't keep waiting for that dumb shit. There's no time to waste. If they find us …' she trailed off. Lalee did not stop to imagine what consequences waited for them. Sonia was looking around as Lalee came and stood next to her. 'Where are the girls? I thought they were with you,' Lalee said, panic rising in her voice, making it loud. Sonia looked in the distance and silenced Lalee. 'Keep that bag safe,' Sonia said, still eyeing the wall and the trees. 'Maybe Rambo has the girls. He'll meet us here. Give it a few more minutes,'

Sonia added, placing a hand on Lalee's shoulders. 'What was your plan exactly?' Lalee asked. Sonia sighed, 'At this point, there isn't one.' Both of them heard the sound of someone approaching fast. Instinctively, they both shrank behind the shadows. Lalee crouched behind a thick trunk while Sonia stood stock-still. Durga stopped a few yards before them, bent over with her hands on her knees and breathed huge gulps of air. Lalee could hear stray shouts and voices getting louder. A few pinpoints of lights – flashlights by the look of them – began zigzagging through the dark trees. Durga looked up at the darkness and the tall walls around them with panic and fear on her face. Lalee shot out of the trees, 'Durga, Durga, this way, here.'

Sonia cursed behind her. 'Come on,' she hissed, even though Lalee's yell had alerted their pursuers. Both Lalee and Durga were now racing back, following Sonia's voice and searching for her in the shadows. She was halfway up a tree, looking for handy branches that she could use to reach the edge of the wall. Lalee and Durga followed, scrambling up nearby trees as fast as they could, while the mob got closer and closer behind them.

'Quick,' Sonia yelled now, pointed at Durga and said, 'jump!' Both Lalee and Durga stared at her and then at the people behind. They could make out faces now. It would take a few minutes for them to catch up. All three of them jumped the wall, one after the other. Lalee held the bag with the money with her left hand. When she landed on the hard, dusty earth on the other side, she couldn't break her fall. Even with the panic and the adrenaline, a sharp pain shot through her wrist. Sonia's tall form was already racing across the highway, disregarding an oncoming truck and escaping it by inches. Lalee looked to her right and saw a car burning. Men with saffron bands tied around their foreheads were screaming in the distance. It was dark, devoid of street lights where they landed. Durga, Lalee noticed, had begun to whimper. But this wasn't the time for tears. If one of those men hunting them through the compound or that faceless, dark mob behind them on the streets were to find them, they would forfeit more than their lives. Lalee placed a hand on Durga's shoulders, urging her gently back towards Lalee. Durga's whimper slowly turned into convulsive sobs. 'Look to your side,' Sonia almost shouted. 'Look at them – do you see them? Those are swords in their hands. What do you think they will do if they find us?' Durga turned her red, blotchy eyes towards Lalee. It was the face of someone who had lost everything. 'My sister,' Durga whimpered, 'she went to find Rambo when we lost you. My sister is still in there.' Durga crawled back to the wall and scratched at it, trying to gain purchase on its surface. Lalee almost jumped on her, dragging her back with both arms. Durga shouted, screamed, strained against Lalee with her bony, malnourished arms. Lalee looked around sure that the men around them had heard the nerve-racked girl. She pulled on Durga with all her strength, the twisted wrist singeing from pain. Lalee almost hauled Durga across the road, praying that they would go unnoticed. One chance at freedom, one chance is all she asked for.

On the other side of the road, Lalee dragged a howling Durga as far as she could through thorny bushes and bristling undergrowth. Sonia stepped out from her hiding spot against a boulder. Lalee let go of Durga, wheezing. She crouched on the earth, trying to steady her fast-beating heart. Durga was whimpering softly on the ground next to her. Her sobs pierced Lalee's mind, bringing back dark memories of women crying, ritually grieving at the cremation grounds in her old village. 'We have to keep moving,' Sonia said and Lalee watched, for the first time, as naked fear cracked Sonia's perfect face. 'They know we're not there, whether or not they found out about ... the other thing.' Lalee didn't know what she meant until she looked at the cloth bag still clenched in her fist. She pushed herself up, calling Durga's name over and over again, urging her to get up. Sonia began walking through the undergrowth, stomping on dry leaves and stepping on twigs. Lalee followed her blindly, watching her like a beacon, like a will-o-wisp. Durga's sobs went on like they would never touch the bottom of her loss. Lalee walked with Durga's hand clenched tightly in her fist. She could hear footsteps and screams from the mob still chasing behind them, though she could not tell anymore if they were just in her mind, men with swords and flashlights forever chasing behind her.

When they reached the end of the badlands, Durga had quietened, following Lalee closely. Lalee felt a lifetime's worth of exhaustion descend upon her. She wanted to sink down, lie on the bed of dead leaves and disappear into oblivion. But she knew it was still not safe. If she closed her eyes, she could still hear pursuing footsteps behind her. Sonia was quiet. Lalee asked, panting heavily, 'Where is Rambo?' Sonia did not reply. After a while, she slowed down and said, 'We need to get out of here.'

Sonia stood on the highway until she could flag down a truck. Lalee had heard several big vehicles pass by while she waited with Durga in the shadows. She watched as Sonia raised her hands, trying to catch their attention. A blonde, white woman on a deserted highway would get a lot of drivers to stop for her. And Lalee knew where that would get them. She hoped desperately that after everything, they could find safe passage.The truck that finally picked them up was being driven by an old, Sikh driver. In its back, the three of them huddled together, partially screened by large black tarpaulins. Lalee had only seen a glimpse of the driver's face in the sideview mirror as Sonia had hurried them into the truck. The commotion seemed to have died up a little. The truck driver may also have taken a longer, more circuitous route, saving them from the inevitable searches by Maharaj's militia. For a long time, all three of them kept quiet. Finally Sonia asked Lalee, 'Do you have somewhere to go?' Lalee nodded. 'That fat bitch, your madam, is neck deep in this. You go to Sonagazi, you're dead; go somewhere else.' Lalee nodded again, hugged her knees and sunk her face into the gap between them. Even in the blasted heat, Durga was shivering slightly from time to time. Lalee looked up at her and sank back again. She'd have to find somewhere to go. In all her life she had dreamt of escaping, sometimes idly, sometimes with all she had got. But she never had to consider where she would go, where she could find refuge. When Lalee found herself out of Shonagachhi, walking in the city, she watched the windows of homes, especially in the evening. The tableaux of quotidian lives – lives she would never know, never live – displayed in these small squares, looked surreal to her. A woman in her kitchen, a TV screen airing the news, children at play or simply sitting at their desks staring at textbooks with drowsy eyes – the trickle of someone's humdrum, bromidic evenings. All those windows and doors in this sweltering, suffocated city and she had nowhere to go. Lalee looked at Durga. She was staring out, catatonic, through gaps in the tarpaulin. Here was someone else who had nowhere to go, someone who was a more valuable export, and a more hunted merchandise. Maybe Sonia was thinking the same thing. She said, 'I can take her. I know where she will be safe. You can come with me too, if you want.' Lalee turned to Sonia. This is the kindest Sonia had ever been to her, and still there was a bitterness to Sonia's invitation, as if she was doing something she didn't want to. Lalee shook her head. She didn't want to go with Sonia and she didn't want to leave Durga with her. But, people who have no beds to lie on don't invite guests.

'Where will you take her?' Lalee whispered.

'Your Deepa Madam, you trust her?' Lalee nodded her head.

Sonia looked at her and said, 'That's the best either of us can do.'

She felt the night air sweep over her head. The truck kept moving like a leviathan on empty streets.

# 42

THE ROOM WAS DARK. RAMBO SAT ON A CHAIR. IT WAS HARD and unyielding, and when Rambo tried to lean backwards, it didn't move an inch. *Must be a wooden chair, not the moulded-plastic variety*, he thought to himself. Rambo smiled, ignoring the wincing pain on his face, which was still swelling, unseen in the darkness. It didn't matter what he was sitting on. The man sitting opposite him was holding a gun. Rambo knew that instinctively, even though he could see almost nothing in the dark. He flexed his wrists, pushing against the thin nylon rope that was cutting into his skin. He struggled frantically, giving in to the rage he felt struggling against his restraints before calming down, breathed out and sagged further into the chair.

The manager cleared his throat. 'Open the windows,' he said. Rambo saw a darker figure move past him, walk to the edge of the room and open the window. A dim glow from the tall lights of the compound flowed in immediately. The madness of commotion on the outside was long gone, but a few spirited yells and sloganeering could still be heard.

Rambo sat up straighter, looked at the manager and tried to smile. 'Shouldn't you be out there? Managing the crisis?'

'There is no crisis to be managed.'

Rambo jerked his head towards the window.

'Hotheads and expendables,' the manager said. 'Meat of any good riot. Some of them will give their lives for Maharaj, and others come like flies whenever something goes down. Either way, there's no crisis. No one will get in here.'

Rambo smiled at him. He wanted to convey that this was all some kind of a mistake, warranting nothing more than a slap on the wrist. But instead he slipped against the manager's implacability in the half shadows of the strangely quiet room. Desperately, Rambo tried to provoke – he needed a reaction. He began to laugh, 'What about that letter that got out, eh? That girl, one of your Maharaj's sevikas who wrote to the president and put the CBI on your trail?' To Rambo's momentary amazement, the manager smiled back. He never imagined that the manager could smile.

'Everyone knows that,' he barked. 'She accused Maharaj of rape, sex trafficking, assault and kidnapping. But what did that accomplish? There's two police jeeps outside and five hundred loyal followers. They call themselves Maharaj's yoddhas. They'll kill every woman in this compound before they let anything happen to Maharaj. You don't understand religion, Maity. Maharaj is their god. And how can a god do wrong? '

Rambo was rocking back and forth on the chair. He could taste the blood pooling inside his mouth. A sudden panic gripped him. The men in the room looked on as he struggled against the straps. When he stopped, slumped forward and exhaled heavily, he noticed a spreading dampness around his crotch. The manager watched him.

'We didn't take you on because you are a good pimp, Maity.

We did so because you were too dumb to do anything other than what you're told. And here we are now.'

A tear rolled down Rambo's eye, without warning, instigated by a gut-wrenching fear he hadn't felt in years. Between spitting blood on the floor and blubbering out of pain, Rambo begged for his life. He only set out to make a little bit of money and he hadn't made a good plan. Sonia had, and all he had seen was an opportunity, a small windfall, a little bucket of water taken from a vast sea. He wanted to plead, to beg for mercy, now that all the bravado had been knocked out of him. But he couldn't find the words to explain any of this to the manager.

The manager laid the gun on his lap, took off his glasses and held them in one hand carelessly. Rambo felt his eyes being drawn to the glasses instead of the gun. *How odd*, he thought, he couldn't really believe he was going to die.

Rambo threw up on the floor. He stared at the pale-yellow puddle, horrified by the sight of it and the globs of blood that dotted it. He closed his eyes. Just before losing consciousness he heard the manager say, 'You'll find that white bitch for us, you'll find the money.'

# 43

TILU WISHED HE COULD SELL A KIDNEY AT THIS LATE HOUR, if that meant he would have a few notes in his pocket and that would buy him a pint of cholai or even bangla. He looked at his chappals; the right one had broken a strap. He would have to limp his way back home. He had gone on a rescue mission, and all he had to show for it was a broken sandal. He had never felt more like a man, more in charge, than when he had set forth with Bhoga to rescue Lalee, putting himself in the jaws of death. His short frame, his caved-in chest and his emaciated arms had expanded, buoyed by the sense of hope and immensity he had always craved but never quite achieved. The band of mongrels that guarded the mouth of his alley in the night had begun their duty. The leader of the pack, a mangy bitch with limpid eyes Tilu called Maagi, stood to a side and bowed her head, waving her tail, wanting to be petted. Tilu sat down on the road, touched the coarse fur of the dog, sinking his fingertips to the bony skull underneath. Maagi nuzzled him, pushing into him further. Tilu sat there for a while, breathing in the warmth of a creature that demanded nothing of him. A soundless wave of lightning flashed across the sky, its brightness dimmed by the day's smog. Tilu heard the thunder descend like the sound of a giant's spine cracking. He held the dog's head between his hands and looked her in the eyes, 'Maagi, a kalboishakhi is coming. You and your friends be safe tonight.' Maagi looked at him with her baleful brown eyes, glowing in the reflected light of the street lamps. She breathed out, filling Tilu's world with her scent, shook her body and tottered off in the opposite direction, her pack following behind her.

Tilu gathered his broken slipper and walked barefoot the rest of the way.

As is its wont, the sudden monsoon showers descended upon Tilu without warning. He stood, getting drenched to the bones in seconds. He turned his face up to the sky. If he walked a few steps ahead and rounded a corner, he would be home. Shelter was near, but he didn't want to move. He waited under the deluge, watching the swaying electrical and telephone wires, imagining them to be tall coconut and palm trees, dripping on him, finally soaking in the rain a whole city was waiting for, breathless in the muggy heat of summer. Tilu started walking slowly, holding on to his slippers in the hope they could be mended one more time.

On the concrete slab that bridged the gap between his doorstep and the small open sewer that ran in front of it, Lalee was sitting, hugging her knees, her hair plastered around her face and her saree clinging on to her body. Tilu felt certain he was dreaming. He could have accepted that if he had a drop of alcohol in his blood – and he keenly wished that he had – but even an empty stomach could cause a hallucination, he knew. This Lalee in front of him, outside his house, must be a mirage; he had thought about her so hard that he had willed her into existence. He walked towards her, approaching with the delicacy necessary to sustain the dream, and fearing that the rain would wash her away. Lalee looked up at him without a word and Tilu sat down beside her, wondering if he was allowed to touch a projection of his overheated, love-infested brain.

Upstairs, in the room and the half-corridor he had inherited, Lalee seemed more real, spreading herself as the water fell off her, flooding Tilu's narrow, squalid world. Tilu watched transfixed as Lalee wiped the rainwater off her hair, her bruised dark skin, the length of her body. Dressed in one of his old shirts, Lalee asked, 'Do you want some tea?'

Tilu couldn't believe a figment of his imagination would make him tea. Lalee caught him staring at her, she smiled, and Tilu was destroyed. He followed her to the corridor, where the tarpaulin was waging a losing war against the twin onslaughts of rain and wind. Lalee managed to light the kerosene stove, find the tea and sugar among the battered, oil-stained containers and made the tea. Tilu thanked the gods when he realized that the small 500 ml pouch of Mother Dairy milk he had bought a day before had not gone bad. Lalee handed him a steaming cup. Tilu encircled its warmth in his callused fingers, sliding closer to Lalee until their shoulders touched. They sat in the shaded corner of his makeshift kitchenette, partially sheltered by the heroic tarpaulin, on its last legs now, threatening to collapse any second, leaving them at the mercy of the elements.

They watched the lights of the billboard displaying the mattress ad flash on and off, the svelte woman still inviting any willing spectator into her warm embrace. Lalee extended her hand towards his, still warm from the steaming tea. Tilu grasped it before she could disappear, holding on to her fingers for dear life. The lady on the mattress flickered amidst lashings of rain, wind and the occasional flash of lightning, until the lights finally went out in an abrupt power cut. 'Fucking load-shedding,' Tilu muttered, trying to get up to find some candles and matches.

Lalee gripped his fingers, refusing to let go. Tilu sat back down. 'The stars will come out soon,' she whispered. Tilu knew they wouldn't. Not with the wind and the thunder growling as they did. That fantasy mattress with the attractive lady was all the stars they were going to get that night, but they sat there all the same, spending half the night watching the rain, shivering as its scattering droplets misted their clothes and soaked them all over again.

In his narrow bed, lying side by side with Lalee, Tilu smiled to himself. He slept peacefully, undreaming, through his long night of warmth, entangled limbs and the rain still whispering through the open, dark windows.

*Once loved is always loved*, Tilu Shau thought, and felt really quite pleased with himself. He felt he had got to the bottom of it – this whole roiling mess of whatever it is everyone was always going on about. Love was love, and it had miraculously remained unchanged through the strange madness of getting to this point.

People loved in the age of the radio and the telegram; his own father had wooed his mother across a distance, and now people loved in the age of smartphones and the internet. Tilu hadn't done any of this, but he knew in the sweltering bog of his heart that all love was big, large, flashing capital letters on a red neon sign. It felt the same, in song and dance and writing – the eternal wait and the indescribable union.

Sometimes he heard the songs. And they seemed to say: yes this is it, this is exactly what it feels like. The words may change but this is the soul and centre of it.

Sometimes he was afraid that this was the end of the road, that he would never feel love like this ever again. It felt like a small death. He had once heard a very learned man say that the French called every orgasm a small death, but Tilu Shau knew in his bare bones that when push came to shove, love was bare-knuckled. Unless you died a little bit a hundred times over, it really wasn't love.

When Lalee touched him, Tilu felt the overwhelming surge of an ocean just waiting to drown him. He was left speechless with a touch. If he had dared open his mouth or tried to put it into words, that huge surge would engulf him, drown him, leave nothing of him. On balance, Tilu thought, Lalee was almost negligible. She was drowned out by his love for her. It didn't matter how she reciprocated, or even if she did, because no one could take his love away from him, not even Lalee. She had been loved, that is how she would remain – always loved.

What kind of love negates the beloved, Tilu wondered. His well-trained heart said all of them. It negated even him, until there was no one doing the loving. In a strange little corner of his soul, a place that was alien to him, he felt incredibly lucky to have even known such a kind of love. How many people had been born, worked jobs, sired children, died without ever knowing that kind of obliteration? Tilu sighed; he could dissect how he felt all day long. He could close his eyes and feel the shape of that great wave of annihilation lurking behind his sense of self, waiting for a moment's distraction to descend upon him. But he still had to reach Lalee, to find her, to touch her one more time, even if it meant that nothing of him would remain in the ensuing deluge. *Once loved is always loved*, Tilu whispered to himself, like a chant.

Without saying anything, he took her hands and held them tightly. For a long time Lalee didn't look up but buried her face between her knees. He kissed her arms. Starting with the wrists and her forearm, till he reached her damp forehead, her distorted face and drew her closer into himself. He held her as she cried.

They sat side by side on the bed in the dark. The moon had climbed far above Tilu's small grime-encrusted window. Droplets of rain fell under the light of the halogen street lamps, each of them distinct, beautiful. Tilu felt he was in a movie; this was everything he knew about love. The madman who lived at the end of the street sang a song. He sounded happy, and completely out of tune. Tilu turned towards Lalee and put his hands around her shoulders, making her look directly into his face. Lalee saw that Tilu was teary. He said with a catch in his throat, 'Marry me. I don't have much but whatever I have, whatever I am, it is yours if you choose. There is nothing I won't do for you.' Tilu's voice cracked in the end, a lump in his throat pushing down on his heart, blocking any words, any breath that might escape.

After a few long seconds, Lalee broke into bubbling laughter. It started with an odd gurgle and became in no time at all a full, unstoppable giggle.

Tilu was staring at her with his mouth slightly open, his jaw dropped a few inches at Lalee's sudden unfettered mirth. Lalee had to wipe her eyes before she could reply, 'Why?' she asked. 'Why do you men think marriage is the solution to love?'

'I wasn't trying to solve anything,' Tilu said in an offended tone. 'I *want* to marry you,' he said, in defence of himself.

'Then my answer is no, Tilu,' Lalee said. 'Don't look at me like that. This is no tragedy.'

She took his limp hand in hers, 'You've been good to me. I ...' she stopped for a bit before continuing, 'but I've not been good to you, and I am touched by your offer, but you see,' she looked into his eyes, 'there's no need for us to get married. And I don't think it is wise.'

Tilu failed to say anything but Lalee spoke again, 'Now, would you like to come with me? I need to get out of that place, but I have some things to do before I go.'

'Can you stay a little while longer?'

Lalee didn't say anything. She stared at the billboard outside the window. She could, she thought to herself. 'Yes,' she whispered.

'We will have a picnic tomorrow,' Tilu told her, staring at the same billboard. 'We will watch a movie, walk in the park and then eat at a restaurant,' he said like a man in a dream. He'd go anywhere with Lalee, walk with her hand in hand, look proud and anxious in an air-conditioned, dimly lit Chinese restaurant. When the grumpy waiter would be quietly rude to him, he'd tip him extravagantly, and walk out the door with his arm around Lalee's shoulders.

'You know, after all these years in this place I've never even seen the Victoria Memorial,' Lalee said.

'You must see it. It is a great piece of our history. They close at six. After nightfall, it's only drug dealers, pimps and …' Tilu stopped.

'And prostitutes,' Lalee finished the sentence.

'I have seen those places from the outside,' Lalee said, a hint of childish excitement in her voice. 'It looks nice – all the people in Chowringhee and New Market. When the bus goes on the flyover, you can see the Maidan, the white dome of the Victoria Memorial with the fairy on top … you can see it all.'

'The fairy used to turn, revolve on the top at one point in time.'

'What happened to it?'

Tilu shrugged, 'Disrepair, or maybe she decided that it wasn't worth the trouble,' he smiled.

'Did you see it turn?'

'Yes, when I was a boy. My father took me, sometimes. On Independence Day and Republic Day we rode horse carriages, ate peanuts and roasted chickpeas and played football. This was when my mother was still alive,' he paused. 'Shall we go?'

'Yes.'

'I have to tell you,' Tilu said with some hesitation, 'I don't have much money.' He was struggling to find the words. 'I mean … I had some, but ... ah, it's gone now.'

Lalee looked at his face, the anxious eyes, the frown, the small, pinched face forever worried about its own insignificance in an uncaring, vastly complex universe.

'Don't worry about money. I can take care of that.'

Tilu added quickly, 'No, no, I have some money, but I don't think I can take you to a restaurant or anything … I just thought you should know.'

Lalee smiled, and let Tilu worry for a moment. 'Who made Victoria Memorial?' she asked, turning on her side, pulling the covers close to her chin to protect herself from the slightly chilly, rain-soaked breeze flowing about the room.

'That's a fascinating story,' said Tilu. And then he told it to her.

# 44

MALINI WAS WALKING AS FAST AS SHE COULD FROM THE Collective's office room towards The Blue Lotus. Chanda was standing outside comforting a crying girl. Malini opened the door and walked in. Some men she hadn't seen before and Shefali Madam's old servant were readying a small van.

She walked up to the pair of girls and asked, 'What happened?'

'Amina killed herself,' Chanda said in a stage whisper.

Malini stared at her, uncomprehending. Chanda repeated herself. There was sorrow in the way she relayed the news, but also an edge of thrill that disturbed Malini. Completely startled out of her morning stupor, Malini took a few seconds to steady herself. 'How?' she asked, as she felt her head spin a bit. She had been on the verge of mentioning that she had talked to Amina the night before.

'She took sleeping pills – Madam found her in the morning.'

Malini didn't believe her. She caught herself just in time before challenging Chanda. The target of her ire, here and now, would have been Chanda, and all she could be faulted for was a macabre glee. Malini wanted to save her rage, to channel it, when the time came. 'Where is she?' she asked. 'Let me take a look.'

'They're just bringing her out. They'll take her straight to the ghat to be cremated,' Chanda added with some surprise, 'I didn't know you were friends.'

'I don't need to be her friend,' Malini yelled, frying Chanda in her stare. 'She was one of us.' Chanda made a face.

As she made a move to enter the house, Malini saw the men bring out the body. Malini noted that Chintu was nowhere to be seen. In lieu of a stretcher, the men used a large white bedsheet. The weight of the dead girl rocked the sheet, moving slightly as it was carried down the stairs.

Malini stood with her arms crossed, next to the women who lined the stairs, staring at Amina's face as long as she could see it. The bloodless, swollen face hollowed her out from the inside in a way that no amount of carnage or battery could. The casual ignominy, the mundane indifference with which this skinny, underfed girl had quietly died and the way she was being disposed of – as if the brothel was being spring-cleaned.

Amina's eyes were closed. Malini thought that whoever came up with the description of dead people looking peaceful had either been very fortunate or had never seen any dead bodies. Then she noticed the marks on her wrists. Her left hand was lying limply to one side while her right lay across her chest. Malini noticed that deep purple welts circled her wrist like bracelets. She followed the body outside and tried to see the girl's other hand. As she bent down to touch the body, Chanda croaked from behind, 'Arrey, what are you doing? Don't touch it. Or you have to go and take a dip in the Ganga. Don't you know the rules?'

Malini looked at her and said, 'Why are her wrists like this? What happened?'

'Don't know. Maybe she hurt herself?'

'That's not possible' mumbled Malini. 'And you can't take sleeping pills with your wrists tied together. Chanda,' Malini said, deliberately touching the body, 'who slept next to her? I know you girls have to share rooms up there.'

'She had her own room. Madam told us that she was sleeping and no one was to disturb her.'

Nothing about this felt right to Malini. She had spoken to the girl less than twelve hours ago, and though she didn't seem to be doing well, she didn't sound like she was going to kill herself either.

The men began to wrap Amina in the white sheet; a few stray sticks of tuberoses adorned the head of the bed frame. Lengths of twine tied her body to the skeletal ribs of the bed, going in and out of the wooden slats, securing her in place. The shroud covered her up to the neck so all that was visible of Amina was her discontented, swollen face. 'Get off the van, we have to go now,' one of the men spat out at Malini without any ceremony.

'Where are you taking her?' Malini asked, a frantic anxiety taking hold of her. 'This is a police case. You can't just burn her,' she yelled.

The men looked at her as if she had gone mad. Chanda and the weeping girl had heard her too. 'The police?' asked Chanda. 'What're they going to do? You want them to take her away and put her in the morgue and cut her open? What good will that do? And we won't get the body till midnight at least. No one will go to all that trouble,' she said. Then she came forward and took Malini's hand, 'Move away; let them take her. Let her have some peace.'

The metal doors of the van shut and the man at the wheel turned the engine on. Black smoke spat out of the exhaust pipe and covered the trio of women in a haze. Then Malini said, almost to herself, 'She was Muslim, wasn't she? Why are they cremating her?'

'It's easier,' Chanda said, looking at the van driving away, turning the corner to the main road. 'She had a Hindu babu. He left her years ago, but she used to wear sindoor and bangles; she always said she was his wife. It's what she would have wanted.' She said after a pause, 'Besides, I think you need a Mullah or someone to bury in the Muslim way. Who's going to do that? We don't have any here right now.' Chanda looked at Malini's blank, unseeing face, 'Come on now, she's better off wherever she is going. You and I have to get through the day.'

Malini moved away from Chanda and began walking towards The Blue Lotus. A few girls were gathered in the balcony, looking at the van that was driving away with Amina Bibi's body. Malini stopped when she saw Shefali Madam appear among them; she was dressed in a starched saree, her mouth full of paan. The two women stared at each other and then Shefali Madam looked away. She said something to the girls that Malini couldn't hear and one by one they disappeared inside. Madam glanced at Malini for a moment and followed her flock.

Malini walked back slowly to the office. She would have to call Deepa immediately. Things had not gone according to plan. She took out her cellphone, turned on the screen and then put it away. She had to do something before calling

Deepa. She went to the Collective's office and moved a steel cabinet slightly to its side. She took out the plastic packet with the two phones Amina had handed to her not twelve hours ago and put it in her bag.

Constable Biswas at the police kiosk on Sovabazar Road, right before it curved into Shonagachhi, was sipping his hot, milky tea when he saw a white van pass by. Since no one was chanting the lord's name in loud yells, as was the custom when carrying a dead body to its last Hindu rites, it would have been impossible for Biswas to know that a dead woman lay inside it. But the van had to stop for a full fifteen minutes at the traffic light, thanks to the early morning rush hour when all of the productive citizenry was trying to circumvent the laws of physics in a bid to reach their workplace under two hours.

Since the van stood motionless right outside his kiosk, Biswas could see the dead body wrapped in white quite plainly through the clear windows of the van. He hadn't thought much of it, until a few hours later when a freelance pimp of his acquaintance dropped in for a chat. He learned that a girl from The Blue Lotus had killed herself and they wondered idly if there was some kind of curse on the place.

Biswas said, 'This Shefali Madam of yours will be left pretty lonely if this goes on, eh? You never know, these unnatural deaths …' he shook his head gravely. 'They call to the others from the beyond.'

'Oh come on,' replied his informant, 'it's nothing out of the ordinary. These things happen once in a while.' He waved at a young boy hovering at a short distance with a kettle and a stack of clay cups. 'Another cup?' he asked Biswas. Handing him a steaming cup of tea, he took a sip from his own. 'If you ask me, my money's on Shefali Madam, Chintu and the girl's babu.'

'Hmm,' said Biswas, 'we're looking into it. Just yesterday Singh sir and Balok-da came over.'

'Yes, I heard,' the pimp yawned. 'Why are you bothering with it? It's going to die down soon, right? Oh you should have seen it yesterday,' he said, 'the whole place was milling with journalists and bystanders. It's bad for business, I'll tell you that much. Had a new john with me, saw the cameras and got spooked. People don't want to come here when they see police jeeps and TV channels.'

'It's just pointless raking of filth.' Biswas contorted his face in disgust. The pimp lit a cigarette and offered one to the constable. Puffing out a cloud of smoke, Biswas said, 'What are they going to do, eh? Stop it all? Every once in a while they'll rake up some shit or other. Fucking news channels.'

Once the pimp had departed, Biswas thought about this new information he had gathered and called a number, just to be on the safe side. 'Balok-da?' he said into the phone. 'It's Biswas, from the kiosk … looks like another girl from the same brothel died today … Yes, Shefali madam's house … I don't know … they're saying suicide … sleeping pills, apparently. I thought I'd let you know … they took her to the ghat about an hour ago, sorry … Sorry, I didn't think it mattered that much … Sorry, yes, yes, of course, I saw you and sir come here yesterday … No, I didn't stop then … I don't think so … I spoke to Bablu, the pimp – you know the guy? … Yes, he said there was no diary, no FIR; they didn't want to go through all that … Okay, okay. Thank you.'

And Biswas gazed out lazily at the still-struggling traffic, safe in the knowledge that he had done more than his duty for the day.

Balok Ghosh, on the other hand, replaced the receiver and sat for a moment in thought. Naskar, who was sitting across from him, pricking up his ears and eavesdropping on the fairly loud telephonic conversation, said, 'Another one, eh Balok-da? It's murder season up there, eh? What do you think?'

'I think that you talk too much and talk without thinking, Naskar, that's what I think.' Balok Ghosh said with a sour face. 'If you want to amount to anything, especially in this job, you'll do well to keep your mouth shut.'

Reprimanded, Naskar went on the defensive, 'What did I say? You were saying the same thing on the phone. I heard you.'

'I never said "murder", did I? It's suicide. Learn the difference; it'll serve you well in the future. Do you know what murder means?'

'Yes, a lot of fucking bother,' Naskar said sulkily.

'Exactly. Which is why it's useful to choose your words wisely.' After a while Naskar said, 'Are you going to call Singh sir?'

Samsher Singh still hadn't shown up at work. He was taking it slow, given the strain of the preceding day's work.

Balok Ghosh shook his head thoughtfully, 'No, I reckon there's no need to trouble the gentleman. He can learn the facts in time. There's no rush; everything is under control.'

'But they already took her to be cremated, no? I heard,' said Naskar.

'Yes, yes, accidental death, or suicide. It's plenty of work doing the last rites and a proper cremation without adding the police to the equation. Let them get on with it.'

'But,' Naskar said, suddenly excited as a new idea hit him, 'if, say, it is not suicide or an accident, but murder, then they'd have burnt the evidence! Don't you see?'

Balok Ghosh gave his young colleague a chilling stare and said, 'I'd suggest you get on with your work too, Naskar. Don't try to complicate things. Life is difficult enough as it is. If things can be simple, let them remain that way.' And Balok Ghosh strolled off for another cup of tea and a well-deserved roll-up away from young, excitable recruits.

# 45

WHEN LALEE WOKE UP, THE LIGHT WAS GRADUALLY changing outside and she could feel a chill inside the room. She pulled the covers tighter around herself, inching closer to the warm body next to her. Tilu Shau was lying on his side, one hand supporting his head, his eyes closed. It was a little before seven and she could hear voices outside, the sounds of Tilu's cramped neighbourhood waking up around them. She shut her eyes tightly against the world, wresting a few moments before the weight of consciousness descended on her. She tried to hold off flashes of memory – the ashram, their escape. Durga's face. She had abandoned a needy child. Against all of that, she tried to think of Tilu. A magical day – a rain-soaked, damp and breezy day. They would take a walk around Victoria, go to New Market, eat at a Chinese restaurant. Lalee sighed. The clock inched forward and the day began to creep up on them. Lalee sat down on the edge of the bed, listening to the comfortable measured breaths of the sleeping man beside her. The sliver of light from the halogen street lamps fell on his face. An aquiline nose etched with two small depressions on each side from his glasses. Dark shadows under his eyes, as though he didn't sleep well. His scant hair fell on his forehead, his mouth was slightly open and he slept curled up as though he were guarding himself from the world. Lalee laid a hand gingerly on the Tilu's face. He lowered his face onto his shoulders so that Lalee's hand was between them, drawing warmth from his body. Lalee stared out of the window at a murder of crows, sitting outside Tilu's window on the sagging electrical wires. She closed her eyes and tried to think of that room in The Park, but though she could remember the patterns on the bedcover and the upholstery, she could not picture herself in the room. In her memory, it was as if an invisible and unknowable person had passed through, but could not inhabit the space. And for the first time in many years, Lalee, her hand growing warm against someone's cheek, wondered how it would feel to pack up her meagre belongings and never return again.

Tilu didn't want to let Lalee go by herself, but she insisted and Tilu Shau had never been a man who would win an argument with Lalee. She pulled her dupatta around her face, hiding herself. She walked with her eyes on the road, criss-crossing her path with unnecessary alleyways and meandering lanes. When she reached the Sex Workers' Collective, the road outside was packed with women. Some were busy arranging chairs, others were speaking to reporters and still more were putting the finishing touches to their placards. Lalee slid in through the crowd, still hiding her face, and went round to the back, where there was another door that led into the office.

Inside, Lalee saw Malini bossing everyone around, like a matriarch at a family event. The whole place had come alive, everyone was busily working together. Lalee stood behind a door, avoiding eye contact with everyone. When Malini finally seemed to have a minute to herself, Lalee came out of the shadows and stood in front of her. For the first time in all the years that Lalee had known her, Malini was lost for words. She stared at Lalee's face for a few seconds, and then she enveloped her in a bear hug. Then she whispered into Lalee's ear, 'Walk with us today; don't say no.' Lalee looked at Malini and said, 'Yes.'

# 46

DEEPA LOOKED OUT OF THE WINDOW AT THE SLOW, jumbled-up traffic, moving at the speed of treacle. She clutched the back of the driver's seat and pulled herself forward. She'd been in a state of controlled panic since the call, rushing out of the NGO office as soon as she could. She wanted to scream at the driver to go faster, annoyed at his nonchalant yawning. 'Bhai, isn't there a shortcut?' Deepa yelled, struggling to be heard above the traffic outside. The taxi driver rolled down his window, spat and settled back into his seat. Deepa began counting down from hundred, hoping the unbreakable knot in traffic would be broken soon.

Before the taxi could come to a complete stop, Deepa opened the door and jumped out. She could make out the two faces inside the cafe, through the hazy glass. She did not wait for her change, crossed the road recklessly, driven by an unreasonable fear that they would somehow disappear before her very eyes. Sonia looked up when she entered the cafe, and then looked away again as if this meeting was of no consequence. Deepa, on the other hand, enveloped Sonia in a hug, surprising herself as much as Sonia.

'How did you get out?' Deepa blurted.

Sonia looked around, sweeping the cafe for possible threats, noticing where the exits were. Deepa noticed a young girl of eleven or twelve looking at her with wide-open eyes, her hand stopped midway to her mouth, still full of food. 'This is Durga,' Sonia said, as Deepa pulled a chair up for herself. She smiled at the silent young girl, hoping she looked reassuring. Years of dealing with the rough-and-tumble world of pimps, policemen, trafficked girls and women, and the viscous, unabating basic violence of the city, had cast her face into a mask of perpetual irritation. Deepa worried about it sometimes, when a knot in her throat threatened to tear through the facade she constructed for herself.

'She needs to go with you,' Sonia said, jerking her head towards the young girl, who was looking from her to Deepa.

'Where did you find her?' Deepa asked.

'From the ashram, where else?'

'How did you get out of there?' Deepa hissed, and not waiting for the answer, she added, 'And why are you here? Do you know what can happen to you if you're out in the open?'

'Relax. I'll be gone before you know it.'

Deepa felt a simultaneous pang of anger and panic. She could never get a handle on this girl; she always seemed too slippery, too caustic, too tart.

'I can't take her where I am going so I am here to hand her over to you.'

'Where *are* you going?' Deepa pressed again, and in the glare of Sonia's eyes, added, 'Yes, of course, I'll take care of her, that's not a problem.'

'All right then.' Sonia stood up and grabbed her handbag.

'Wait.' Deepa nearly blocked Sonia's way. 'Tell me what you found – what happened to you?'

'Short version? Girls come from your madam, go straight to your godman, then the best of them go all the way to Bangkok and sometimes Dubai. That's as far as I know. It could be the other way round. It's not like I know everything.' She laughed. 'Take care of this one for me.' Sonia walked out of the door, never looking back at either of them.

Sonia ran her hand over the hard, plastic-wrapped bundle inside her handbag and pulled out a scarf. She draped it over her head and face and covered her eyes with sunglasses. She could pass for a local girl now, albeit an exceptionally pale-skinned one. She hailed a cab and got into the first one that stopped. Before the driver could ask her for her destination, refuse to take her and start a squabble, she planted herself in the back seat. The driver announced sullenly that he'd need double the fare, before he put the meter down. Sonia dismissed the demand with a wave of her hand, sighing in the privacy of her veil. This strange country could overwhelm you with kindness one minute and skin you alive the next. Just like her own, she thought. When the taxi stopped in front of a small three-storey building on Ballygunge Circular Road, Sonia showed no sign of getting out of the cab, staring intently outside at the upper storeys of the building from the taxi window instead. The driver had already turned the meter off and was about to voice his annoyance when Sonia dropped the fare on the seat and stepped out, carefully closing the door behind her.

Sonia waited for the taxi to turn the corner and disappear. She liked this neighborhood and its leafy avenues and old art-deco houses. The old man who ironed clothes for a living was preapring his antique iron as his scrawny, prepubescent assistant fanned coals on a burner. They looked up at her as she removed her veil, but quickly went back to what they were doing. The two of them were witness to a great number of goings-on in the neighbourhood; Sonia wasn't of particular interest. She proceeded to pull a key out of her bag and used it to open the collapsible iron gate. Inside, she knocked on the painted green door. Three knocks, in short, measured intervals.

A slight young man in a vest and long pyjamas opened the door. He looked up from his phone at Sonia, gave her a perfunctory smile, and went back to his phone again. 'What's happening, Maxo?' Sonia asked, in a perky voice that sounded hollow even to herself.

'Yeah, the girls are out. Anna and Maria are inside.'

Sonia pushed the curtain back and entered the living room. Two young women, both pale-skinned and dark-haired, were lounging on a sofa, staring at reruns of *Friends* dubbed in Russian on a widescreen TV across from them. Sonia sank into the old couch next to them, removed her shoes and put her feet up on the coffee table in front of her. She closed her eyes and placed a hand casually on top of her purse. She had things to do. And she needed to get away from Calcutta as soon as she could. She remembered the young girl they had to leave behind in the ashram, but she had brought one, that, she thought would even out the score. 'Where is Charlie?' Sonia asked the girls. Anna didn't look away from the screen, but Maria said, 'He'll be back. He's setting up something for Maxo this evening. The market for boys is picking up, and he gets better clients than us.'

Sonia laughed softly. She had come out of Uzbekistan and into Russia on her own, and had picked up this bunch of Uzbeks somewhere down the road. The burly Punjabi man who called himself Charlie was their handler. He found the gigs, the apartments and the rental car drivers who ferried them around. He also had contacts. Sonia would wait for him, and figure out a quiet, unobtrusive path to Bombay, then maybe back to Dubai, far away from the reach of Shefali Madam or her Maharaj. All she had to do was wait it out and then get away in time. It would not be safe to cash in the gold or use the notes she had found in the ashram. Everything was too easily traceable. But Charlie would find a way, especially for a price, and she would have made her escape.

# 47

SAMSHER SINGH SAT RAMROD STRAIGHT IN HIS CHAIR. Deepa was sitting in front of him once more and Samsher was smiling politely at her. Deepa was saying a number of things, none of which Samsher wanted to hear very much about. He was idly wondering if Deepa would really reach over at any point and slap him in the face. It seemed like a distinct possibility, and Samsher didn't feel confident enough that he could arrest her in such an event. He was singing in his mind, concentrating hard on the lyrics of the new item number the constables had been playing on their phones that morning. It helped him get through this exchange.

Deepa started shouting. Samsher decided to interrupt her, 'But these videos prove nothing, madam. The pictures are not clear, someone could have made their in their own living room … we can't use them at all.'

'I've been doing this for decades, OC Singh. I've seen the police manufacture evidence out of thin air, and I've seen them lose water-tight evidence in laughable ways. You can see the ashram clearly in that video, you can read the words Nandankanan Ashram. It's all been in the news so you can't tell me you don't know about the recent CBI raid. And you can see the now-deceased Mohamaya Mondal in the videos too, with a split-open face, if nothing else. This is still circumstantial evidence in a murder case. You are supposed to know this yourself.'

The child next to Deepa was staring at a corner of Samsher's table, sometimes twining her fingers and scratching her hands. White marks formed wherever she scratched her skin and Samsher couldn't help but steal a glance at them every now and then.

'It's not enough for an arrest warrant, madam,' Samsher said with exaggerated politeness.

'Not what I'm asking. Just get a search warrant. Her twin sister is still trapped there, officer. We have confirmed news there are new girls being brought in and that the transfer will happen today. We have been working on this for months. The CBI are all over the ashram; the situation is in your favour, officer.'

Not imperiousness or condescension, Samsher was startled to find a note of pleading in Deepa's voice.

'Yes, madam, sure. Yes, sure,' Samsher repeated himself, still smiling beatifically.

Balok Ghosh walked slowly towards Samsher and stood next to him. He lowered his mouth and whispered in Samsher's ear. 'Call came from the DCP's office, sir. I said you will call him back.'

Samsher's smile faded. He glanced back at Deepa. He couldn't even have a frank conversation with his constable in front of this woman and she gave no indication that she was moving anytime soon. He sighed. He looked up to meet Balok's eyes and the old constable blinked at him in confirmation.

Samsher turned towards Deepa. 'Excuse me a moment, madam,' and he walked away, towing Balok Ghosh along. Trailing after Singh, Balok said, 'Media attention is high, sir; there is a lot of tension in the area.'

Samsher walked into the small office at the opposite end of the police station and yelled at Naskar and the other constables to leave him alone. He held the telephone receiver to his ear for a few seconds, listening to the buzz before his hands slowly found the buttons to press. 'DCP's office?' he asked, doing his best to sound confident. 'Burtolla OC calling.'

Samsher pressed his temples with his right hand and concentrated on keeping his voice steady and controlled. He didn't have opportunity to say much more than 'yes, sir' and the occasional 'of course, sir', and he found himself nodding vigorously at certain points. The ashram was out of bounds. It went too deep and too high for someone like Samsher. He was a small man with small powers and had no business going after the sharks. He let out a breath he didn't realize he had been holding. If he went to Nandankanan, he wouldn't come out of it unscathed. Ever since the letter from that wretched sevika had reached the media and was made public knowledge, he had been expecting something like this. He might be small fry, but he heard things. Disappearances, threats, the death of a reporter who was looking into the matter – he had heard the rumours, but he had never thought he would have anything to do with it. He exhaled.

Balok Ghosh was standing outside mushing a clot of chewing tobacco on the palm of his hand. When Samsher threw the doors open and strode out, Balok ran after him. Samsher said, lowering his voice, 'DCP wants the situation to be under control.

Sala I have a magic wand – I wave it and everything becomes okay, but high-profile raids Bose will go to and eat all the footage … the CBI is over there, in the real tiger's cave. If I go there, they'll laugh at me. Sala, they hand over these fucking decisions at the last moment like I'm some bokachoda waiting to be shat on. Apparently, these NGO people have some informant inside. Bnara, even the home minister is getting involved.'

'Of course, syaar,' Balok said. 'That sevika woman, arrey, those women that babaji would … you know … use, she wrote straight to the prime minister, home minister, everyone, sir. All big fish, now with media and everything – everyone is involved.'

Samsher walked back into his office. 'We will be there, madam. It is our public duty. We cannot let this continue after all.'

Deepa stood up. She was looking at him directly and Samsher knew he wouldn't be able to fool her, whatever he did. He would be there. But he wouldn't be in front of Nandankanan. Samsher was a lot of things but what he most emphatically was not, was a fool, or an idealist. He would wait just outside Shonagachhi on the main crossroads with his jeep and maybe another one with underlings, watching the march as it would pass them by. Police presence would be good; he could ensure that nothing untoward took place. High-profile thing like this after all, maybe when the cameras panned, they'd catch Samsher's face as well. All Samsher had to do was iron his uniform and follow orders, turn up at the right time in public to see that the police were out and about, making the world a better place.

Later, Samsher sat, quite at peace in the front of the jeep.

Balok Ghosh sat in the back, his chin resting on the barrel of his rifle. 'What do you think, Balok-da?' asked Samsher.

'Good for image, sir – all the news channels are there. Whole night's news and talk-show material covered in a few hours' work tonight.'

'Yes?' Samsher asked.

'Yes, sir. The real stuff is not here. It's somewhere else, sir. That NGO madam is right, syaar. The girls are somewhere else. If I steal a trunk full of money, will I keep it in my bedroom?' Balok Ghosh scoffed. He had told his wife he was going to be on TV tonight. She was excited about it. His wife and her sisters were in the house right now, sitting in front of the TV, waiting for him to appear.

# 48

LALEE MERGED WITH THE PASSING MULTITUDE OF WOMEN, each walking with a candle. She had come empty-handed but someone lit a candle and handed it to her. Without speaking, Lalee walked with them, not listening to the words but following the rhythm of footsteps, irregular and uncoordinated, but all marching in the same direction. She saw faces in the crowd she recognized, and ones she didn't, faces that looked familiar as if in some way she knew them, and faces she had forgotten. She saw the old midwife, jerking her bent body forward in a peculiar lurching motion. She smiled toothlessly at Lalee. As she walked, without warning, uncharacteristically and with abandon, Lalee began to cry. Light tears gave way to full sobs, allowing her no air to breathe. She kept on walking, hot wax dripping on her fingers, both hands clutching the white candle tightly. She cried like she hadn't done in years; in the early days, when she had just begun in the trade, she would cry like this in the long afternoons between shifts. By evening, her face would swell and her eyes would redden. Those days Shefali Madam would either force a few stiff drinks down her throat or hit her. She soon learned how to cry silently. In time, she cried in the early hours when she could finally go to sleep. She found herself turning into the young girl who knew nothing, understood nothing and was afraid. Afraid of the men who touched her, afraid of that new life, of the nightmare her life had become. No core of rage, no amount of anger was safeguard against this sudden and utter breakdown of walls she had built around herself. She whimpered as Malini walked next to her. She placed a hand on Lalee's back, and urged by that small act of kindness, more tears came with renewed force.

Those early days were never quite far behind for her. Lalee walked. She had things to do – go to a pawn shop and exchange some of that gold for cash, shop at New Market, eat Chinese, sit on the lawns of Victoria Memorial with Tilu. Her bag of treasure was with Tilu. No one would look for it there, and he was the only person she could trust. A soft affection dropped over her like a blanket. Tilu's slightly anxious face flashed before her eyes. She would buy him a pair of new chappals, a pair of expensive leather chappals that would not tear so easily. Tilu would worry about the price but Lalee would shush him, forbid him to say a word, and he would sit back down defeated, frowning, and he would walk out of the shop with a new pair of comfortable slippers.

# 49

LALEE MOVED WITH THE SLOW, LONG QUEUE IN FRONT of the dark window of the ticket counter like a sleepwalker. Crowds of impatient people, moving and elbowing, small arguments, shoving and the background strain of railway announcements didn't touch her. She closed her eyes and saw a field, a glaring sun in midheaven, the old banyan tree, the mud lane that turned into a small row of houses. She could almost feel the burning heat from the ground singeing her bare feet, the small, brown, dusty feet of a child. At the end of the lane would be a small house, three rooms in all, where she and her five brothers and sisters lived. She opened her eyes and wondered if it really would be the same. No, things would have changed. A new room here, another thatch there – just as she had changed. Would she recognize it when she saw it? Would it recognize her? Would her brothers, her sisters? Would her mother know who she was?

A tired man on the other side of the window said unhappily to Lalee, 'Where to?'

Lalee blinked a few times; she had been far away, thinking about a place she used to call home. Just at this moment, she couldn't remember its name. Where? What was the name?

'Village Kalipur,' she said.

'Where is that?' the man asked sourly, motioning for her to stand aside.

'Puncha,' Lalee said hurriedly, 'in Puruliya.'

The man pushed back his glasses on the bridge of his nose and began typing into a machine.

'Fifty-three rupees and fifty paisa,' he said without looking at her.

Lalee handed him a 100-rupee note; he returned the change and handed her the ticket. People in the queue began to yell at her until a large woman elbowed her out of the way.

Lalee put the ticket in her handbag and tried to remember how to go home. It was something her grandfather had taught her when she was still a child, in case she got lost. The name of the village, the local post office, the name of the district. That must have seemed the end of the world to her grandfather, Lalee thought. Lalee tried to remember what he looked like. He was tall and lanky, that much she could recall. He always wore a white kurta and a short white dhoti. The clothes always smelled fresh. But she couldn't remember his face.

A mile's walk from the Kalipur station – that was the way home. One mile eastward. That was a long time ago. Surely, by now, there must be a better way to get home and there wouldn't be any need to walk.

She looked around for Tilu and saw him standing under the big clock on an old archway at the Howrah station. *Built by the British*, she thought. Did my father ever come here? Did he ever see this? She walked slowly towards Tilu and stood beside him. In the middle of the passing multitude, only the two of them stood still.

'Got the tickets?' Tilu asked.

Lalee nodded.

'I can come with you,' he said, 'if it makes things easier. You can say I'm your husband, or … something …' he trailed off. 'They don't need the truth.'

'I do,' Lalee said in a soft whisper.

'I'll wait then. Until you come back.' Tilu stole a glance at her. He did not know if she would come back, but he was hoping with all he had that she would. He tried to make it sound like a statement, but a question mark floated in the air. 'When you come back, you don't have to go to Shonagachhi. You can stay with me.'

Lalee looked at him and opened her mouth to protest but Tilu pre-empted her thoughts, 'No, no, I don't mean … I'm not going to …' After an awkward silence, he continued, 'Just come and stay with me. There's enough room and no one will ask anything. And then, whenever you are ready, if you want to, you can leave.' He looked down at his old, worn-out chappals, unable to meet Lalee's eye.

Lalee smiled, but Tilu didn't notice that. 'We'll see,' she said, 'but it sounds like a good idea. For everything you have done ...' Lalee tried to find the words. But this was an alien language, a warmth and faith she didn't know how to wrangle into words.

Tilu's face grew warm. He looked up and spotted a tea seller walking around with a bucket of kettles and plastic cups. He ordered two cups and handed one to Lalee.

They sipped in silence. Tilu made loud sucking noises, and Lalee smirked at him. Sweet, milky tea had never tasted this good to Tilu. Lalee looked around the station and thought about how many girls, how many women in this station right now might end up in Shonagachhi in a week.

She looked at every passing face, trying to etch them into memory. 'This is a strange city,' she said.

'Isn't it?' Tilu replied, and Lalee saw that his eyes were shining with a light that hadn't been there. He was gazing out at the city as if it was his personal masterpiece. *We love strange things*, she thought. She thought of her room in Shonagachhi – her old room – and knew that for whatever it represented, she was grateful for that home, that shelter. And that she would miss the certainty of belonging, even if it was to a place like Shonagachhi. Homes are always odd places.

In a few minutes, she would disappear in the teeming crowds, sit on a train and be on her way to another place and, if she was lucky, another phase of her life.

For now, standing in the thick of the sweaty five o'clock rush-hour madness of Howrah Station, she looked up at the distant pre-dusk horizon and hummed a song to herself.

# Before ...

*'I DON'T LIKE THIS, I'M NOT OKAY WITH THIS.' MOHAMAYA waits on the other side while Deepa falters through the sentence. It is muggy, and the smooth surface of the cell phone sticks to Maya's cheek. Outside, Amina is explaining something to Lalee. Hands flying through the air, gesturing as she speaks and the two of them are silhouetted against the fading sky, against the painted sacking of chicken-coup buildings and blinking lights.*

*Maya smiles, something Deepa will never see. 'You talk a lot about choice, Deepa-di. The first time I saw you, at the Collective's class, you talked about choice. I didn't get it at the time, but I think I do now. But you have to believe in it too. I'm choosing to go.'*

'Phir bhi,' *Deepa says and Maya thinks her bullish, but with affection. That's what Deepa-di is like, unwilling to let go without an argument, with a countering dissent. 'You were all alone there, and if I knew I wouldn't let you go,' Deepa breathes hard into the mouthpiece. 'We're this close to finding our way in. The Crime Branch is telling us to wait. They don't want anything to shake their case. Look, there is going to be a riot when they go in. I can't ...'*

*Maya cuts her off. She speaks indulgently, with the optimism of the young. 'Didi, see, I have two kids. They're well away from here. No one here knows where they are. I have some money at the Collective but I have some more elsewhere. Everything is taken care of, you know that. If I didn't, who would? They were asking me to, they were literally begging me to take this job. It would be very stupid to dismiss this opportunity. Besides,' Maya waits for a breath, hesitates at the threshold of confidence. 'Besides, my daughter is almost eleven. I've seen girls that young here, Deepa-di. Are you telling me to wait? Would you? If you could do something, anything, for another girl like that?'*

*Deepa is quiet. The noise of the city pervades the line. It travels dancing on distant telephone towers, flickers across wires, shines like dust in the twilight. Deepa breathes into the phone. It is past 6:30 and Calcutta is blue like the city has hanged itself over a heartbreak. Deepa stares into the distance, at the ochre cabs stuck in gridlocks, the men who hang unperturbed out of red and yellow minibuses, calm in the face of death. She looks up at the sky, above the jumbled electric wires where crows return to perch in the gloaming. Her eyes burn and she thinks,* fuck this goddamn pollution, *and wipes her eyes and swallows furiously so Maya would never hear the catch in her throat.*

*'Where are you now?' Deepa asks, her whole body seizing with fear. 'In Shonagachhi?'*

*Maya laughs softly. Where else would she go? All that is her's is here, some cash strewn here and there. Clothes she had lusted over, collected when she could afford them. She would contact the Collective's cooperative bank later, but still, life gathers its trinkets, its keepsakes. Her presence is only temporary and no one will know.*

*'I'll come and get you now Maya, it's not safe,' Deepa shrieks into the phone. 'I'm coming, I'm coming,' she breathes.*

*'It's okay, Deepa-di. Come tomorrow I'll go wherever you decide, okay? Tonight, I'll get all my things … you know I'll probably never come back here, na?'*

*Outside, Amina is doubling over with laughter, her giggles spilling over the loud bollywood tunes and the babel of the streets. Maya wants to hear what is so funny. She feels slightly impatient with Deepa-di, but they aren't finished yet. Even Laal didi is smiling a little, watching Amina.*

*'I understand what you're saying,' Deepa says, and Maya smiles to herself. She's just won a not-quite-argument with the formidable Deepa-di. It makes her feel warm and secure, like she's become a whole person, a person of consequence. 'If you say it's your choice, I won't be the person who tells you what you choose. Just call me when you get back, and don't contact me when you're there – it won't be safe.'*

*Maya leaves her phone on the table, splotched from the oils on her face and now so hot that she doesn't want to touch it anymore. Outside, on the long verandah where Amina is still giggling, the big mattress on the advertisement has just lit up, the lights illuminating half of Amina's face. Other girls are leaning out, breasts hanging over sand-casted railings, chatting to each other, hurling things at passersby. 'What are you laughing about?' she asks Amina.*

*'I'm telling Laal didi to charge her babu phantasy rates – I've heard what they do.'*

*'He's not my babu,' Lalee said.*

*'*Oi holo*, regular customer who's fallen in love with you.'*

*Lalee makes a face, but Maya suspects that Laal didi's*

*normally prickly mood is diluted. She puts her arms around both of them, bringing them together in a rough, makeshift hug.*

*'Aah, stop. My skin is so sticky with sweat – don't cling to me like this,' Lalee says with perfunctory annoyance.*

*'Oh,' Amina elongates the 'o' and falls needlessly on Lalee's shoulder, 'and when your writer babu comes and wants to lie on top of you? Then what will you say, ha?'*

*Lalee lights a cigarette and says very solemnly, staring at the girls in the house across, 'I'll charge him double phantasy rate.'*

*All three of them laugh until their eyes stream. They watch the giant billboard with a nightie-clad woman sitting suggestively on a bone-white, fluffy mattress.*

'Eai shon, *you know what that writer babu told me?'*

*It is going to rain. It threatens, it darkens in the corners, where the eye doesn't go unless it is afraid. Above the tangled electric wires, above the BSNL towers and the CESC poles that sway like twigs on the first day of the monsoon, pewter ink descends in clusters, congregates in a future forever suspended. This is what a death is. It is a drop of ink in undisturbed water. It sinks, spreads its tendrils, exhausts itself, replicating in curves and sinews. The three of them don't know it yet, but they know its shape, somewhere deep in the bones where the mind hasn't reached.*

*'He says there was a fakir here once, Shona Gazi – you know that dargaa, arrey, after Durga Charan Mitra Street, that way,' Lalee points.*

*The other two look at her, smiling, on the edge of teasing. 'He said that's why it's called Shonagachhi. The sahibs made this place exclusive. Only girls who serviced the gora sahibs could live here at the time,' Lalee finishes, inhales the cigarette. It tastes like air laced with softly burning metals, filling her with an idea, an image of what she could be, what is yet to happen. A luxury, and a style of herself she can envy.*

*Amina starts laughing, and Maya doubles over. Lalee frowns at them. 'Your writer babu is too much,' Maya says and Lalee feels annoyed because she felt secretly fascinated when the man had said it nervously, stuttering a few times while he tied the rope in his pyjamas into knots, lowering his voice like he was confiding some great secret to Lalee.*

*In a few hours, Tilu will mumble unintelligibly about money just there, outside. 'Phantasy sex will cost you more,' Lalee will say, annoyed, loudly enough for everyone to hear. Maya will smile softly in her room, tapping her foot to the beat of a Hindi song she really likes. In a few hours she will switch off the light, pretend that the room is empty. She does not feel like entertaining a visitor. She thinks of her children. The boy is thoughtful and slow but the daughter is a firecracker. She has a talent for dancing. Maya thinks she'll need to ask around for a good dance master, someone old and innocuous.*

*For now, the heat rises from the concrete. It rises from the heart of the soft loam of the lower Gangetic plains buried under the asphalt, reaches its tendrils upwards to the three women, standing on a balcony that should have been condemned by a municipality that cared. They lean over. They laugh. Tomorrow is Sunday and Amina wonders idly if she should get some mutton. The heat touches their skin, melts on contact, rivulets of sweat trickle on charted territories of the body, down the slope of their necks, pausing over the mounds of raised breasts, losing itself in the folds of flesh. They laugh and fall over one another.*

*And the scent of their skin rises like a cloud. It is one of those truly blue evenings. The moon isn't quite full yet – just a few more days, all three of them think. But it is a thought too fleeting, too inconsequential.*

# Acknowledgements

I WROTE WHAT WAS TO BECOME THE FIRST CHAPTER OF THIS book on a train from Norwich to London in the winter of 2014. I didn't have internet access. I was bored, I thought the scene was funny. I wrote to amuse myself, like a storytelling child.

A year later, I was at a reading organized by the Division of English at Nanyang Technological University, Singapore, where I was a PhD candidate. With trepidation, I read the first chapter in front of an audience for the first time. Everyone laughed, and at the right places. I'd never been considered particularly funny before that moment in my life. So, my very first thanks go to those twenty-odd people who came to that reading in 2014. Without you, I would never have written this book.

I wrote and rewrote *A Death in Shonagachhi* over a period of six years. A debut novel is a leap of faith, a jump into the abyss, and I have many people to thank without whom I would never have got this far. Thanks are due, in no particular order, to all the people who shaped me into a writer.

To Nanyang Technological University for funding my research, for allowing me to write my first book. To the

Michael King Writers Residency for giving me space and time to work on this book.

To the women, children, transpersons, shopkeepers and workers of Shonagachhi for talking to me, for telling me the best jokes and for the endless cups of tea and fried snacks.

To my supervisor, Dr Barry Sherwood, who encouraged me to tell this story. To Dr Neil Murphy for his unwavering support. For saying 'You can write' when I needed to hear it.

To Dr John Tangney for everything – sandwiches and ginger beer, a warm bed in times of great distress, for reading everything I wrote, for treating me like a Real Writer, for the echinacea tea, for the reality checks and tarot card readings, for letting me comment on rugby, and for being there.

To my editor Teesta Guha Sarkar, for her grace in difficult times, her faith in my work and for giving me free rein in how I wanted to tell this story. To Kanishka Gupta, for believing in the book and for being a great friend and advocate. To Rahul Soni, for his kindness and his faith in this book.

To Maria Cardona Serra, who manages to perform miracles every minute of every day. Thank you for everything you've done.

To Dr Rittvika Singh, for her life-changing friendship, for reading the book with care and love, for showing me things I would not have seen had it not been for her. For being my person. To Dr Amit Kumar, for reading my book with so much enthusiasm.

To my writing group in Wellington: Fiona Clark, Whitney Cox, Meryl Richards, Pallas Cotter and Catherine Robertson for reading my book and giving valuable feedback. For the wine and the chats. For a sense of belonging and community. For helping me find my place in a new country.

To Dr Puja Bhattacharya, Dr Koyel Khan and Suddha Prasad Bagchi for believing I could write, for being impressed with everything I wrote in those early, juvenilia-filled days. I needed the faith you showed in me.

To my best friends Suchandra Ganguly and Prithwish Barman, for making me deliriously happy and extremely crass and insanely funny every time I meet them.

To my partner Eric, for doing the dishes, cooking dinner and cleaning the house while I wrote. For telling me to stop wasting time and write. For being happy every time something good happened and acting like he had known it all along. For living with my mercurial moods.

To my father, my brother, my sister-in-law and my nephew.

To my mother who expected exceptional things of me. I wish you were here.